Our L.I.F.E.

L.I.F.E., Book Three

Felyx Lawson

Winnipeg, Canada

Editors: Craig Gibb & Francisco Feliciano

Published November 2023 by Deep Hearts YA, an imprint of Deep Desires Press and Story Perfect Inc.

Deep Hearts YA
PO Box 51053 Tyndall Park
Winnipeg, Manitoba R2X 3B0
Canada

Visit deepheartsya.com for more great reads.

Our L.I.F.E. was partially inspired by this playlist…

Mad World by Michael Andrews & Gary Jules

Time Warp by Nell Campbell, Patricia Quinn, & Richard O'Brien

Baby Got Back by Sir Mix-A-Lot

Touch-A, Touch-A, Touch Me by Susan Sarandon

Never Gonna Give You Up by Rick Astley

Lay All Your Love on Me by Dominic Cooper and Amanda Seyfried

Escape (The Pina Colada Song) by Rupert Holmes

Breathe by Blu Cantrell, feat. Sean Paul

Defying Gravity by Idina Menzel

Take a Chance on Me by ABBA

Good Riddance (Time of Your Life) by Green Day

99 Red Balloons by Nena

Our L.I.F.E.

Chapter 1

R ider dashed from his bedroom to the bathroom. His mother had already shouted for him three times. He was running thirty minutes late after sleeping in, having stayed up way too late facetiming Cam and had lost track of the time.

Cam, after being offered a basketball scholarship to Kentucky University, had left a whole week before Rider was due to leave for Houston University and Rider was missing him greatly. It also hadn't helped that last night had been the first time they could talk without being interrupted by his parents, hence the late night. They had promised each other no crying and Rider had made it a whole fifteen minutes.

As Rider tried to get his hair under control, his phone vibrated with a photo message from Cam, which immediately drew a smile and caused Rider to blush. He quickly checked around him before sending his own seductive picture back to Cam.

"Rider, will you hurry up! Your father is waiting in the car and if you don't leave soon then you'll hit traffic!" his mom shouted from downstairs.

Rider let out a deep sigh and slid his glasses back onto his face. He wasn't going to miss the constant complaining from his parents. As Rider came down the stairs, he could see his mom's eyes were already wet. She had thrown a going away party last night, during which she had got extremely emotional and pulled him into a tight hug, refusing to release him for a good five minutes. He had also spent two hours embraced in a hug sandwich between Sam and Jane, even the tough Latina had broken down in tears before she had left. The one thing that had upset Rider was the lack of a short blond-haired teen; Lloyd was still extremely distant from the group. Rider had seen him a total of three times during the summer.

Before Rider could say anything to his mother, she had him in a hug so tight he was sure she would bruise his ribs worse than when Darwin Brown had attacked him over his sexuality. She only released him when he started gasping for air. Receiving a kiss on his cheek, he was instructed to call home at least once a week.

"I'll miss you so much, Ri."

"I'll miss you too, Mom." Rider pulled his mom in for one last hug. "Love you."

"I love you too."

Stepping out into the warm August sun, his father smiled from behind the wheel of the car, jokingly tapping his watch to try and speed his son up. Once everyone had left the going way party, he and his father had fully packed all Rider's belonging in the car to make the journey easier. Before Rider could slip into the car, his phone vibrated again.

Hey Ri, sorry I couldn't be there yesterday. I know you'll have an awesome time at college. Don't forget about me.

Rider smiled at Lloyd's message. Out of everyone in Belmont, it was going to be his best friend he was going to miss the most. Rider just wished had had been able to see the smaller teen one last time before he left. He had just finished letting Lloyd know that when his father leaned out the window.

"Let's get going, Rider. We have a long way to go!"

Letting out a sigh, he climbed into the car. It felt cramped with the chair pushed forward to accommodate his belongings. He hadn't even packed that many items. When first asking his father to drive him, he had thought the trunk would fit multiple suitcases, his guitar, and his amp but once the guitar had been placed in, he didn't want to risk it getting crushed, so he put his second suitcase behind his seat.

Rider waved at his mom, who had tears in her eyes, as the car pulled out the driveway. Merging onto the highway, his father went over the plan again although Rider already had it committed to memory. They would drive continually, only stopping for lunch and dinner; his father had even threatened to bring plastic bottles to avoid toilet breaks. They would stop around 9:30pm to find somewhere to sleep before rising early and arriving at Houston the following day, allowing Rider almost the full week to explore campus before classes started.

"Are you excited, Ri?" His dad smiled while keeping his eyes on the road.

"I'll miss you and Mom but yeah. Everyone says college is the best time of their life so I can't wait to see it."

"How's Cameron settling in?" The last syllable was drowned out by the horn and his father shouting at the guy who cut them off.

"It's technically his first day today. He sounded extremely excited on the phone last night."

"Technic—Get out the way, you jackass. Technically?"

"He doesn't start his classes today. He's meeting the team and the coach today."

As the duo drove, Rider watched out the window as the country passed him by. He had always wanted to travel the country but so far had only been to Belmont and New York. The journey went quicker than Rider had expected; they were soon parked up in front of a motel. Although he had done nothing but sit all day, he felt extremely tired. He hardly had the energy to finish his In-N-Out burger before sliding into bed.

When his phone lit up the room, a smile spread across Rider's face as Cam's name appeared on the screen. As Cam talked about how his day, the soft warm voice of his boyfriend caused Rider to briefly close his eyes, but it was enough to pull him into slumber, a smile on his face. Jeremy laughed quietly at Rider as he grabbed the phone.

"Hey, Cameron, it's Jeremy. Rider's fallen asleep."

Cam laughed. "Ah that would explain the snoring. Well, when he wakes, tell him I said good night."

"Will do, Cameron. You have a good evening."

Rider struggled to hide his blush in the morning when his father handed his phone back. He wanted to call Cam and apologize, but there was no time. Within ten minutes of waking, they were back on the road heading toward Houston. As they approached campus, Rider's breath got caught in his throat. The large buildings and the number of students already moving around the place was very off-putting. Following the signs directing them to the parking lot next to the dorms, his father managed to find an available spot right in front of the building.

The dry heat hit Rider as soon as he stepped out of the car. He already knew Houston would be a warmer than Belmont, but not this hot. Rider was shading his eyes from the sun that was bearing down on him as an extremely peppy girl suddenly appeared in front of him, welcoming them both to the university. Rider had only just gotten his name out before she was scratching something off on a list. Shuffling through the large box of envelopes, the preppy girl pulled out the one named *Williams, Rider* and passed it over to him. Inside the envelope Rider found an information pack, including details of the dorm and what room he was in.

"Your Resident Advisor will be around soon to greet you and let you know more about the campus," the girl said with such energy Rider wondered how she kept it up all day. "So, Mr. Williams, welcome to Houston and please enjoy yourself."

The peppy girl was gone before he could even thank her. Rider's room was on the third floor but it took him some time trying to locate it as he dodged all the people coming and going, boxes filling the hall as new students moved into their rooms. Soon he stood in front of the pine door, 327 emblazed black on a silver plaque. He slid the key into the lock, turning it and pushing the door open to see the room that would be his home for the next year.

Rider's face dropped as he entered the fairly small room, the smell of the fresh white paint still lingered in the air. The room had no personality at all, but this wasn't what caused Rider's sadness...there were two beds in the tiny room. When Cam had video called from Kentucky, he had a dorm room to himself. Living so close to another person and having to hide his sexuality wasn't something Rider wanted to do.

"Now this takes me back," his father said as he dropped the suitcase down and looked around. "Same size as the dorm room I had in college."

Opening the case, Rider started pulling out his clothes, placing them on the bed to the right. Due to the new student congestion, it took them forty-five minutes to fully empty the car, by which time Rider was drenched in sweat due to the heat outside. Each trip, Rider had stopped by the elevator, but it had always been full, and his father refused to wait around. By the time his father was ready to leave, most items had been stowed away, his guitar slotted into the gap between the end of the bed and wall. Rider walked his father back down to the car.

"So...erm...I hope you have a wonderful time here, Ri." His dad's voice cracked slightly. "Don't forget to call and we'll see you at Christmas."

With how difficult it had been to leave his parents and friends and that Cam wouldn't be returning for Thanksgiving due to his training schedule, Rider had decided to stay at college for that week. He wanted to avoid returning home, seeing Lloyd, and then not wanting to leave again. Rider nodded at his father, knowing that if he opened his mouth to say anything he might change his mind and go back home with his father. The duo hugged tight before his father climbed back into the car. Both men wiped the tears from their eyes. Rider waved as the car pulled out of the spot. His eyes were still a little blurry from the tears as he turned to head back toward his room when he bumped into someone.

"I'm so sorry," Rider said a bit too loud.

"It's okay," a calm voice replied.

Rider looked at the older guy in front of him, his dark hair pulled into a tight ponytail that cascaded down to his shoulders, a streak of electric pink running through the length similar to what Jane had done with her hair last year before college interviews. His build was thin as if he was a runner. Rider could see muscles under the tight top he was wearing.

"Fresh meat, I see. Name's Jacob but you can call me Jay," he said with a smile.

"Rider Williams."

"So, what's a cute guy like you doing in a dump like this?" Jay asked while waving at the dorm with a stretched-out hand.

"Erm…I…" Rider was taken back; he wasn't used to getting compliments, let alone from a guy. "I'm here to study journalism."

"Ah, cool. I got to head but hopefully I'll bump into you again."

Jay winked before he disappeared down the path. Rider swallowed hard and headed toward his room. Had he misheard Jay or did he actually call him cute? Shaking his head as he entered his dorm room, Rider wondered when his roommate was due to arrive. He hardly had time to sit down on his bed before there was a knock on the door. As he opened the door, Rider's jaw dropped when he saw the guy standing in front of him. Rider was still in shock as he was pulled into a tight hug.

"Yuki?"

"Hello, Rider. It is a pleasure to see you again. When I saw your name on the list, I could not wait for you to arrive." Yuki smiled as he released Rider from his hug.

"What? What you doing here?"

"I go to college here. I am your resident advisor."

"But what about you and Lloyd?"

A confused and sad look spread across Yuki's face. He walked over to the empty bed and sat down as Rider sat on his own bed. It was a couple of minutes before Yuki spoke again, his eyes were wet, and his voice cracked slightly as he explained how he and Lloyd had broken up on Lloyd's birthday. Rider was shocked—that was six months ago, and Lloyd hadn't said anything. Over the summer during one of the few times he had seen Lloyd, the younger boy had said they were doing well but Yuki had been busy with work and couldn't attend. It had to be the reason why Lloyd had been pulling away from the group.

"I am guessing Lloyd did not tell you. I hope he is doing okay; I do miss him a lot."

"I'm sure he misses you also," Rider said with a weak smile.

Yuki soon changed the topic, trying to distract from memories of the younger teen. He started talking about the university that he and Rider now both called home. He went over Rider's timetable, giving him a description of which buildings his lecturers would take place in and the quickest way to get there. Rider was sure Yuki didn't spend this long with every new student, but he was happy for the advice. As Yuki started to explain the rules of the dorm, Rider interrupted him.

"What about my roommate?" he questioned.

"From my paperwork your roommate is called …erm…I think it is pronounced Giasone Alighieri. He should also be arriving today. Are you worried about having to share the room? I know you did not come out until last year and it can be a bit daunting having to share a room with someone."

"Slightly. I spent so many years hiding my sexuality and struggling to come out. Now that I am, I really don't want to go back into the closet." A slight frown formed on Rider's face.

"You do not need to worry about that, Rider. The university of Houston is accepting of all sexualities. If your roommate has a problem, come and see me. If I cannot help, then we will move you to a different room." Yuki smiled, relaxing Rider slightly.

"Are peoples' sexuality common knowledge at Houston?"

"No. I am not out to anyone here. Why do you ask?"

Rider found himself telling Yuki about his run in with Jay. How he had been called cute even though he hadn't done anything to reveal his sexuality to anyone in the campus. The only proof that existed at this moment was the homescreen on Rider's phone of him and Cam sitting on a bench in The Met, which Trish had taken when they had visited New York.

"I would advise you to stay away from Jacob Augustus. He is currently on his fourth attempt at his third year of his degree and is known for selling narcotics around the campus. The only reason he has been allowed to remain at Houston is his father is a lawyer who annually donates a large amount of money to the university. Anyway, I must get going. I have a number of students I need to greet. See you again soon, Rider."

The duo hugged again as Rider followed Yuki out of the room in search of a bathroom. When he returned to the room, there were voices on the other side of the door. Pushing open the door he was greeted by two guys who were facing the other way, currently laughing at bedding being thrown around. They hadn't even noticed Rider enter the room till the door clicked behind him. The one closest to him was tall with a deep natural tan to his skin, short blond hair, and blue deep eyes that reminded Rider so much of Cam. The second guy was shorter, his dark brown eyes complimenting his dark skin. His hair hid under a hat with what looked like a trucking company logo on it. The partial beard made Rider question if the teen was a trucker himself. Whereas the first guy was wearing a long-sleeved black shirt despite the heat outside and smart dress pants, the second guy had an extremely short-sleeved T-shirt that looked more like a vest than a T-shirt. Rider could see the muscles under the top, causing him to blush.

The shorter guy soon sat down on Rider's bed, ignoring him in the doorway. "And this will be my bed," the stranger said bouncing up and down on the bed a couple of times.

Panic quickly set in and Rider lost for words. Had they gotten the wrong room? Rider was definitely in the correct room, else Yuki would have let him know. Rider tried to say something but no words would come out of his mouth. The short guy started to laugh, and the tall guy rolled his eyes as he turned to face Rider.

"Ignore Elliot. He's joking, he's actually only here to help me move in." the tall guy said as he extended a hand to Rider. "The name's—"

"Giasone?" Rider asked hopefully.

"Yeah. but you can just call me my American name, Jason," Jason said with a smile. "And you are?"

"Oh, I'm sorry. I'm Rider, Rider Williams. I guess I'm your roommate."

"And I'm Elliot McFarlane," Elliot said proudly, causing Jason to chuckle.

Elliot climbed off Rider's bed before dropping down onto the bed Jason was currently in the middle of trying to make. Jason rolled his eyes at his friend as Rider sat down and watched the dynamic between the two; the laughter and closeness remind him of himself and Lloyd. Rider was reminded of what Yuki had only told him an hour ago, he had to make sure his best friend was okay. He excused himself, allowing Jason the time he needed to settle in and the privacy he needed to call Lloyd. On his was out Rider was sure he heard Elliot whisper to Jason. *What about him? He's cute, don't you think?*

Rider found a bench outside his dorm and sat down, despite it been late into the afternoon the sun was still warm. He pulled out his phone and held his breath as he called his best friend. It had been very hit or miss if Lloyd would answer of late. He released the breath just as he heard the click of the phone, Lloyd's normal friendly voice coming through the speaker.

"Hey, Ri. I didn't think I would hear from you so soon. Everything okay down there in Texas?"

"Hey, Lloyd, I'm all settled in, Dad is already on the way back and I don't know anyone yet so thought I'd give my best friend a call. See how everything is going in Belmont." Rider swallowed, wondering how to bring up the topic of Yuki.

"I'm good, just got out of class. It's weird being at school alone. I'm sure it won't take you long before you make a lot of friends and forget about the people back in Belmont."

"Actually, I do know someone here. You'll never guess who the resident advisor is... It's Yuki." Rider could hear Lloyd swallow hard. "You okay, Lloyd?"

"Yeah. Why wouldn't I be?"

Rider could hear Lloyd's voice crack. "Because Yuki told me that you had broken up. He said it happened on your birthday. Why didn't you tell me?"

"I...I...I got to go, Ri." His voice was raw with emotion. Rider was sure he could heard tears coming from the smaller teen.

"Lloyd, please don't go. I'm here—"

The call dropped as Lloyd hung up on Rider. He tried calling back a couple of times but each time he was sent through to voicemail. He let out a sigh when he finally accepted Lloyd wasn't going to answer again.

Lloyd I'm here if you need me. You're my best friend don't forget that!

Rider remained where he sat as he thought about how his best friend was home alone. Taking a couple deep breaths and trying to clear his head, he knew who he could talk to that would cheer him up. Rider pulled out his phone again and dialled another number, struggling to not smile when his boyfriend answered.

Chapter 2

Cam

Last night, the call had gotten slightly steamy, and Cam had meant to send Rider a teasing picture but had accidentally fallen asleep. Instead, he just sent the photo now hoping it would arrive before Rider left for Houston. A knocking on his door caused him to almost leap off his bed. He pulled up his jeans and threw on a T-shirt, as he tossed his phone on the bed. Taking a deep breath and trying to look casual, he opened the door to his dorm room. He was greeted by the extremely happy face of Quintin Matthews, who pushed their way into the room. Cam wasn't even sure how his best friend had managed to get hold of the white basketball jersey hanging off his dark shoulders before they had even met the team.

"Did I interrupt you at the wrong time?" Matthews pointed at Cam's flushed cheeks.

"No…I was just doing some push ups."

As Matthews walked across the room, Cam's eyes went wide when he noticed his phone was still unlocked, the photo he had sent to his boyfriend on full display for anyone to see. Cam quickly dashed forward, scooping up his phone just as Quintin dropped down onto the bed.

"I didn't know push ups was the new code for sexting." Quintin smirked.

"How's Carrie-Ann?" Cam asked, quickly changing the topic.

"She's doing well. When her parents kicked her out, her plans for college went with her but she's found a job at a restaurant and a cheap place to rent. Sasha has also been helping her out. My parents said she could stay with them, but she refused. She wants to be independent. Shame she couldn't just come stay here with me."

Cam couldn't understand the thought of not loving a child just because of who they fell in love with. No matter how much of a bitch at times Carrie-Ann had been, she didn't deserved to be kicked out of her family home because she loved Quintin and her father had problems with Quintin's skin color. From the end of the last year, Carrie-Ann had grown on Cam. She had defended Rider against Spencer, then at the prom not only had she encouraged Cam to go to Rider, she actively shut down any cheerleaders who had been bad mouthing the couple. He wasn't sure what had happened to change her opinion of Rider, but he was sure Quintin had something to do with it.

"What about you and Williams?" Quintin asked.

It had been just six days since Cam had last seen his boyfriend and it was already difficult. The first night at Kentucky, he had rolled over in bed and was confused when there wasn't a warm body next to him. During the summer the couple had been inseparable, including sharing each other's beds. In the last week, he and Rider had messaged each other constantly when they weren't talking on the phone. Cam was sure if he didn't have unlimited minutes, his cap would have been hit within the first two days.

Matthews gently punched Cam's arm, bringing him back from his daydream. From the smile on Quintin's face, Cam knew what his friend wanted to discuss. He wanted to rush a fraternity with Cam, have the full college experience. Quintin was in the middle of explaining why playing beer pong every weekend was a good idea when there was a knocking on Cam's door. Cam was a lot more relaxed this time when he opened the door, revealing Mr. Olivers, the scout that had recruited them. Next to Mr. Olivers was another student who was tall, with pale skin and high cheekbones, silver hair just above his shoulders held back from his eyes by red headband, and a clean shave compared to the stubble that Cam and Quintin currently wore.

"Mr. Walker and Mr. Matthews. I want to introduce you to Mr. Morales."

The student walked forward and offered his hand to Cam and Quintin.

"Name's Fernando," the student said with a smile.

Fernando was the third recipient of the Issel Scholarship and would be joining them not only on the basketball team but also in history studies. As Quintin asked where Fernando was from, Cam couldn't help but focus on Fernando's family name, it sounded so familiar to him. It was when Fernando started talking about being from a small town in Kentucky called Murray that Cam realized where he had heard the name before.

"By any chance do you have a cousin named Dave?" Cam asked, causing a confused look on Quintin's face.

"Yeah. Dave's studying chemistry here at Kentucky. How did you know that?"

Cam smiled softly remembering when he had met Rider's sister Becca and her boyfriend Dave Morales last Christmas. Rider had been afraid to introduce Cam as his boyfriend and although he himself had been nervous, Cam said the words out loud while sliding his hand into Rider's. Whereas Becca was fairly loud and happy to try and embarrass Rider, Dave was a calm quiet guy. Cam's favorite moment had been when he and Dave had been sat on the couch, looking through old family albums of the two siblings, both agreeing how cute their younger partners had been.

"My...erm...my friend's sister is dating him."

Cam caught the look of sympathy of Matthews's face. For his last couple weeks at Belmont High, Cam had been out and proud, but at the moment he was back in the closet. Attitudes around LGBT athletes still hadn't caught up to the general public's, and until he knew more about his new teammates it was going to stay just between him, Matthews, Becca, and Dave. Matthews nudged Cam with his elbow, pulling back into the room; Mr. Olivers was already discussing the coming month's training while trying to find the schedule sheets in his large folder.

"I must have left the schedules in my office. If you

excuse me, I will be right back," the scout said, quickly turning on the spot and heading out.

"So, where are you guys from?" Fernando looked between them.

Cam's phone buzzed, distracting him from the conversation, while Matthews diverted the conversation to how Belmont had won their state's championship. Cam couldn't help but smile when he saw the name on his phone. As he opened the message, his eyes went wide, and his cheeks flushed a deep crimson as he was greeted by a photo of Rider in front of the mirror in nothing but Cam's jockstrap. Cam slammed the lock button as Matthews started to lean over, but he wasn't quick enough—Quintin's wide eyes revealed he had seen the image.

"Fernando, can you show me where the toilets are on this floor? I live the floor above." Matthews stammered quickly, looking flush himself.

Before Fernando could confirm that each floor of the dorms was identical he was pulled out the room by Matthews. Cam let out a sigh and reminded himself to thank Matthews later. He was just glad his new teammate hadn't caught the image; there was no way Cam would have been able to explain it. Accessing his phone again, the image of his boyfriend reappeared. Cam wished he had more than a couple minutes so he could fix the instant reaction the image had caused.

> You look extremely hot in that image. Shame I opened it around my teammates. Love you and I'll put better use to the photo later ;)

Cam slipped his phone back in his pocket, adjusting his jeans just as his door swung back open. Cam nodded at Matthews, allowing him to know everything was okay as he and Fernando came back into the room. The trio hardly managed to get another word out before Mr. Olivers came strolling into the room without knocking.

"Okay, gentlemen, here are the schedules. Now, let's go introduce you to the rest of the team."

The University of Kentucky's gymnasium was a lot larger than Belmont High's. Cam's head swivelled in all directions as he took in the grand scale, with a smile permanently etched onto his face. It wasn't long before Cam heard a voice echoing around the room. A number of basketball players started to line up, the majority Cam already knew due to the week he and Matthews had spent at Kentucky last year. The three new players were soon standing in front of the team with all eyes focused on them. Cam's gaze moved to the left as footsteps echoed around them. A short, plump woman walked across the hall, clipboard in hand, with a stern look on her face. The energy she gave off made Cam swallow hard; she hadn't even said a word and he already knew she wasn't someone to be messed with.

"I'm sure you all know me by now but let me reintroduce myself again. Oseman! Shut up and pay attention." The short guy on the end of the row instantly silenced and his eyes went wide. "I'm Coach Lieberman. If you're here, then congratulations on making the team again. Some of you only just made it." Coach's eyes fell on Oseman again. "First order of business, everyone please welcome

Walker, Matthews, and Morales. These are the freshman joining the team this year."

The coach handed Cam and Fernando their official team jerseys. Cam looked down to see the black number emblazoned on the white material. A smile spread across his face; he could never escape the number twenty-two. The number was everywhere in his life—his birthday, every team number he had, the day he lost of his father. Once the three had changed into their gym gear, Coach split the team and put the "newbies" through their paces. Cam gave his all, fighting harder than he had against Red Bay in the championship match. By the time Coach blew her whistle, Cam was struggling to breathe but he couldn't help smile.

"Good going out there, Walker. Olivers said you play Point Guard."

"That's correct, Coach."

"Good. Oseman is our main point guard, but you just dominated him, so there may be some changes. Go get cleaned up, then meet me back in the hall with the rest of the team."

Cam nodded to the coach before heading to the showers. He was amazed by the facilities as much as he was the gymnasium. Instead of having an open area like Belmont, there were individual stalls protected by a frosted glass door. The shower jets were powerful, instantly relaxing Cam's muscles, taking away the aches and pains. It wasn't until he heard Coach shouting into the changing room for people to hurry up that he finally decided to exit the shower cubicle.

"Good playing out there, Walker," Fernando said, offering Cam a high five.

Cam's left hand wrapped tight around his towel as his right hit the outstretched palm. Quickly changing back into his clothes, Cam found Matthews speaking to a few players. Alek Patel was the small forward, Hugo Livingston played center, Rhys Cox was power forward and captain of the team, and Jean Livingston the equipment manager and Hugo's non-identical twin.

"Good to see you again, Walker. If anyone deserved to get the scholarship, it was you and Matthews." Rhys slapped Quintin's back. It had been Rhys that had showed Cam around Kentucky last year.

"Sorry, guys, Coach wants to see you all now," Jean said.

"Sure thing, Twist, be right there," Hugo said to his brother.

Jean had tried out for the team with Hugo during their first year, during his trial he had slipped and twisted his ankle badly, ruling out any chance of joining the team. Coach Lieberman had found Jean's passion moving, so she assigned him equipment manager. Jean had enjoying the role so much that even after his injury had healed, he remained the equipment manager for the last two years rather than retrying for the team.

Each of the team had their own nicknames. Hugo's was "Wall" because during his first match an opponent had run straight into him, ending up on the floor with a broken nose. Rhys in his sophomore year went on a juice detox after getting extremely drunk at a frat party and losing all memory of the weekend; since then he had been nicknamed "Decox". Cam was sure it wouldn't be long before he and Matthews would be given nicknames.

The team all walked out together, soon finding themselves on the midcourt line. Coach Lieberman flicked through her clipboard, making the whole team wait on her.

"Okay, that was a good start to the year. I want to run a couple more drills before I decide on the starters. Now, to go over the rules, not only for the newbies but for some of you who seem to have forgotten them by the end of the last semester." Coach glared at Oseman and Hugo. "The team practises twice a week minimum, if we make it into the NCAA championship then that will go up to four times a week. If you miss two practises in a row you are cut from my team. If you act like a clown, either at practise or in your classes, you are cut from my team. If your grades fall too low, you will be cut from my team. If I hear about any racists or homophobic…" The pause cut into Cam. "…behaviour, you are cut from my team. That means if you are lucky enough to be here on a scholarship, you can say goodbye to your funding. I make the rules and my decision is final."

Cam would follow any rule Coach Lieberman made if it meant he could study history and do his father proud.

Chapter 3

Lloyd

The sun bore down on Lloyd as he sat on a bench overlooking the lake, his fingers swiping through the photographs on his phone, a weak smile on his face as he looked over the photos from Rider's birthday last year. The look on Rider's face as he stared at Cam…how had Lloyd not realized his best friend had been in love? Lloyd kept looking through the images till his heart shattered; it was from the evening that Cam and Rider had gotten back together. After the two had vanished, Lloyd had slipped next to Yuki whose arm was soon wrapped around him. Yuki had pulled him close and kissed him, during which Sam had snapped the photograph he was looking at now.

Locking the phone, he shoved it deep into his pocket. It had been six months, but it still felt like only yesterday since his heart had been destroyed. Last week, Rider had called, revealing that not only was he at the same college as Yuki, but that he now knew they had split up. Rider had tried calling a couple of times since, but Lloyd couldn't answer. Every time, his hand started shaking and he broke down in tears. Lloyd didn't want to bother his best friend with his problems. Moving across the country, starting college, leaving his boyfriend...Rider had too much to worry about already.

Lloyd rose from the bench and started walking toward the store. He had promised his father he would bring some groceries home. He moved around the store quickly and quietly, hoping to avoid anyone he knew. Averting his gaze from the cashier's eyes, he slipped the money across the counter and grabbed hold of the groceries, heading out into the warm sun again. Distracted by his feelings, Lloyd almost walked into someone as he exited the store. The man's gray suit clashed with the bright sky, but his sandy-brown hair was styled perfectly with not a single strand moving in the breeze.

"Mr. Keats, I'm sorry. I didn't notice you there," Lloyd said.

Lloyd's smile was not returned. Mr. Keats glared at Lloyd before grabbing him by the arm and pulling him around the corner of the store. The building casted a shadow over the two of them, removing them from the public eye.

"Mr. Keats?" Lloyd was frightened of the look on the older man's face.

"Shut up!" His dark eyes bore a hole into Lloyd. "What the fuck did you do to my daughter?"

"What? I...erm...what do you mean?"

Mr. Keats stepped forward, pining Lloyd against the wall. Lloyd swallowed hard as he tried to keep eye contact with Sam's father. Lloyd could feel his legs shaking, terror coursing through him. The bag slipped from his hand, but he didn't move to pick it up.

"You! You infected Samantha somehow. She was normal till she started dating you!" snarled Mr Keats, flecks of saliva landing on Lloyd's face.

"Sir. I…erm…I don't know what you mean."

His bony finger started pressing into Lloyd's chest as he demanded answers, Lloyd's head bounced off the cold brick of the store as he tried to put distance between them. Vile language was launched at him at such speed Lloyd struggled to understand everything that was being said. The verbal onslaught attacked his senses making the terror he was feeling multiply. Mr. Keats's daughter had come out as a "dyke", but that was impossible, his daughter was "normal". She would grow up normal, have a normal life. No matter how much a "stupid idiotic waste of space" like Lloyd infected her mind.

Lloyd's legs almost gave way; it was only the manic look on Mr. Keats's face that had Lloyd stuck to the wall. Sam had come out to her father. She had been so brave, and her father couldn't stand it. Lloyd's fingers pressed hard into his leg to try and stop his arm from shaking. All air seemed to have been pushed from his lungs, his chest became tight. The pounding in his chest started echoing in his ears. Gasping for breath, each one feeling like breathing volcanic fumes. A panic attack was imminent, and there was nothing that Lloyd could do to prevent it.

"My daughter tells me she's a dyke. That Williams boy is a faggot. What's the common denominator? You!" Mr.

Keats's finger pressed hard against Lloyd's sternum, making him hit his head against the wall again. "You infect everyone you come into contact with."

Lloyd bit his lip hard, trying to stop it from quivering. He could feel hot coppery liquid flow into his mouth, as he failed to hold in tears. He could no longer keep eye contact with Mr. Keats and his gaze fell to his shoes. It felt like he had been kicked in the gut, the wave of guilt ballooning in his chest. Maybe it *was* all his fault; if he wasn't around, then Sam might not be in this mess, Rider might not have been beaten up in school, and Yuki would never have had to feel the pain of breaking up with someone.

"Stay the fuck away from my daughter, you freak!"

Mr. Keats turned and walked away, a calm look crossing his face as he stepped back into the sunlight, as if nothing had just happened. Lloyd's legs gave up and he slumped down to the ground. Pulling his hand away from his thigh, his fingers were tinged red, blood starting to stain his jeans from the wounds now in his thigh. His head fell into his hands, defeated. The tears flowed as Lloyd wiped the blood from his mouth, trying to stem the cut from his lip with his tongue. As Lloyd sat on the cold ground all he could think about was how everyone would be better off without him. His hand shook as he pulled out his phone, tears sprinkling the glass as he punched out a message to his best friend. He quickly received a response.

Hey Lloyd, I'm so sorry but I'm just about to head into a lecture but I'll give you a call after it finishes.

Lloyd stayed where he was until his breathing returned to normal and his shaking was back under control. It had been a couple years since his last panic attack; it involved him in a bathroom crying until Sam had come in to check on him, ending with him coming out to her. He climbed off the ground, picking up the items that had spilled out of the bag, and proceeded to walk home. He wiped away the last of his tears just as he reached the door. He could hear his father in the kitchen as he entered the house.

"Hey, Lloyd." His father smiled. "You okay? Your eyes are red and your lip looks a little swollen."

"Hey, Dad, I'm fine. Some dirt got in my eye and I rubbed it a bit too long."

Faking a smile seemed to relax his father as Lloyd put the groceries away before excusing himself. He locked his bedroom and slid into his bed, pulling the covers over his head. Lloyd closed his eyes; his world was devoured by darkness as he slipped into a dreamless sleep, waking only when his father knocked on the door four hours later.

"Lloyd, are you hungry?"

"Not at the moment, I'll grab something later on," Lloyd called from under his duvet

"Okay. Don't forget, I'm at work in a couple of hours." Lloyd heard shuffling outside his room. "Lloyd, you know I'm always here if you need to talk. Okay, buddy?"

Lloyd didn't respond to his father. Instead, he pulled out his phone. No notifications, no messages, no missed calls. It was as if his best friend no longer cared about him. Lloyd bit his lip again, reopening his wound, and tried to hold back the tears. He pulled his journal out from under his bed and started to write. It had been the only way Lloyd had found recently to cope with the dark thoughts going through his head.

Jane

Jane was in the kitchen reading a book to her younger sister, Sofia, when the doorbell rang. It was strange for the Gomezes to receive a visitor after 7:00 pm. Val passed her daughters, kissing each on the forehead as she headed for the door. Jane turned her attention back to the book she was reading, Sofia smiling at the knight that had just arrived to save the princess. As the door opened Jane could hear crying echoing down the hallway.

"Juana, can you come here, please?" her mom called from the door.

"What about the princess?" Sofia looked up at her sister as she rose.

"I'll be right back, and then we will find out what happened to the princess."

Smiling at her sister, Jane left the book open on the table and moved toward the door. Once out of sight of Sofia, the smile dropped and was replaced by worry. A visitor so late who was crying…it brought memories of rushing home to find her mother on the floor in tears at the news of her father. As she approached, Jane could see her mother holding someone close, the crying becoming louder. Jane's eyes went wide when she noticed it was Sam wrapped in her mother's arms.

Jane ran toward the door. "Sam! What's wrong?"

Sam looked up, breaking the hug from Val and falling into her girlfriend's arms. Jane pulled Sam close to her, kissing Sam on the forehead just how her mother had done to her only minutes ago. Through the sobs, Sam explained how she felt she was finally ready to come out as bisexual to her parents. She had waited until her brother had taken the twins out the park before she had sat her father and mother down and broke the news. It wasn't the same as when Rider or Jane had come out; her father was furious, bursting into shouting before she could finished explaining how she had felt. He had thrown slurs at her, making her feel not normal, before he had to leave for work.

Her mother had remained quiet while the shouting happened, once her husband had vanished, she had pulled her daughter into a tight hug. When her father had returned home from work, he had remained silent, not even looking at her and concentrating on the twins. Only when they had gone to bed did his façade drop. He was angrier than when he left, spitting vile insults about finding the person responsible for corrupting his daughter. When Sam tried to explain how she wasn't corrupt, that she was still the same daughter she had always been, her father gripped her by the arm, taking her to the front door and throwing her out. Her brother Ant had tried to fight for his sister but received a backhand from his father. Sam left in tears to protect her brother. The red mark was still visible on her arm where she had been grabbed. Anger flowed through Jane, but she fought it back, Sam needed her to be calm right now.

"Oh, Samantha," Jane's mom rubbed Sam's arm as Jane hug her girlfriend tight.

"I...I...I didn't know where to go, what to do. I didn't want Ant to get hit again because of me." The tears were coming heavy and fast. "I'm so sorry, I have nowhere else to go."

"You don't need to be sorry. You are always welcome here. Isn't that right, Mama?"

"Absolutely. Juana, you take Samantha into the living room. I'll put the kettle on."

Sam was soon seated in the living room, Jane on one side of her and Sofia on the other. Her cheeks were stained with tears, but Sam had calmed down slightly. Jane squeezing her hand while Sofia rambled about the most recent argument she and a boy called Aaron had gotten into at the grief group.

"He said Twix was the best but everyone knows it's Kit-Kat," Sofia said adamantly crossing her arms over her chest

Jane slipped away to "check" on the hot cocoa. Her mother was on the phone, her voice quickening and Spanish slipping in, a sign of her mother's worry. As the call came to an end, her mother took a deep breath before explaining how Sam's mother had tried to stand up to her husband, but he had shouted her down. From the look on her mother's face, Jane was sure it was more physical than just shouting.

"He says that if Samantha isn't normal then she isn't welcome home. I promised Julia I would look after her daughter till everything calmed down." A scowl spread across Jane's face, causing her mother to pull her into a tight hold. "I know what you are thinking, Juana. Please do not go over there. Don't do anything to Mr. Keats. It may make things worse."

"Fine," Jane said to her mother as she tried to let the anger go. "Thank you, Mama, for letting Sam stay," Jane said as she hugged her mother back before they joined the two girls in the living room, a cup of cocoa in each hand.

Sam gave a weak smile as Jane explained how she was going to be staying here for a while. Sofia on the other hand was ecstatic about having Sam staying with them. She pulled Sam up to Jane's room as she explained all the stuff they could do together that Jane had refused to do.

"We can make each other look pretty with makeup."

"What about Jane?" Sam said, a gentle laugh escaping.

"She's too much of a boy to use makeup."

"Hey!" Jane shouted, causing Sofia and Sam to laugh out loud.

Sofia had argued that she was cheering up Sam, which resulted in being allowed to stay up past her normal bedtime. Jane eventually bribed her sister with the promise of ice cream for her to finally go to bed, leaving the two girls alone. It didn't take long before they were both lying on Jane's bed, Sam wrapped tight in Jane's arms.

"Everything will be okay, Sam." Jane kissed her girlfriend passionately.

"I just…I don't know."

"We'll get through this together. I'm sure your dad will come around. Till then you're all mine."

Chapter 4

Rider

It was the first day of his college experience and Rider was already in trouble.

He had arrived at what should have been his first journalism lecture fifteen minutes early, but he had misread his timetable and went to the wrong room. Rummaging through his backpack while crossing the quad, he pulled out the paperwork as the rain hit him in the face. He adjusted the hood on Cam's hoodie to try and protect him as he looked for the correct building and room. His eyes went wide as he noticed he was supposed to be the other side of campus.

As he shoved the soggy paperwork back in his bag, his phone vibrated in his pocket. He shielded his phone from the rain as best he could as he saw a text from Lloyd. This had been the first message he'd received from the younger boy in the last week, despite the numerous messages Rider had sent.

Hey Ri. Hope your first day is going well. Any chance you're free? Could do with a chat?

With only ten minutes to make the fifteen-minute journey, no matter how much Rider wanted to call Lloyd right now, he had to make it to his lecture. Rider sent an apology message and promised to call his best friend afterward. He pushed the phone into his pocket before he picked up speed, running in the direction of his class, the rain coming down heavier with each step. He was out of breath by the time he got to the correct room, with his phone saying he was four minutes late. Taking a deep breath, he pushed the door open slowly hoping to slip into class unnoticed, but his bad luck thanks to the water curse had other ideas. The door creaked loudly, pulling the attention of everyone in the room including the lecturer who had been writing on the board. Rider froze on the spot as everyone glared at him.

"In or out?" the lecturer said.

"Excuse me?" Rider asked, confused. A wave of hushed laughter spread through the room, causing his ears to glow red.

"Either come into my lecture or get out," the lecturer reiterated.

Her blonde hair was pulled up into a tight bun, her glasses rode halfway up her nose, and her amber eyes focused sharply on Rider. The tapping of her boot on the floor echoed as he opened the door fully and entered. The door was positioned at the back of the room, with a staircase leading down into the room with seats on either side. With

no free seats by the door, he moved down the stairs, his wet
sneakers squeaking with each step. Rider made sure to avoid
Professor Hudson's gaze; her eyes were like daggers. She
remained silent as Rider moved closer to her, finally
shuffling into the first available seat, three rows from the
front, his face still burning.

After a moment, Professor Hudson continued writing
on the board. Rider's eyes went wide when she wrote the
course code, *Jour 307*. Yuki had explained course codes
when he'd arrived, the higher the number, the more
complex the course. Freshmen courses were always in the
one hundred range, sometimes slipping into two hundred,
but never up to three hundred. As quiet as he could, he
pulled out the soggy timetable, right below the room he saw
the course code, *Jour 307*. *There has to be some type of mistake.*
Professor Hudson's voice pulled Rider back into the room.

"If you are in my class to become famous, then leave. If
you are here because you want to meet famous people, then
leave. This is a serious journalism course for serious
students. Before I start our first lecture, let's see how astute
you students are. Mr. Late, what's your name?" Professor
Hudson asked, looking at Rider.

"Rider Williams," he said.

"So, Mr. Williams, who said the difference between
literature and journalism is that journalism is unreadable
and literature is not read?"

Rider could tell she hadn't chosen him only because he
was late but also because she wanted to know if he could
handle the course. Rider felt every pair of eyes in the room
on him, but he wasn't nervous. Confidence flowed through

him. Simply smiling back at Professor Hudson, he responded, "That would be Oscar Wilde."

"That's correct." The professor nodded at Rider as a hushed whisper went around the room. "So, why are you all here? It is to prove Oscar Wilde wrong. The goal of this course is for you to be able to write journalism that's readable."

Rider let out a relaxing sigh as he removed the soaked hoodie and settled back into his seat, pulling out his notebook and pen. As Professor Hudson asked the class more questions, Rider couldn't help but smirk as he mentally answered questions that others in the room couldn't. It was around halfway through the lecture when Rider felt a pair eyes on him coming from the left of the stage. Someone sat to the side of the table that hosted Professor Hudson's notes, a nod from the professor caused the guy to jump up and start passing out study material.

As the Teaching Assistant moved around the room, Rider's eyes followed him. His slim build matched that of Rider, but he was taller, and his skin had a deep tan compared to Rider's paleness. He wore his unnaturally dark hair in spikes that seemed to shimmer a dark blue as the light caught it. Rider was sure it had been dyed. As he reached Rider, a smile appeared on his face, and with a simple nod he handed over the course notes. Rider couldn't help but be drawn to his deep emerald eyes. As the older student moved on, something shiny caught Rider's eyes; a small silver stud sat in his right ear.

There was an aura about the student that enraptured Rider, and he couldn't look away. He wasn't sure how much of the lecture he missed, it was only when he caught a glimpse of emerald eyes looking back at him that he quickly looked toward Professor Hudson and the writing on the board. Focusing on the lecture, Rider found himself raising his hand more often to answer the questions Professor Hudson asked the class, although he wasn't sure if the question on what the 5Ws stood for was rhetorical when only himself and one other person had raised their arm. He could see the TA in the corner smile and shake his head every time Rider got a question correct.

"Some of you have never been in one of my classes before so you won't know, but my classes are reliant on assignments. Your first assignment is…" Rider could hear a number of murmurs around the room as if they had expected an easy first day. "To write a four-page article about the difference between last year and this year, as well as what you are looking to get out of this course. Please submit all work to my office before four on Friday and you will receive your mark back next week."

A simple nod from the Professor caused the students to rise from their seats as they started leaving the lecture, all confusing Rider slightly. He had expected some type of bell to signify the end of the class. Rider quickly gathered his belongings and was barely out of his seat before Professor Hudson stopped him. Rider found his eyes focusing on his feet, it was difficult to keep eye contact with the Professor and he was worried if he looked around the room it wouldn't be long till his eyes settled on the TA.

"Mr. Williams, I am not used to students turning up late for my lectures."

"I'm sorry, Professor." Rider remained looking at his sneakers until the silence was too much. When he raised his head, he realized Professor Hudson had been waiting for him to look at her.

"I was surprised by your answers in class; you are younger than most in this class, but your answers were very thought out. Some of the questions I threw out even my third-year students would have struggled to answer. You are definitely more than you first appear, but please remember, Mr. Williams, first impressions often kill an interview."

"Erm...Yes, Professor, thank you." Rider was taken aback by the professor's words. "Professor, I do have one question."

"Sure, shoot."

"The course code indicates this is an advance course. I'm just wondering if I'm meant to be in this class."

Professor Hudson smiled, indicating for him to follow her as she wandered back over to her desk and collected her belongings. The course was, in fact, a second-year course and apart from himself all the students were in at least their sophomore year.

"Your application caused a stir among the staff. Professor Ren was impressed by your interview and the articles that he received from you high school, he believed the basic journalism course would have been too easy for you. Some students skip classes, but not normally freshmen, so you are lucky. There were arguments in the department, but eventually it was agreed you would be moved to my class." Professor Hudson laughed at the shocked look on Rider's face. "Don't worry, there is an ongoing pool to see how long it takes for you ask to be moved to the freshman course."

"I will do my best, Professor."

"That's all I ask. Okay, Mr. Williams, I have a lot of work to get on with, but I'm looking forward to reading your first assignment."

Rider couldn't help but smile as he climbed the steps to the exit. As he pulled open the door, this time it swung smoothly open, not emitting even one squeak. He almost jumped back into the closing door when a shadow appeared beside of him.

Rider found a smiling face looking at him. He had missed the TA pass him while speaking to Professor Hudson. "Nice answers in there, Peter."

"Peter?" A confused look spread across Rider's face.

"Nice shirt, Parker." Rider looked down at his shirt, the one that Cam had bought him for Christmas, which had a small spider-man hidden in the bottom corner

"Oh, thank you," he said, blushing slightly.

"Keep up the passion and you will make Professor Hudson proud. She did go up to bat to get you assigned to her class, after all. Anyway, catch you around, Rider."

With the TA heading off, Rider was left to reflect on what he's just heard. From the cold reception when he'd first arrived in class, he would have never expected it was Professor Hudson who had fought to get him assigned to a second-year course. The confidence he had felt answering the first question burst alive again as he started heading out the building. He was glad to see the rain had stopped, but as he was looking up at the sky, Rider accidentally bumped into someone.

"Are we always going to run into each other like this?" Jay smiled at Rider. "What you doing in this building?"

"I'm taking journalism. What about you?" Rider asked.

"Taking my third year of law. I thought we would have more likely seen you in front of the camera rather than the one doing the interview."

Rider felt a bit weird as he slipped on Cam's hoodie on before they started walking over to the quad, he wasn't used to guys hitting on him. The only person to ever show him interest was Cam. Jay's arm landed on Rider's arm as he finished a joke, it lingered until Rider felt uncomfortable and he shook it away.

"How did you know I was gay?"

"Sixth sense." Jay laughed again, raising his arm back up, but Rider pulled back to avoid it.

"Well, I have a boyfriend." Jay's arm fell, but the smile remained on his face. "But thank you for the compliments. It's very nice of you."

"No problem. Who knows, maybe in the future?" Jay looked around to check they were alone. "If you're not interested in me, what about my wares? Can I tempt you with some weed?"

Rider declined and said goodbye to Jay, breathing a sigh of relief once the door to the dorm building closed behind him. He walked back to his room, his mind focused on his boyfriend in Kentucky. The room was empty as he entered. Pulling out his notes from the class, he started to work on his first assignment of the year, the phone call he had promised Lloyd accidentally forgotten about.

Chapter 5

Cam

Cam doubled over as he gasped for air. The practises at Kentucky were more intense than Belmont. Not only did they train for three hours solid, but each session ended with a full match. As he rose back to a standing position, Rhys slapped him on the back in celebration. Cam had managed to clinch a last-minute three-pointer which had managed to secure victory for their team.

"I see you haven't lost any of your skills, Python."

The team couldn't seem to settle on one nickname for Cam. It had first started as "Long Shot" due to his ability to sink baskets from beyond the midcourt line. It had evolved into "Shooter", followed quickly by "Revolver", "Colt", "Colt Python" and finally just "Python". Matthews, on the other hand, the team had decided on one name, and it had stuck, "Q-Tip".

"Thanks, Decox," Cam said, giving the captain a fist bump.

The duo quickly lined up at midcourt, along with the rest of the team. Coach Lieberman liked to highlight all the spots in the game where each team had made mistakes and how they could improve. Cam had quickly come to realize that Coach rarely gave out any praise, and this only seemed to spur everyone on, including Cam.

"That's it for today's practise. The starting list will be going live in a couple hours. If people do not agree with the decision, you know how we settle it. Now get out of here."

Hugo caught the confused look on Cam and Matthew's faces as they all headed back toward the locker room. "A couple years ago, one of the seniors lost their starting position and refused to accept the coach's decision. He challenged his sophomore rival to a one-on-one match. When Coach found out what happened she made a ruling, whoever won was the starter."

Matthews laughed. "Maybe I'll challenge if I don't make starter."

"No go, Q-Tip. Only someone who lost their position can challenge," Hugo said.

Cam couldn't help but laugh when Matthews' face dropped. They had both come to the realisation that neither would be starters in their freshman year, even Rhys hadn't been able to tell them the last time a freshman had made starter. The atmosphere in the changing room felt electric as Cam climbed out the shower; people were already arguing over who was most likely to get a position. As Cam slipped his T-shirt over his head, a shadow blocked out the light; Matthews' smiling face greeted him.

"Guess what?" Matthews said with a smile.

"You hate you nickname Q-Tip?" Cam smirked causing Matthews to roll his eyes. After first receiving the nickname, he had spent the entire evening in Cam's room complaining.

"The guys invited us out for a few drinks, it's a team tradition before the list goes up. Fernando is up for it. What about you?" Cam had barely enough time to even nod before Matthews was shouting at the group forming by the door. "Python's in."

The team was soon located in a bar off campus, beer in everyone but Cam's hands. Hugo had offered to buy him one in case he was IDed, but Cam had declined to a round of booing from the team. Jean had asked Cam and Matthews about Belmont, but when the team found out Cam was originally from New York, the conversation quickly derailed. After thirty minutes of talking about his home city, Cam wasn't the only one bored. Oseman quickly changed the subject to something he knew more about: women.

"So, Wall, how's Steff?" Oseman asked.

"No clue, ended it with her just before summer. I'm all about Beth now." Hugo smiled as he finished his drink.

"Wait! Isn't Beth, Steff's sister?" Rhys asked while shaking his head. Jean simply rolled his eyes at his brother.

Hugo wasn't the only one dating. Jean was in a long-term relationship with a girl called Jo, they had met in their economics lecture in freshman year and had been steady since. Hugo seemed to change girls every couple months, Beth his current conquest. Oseman was in an on-and-off relationship with Ava, one of the cheerleaders. Fernando was currently single, enjoying sleeping around rather than staying in any steady relationship.

"What was the magic number for last year?" Oseman asked with a wink.

"Seventeen." A round of applause went through group. "What can I say, if I want something I take it."

"Q-Tip? What about you?"

Cam rose and went to the toilet as Matthews started talking about Carrie-Ann. By the time he returned, Matthews phone was making the rounds, showing off Carrie-Ann. A number of wolf whistles came from the team, mainly from Hugo and Oseman, before all eyes quickly fell onto Cam. He could see a worried look in Matthews' eyes. Cam smiled to show it would be okay.

"I'm dating someone, although they go to a university in Houston. We're doing the long-distance thing, although it's difficult. I miss them."

"What's her name?" Rhys asked.

Cam could see Matthews biting his lip. "Erm...Trish."

Unlocking his phone and moved through the pictures. He hovered over the picture that Trish had sent to him earlier in the year of Rider and him sat on a bench in the met. His heart ached that he couldn't share this with his teammates, but Coach's words about homophobia echoed in his head. He moved to the next picture, the photo Rider had taken of him and Trish in front of a painting, mimicking the expressions of the characters. He passed his phone around, shock and confusion on Matthews' face.

"She's hot!" shouted Oseman.

Cam swallowed hard as he took his phone back. He

hated lying not only to his teammates but also about Rider. They had spent most their final year at high school hiding their relationship from the world and here Cam was shoving it back into the closet. Excusing himself, he headed to the bar, but then detoured out the front door. Crossing the road, he sat on a bench, phone in hand. Pulling up his contacts list, he selected the number that was set as his first favorite, Riders and hit the call button. Cam let out a sigh when Rider's phone rang out, instead he called the next best person.

"CJ, CJ, wherefore art thou, CJ."

"Hey, Trish." Cam chose to ignore any and all Shakespeare references. "Wait, is that Yorick in the background?"

"Oh...erm...I'm still at college. Anyway, how is your college going, CJ?"

He wasn't sure how to answer, he could still feel his guilt over hiding his relationship with Rider. Trish must have sensed something wrong as she instructed whoever she was with that she would catch up, giving Cam her full attention. He was soon telling her everything, from lying about Rider's name to showing her photograph.

"CJ, breathe and relax. I don't mind that you used my name, it was sweet that I was the first girl you could think of. Also, don't worry about Rider, I'm sure he will understand. I mean, I get why you would want to hide your sexuality from your teammates. Sometimes it's just hard to tell people things."

"I just hate it. We had to sneak around most of last year.

I don't want to have to force our relationship back into the dark. Why do jocks have to be homophobic pricks?"

"Do you know if your teammates are?"

He was soon explaining the way Coach had worded her welcome speech and the pause around the homophobic attitude. Cam couldn't help but let out a small laugh when Trish started tutting. She always had this magical ability to cheer him up. The phone vibrated in his ear, as Cam pulled away, he could see a message from Rider apologising for missing his call.

"Rider by any chance?" Trish laughed.

"How…? Actually, keep your secrets. I'll call you later."

Trish wished him luck before ending the call. Cam took a deep breath as he called Rider, this time being answered almost immediately.

He swallowed the lump forming in his throat. "Hey, Rider. You free? I just wanted to talk to you about something."

"I'm sorry for not answering earlier, I was using my lunch break to complete an assignment that's due by five today and I'm currently on my way to my afternoon class. You're lucky you only had morning practice today." Rider huffed as he ran across his campus. "Is it serious?"

"No, no, it's nothing serious. It can wait, although I do have to go back to practise soon as they are finalising the starters list today. I love you, Ri, I miss you like crazy."

"I miss you too. I love you, Cameron James Walker. Good luck with the list and call me later, okay?"

Agreeing, he let out a sigh once the call ended. The phone had just reached his pocket when someone jumped over the back of the bench, landing next to him. Oseman had been sent to locate him as the starting list should be posted. Cam followed the shorter teammate back into the bar, grabbing his jacket from the seat by Matthews before the team headed back toward campus. He and Quintin hung back, allowing the older students to check the list first.

"No way! How?" Oseman spat at Rhys who just shrugged.

Jean walked over to where Cam and Matthews stood, a smile on his face. "You might want to check the list."

Cam looked at Jean then the list. His feet only engaging once Quintin gave him a nudge forward. The group around the sheet seemed to separate as he approached, his eyes scanned down the list until they settled on the bottom name. Cam's confusion only increased. *Starting Point Guard————Cameron Walker.*

"How did Python beat me?" Oseman glared at Cam. "I challenge it!"

Hugo slapped the back of Oseman as he glared at Cam before disappearing toward the changing room. Cam was still looking at the sheet until he felt the captain's hand on his shoulder.

"You heard him. He's challenged you for his spot back. Better go get changed," Rhys said.

Cam's stomach churned as he got back into his uniform. Matthews was trying to give him a pep talk, but Cam couldn't concentrate on anything, it was background noise. As he stepped on the court, a calm feeling flooded over Cam, the same feeling he had when Rider had kissed him for the first time. His eyes focused on Oseman who was ready, passing the ball to Cam.

"Okay, the rules are simple," Rhys said, coming forward to referee. "First to five baskets wins. Once the match starts it can't be stopped until there is a victor, if a player calls it quits then they lose. Both defender and challenger must accept the result of the match. Defender starts with the ball. Keep the roughness to a minimum."

Bouncing the ball a couple times, Cam nodded indicated he was ready. As the whistle blew, he didn't move. Instead, he jumped, launching the ball down the court straight into the basket. A wave of cheers echoed around the court. Cam remained focused on Oseman, not allowing his advantage to go to his head. They both charged down the court, Cam trying to guard any opening the smaller teen had. A shot ricocheted off the backboard but using his speed, Oseman was around him and scored the rebound before Cam could even turn.

As the one on one carried on, each point guard closed down the other. Cam lost track of the time and the score. This was no longer about the starting position, it was about pride. Oseman tried for a long shot but wasn't accurate. Cam scooped up the ball, turning to shoot as Oseman's arms came up wide, catching Cam off guard. An elbow connected with Cam's nose. Recoiling backward, he could feel the blood already starting to flow, his eyes watering. Oseman took advantage and scored a basket.

"Walker, you okay?" Matthews shouted from the sidelines. "We have to let him sort that out."

"Sadly, we can't. The rules state if he can't play then Oseman wins," Rhys said, sympathetic.

Cam wasn't going to go out so easy. He wiped the blood away with his arm as he took the ball back to the starting point as Rhys announced it was four-all, who ever got the next basket would be Kentucky's starting point guard. Using his clean hand, Cam wiped the tears out of his eyes. Bouncing the ball a couple times, a smirk spread across Cam's face. He faked left, then spun to the right, running straight past Oseman, who was still going to Cam's left. Charging down the court, he could feel his mark just behind him. When he wouldn't make it any further forward, Cam leaped, pushing the ball with all his might, sending it through the basket.

"Fuck!" Oseman's defeat echoed around gymnasium.

The team was over to them before Oseman could complaining that he had been cheated. The captain wouldn't have any of it, Cam had won even with a bloody nose. Matthews was already shoving tissue up Cam's nose to stop the bleeding.

Matthews laughed. "How? I mean, how many people have you beat with that move?"

Cam held his nose back, trying to stem the flood as he watched his challenger storm off toward the locker room, only stopping to glare at Cam before carrying on. Cam couldn't help but smile through the pain in his nose. He was now the official Kentucky starting point guard.

He couldn't wait to tell Rider.

Chapter 6

Jane

Jane had a smile on her face as she sat in the cramped office, a stack of documents on the table in front of her. An ancient computer made noises as it sat idle.

She had met Abe Hancock at the grief group she went to after losing her father, which Abe ran in memory of his wife. Abe also ran the Belmont homeless shelter. With all the help the group and Abe had given Jane and her family, she had happily agreed to volunteer some of her time at the shelter. She had only been here for thirty minutes, but the fuss Abe had made when she had arrived made her want to donate even more of her time.

"Okay, Jane, I think that's all the paperwork done," Abe said, closing the file that sat on his lap. "We will start you with something easy for your first time. Wouldn't want to scare you straight away with having to do the laundry."

The duo rose to their feet and headed toward the kitchen. Abe had already given Jane a tour when she first arrived. The building had two large open areas with three-tier bunk beds, a number of private rooms that could be rented at a discounted cost, and a large industrial laundry room. Jane had been surprised when she first arrived how few people it took to run the shelter; at the current time there was one person on the reception, two people stripping the rooms, Abe who had been working on the finances, and Adele who was currently shaking Jane's hand.

"Adele will show you how to get the food ready for this evening. Once you finish, come back to the office and I'll find something else for you to do."

Abe quickly vanished, leaving Jane to peel and chop potatoes before dropping them into the pot while Adele worked on some type of undistinguishable meat. The goal was to make somewhat edible stew out of the very minimal ingredients that the shelter currently had.

"So, what made you decide to volunteer, Jane? We don't get many young people giving up their time."

"I lost my father earlier this year. Abe and his support group have been so helpful, and I wanted to give something back." Jane's voice cracked slightly. It was still painful to think about.

"I'm so sorry for your loss. It is very sweet that you want to help. We definitely need it."

"What do you mean?"

Jane was shocked as Adele revealed the truth. The Shelter was in financial difficulty, each month only just barely paying the bills, often thanks to Abe put his own money into the shelter. The shelter had yearly fundraisers, but the amount raised had slowly being reduced each year since the loss of Abe's wife. Jane had been so invested in the details, she had finished all the potatoes without even noticing.

Once everything had been added to the pot, Jane tried to light the stove but all that happened was a clicking sound. Everything in the kitchen was at least twelve years old, the majority of the items being donated to shelter. The newest item was the refrigerator which was coming up to its eighth birthday. Adele noticed the difficulty Jane was having, she flicked the lighter while hitting the gas at the same time, causing a flame to burst underneath the pot of stew.

"The stove can be a bit tricky the first couple times. I'll finish up here if you want to go find Abe." Adele smiled before filling the sink with water.

Entering the office, there was no sign of Abe. Jane turned to head back out when her elbow caught a stack of files on the table causing them to crash down to the floor. Crouching to collect the paper, she couldn't stop from looking. The paper was a mix of financial documents, spreadsheet printouts of shelter outgoings, several bills— some of which were second and third requests for payments—and IOU notifications from people who owed the shelter money. Adele was right, the shelter was struggling. Jane wasn't sure how long it could keep running with such a shortfall. She leapt to her feet, paper in hand when she heard a noise behind her.

"Abe, I'm so sorry. I didn't mean to—"

Abe stopped Jane with a wave of his hand. "It's okay, Jane. It's no secret about the shelter." He sat down, signalling Jane to join him. "I try my best running this place but I'm struggling. It has been decades since I studied business and it's drastically changed since my heyday. The volunteers are wonderful people but most only finished high school."

"I'm studying business at college, I could take a look if you don't mind." Jane smiled weakly,

Abe just nodded handing her the most recent folder. Jane's eyes flicked over the paperwork, her brain looking for anywhere she may be able to save the shelter any amount of money. The current rate for electricity seemed high and according to the bills, which dated back three years, the shelter hadn't looked for a better deal. There were invoices for bedding cleaning company, which made Jane question if there might be cheaper options available or a discount for charities. A little smile appeared on her face when she looked over the invoices for the food deliveries. The shelter ordered food on a weekly basis, but if they ordered in bulk and froze the produce it would save some money.

"My mother is also a manager of Paulo's, the Italian restaurant at Third and Main. Due to policy, they toss a lot of food in the garbage that is still perfectly fine. I could speak to her about donating the food. That way the shelter would get some better-quality food but also save money."

The old man smiled as he sat back in his chair. Jane returned to looking over the paperwork when there was a knock on the door, Abe was needed at reception, someone who had been banned from the shelter was trying to enter. As he rose, he logged into the computer so Jane would have access to all the documents. Jane positioned herself behind the computer, surprised the ancient machine connected to the internet.

She got lost in all the documents and ways she could help the shelter until she heard a humming coming from the doorway. The harsh florescent light cascaded down on the soft, dark face of a boy who looked confused at why Jane was behind the desk.

"You're in my dad's seat," he said, walking into the room.

"I'm helping him out with some paperwork." Jane smiled

"Wait. You're Sofia's older sister. Does she still think Kit Kats are the best?" He laughed, shaking his head as he dropped into the seat Jane had previously filled.

"Yeah, that's me. My name is Jane and I'm guessing you're Aaron."

Aaron looked at Jane with even more confusion, he demanded to know how she knew his name. No matter how many times Jane confirmed it was from Abe, Aaron was adamant that Sofia must have been talking about him. She laughed, her eyes fell back to the paperwork in front of her, Aaron remained where he sat, looking around the room. It wasn't long till Jane was distracted again, Aaron singing jingle bells at the top of his voice.

"You do realize it's not even October yet. You still have three months till Christmas."

"It doesn't need to be Christmas to sing the songs. They are fun to sing and always make people smile."

Jane had a huge grin on her face; all she could do was shake her head, but Aaron was right, his singing had made her smile. Aaron kept her company as she worked, telling her all the stuff he was currently interested in at school and all the subjects he hated. The split was simple if it had anything to do with playing, like recess, then Aaron liked it, if it required him sitting still and studying then he didn't.

"How's it going…" Abe paused as he entered the office. "Aaron, why are you bothering Jane? You should be doing your homework."

Aaron glared at his father before slipping out of the chair, buying himself just a small amount of extra time by giving Jane a hug rather than saying bye. Abe sat down as Jane went over what she had found so far. She had managed to find cheaper water, gas, and electric deals, as well as articles online about companies who provide corporate sponsorship or, in simple terms, provide certain items such as phonelines and internet for free for charities. In total, she had found ways that would save the shelter around three hundred dollars a month. Abe's jaw dropped as she went through a number of different potential solutions, they weren't guaranteed but it could possible ease the burden on the shelter and Abe.

"Jane, wow. I mean wow. Thank you. With running the shelter full time, organising the grief group, looking after Aaron, and worrying about Peyton in New York. I guess it was easier to just leave things how they were and expend my energies elsewhere. Also, I hate those machines," he said, pointing to the computer. "Always struggled with them. Last month I had just finished doing the new timesheets only for it to freeze."

Abe went around the table and pulled her into a tight hug; a tear appeared in the corner of his eye. She couldn't help but feel a little emotional herself. Abe was a great man, what he was trying to do for the community was amazing. Any little thing she could do to assist was worth it. The duo spent the next two hours going through the paperwork trying to find even the smallest amount they could save. By the time Jane was ready to leave the shelter they had made seventeen phone calls and the grand total would be around six hundred and fifty dollars better off a month. Even Aaron came so see Jane off.

"Thank you so much for everything you have done today, Jane," Abe thanked her.

"Not just today. I'll be back next week."

Aaron burst into a smile when he heard Jane was going to be back, and even Abe struggled to hide his smile. The duo walked her out of the shelter, organising times for next week as her mom's car pulled up to the curb. Jane hugged them both before she climbed into the back of the car where Sam was positioned, having given up the front seat to Sofia. Sofia knocked excitedly on the window waving at Aaron, who was obviously trying to ignore her but failing. His eyes kept glancing into the front window. Sam squeezed Jane's hand before the car pulled away from the shelter.

"How did your day go?" Sam asked.

"I'm so proud of you, Juana, for volunteering," her mom said.

"Did Aaron mention me?" Sofia shouted over Sam.

Jane rolled her eyes at her sister before telling her mom and Sam about everything that had happened and the proud feeling she had in her chest. Sam's jaw dropped when Jane explained how much she had managed to save the shelter.

"Jane, that is amazing," Sam said, giving her a quick kiss on the cheek

"Thanks. While I sat there looking for solutions, I felt…it was challenging, to be sure, but I just felt great, like I was doing something worthy. The feeling of trying to save the shelter was amazing."

"Maybe that's your calling. After you graduate, maybe you can go into business consultancy."

The idea caused the smile on Jane's face to grow. Sam already had the plan to go into social work and Jane originally had no idea what she wanted to do, but now she wanted to help people. Things were definitely looking up.

Chapter 7

Rider

It was only the third Monday of the semester, but Rider was confused why Professor Hudson had instructed him to remain behind again. He had arrived early, answered any question thrown at him and even apologised for sneezing. There was only Professor Hudson, Rider, and her TA left in the room before she started talking.

"So, Mr. Williams, held back again."

Rider swallowed the lump that was forming in his throat.

"You don't need to look so worried. Your assignment was extremely interesting. The format and structure...the way you turned a phrase was extremely well done. Your ability is already well ahead of many of the students in this course. At one point there was questions if your work had been plagiarized, but when it was processed through plagiarism software it came up clean."

"Thank you?" Rider wasn't sure if he should be

offended at the idea of plagiarizing his assignment or be complimented.

"So, the reason why I asked you to stay behind is I have a proposition for you. It is extremely rare, but I would like to offer you the position as my third TA."

"You want me to be your teaching assistant?"

"Yes. My third TA graduated last year and, out of the class, I believe you are the best choice. You'll assist in classes and sit in on some more advance classes, which I'm sure you are ready for. You won't have to teach a class, but you will support Nixs when he has to. Being a TA is a lot of work, but can be very beneficial, especially if you are serious about journalism."

Rider was still in shock when he agreed to do it. Professor Hudson smiled before leaving for a meeting. Rider soon found himself sitting in the empty lecture hall across from the TA that had been watching him the first lecture. He was in his senior year and had been Professor Hudson's TA for the last year. Rider struggled to maintain eye contact as the emerald eyes looked over him.

"You must have really impressed Michele for her to offer you the TA position."

"Michele?"

"You didn't think her first name was professor, did you?" The TA laughed. "Well, you impressed me anyway. Your take on the ethical implications of giving everyone an equal platform even if it was a hate group was very interesting."

"Thank you." Rider's ears started to blush, he wasn't used to getting compliments on his writing.

"We haven't officially been introduced, I'm Nickolas Nicholson. It's a pleasure to meet you, Rider."

"Cool name. So do you prefer Nickolas or Nick?" Rider smiled, causing a weird look to come across the TA's face. "Sorry? Did I say something wrong?"

"No, not at all, I'm just used to people laughing at my name. Anyways you can call me Nixs."

The duo started going over what Rider's requirements as TA would be, but were soon derailed into hobbies and interests of both of them. Nixs was also a geek, having collected comics since he was very young. His favorite character was Wiccan, followed by Spider-Man. A smile spread across Rider's face at the name Wiccan, one of the few gay superheroes. In fact, when he had been younger Rider had a major crush on Wiccan.

"So, you always been a nerd?" Nixs smiled.

"I'm not a nerd, I'm a geek," Rider said defensively, drawing a laugh from the older guy.

"Oh yeah, you are definitely a geek, but I saw the mark for your assignment. You are also definitely a nerd." Rider found himself blushing again, a smile on his face.

Nixs had also written for his high school paper and had dreamed of writing for a newspaper all his life, despite that his parents had wanted him to join the Marines. In his first year at college, he ended up writing for the university paper, but once he became a TA it had taken up too much of his time, requiring him to drop the paper. Overall, Nixs was an older, slightly taller version of Rider. A ringing caught Rider's attention, he was sure he had heard the tone before. It wasn't until Nixs pulled out his phone that he realized it was a 16-bit version of the Spider-Man tune. The smile on Nixs face disappeared quickly as he looked at his phone.

"Sorry, I've got to take this."

Nixs disappeared over into the corner of the lecture hall. Rider tried to give Nixs some privacy by concentrating on the notes he had taken during class, but when Nixs' voice got louder, he couldn't help but listen in to the conversation.

"No, Jordon, no! I told you at the beginning of summer it's over between us. Why? Because I said I said I loved you and you responded by sleeping with two other guys—at the same time. You're sorry? No! You don't get to be sorry. Fuck you, no, I won't drop by. Yeah? Well, screw you too."

Rider's gaze dropped back to his notes as Nixs walked back over slowly, breathing heavily. Nixs dropped his phone on the desk in front of Rider as he started to pace, letting out a long, controlled sigh. Rider remained looking at his notes, giving the older guy some time to calm down, not looking up till Nixs spoke again.

"I'm sorry you had to hear that," Nixs said as he slowly slid into the chair next to Rider.

"Hear what?" Rider playing innocent.

"Cute." Nixs laughed, a smile reappearing on his face. "My ex, rough break up."

"I'm sorry, she—"

"He. It's okay, I'm better off without him."

Rider's jaw dropped; he was lost for words. From all the glances he had taken of Nixs, Rider knew Nixs was cute, but he had never once thought he might be gay. The confidence, the way he spoke his mind; Rider wasn't used to seeing that in any gay guy he knew. Nixs' smile dropped off his face as he waited for Rider to say something. When Rider didn't say anything, Nixs bit his lip, a slightly worried look on his face.

"You don't have a problem with me being gay, do you? My roommate in freshman year had a major problem with it." Nixs laughed nervously.

"No, no, no." Rider waved his arms around, almost hitting Nixs in the face. "I mean...erm... That would just be strange. I don't mean you being gay is strange...erm...I mean it would be strange if I had a problem, because I do. I mean I don't...erm...I am. I mean I'm also gay."

"Oh, cool." Nixs laughed at Rider's ramblings, causing Rider to blush again. "Good to know."

"What happened with your roommate?" Rider asked.

"Well, we got in a fist fight, then it got...well, complicated is probably the best way to describe it."

A noise from behind them caused Rider to jump. Students were starting to filter into the lecture hall. Nixs checked the time and realized another lecture was imminent. Rider quickly scooped up his notes and shoved them in his bag before the duo headed outside, the dye in Nixs hair reacting with the sun, the blue becoming vibrant. There was something about it that Rider found cute.

"Sadly, I have another lecture in about thirty minutes, so I've got to head. Catch you around, Rider."

"Bye, Nixs."

Rider started to walk in the direction of his dorm but instead found himself watching Nix walk across the quad. It wasn't until Nix turned and looked back at him that he panicked, looked away, and started to walk at double pace.

Rider took a deep breath as he reached his room, trying to focus himself. Pushing open the door, his eyes went wide as the scene that greeted him. Jason was currently lying down on his bed, someone straddling him, leaning over, their mouths pressed together, hands running over each other's clothed bodies. Rider's phone accidentally slipped out of his hand, which snapped the two out of their make-out session. Rider was sure, the person kissing Jason was part of the football team.

"I'm sorry," Rider said louder than he had meant to.

The jock jumped off Jason, a panicked look on his face before he quickly disappeared, passing Rider on his way out of the room. The door slam echoed in the small room. Jason's hands came up, covering his face as he let out a long sigh. Rider stood still looking around the room, he noticed a bottle of open vodka on the desk. *Was this just a drunken accident?*

"Jason, I am so sorry, I didn't mean to."

"It's fine, Rider." Jason smiled as he sat up. "Not your fault. I should have put a tie on the door handle or something. I knew the risk of making out with a closeted guy. I guess he won't be coming back anytime soon." Jason let out a small awkward laugh. "So, I guess you know, I'm gay."

"Is it national coming out day?" Rider joked, confusing Jason. "Someone else told me they were gay today." Jason's gaze remaining on Rider, waiting for acceptance or rejection. "Don't worry about being gay, I'm also gay."

They both laughed as they described how they had both been too afraid to bring up the topic with each other.

Rider soon found himself telling Jason everything about what had happened to him last year and how he and Cam had ended up together, how since the attack and moving to Houston he wasn't going to hide the fact he was gay but wasn't going to go around shouting it from the rooftops either. Jason's parents had happily accepted him, but his brother, Virgil, had taken it badly, accusing him of just wanting special treatment. He also hoped his youngest brother would accept him, but Dante was only a year old, so he still had a while to find out. What surprised Rider more than Jason being gay was the discovery of how he and Elliot had been a couple and only split due to Jason coming to college.

"I'm sorry about, Elliot."

"You don't need to be. We couldn't do the long distance, even thought it would have been closer than you and Cam. Elliot is extremely sweet, he would rather have me find someone on the football team than pine for him," Jason said with a smile, his cheeks blushing. "Long distance is hard when all you can think about is kissing the guy you love."

The evening passed quickly as they discussed when they had realized, celebrity crushes, and first loves. Rider struggled to hide the smile on his face as he climbed into his bed later on.

"I've never been so relieved in my life," Rider said as he lay down on his bed.

"How come?" Jason said from his own bed.

"Well, I was worried about telling you I was gay. I thought it might make living together uncomfortable. I guess I was mistaken." They both laughed. "Although, we have to come up with some type of signal for if you are making out with a closeted guy."

Chapter 8

Cam

Cam sat on the bed breathing heavy, phone still in his hand. He pulled up the call list but decided against calling Rider back. He was still angry, and it could cause the fight to get worse. Their daily call had been pushed to weekly due to both being extremely busy. He had been telling Rider how he and Matthews were interested in trying to join a fraternity that a number of the basketball team were a part of, but Rider had got upset saying it would take up even more of Cam's time. Cam had only simply highlighted that the reason they had slipped to a weekly call was due to the extra time Rider was putting into his TA work. Cam let out a sigh, he could still hear the conversation in his head.

"Being a TA will help me get a job in the future. A frat is only used to drink and sleep with women. What happens if they find out you have a boyfriend? That Trish isn't your girlfriend?" Rider snapped.

"If they find out about you then so be it. I love you,

Rider, but you haven't given me a good enough reason not to rush," Cam said, trying to remain calm.

"I don't even know what you mean by rush." Rider's volume rose enough to allow the phone to echo around Cam's dorm room.

"Join, Ri. Rush means to try and join."

"Fine, do whatever you want!" Rider said, his voice cracking slightly.

That's when Rider had ended the call. Cam hated being so far away from Rider; little things that shouldn't be a problem seemed to balloon due to the distance. He had a twisting feeling in his gut, although they had squabbles before this had been their first proper fight. Cam enjoyed the time he spent with the basketball team, but it also felt like he still needed to hide a part of him. That he had thrown Rider and his love for him into the closet just to try and be a jock again... Letting out a sigh, Cam went to press redial, but his phone burst to life, Rider's name lighting up the screen.

"Cam, I'm sorry."

Cam could tell from his voice, Rider had been crying. "Ri—"

"I mean it. I just miss you so much and don't want to lose you." Rider started crying again, causing a couple tears to appear in Cam's eyes. If he had known being so far from Rider was going to be so hard, Cam might not have accepted the scholarship.

"I miss you too, Ri. I love you so much. I know rushing a frat may take up more of my time, but I'll still be here for you. No matter what happens, I will always have time to call you. I know your TA work is amazing and I'm so proud of you. If you really don't want me to rush, I won't, I just don't want Matthews to rush alone."

"No, Cam. I want you to do it. I don't want you to miss out on anything because of me. I'm just worried what will happen to you if they find out about me."

"Don't worry, Rider, I look after myself. But if anything happens, you'll be the first to know."

Rider was the sweetest person Cam had ever known. The fight wasn't about not being able to talk, it was the worry Cam might be bullied or worse. The duo agreed to changed topic, talking about how their week had gone. Rider had fully embraced his TA work; although he wasn't allowed to grade the assignments of his classmates, he had helped prepare the presentations. Cam hardly understood anything about the extra classes he was taking, but from the passion in his voice, Cam could tell how much Rider was enjoying himself. It was only a knocking on Cam's door that ended the conversation.

"I'm going to have to go, but I love you, Rider. FaceTime later?"

"Love you too. Sure, I've forgotten what you look like."

Saying goodbye, Cam slipped the phone back in his pocket. He could hear a noise from outside his dorm room. Walking over to see what was causing the commotion, the door wasn't even fully open before Matthews burst past Cam and jumped on the bed. Cam shook his head as he closed the door and came to sit on his desk chair, glaring at his teammate for taking his bed.

"What? You snooze, you lose. So, what did Williams say? He give you permission?"

"How do you know I was on the phone with Rider?"

"I tried calling but it was busy and you don't have call waiting. Who else were you going to be on the phone with for forty minutes?"

Cam let Matthews hang while he changed the topic to their current history assignment. He had to duck when a pillow came toward him, colliding with Cam's bottle of water. As the bottle started to fall, Matthews dove off the bed to catch it, but he wasn't quick enough. The bottle split open when it hit the floor, the contents splashing over Matthews and the floor.

"Shit!" Why is it I seem to end up wet when it involves Williams? I thought that was your job?"

Shaking his head, Cam grabbed a towel and threw it over Matthews. "You got drenched once helping me find Rider in Central Park, and you're never going to let me forget. Anyway, yes, we are rushing."

"Awesome!" Matthews forgot about the pool of water by his feet. "They are recruiting today, we need to go!"

"Don't you want to change your pants first, you look like you pissed yourself." Cam laughed.

Thirty minutes later and a new pair of jeans, Cam and Matthews found themselves in front of a large house about fifteen minutes' walk from the gymnasium. It was one of the houses that belonged to Kappa Alpha Theta, and was currently the home of Oseman, Hugo, Alek, and Jean. A hand tapped on Cam's shoulder, he turned to be greeted by the smiling face of Fernando.

"I see Q-Tip convinced you to rush too?" Fernando asked. Cam laughing at the glare Matthews was giving them.

"Yep, but I have no clue what it will entail."

"But we are ready!" Matthews said slapping them both on the back.

The trio advanced toward the house. Alek greeted them before escorting them into the sitting room to join the row of students who were also eager to join the frat. A couple faces dropped when they noticed the three basketball players join their ranks. Kappa Alpha Theta was notorious for selecting jocks over any other pledge, and with three players already in the house, the chances of Cam, Matthews, and Fernando were high. A silence spread across the room when three frat brothers wearing robes entered the room, Cam could make out Hugo and Oseman under the robes. The third hooded member moved past Hugo and Oseman before lowering his hood.

"Pledges, I am Brother Turner. You have decided you want to try and join Kappa Alpha Theta." A few pledges flinched as *Kappa Alpha Theta* was echoed loudly around the room by other members of the frat. "Well, I wish you all luck, but not all of you will make it through hell week. If one of the brothers gives you a command, you will do it without question, if not, then you are gone. So, why don't we start now, brothers?"

A number of brothers came forward with tins of paint and artist paint brushes. Jean laughed at the confused look on Cam's face as he dropped the items in front of him. Once each pledge had received a can of paint and a small brush, all eyes returned back to Brother Turner.

"The outside of the house needs a new paint job. You are all to paint it with the brushes you have been given."

It would take a while, but Cam couldn't see this being that challenging.

"One last thing. You have to do it in your underwear. If you have a problem with that, you can forget joining this frat." Turner spun on his heel and walked out of the room.

"You heard him, pledges!" Oseman shouted, glaring at Cam.

Cam looked to his left to see Quintin was already stripped down to his boxers. Removed his T-shirt, he let it drop it to the floor before pulling his jeans off. The pledge to his right wore a sad look on his face, Cam's abs were a drastic difference compared to the pledge's round tummy. The pledges weren't even out the house before two of them had already dropped out of the rush, feeling uncomfortable being just in their underwear with the world to see. Fernando didn't seem to have any issue, despite wearing a jockstrap.

The Saturday sun beat down on the pledges as they started painting the front of the house. The yard had no trees or bushes to protect from the sun. Cam had only gotten around ten inches painted before the first car horns came. Soon students started passing the house, wolf whistles joining in with the car horns. As the temperature started heating up, the pledges battled on, slowly being called into the house. Matthews smiled at Cam as he vanished into the shadow of the house.

"Fernando, any clue what they are doing once they get called in?"

"My cousin pledged once, he said they do kind of an interview and if you don't bring anything to the table, they can drop you right then."

"Fuck you, guys, I don't want to be part of your shitty frat anyways!" shouted the larger guy who had been next to Cam.

He was now leaving the house, fully dressed, giving the brothers in the doorway the middle fingers. Cam watched him leave before the brothers shouted at the pledges to continue painting. Three hours later and he still found himself in the heat; he had been the only pledge left outside for the last thirty minutes. *Have they forgotten about me?*

"Python, get your ass in here," Hugo said, standing at the door.

As they entered the house, all the lights were off and the curtains were drawn, making the whole house dark. As they walked through the house, it looked like a scene from a horror movie, pledges stood in the corners of rooms facing away—not moving, looking, possibly not even breathing. Cam was stopped in front of a closed door.

"You're on your own from here pledge," Hugo said.

Cam placed his hand on the door handle but quickly yanked it back. The handle was hot. Cam spit into his hand and opened the door as quickly as he could to stop any burn. Entering the room, he was greeted by seven hooded figures. As Cam took a step further forward, two grabbed his arms and pushed him down to his knees.

"Pledge. You have chosen to rush Kappa Alpha Theta.

This is a brotherhood, once you are accepted, you are bonded by blood. Pledge, do you promise to always be truthful with your brothers?"

"Yes." One of the hooded figures smirked at Cam's acceptance. A silence hung in the room, Cam knew they wanted more. "Sir."

"Good. Why do you want to join us?"

"I want to join my fellow teammates, I want to be their brother."

Cam tried to swallow, his throat dry from being out in the sun. It wasn't all his teammates, it was Matthews. He had helped and supported Cam and Rider's relationship from the shadows in Belmont. That evening in Central Park, not only had he accepted Cam without question, Quintin had shown Cam something so personal and raw. Cam would do anything for Matthews. The hooded brothers seemed to be nodding, accepting Cam's bending of the truth. He was pulled back to his feet before he could say anything else.

"You will now be shown your corner. You are to remain looking at it till told otherwise. Do not close your eyes longer than a second or we will know."

Being directed to his corner, Cam could see Matthews in the living. Quintin's legs were shaking. He wanted to check on his friend, but it could void both of them joining the frat. Quintin had been so passionate when he had tried to convince him to join, Cam wasn't going to cost him that. Cam was soon standing in a corner in a room by himself, on his right a radiator pumping out heat hotter than the sun, on his left an air conditioner blasting out ice cold air.

Time soon meant nothing, his eyes focusing on the single rose in his vision. The exhaustion started to manipulate his sight. The rose split into two and they started dancing with each other, finally coming back together and spinning in place. A large smash behind him caused the rose to return back to its starting point, He wanted to turn and look but something inside him refused, instead increasing his focus on his rose. His legs began to get heavy, having been on his feet since leaving his dorm. It felt like days he had been stood in the corner. Cam started to question again if they had forgotten about him. Just as it felt like his legs were about to give way, a hand landed on his shoulder. Jean was smiling at him as he escorted him back to the living room where the rest of the pledges were sat down, cool drinks in their hands. Cam slid into the seat next to Matthews, his feet and legs screaming in agony.

"You pledges did well for your first day. We only lost a grand total of five, but it's just the start of the week. Now get out of my sight!" Turner shouted before turning and leaving the room.

Cam struggled to walk back to the dorms, just glad he was now fully clothed. Matthews had to prop him up on the way back. Not only did his legs ache but Cam was mad. Quintin had revealed not only had he stood outside for an extra thirty minutes longer than anyone else, but in the corner at least forty-five minutes longer than any other person. Matthews had been sat down on the seat for almost two hours before Cam had joined him.

"What the hell?" Cam shouted as he perched against the wall as Matthews opened his door for him.

"If I had to guess, it's Oseman. He's third in command at the frat and not too happy you took his starting spot. But once we pass hell week, he can't do anything else, we'll all be brothers and he has to treat you like one or get kicked out."

"Don't worry. I can outlast Oseman and anything he can throw at me"

Dropping down onto his bed, Cam struggled to even lift himself up on his pillow. Mathews was still laughing as he slipped out the door. All he wanted to do was close his eyes and sleep, but he had promised Rider. He pulled out his phone, the home screen quickly replaced by Rider's smiling face.

"Hey, handsome or should I say lobster? Why is your face so red?" A worried look spread across Rider's face.

"Oh…" Cam patted his face, he could feel the heat in his cheeks. "I was out in the sun for a good couple hours. You know what I'm like with my fair skin." Cam smiled, easing Rider's worry.

"So, how was the rush? Did it go well?"

"Yeah, but let's forget about that. What about you? How's your day been?"

As Rider started telling Cam about what he and a student called Nixs had done this afternoon, Cam could feel his eyes getting heavy. He struggled and fought to keep them open for as long as possible, but he lost. Sleep took him, his phone landing on his face without waking him up.

Cam woke up to a bright room, his legs ached from being in the same position all night, but the pain subsided after he stretched a couple times. Scooping his phone up off the bed, Cam poked at the screen, but nothing happened. Cam shook his head as he plugged his phone into his charging cable, he couldn't even remember how long he had talked to Rider. Once the screen flicked to life, the phone vibrated, signalling a message.

Looks like you feel asleep but you're too cute to get mad at. Sleep well Cam, love you. Xxx

There was a photo attached to the message that caused Cam to blush. It was a screenshot from Rider's phone of Cam's face fast asleep, Rider with a smirk in the bottom corner. He sent a quick message back apologising and how much he loved Rider before heading for a shower, not knowing what today and hell week might bring him.

Cam found himself standing outside the frat house with Matthews on the following Saturday evening, the toga party in full swing. Each day of the week had been just as chaotic as the first. The pledges had to continue to paint the rest of the house on Sunday, which was then followed up by a trip. Turner, being on the hockey team, had access to the rink outside of the normal times. The pledges soon found themselves stripped naked on the ice, only allowed to get off and warm up once they had moved the puck all the way down the end of the rink and scored with only their face. Again, Cam had found himself left till last but had to remain on the ice all the time.

Due to being on the basketball team he had lucked out

on Monday, only needing to do the lunch time challenge, which was to go to lunch in the cafeteria in a cheerleader outfit, which earned him a lot of whistles. The other pledges ended up playing a game called "Wizards" while Cam, Matthews, and Fernando were at practise. Cans of beer were taped into each of their hands, after they finished both, another two were taped on top of the current cans. The challenge was to see how many cans could be duct taped to their hands and still manage to drink, the bottom two were cut and the next two losers had to walk back to their dorm naked. Wednesday had found the pledges lined up, Hugo standing in front of them holding an onion that had been covered in chili.

"Okay, pledges, time not to fuck your brother. All you have to do is take a bite of the onion, as big or small as you want. All that matters is that the onion has to be gone by the time it gets to the end." Hugo had declared.

Most of the pledges had done a good job and there should have only been a small mouthful left for Cam, but as it was getting passed to him it was knocked out of his hand, landing on the floor. Oseman had come forward and claimed that allowing it to drop caused a penalty in the game with a new onion being required to be eaten, starting at the place it had fallen. Oseman pulled out an onion, one and a half times the original's size, covered in chili. Being at the back of the row required Cam to eat the whole onion, or else all the pledges would fail. He had glared at Oseman with each bite until he had finished the onion.

When the onion was finished Cam had been glad, but the onion was soon replaced with a bottle of Jack Daniels.

Cam had never tasted something so vile; onion, chili, and whiskey did not mix well together. Thursday had been difficult challenge for Cam, not only did he have basketball practise again, but he had been forbidden from eating from sun up till sun down. He was running on almost empty by the time practise had come to an end. Him, Matthews, and Fernando had quickly found the closest fast food place and had waited outside, ordering the minute the sun had set.

Friday, all the pledges had found themselves at a bar, the challenge was a very simple one. Collect as many girls' numbers in one hour as possible and the person with the lowest number would be dropped as a pledge. The challenge, each pledge was given an instruction that they had to follow. Matthews could only speak with a southern accent, which Cam was surprised Quintin pulled off so well. Oseman had smirked when giving Cam his instruction, Cam wouldn't speak at all.

"You want me to try and pick someone up without being able to speak?" Cam challenged.

"Pick up girls, yes."

"Fine. Let's do this." Cam's smile caused the smirk to drop off Oseman's face.

Cam had managed to somehow claim four numbers by the time had ticked down. The first, he had used his phone saying the music was too loud to hear them. Two he had pretended to be mute and had won their numbers out of sympathy. Then final one, all he had done was smile and she had given her number. Matthews had managed to get seven with his southern accent but out in front of everyone was Fernando who had somehow only using Joey quotes from *Friends* had ended up with a grand total of fifteen numbers. One of the shyer pledged sadly lost the challenge having gained no numbers with him having to act like *Harry Potter*.

The frat house was overflowing, the party in full swing as people entered and exited the house. Cam adjusted his toga before he and Matthews ventured into the house. A number of brothers staggered past the duo; Cam wasn't sure when they had started drinking. The furniture in the living room had all been pushed to the edges of the room but Cam was still able to find a seat on one of the battered couches, beer in hand. Matthews had been cornered by Oseman. Hugo soon appeared in front of Cam with a girl in each arm.

"Python, I would like you to say hi to Steff. Steff, this is Python."

Hugo winked at Cam and walked off with the other girl, leaving Steff on the couch with Cam. It turned out Steff had been angry at Hugo for dumping her for her sister, but he had promised to set her up with one of the other basketball guys. The conversation quickly died out when Cam informed her that he currently was dating someone.

"She must be a lucky girl."

Cam's smile was fake, he missed Rider. "Yeah, they are."

It didn't take long for Steff to vanish, leaving Cam sat alone on the couch, his mind wandering to his boyfriend, miles away. *What is Rider up to this evening?* Probably having more fun than Cam was. Cam's eyes focused on the bare feet in front of him, as he raised his head, he saw a smile on Jean's face.

"The announcement is about to start. Come on."

Cam followed Jean into the living room. There was an empty space in the middle of the crowd for the pledges. Turner, Oseman, and Hugo stood on a raised platform, looking over the group. Cam jointed the pledges, flanked by Matthews and Fernando. After hell week there were only seven pledges left out of the fifteen that had started. The first person accepted into the frat was Matthews, the crowd cheering as he took a deep bow. Fernando quickly followed suit. Cam stood patiently waiting, knowing he would be last, like he had been all week. Four new brothers, two failed pledges.

"Cameron Walker." Turner looked at him as he spoke. "You have not made it into this frat, and unlike the others, you can't try again."

"What!" shouted Matthews from over Cam's shoulder. "He did everything you asked, in fact he did more than you asked. Oseman, is this all over the fact that he took your position off you?"

Cam realized something was off. Oseman was smirking in a wicked way. This may have started due to the position, but it was not the reason he wasn't getting into the fraternity. As Oseman stepped forward and pointed at Cam, the realization dawned—it was a trap.

"We don't let fags into our brotherhood."

A gasp went around the crowd. Hushed whispers followed, but Cam ignored them, keeping his eyes focused on Oseman, biting back the emotions that were building.

"Not going to defend yourself? Or you got a cock in your mouth?" Hugo said, laughing from behind Oseman.

"Good luck trying to deny this," sneered Oseman. "You say you're dating Trish. Then who is Ri? I heard you on the phone saying you love and miss them."

Cam swallowed the lump in his throat, his fist clenching into a ball. He couldn't believe Oseman had been spying him on him. Cam flinched as he felt a hand on his back; Matthews tried to relax him. He unclenched his hand and tried to ease the rage he felt. He was only here for his friend. He took a deep breath before he said his next words.

"It's short for Trish. It's the middle part of her name." Cam felt guilt flood him immediately.

Oseman's face burst into a giant smile, as if he had been hoping Cam would answer like that. "That's strange because at the start of the call you specifically said the name Rider. Last time I checked, Rider is a guy's name."

"Then there was Steff. She told us that not only did you not flirt with her at all, you avoiding using any pronouns and didn't even give your supposed girlfriend's name. Only a fag would hide who he's dating. Bet this Rider is another faggot," Hugo condemned, shaking his head as if what he had caught was Cam making out with another guy.

Cam's eyes flicked between both his teammates, a snarl starting to appear on his face. People could say anything they wanted about him, but not Rider. Cam went to step forward, but a hand wrapped around his wrist. As he turned, he saw the hand belonged to Matthews, sympathy and sorrow etched in his eyes. Cam let his fist relax again, nodding to Matthews before he turned back to the platform.

"You want to know the truth, fine! I'm not only *dating* a guy called Rider—I *love* him. If that means you don't want me in your frat, then fine, because the man I love is worth a million times more than this frat."

Cam turned and headed toward the front door to the frat house, shocked looks on the crowd as they split to allow him through. Cam could hear footsteps behind him, he readied a fist just in case it was Oseman, but Cam froze and turned when he heard Oseman's voice still on the platform.

"Q-Tip, where are you going?"

"You don't want Walker, then you don't get me. I'm not going to abandon my friend just because you think dating a guy is wrong. You all need to pull your heads out your asses."

Matthews patted Cam on the shoulder, signifying he was ready to leave. Cam held his head high as the duo walked out of the house, only taking a deep breath once the door had closed behind him. Rider had been right all along, he should never had tried to rush the fraternity. They were only at the end of the path to the house when Matthews stopped him, a worried look plastered on his face.

"Cam, are you okay? They had no right to speak about you or Williams like that. If we wouldn't lose our place on the team, I would have kicked their asses. Its shit like that… that's the reason Archer isn't here anymore." Quintin's voice cracking slightly at the mention of his brother.

Before Cam could comment, a noise came from the house. They both turned to see the door opening. A sad face came toward them, hands held high to show that he meant no harm. Jean approached, but struggled to find the right words, restarting his sentence a couple times.

"Walker, I'm sorry for what my idiot brother said to you. Not everyone in the frat thinks like him and Oseman, sadly they make the calls who gets in and who doesn't. Matthews, they say that if you come back now, then you can still join, but I understand if you don't want to."

Matthews didn't even respond. Turning on his heel, he started heading toward the campus and back toward the dorms. Cam shrugged before nodding a goodbye to Jean, jogging to catch up with Matthews. He struggled to hide his smile from his friend as Matthews punched him in the arm. As it started to rain, Cam really wished he was wearing more than just a toga. Twenty minutes later and Cam was in his room, towel in hand, drying himself off, when there was a knock on the door.

"Matthews, I told you I'm fine. Go get yourself dry."

As he pulled the door open, Cam was surprised to see a wet Fernando standing there smiling. Moving out the way, Cam allowed him to enter the room. Fernando had only ever been friendly to him so far. Even when he had left the frat house, Cam had noticed the sympathetic look on Fernando's face.

"What are you doing here?" Cam asked as Fernando picked up the towel that Cam had discarded.

Fernando used the towel to dry his face before replying. "I came to make sure you were okay."

"Did you get kicked out like Matthews?"

Cam walked over and dropped down on the bed joining

Fernando, who shook his head. After the party had restarted and the pledges were made part of the brotherhood, he had snuck away out the rear door. The darkness from the rain covered him as he returned back to the dorms.

"I'm not like those guys, don't worry. I won't give you shit for dating a guy." Fernando smiled again. "So, you're gay?"

"No. I'm bi."

He wasn't sure why, but it really annoyed Cam when people assumed he was gay just because he was dating Rider. Taking a deep breath in, he tried to flush all the negativity out when he felt something tickling his arm, shaking it didn't seem to solve the issue. As he looked down, he could see Fernando's finger tracing up and down his arm. He pulled it away and jumped to his feet.

"What the hell!?"

"As I said, I'm different than those other guys. I'm gay, just a lot better than hiding it than you."

Cam was shocked. He couldn't understand what Fernando had just said. "But what about the seventeen girls you slept with?"

"I never said they were girls. So, what about it, me and you?" He winked at Cam.

"I have a boyfriend, Fernando, who I love. Just because he's in a different state doesn't mean I'm going to just sleep with anyone who comes knocking."

From the look on Fernando's face, it was obvious the teenager wasn't used to hearing the word no. With the smugness and arrogance Fernando carried on his face, Cam knew without a doubt that Trish, Rider, and Lloyd would have easily said no.

"I like a challenge," Fernando said with a smirk.

Cam grabbed him by his toga, pulling him over to the door and throwing him out of the room before slamming the door shut. *What is wrong with basketball players?* Dropping back onto his bed he reached for his phone and quickly hit the call button. It only took a couple rings before there was a voice on the other end of the line.

"Hey, you, I didn't think I would hear from you this evening. I thought you had that frat party?" Rider sounded a little disappointed mentioning the party.

"You don't need to worry about that anymore, Ri." Cam let out a soft sigh as he lay down on his bed, allowing the calming effect of his boyfriend's voice to wash over him. "I didn't get into the frat."

"What? Why? You're awesome. Any fraternity would be honoured to have you."

"Well..." Cam took a deep breath. "They found out I was bi and they didn't want me."

Rider immediately started to apologise, believing it was his fault that the jocks had such ignorant views on the world. Cam smiled as Rider continued to talk. In that moment he knew he had made the correct decision. The frat could have been the most welcoming group in the world, but Cam would have still chosen Rider over them.

"Rider, stop apologising, this isn't your fault. I'm sick of pretending to be someone I'm not. I want to be with you, not in some random frat with drunk idiots. If the team can't accept that, then screw them."

Cam found himself telling Rider everything that had happened at the party, laughing when Rider gasped at what Matthews had said. Cam even proceeded to tell his boyfriend about what had happened with Fernando but immediately regretted it when he could hear the panic and worry in Rider's voice.

"Ri, I love you so much. You are the only man for me."

Chapter 9

Cam

As he walked across the campus toward the Coach Lieberman's office, Cam had a sad look on his face. He was supposed to be calling Rider in the thirty minutes his boyfriend had between lectures to wish him a happy birthday, but he had been summoned to speak to the coach. Cam's fingers moved across the screen, head down as he composed a message.

> Hey Ri. Happy Birthday. Our call is going to have to be postponed, coach needs to see me and with our first match this afternoon it could be anything. I'll call you later. Love you so much.

Cam slipped the phone into his pocket and looked up just in time to avoid walking into someone. Fernando smiled, stepping forward and making sure to complete the connection between them. Cam just shook his head. It had been two weeks since he had come out at the toga party and Fernando had so far hit on Cam six times. The number would have been a lot higher if Fernando wasn't avoiding doing it around the rest of the team.

"If you want to get that close, you can just ask, no need to pretend to be on your phone."

"Not got to happen, Fernando. You're not my type so you can just drop it now."

"Come on." Fernando started rubbing Cam's arm.

Stepping away from Fernando, Cam glared at the taller boy. Before Fernando could step forward, a swam of students burst from buildings around them. Cam walked with the flow, leaving his teammate standing alone. Less than ten minutes later, he was in front of a mahogany door.

"Come in," a muffled voice beyond called out.

Cam walked into the office; this was the first time he had seen Coach Lieberman's office. It was drastically different than Coach McClay's. Every surface was clean, everything had its place. All paperwork was stored in the filing cabinet and not scattered across the desk. Coach Lieberman signalled to the chair in front of her, mouthing for Cam to sit while she was on the phone. Cam remained quiet as the phone call was finished.

"Sorry about that, Walker." Coach Lieberman shuffled a couple of loose papers before closing the folder. "Thanks for coming to see me. I wanted to talk to you about a sensitive matter and thought alone in my office would be easier."

Cam's heart started pounding and he swallowed the lump forming in his throat. He nodded his understanding, he had already guessed the subject matter. He had been stopped a number of times in the library and the canteen with students asking if he was dating a guy. It was eventually going to get back to Coach Lieberman.

"So, it's come to my attention that a couple weeks ago you came out to a number of the basketball team, as well as a number of other students at a party." Cam stared at Coach, the neutral look on her face not giving any help at the direction the conversation was headed. "Any reason why you chose to come out at a party?"

"A couple people called me out at the party. I was tired of pretending Rider didn't exist."

"And Rider would be your partner?"

Cam nodded, his hand grabbing his thigh trying to stop it from shaking. The smile on Coach Lieberman's face confusing him.

"I'm not sure if anyone else had said it yet but congratulations on coming out. I know how hard it can be to come out in such a masculine environment, especially where people's differences are looked down upon. The world is slowly changing and accepting the LGBT community, I just wish the sports world would catch up."

"Thank you, Coach. I hid my relationship most of my senior year from my team and peers, and now I just want to be the person I am. I hate the idea of making Rider hide in the closet again."

"That's the best way to be. So, now the difficult topic, have any of the team said anything to you about your sexuality? Last year we had a few reports of homophobic incidents, but due to lack of witnesses I wasn't able to do anything about it."

Taking a deep breath, Cam knew the correct thing to do would be to call out his teammates, tell Coach Lieberman exactly what had been happening, but that could cause worse problems. During practise nothing had changed between the team, outside of practise there was a divide. Oseman, Alek, and Hugo kept their distances from Cam and Matthews, but they weren't against throwing insults when they thought no one would hear. Cam's nickname had evolved once more, they now called him Python Licker. Jean, Rhys, and Fernando would bounce between the two groups, trying to keep everything civil.

"No, they haven't said anything," Cam lied.

Coach Lieberman held her gaze, causing Cam to swallow again before faking a smile, trying to ease the suspicion he was under. She did not speak for a couple minutes before finally nodding acceptance. Cam was sure Coach Lieberman hadn't truly believed him.

"If you say so. I need you to be on top form today, show everyone there is a reason why a freshman is a starter."

"Yes, Coach."

Once Cam was dismissed, he noticed a simple one-word response from Rider on his phone: *Okay*. The guilt reappeared, he felt bad that he couldn't be there for Rider on his birthday, it was the first birthday Rider would be spending alone. Cam tried to call his boyfriend, but he didn't pick up, signifying that Rider must have been in class by now. Cam then tried a different number.

"CJ! It seems like ages since I last spoke to you, I only

found out you were trying to join a frat from your lovely boyfriend. How have you been?" Trish's voice blared from the phone loudly.

"Hey, Trish, are you ever in class?" Cam laughed. He couldn't remember the last time he'd called her and not gotten through. "I've been better. I didn't get into the frat because I'm dating a guy."

Trish's response caused him to laugh again. He was sure that Trish wasn't joking about beating them all up for him. The conversation instead changed to a more positive one: Christmas. The duo planned for Trish to come visit Belmont for Christmas. Despite messaging a lot and also talking at least once a week, neither had seen each other since the trip to New York with Belmont High and were excited to spend time with each other.

"I love that we are spending Christmas together again but why did we choose Belmont. New York is so much more entertaining during Christmas. We could come visit you?"

"No...you don't want to do that. You've both been away from your parents. This way you get to see them and I see you," Trish said. "Does Rider know I'm coming yet? I haven't said anything to him, just in case."

"Not yet, I was saving it as a special surprise. I can't wait to see his face when he answers the door and you're standing there." Cam laughed at the image in his head.

"December can't come fast enough. I can't wait to see you both."

"I can't wait to see you too." A chirping in his ear got Cam's attention, a message from Quintin about lunch. "I'm going to have to go. I still need lunch and have a lecture in about an hour before my first match of the season."

"Okay, CJ, good luck for later."

Cam's nerves started building during the middle of his local history lecture. Coach Lieberman had taken a chance on putting a freshman on their starter line and Cam didn't want to let her down. He also wanted to show his teammates he was good enough to be out there with them. By the time he and Matthews were standing outside the gymnasium, Cam was more nervous than he had ever been. As he took a deep breath, he let it out slowly when he heard voices coming from behind them.

"Jeez, Walker, what did you have for lunch? Cock?"

Oseman's questions sparked laughter from Hugo and Alek. As duo let the three pass into the gym, Quintin turned and glared at Cam.

"You should tell Coach what they are saying to you. I know you're strong, Walker, but stuff like this will get to anyone."

"I'm not going to snitch. It will just cause more problems. Remember, we are here for another four years." A cough from behind them caused Cam to spin on his heel. "Decox!"

"Walker, Q-Tip. Not heading in?" Rhys smiled at them both.

The trio walked in and headed toward the changing room. Rhys had stopped using the nickname Python after the others had twisted the meaning. Cam quickly changed into his gear, keeping his eyes focused on his locker. Oseman had already joked about Cam spying on them when getting changed and building up fantasies in his head. He wasn't planning on giving them any ammunition. He only turned around when he heard Coach starting to speak.

"We all know how difficult Tennessee can be. You may have been giving me a hundred percent in practise, but now it's time to give me even more. If you don't go out there and win, then you will be running lengths till you vomit."

Cam lined up with the team and walked out into the court, the size of the crowd slightly intimidating him. Rhys went forward for the tip-off as Cam's eyes slipped from the ball to the crowd for only a second, trying to find the gray hoodie that had supported him for so long, only to remember Rider was not here. In that time, he missed the whistle, and the ball was coming at him. Cam tried to react, but he was too slow. He fumbled, allowing his mark to scoop up the ball and take advantage. Tennessee went two points ahead.

"Walker! Get your head in the game!" screamed Coach from the side line.

Shaking his head clear of the doubt and distractions, Cam took a deep breath and focused on the ball. Rhys passed him the ball and Cam charged down the court. His mark blocked a three-pointer attempt, and Cam instead flicked the ball to his left, sending it into Alek's hand and straight into the basket. Tennessee was immediately on the retaliation, but Cam was ready. He jumped, connecting with the ball and sending it into Hugo's hands. In seconds, Hugo was pinned down, the only open person he could pass to was Cam, but he chose not to. The whistle sounded for a five second penalty.

"Wall! What the hell, I was open!" Cam walking over to Hugo.

"My bad. I was blinded by the rainbows," Hugo whispered to Cam.

"Hugo, drop the insults. We're in the middle of a match. Sort it out off the court," Rhys interjected sending them both to their positions.

Coach wasn't joking when she said how difficult Tennessee was. Cam and the team were constantly on the defence. His lungs ached, only relieved when he managed to make a break up the court. As the whistle called for the end of the first half, Kentucky was down by twelve points, despite Cam's fifteen points. As Cam entered the changing room, he could see a smirk on Oseman's face.

"Nice fumble out there, I thought you would have been used to handling balls"

"Who the hell I'm dating has no bearing on my ability to play basketball. I kicked your ass, didn't I? And now I'm going to go out there and kick their asses."

Cam tuned and headed out of the changing room before Oseman could even respond. He sat down on the sub's bench. The crowd was still shouting as cheering even during half time, but Cam tried to tune it all out. He closed his eyes, blocking out the sound surrounding him. Instead of calming himself, he stoked that rage he felt deep down. By the time the bell chimed for the teams to come back out, he could already feel the fire flowing through his veins. He was out on the court before anyone from Kentucky joined him.

The tip-off was played, Rhys only just getting his fingers to the ball, but Cam was already moving. He snatched the ball mid-air and charged down the court. Ignoring the shouts from his teammates, he shot before the line, sending the ball soaring deep into the net for three points. Cam could see the look on Hugo and Alek's face, they hadn't expected him to be so vicious, but he ignored them, pulling back up the court. The next play the ball tried to end up with Cam's mark, but Cam moved like lightning, catching the ball before it hit its target. This time he hardly moved before shooting, sending the ball down the court and into the basket.

It wasn't long till both teams were drawing points, but Tennessee changed up their play style, focusing on keeping the ball down on the other side of the court and away from the monster that Cam had become. Coach Lieberman called time out with only five minutes left of the match.

"Walker, I don't know what's gotten into you but keep it up. Cox, they are hitting you hard so I'm pulling you off for the last five minutes. Matthews, you're on. Same with you, Patel, I can see you're winded. Oseman, you're playing small forward for the last five minutes. Hands in"

Oseman stuck his hand at the bottom to avoid having to touch Cam's hand, but this stoked the fire in Cam more. Within twenty seconds after taking the court again, he had scored another three points. Tennessee took advantage of Matthews and Oseman not being fully warmed up, scoring a couple of baskets themselves. Matthews made his way up the court, being closed down faster than he had expected. He passed the ball to Oseman who jumped and shot, the ball ricocheting off the backboard and into the hands of Tennessee. It didn't stay there for long, Cam was already on top of the play and smashing the ball out of their hands. He grabbed it, spinning to the right and sending the ball into the basket, making up for Oseman's failure.

Cam's lungs burned, his legs aching harder than they did after the first day of hell week, but he ignored the pain. As the fever of the crowd started to swell, Cam could tell the match was coming to an end, but he didn't dare look at the scoreboard. Tennessee hit the team hard. Matthews closed down, but Oseman had allowed his mark to slip past him and the ball was soon in Kentucky's basket. Matthews took the ball, only making it ten paces before he started to be closed down again, this time sending the ball to Cam, ignoring Oseman. Cam could hear a countdown thundering from the crowd. Pulling his arm back, he launched himself into the air and pushed with all his might, sending the ball down the court. It bounced off the backboard and slipped through the hoop just as the buzzer sounded the end of the match.

The crowd went crazy, cheers from the home side and boos from the away thundered around the arena. Cam allowed his gaze to flick up to the score, 60–58. Kentucky had won with Cam's final shot sending them ahead. Cam let out the breath he had been holding since the buzzer. He shook the hands of the opposition team around him, but ignored the ongoing celebrations, even when Matthews called for him. Cam headed toward the changing rooms, grabbing his towel and heading to the showers.

As soon as the warm water hit his muscles Cam could feel the pain shoot through him. He had pushed harder than he had ever done in any match. He could hear cheers coming from the changing room, so he increased the water flow to drown out any noise. The water cascaded over his face, washing through his hair and down over his shoulders. The sensation pulled him out of the room and back to the weekend before he left Belmont. He had gotten in the shower that morning when he felt a cold draft on his back. Turning around, he'd found Rider had slid into the shower to join him. A wicked smile on Rider's face soon infected Cam, and he pulled his boyfriend toward him and kissed him as the water flowed over them. Their actions quickly got steamier than the shower, both enjoying themselves and allowing their hands to explore everywhere.

They had exited the bathroom together, Cam's arms wrapped around the waist of his boyfriend, when they both came to a stop, horror on both their faces. His mom hadn't been home, but they'd forgotten that Uncle Roy had been staying with them to help with the drive to college. It wasn't the look on his face that made them blush or even that they had been caught, it was what he had said.

"It's good to see you're caring about the environment by saving water, but next time maybe keep the moaning a little quitter. Your mom would have fainted if she heard what I heard."

Rider had sprinted back to Cam's bedroom so quick that his towel almost fell off, causing both Cam and Roy to laugh. Rider had spent most of the day not wanting to leave the room in case he bumped into Roy again. Cam had been happy to spend the afternoon snuggled up in bed, just watching TV.

A banging brought Cam back to the present; he was still alone in the shower room. Shutting off the water, any pain he had felt when first climbing in had vanished. *I need to convince Mom to buy one of these showers*. Drying himself off, Cam wrapped a towel around his waist before walking into the changing room to see his teammates waiting for him. The only people missing from the group was Coach Lieberman and Oseman. Choosing to ignore the group, he instead headed to his locker and pulled on fresh boxers and his jeans, and slipped on the Batman shirt that Rider had given him. The group was still waiting once he finished getting ready, a huge grin on Matthews' face.

"Walker. You were amazing." Rhys came forward, punching him in the arm, a huge smile on his face. "Coach said out of the sixty points you scored forty-two by yourself."

"Decox is right. You were unbelievable." Alek came forward with his hand outstretched. "I want to apologise for the stuff I said in the last couple weeks. I was being a dick."

Cam reluctantly shook Alek's hand, his eyes on Hugo as he stepped forward.

"Q-Tip told us that Coach pulled you into the office and asked about our behaviour and you covered for us," Hugo said sheepishly.

"Yeah, I did," Cam said confidently, which put a smile on Hugo's face.

"That's cool. And your performance out there—not bad for a gay guy!"

Hugo slapped Cam on the back, causing him to take a couple steps forward. "I never said I was gay".

Cam straightened himself up, picking up his fallen backpack. As he looked around the group, the only person without a confused look was Matthews, who was in the middle of rolling his eyes.

"You already admitted to dating a guy," Hugo stammered, the most confused out of the group.

"Rider? Yes, I'm dating him but that doesn't make me gay. I'm bisexual."

"So, you still like girls?" Cam nodded to Hugo. "Cool. Patel is right, we're sorry for calling you a fag. I mean you were a monster out there, and to cover for us with the coach…anyone like that is cool in my book."

Cam looked over to Matthews, who just shrugged. *Covering for them, being good at basketball, and there still being a chance I would hook up with women is enough to change what they think about me?* Cam hid the hurt he was feeling on the inside. There was more to him than being good at basketball, but it was the only thing that had stopped the insults. He wanted to snap back at them and put them in their place, but that would just cause the rift again. Even though he hated it, sometimes it was easier to just go with the flow. Cam just sighed and accepted, at least he could vent to Matthews when no one else was around.

"We're going to celebrate our first win and we can't go out without our star player," Rhys announced, with everyone nodding in agreement. "You coming?"

Agreeing to a round of cheers from the team, Cam slipped his backpack on and followed his teammates out into the night, Hugo patting him on the shoulder. Laughter soon surrounded the group, pointed at the Oseman and his failed shots. Compliments came from all directions at Cam, a number from both Hugo and Alek trying to make up for the last two weeks. In the haze of team bonding, Cam soon forgot about the phone call he had promised Rider for his birthday.

Chapter 10

Rider

Rider sat on his bed watching the seconds tick away on his phone. Cam had promised to call him after his game, which should have ended thirty minutes ago. His parents, Becca and Lloyd, had been too busy to call him and just sent messages. Jane and Sam had called around lunch, but the call hadn't lasted long, Sam had a lecture coming up and Jane was due at the homeless shelter for her volunteer shift. Only Trish had dedicated time to his birthday call, she had kept him talking so long he had to create a fake lecture just to end the call. He loved chatting to Trish, but his ear had felt like it was on fire.

He dropped his phone onto the bed, his head falling into his hands as tears started to flow. He missed Cam so much and being so far away just made it even more difficult. It felt like they were slowly drifting apart. A knock on the door caused Rider to lift his head. Wiping the tears away, he opened the door to see Yuki.

"Good afternoon, Rider." He pulled a wrapped box and a card from behind his back. "And happy birthday."

As Yuki entered the room and handed over the present, Rider's jaw dropped in shock. The card was a cartoon of an editor demanding something of his staff. Opening it, Rider read the message. *To Rider, I am bad at writing messages so I will leave that for you. Have a wonderful birthday. Yuki.* The present was the perfectly wrapped. Opening it carefully, he was greeted by a Spider-Man alarm clock, drawing a smile from Rider.

"I am sorry I could not give you these earlier. I have been in classes all day."

"Yuki, you didn't need to get me anything. But this is wonderful, thank you."

"I know I did not need to, but I wanted to. You are a friend." Yuki smiled.

Rider placed the clock and card gently down on his desk and pulled Yuki into tight hug, not letting him go until he was sure he wouldn't cry. Yuki seemed happy to keep his arms wrapped around Rider until the hug was broken.

"Oh, what's happening here?"

Jay was at the door frame, a smirk on his face.

"I was just wishing Rider a happy birthday," Yuki said.

Jay entered Rider's room without being invited, the smirk still not dropping from his face as he came over and pulled Rider into a tight hug while wishing him a happy birthday. As the hug ended his hand dropped down touching Rider's butt. It could have been an accident, but Rider wasn't sure. Jay dropped down on Jason's bed, not caring about the paperwork that he scattered.

"I wish I had known it was your birthday, I would have got you a present. Sadly, I've got nothing on me I can give you. Actually, I do have one thing…" Jay winked at Rider before moving his hand down to his crotch and grabbing it.

Rider shook his head and sighed. Yuki was glaring at the man on the bed.

"Jacob." Yuki's tone caused Jay to laugh.

"I was joking. It's not even wrapped, but it could be." He looked at Rider and winked again. "If you catch my drift."

"I will see you later, Rider. I have to begin an assignment." Yuki said, shaking his head in the direction of Jay.

Yuki didn't say anything to Jay, instead grabbing hold of his wrist and pulling him off the bed and out of the room. Rider couldn't help but smile at Yuki's actions. Collecting the papers on the floor, Rider scooped them up and placed them back on Jason's bed before dropped down on his own, landing on his phone, he jumped up and checked for any sign of Cam, but his phone still showed no new messages.

Any happiness that had been brought by Yuki's present was quickly destroyed. Rider reached to the end of his bed, pulling his guitar into his lap. He let his mind go blank as he started playing, his fingers sliding over they strings as *Mad World* slipped past his lips. As the song came to an end, he placed the guitar down on the bed and wiped away the tears that had formed in his eyes. It was only then that he noticed the shadow in the doorway.

"Wow! That was hauntingly beautiful." Nixs had a soft smile on his face. "What's made you feel so melancholy?"

Nixs was summoned into the room, closing the door behind him. With a little more probing, Rider soon started telling Nixs what had made him cry, although he chose to avoid mentioning Cam, just how it was his birthday and people seemed to have forgotten about it. How he was just feeling a sorry for himself.

"Oh no, we can't have you feeling sad on your birthday. I'm taking you out for a drink."

"But I'm only nineteen," Rider said, trying to hide the smile Nixs had brought to him.

"That doesn't matter. You get ready while I head to the toilet and then we will get going."

All Rider could do was nod as Nixs walked out the door. Rider picked up the gray hoodie he always wore but decided against it, putting it back down on his chair. Instead, he pulled a thin navy jacket out of his closet. Grabbing his wallet and keys as he exited the room, he found Nixs waiting for him.

Nixs

Nixs wandered through the maze of corridors that made up the student dorms. He hadn't been in them since his first year and he planned to keep his time here to a minimum. He was sure his ex-roommate still lived here. Nixs knew which student he was on the hunt for, but had no clue which room Rider was in. He had some time to kill before he needed to help Michele with assignments so had decided to surprise Rider, although he was now thinking maybe this was a bad idea.

He had been walking in circles for about twenty minutes hoping to catch a glimpse of Rider. Just as he was about to give up on the plan, Nixs noticed someone getting off the elevator. A Japanese student that seemed older than most students in the dorms was heading down the corridor. From his age and the aura around the student it was obvious to Nixs he was a resident advisor.

"Excuse me!" Nixs shouted down the hallway, getting the advisor's attention. "Hi, my name is Nickolas Nicholson. I'm Professor Hudson's TA."

"Yukitaka Ito. It is a pleasure to meet you."

"I'm wondering if you could assist me. I'm looking for a student in the dorms. A Rider Williams."

Nixs was in luck, Yukitaka not only knew exactly who Rider was but had only just come from there, confirming the trip wasn't wasted. Riding the elevator up, as soon as Nixs stepped out, he felt like he had been sucked back in time. It was the exact floor he had lived on during his freshman year, the floor where so much confusion had happened. Nixs took a deep breath and turned right, heading down the hall, passing the room that used to be his and continuing on to his intended target. The door was already open, music coming from within the room.

He soon found himself resting against the doorframe, Rider had his eyes closed as he played the guitar. During their discussions of hobbies and interest, Rider had kept this quiet from Nixs and he wasn't sure why. Rider was good, his playing smooth and elegant and his voice hypnotic. Nixs couldn't help but smile as he listened. Rider sang softly as he held the last note of *Mad World*. His eyes shimmered with tears as he tried to hide the evidence. Nixs' smile fell slightly, into a softer one, for a moment. He wasn't sure what had gotten the teen upset, but it just made Nixs want to help.

"Wow! That was hauntingly beautiful."

Rider turned to look at Nixs, his eyes wide in shock at seeing someone listening to him play. As he placed the guitar between the bed and wall, Rider's gaze fell back onto Nixs.

"Nixs, I didn't realize you were there. Come in."

Closing the door behind him, Nixs walked into the room and took a look around before sitting at the desk that obviously belonged to Rider. The Spider-Man clock was the giveaway. Sitting on the bed with Rider felt to intimate in the state that Rider was in. He didn't want to make Rider feel like he was being taken advantage of.

"Come on, tell old Nickolas what's wrong..."

"It's my birthday today. I was expecting a phone call from...from my friends back home but it hasn't come through. I'm just worried they've all forgotten about me and I kind of got a little sad, hence the song."

Nixs couldn't help but smile, he had the perfect plan to cheer up Rider. He could take Rider for a drink, allowing him to forget his sorrows. It also meant Nixs wouldn't be stuck marking assignments all night. Swallowing the lump forming in his throat and biting his lip, he pushed the idea of a date out of his head. *This is just a friendly birthday drink.* Nixs laughed when Rider tried to decline due to his age.

"Plenty of bars in the area don't check ID due to being so close to the college. Allowing the students to drink brings in a lot of business. You get ready while I head to the toilet and then we will get going."

Rider finally nodded in agreement, causing Nixs to smile as he headed toward the door. He wasn't even fully out of the room before his phone was in his hand. After only a few rings the professor's voice came over the line.

"Nixs, good evening." Michele's voice sounded bubbly. Nixs was sure she had already finished her first wine of the evening.

"Evening, Michele. Sadly, I need to cancel tonight."

"Oh, okay. Can I ask why?"

Nixs took a deep breath. "It's Rider's birthday today and he was planning on spending it by himself in his dorm room. So, I thought I would take him out to celebrate."

A laugh from the other end of the call caught Nixs off guard; Michele had definitely had more than one wine. "Oh, okay. Well, Nixs please don't scare away this one."

Nixs let out a long drawn-out sigh. Before he had started dating Jordan, he had gone on a date with a potential TA applicant. They had gone for a meal and ended up at a bar for a few drinks. Everything was going well until they had got back to Nixs' apartment, the guy had leaned forward to kiss Nixs and ended up covering him in vomit before running away in embarrassment. After that, he withdrew his application to be a TA, being way too embarrassed to work with Nixs. Michele had blamed Nixs, despite it being him that got covered in vomit.

"You know that wasn't my fault and I also regret ever telling you what actually happened."

Michele laughed again, causing Nixs to laugh. "Okay, you and Rider have fun. Don't do anything I wouldn't."

"It's just a friendly drink. I don't even know if he likes me."

"He likes you. I've seen him look at you; it's the same look you give him."

Nixs was glad he was alone in the hallway as his face had turned a deep scarlet. He couldn't lie to himself, Rider was cute, sweet and they had a lot in common, but with how much bad luck he had with relationships, he wasn't going to rush anything. If something naturally builds between them then he would see where it goes, but at the moment they were only friends.

"Okay, go get lucky."

"Professor!" Nixs said sounding too much like his father. "Anyway, I'm going to go. I'll talk to you tomorrow."

Taking a deep breath, he slipped his phone away. He needed to splash some cold water on his face. Walking down the hall, Nixs entered the bathroom. The cold water felt good on his cheeks, taking some of the heat away. He used paper towels to dry off, and when he turned around, Nixs froze as a person came out the cubicle. The red hair and wide build were immediately recognizable: his ex-roommate, Bane.

"Nixs? What are you doing here?"

"I'm here to see a friend."

Nixs started to head for the door before a hand on his

shoulder stopped him. "Nixs, please. I miss you." Bane's hand squeezed his shoulder.

Nixs lets out a sigh before shaking Bane's hand off him. What they had together was bad for both of them. Nixs wanted a boyfriend, someone he could love and show the world that love. Bane, due to his upbringing, was so deep in the closet he could see Narnia. During the dark of night, they would make out, be together, and it felt good, but once the sun rose, Bane acted like it never happened. Nixs had even given him one last chance—Bane didn't need to come out but he had to accept and admit what they had been doing together, but he couldn't. Nixs had chosen to walk away and start anew.

"I'm sorry, Bane. What we had is over, but if you ever need someone to talk to about what you're going through, I'm here for you."

Bane face twisted into disgust like it did every time after they had done something together. Nixs rolled his eyes. He wanted to help Bane with what he was going through, there had been something between them, but Bane's own inbuilt homophobia had stopped them ever having a future.

"Fucking faggot," Bane spat.

"You still haven't changed then."

Bane walked past Nixs, forcing his shoulder into Nixs', who stood his ground. Once Bane was out of the restroom, Nixs took a few long deep breaths, trying calm down. He hated how easy his ex-roommate could rattle him. He exited the restroom at the same time Rider was coming out of his room. Nixs couldn't help but smile at the navy jacket Rider was wearing. He had never seen the student without his gray hoodie.

Rider's eyes went wide as they entered the bar, causing Nixs to let out a small laugh. "Never been in a gay bar before?"

"Nope." Rider shook his head as he looked around the room, a smile on his face.

"You try and find us a table and I'll get us a couple beers."

Nixs was surprised at how busy it was for a Tuesday evening. As he waited to be served, he watched Rider, who was walking through the bar taking in all the small little pieces. Nixs remembered the first time he had set foot in a gay bar. He had been invited out for a meal by Jordan but somehow ended up in a gay bar. He had felt out of his depth, his eyes wandering over all the guys who had decided it was too hot for tops before remembering he was on a date and returned looking at Jordan.

With two bottles of beer in his hands, he thanked the bar staff before turning to locate Rider in the crowd. He had shuffled further into the bar and was talking to someone who looked double his age. As Nixs approached he could see how uncomfortable the shaggy-haired teen looked; the stranger was too close to Rider. The stranger's hand was rubbing along Rider's arm. Nixs reached the duo just as the hand dropped and went toward Rider's ass. Rider tried to jump back but he wasn't as quick as Nixs.

Using just a thumb and finger, he grabbed hold of the stranger's thumb, pulling it back and bringing the hand and arm up behind the older man's back. The stranger struggled but couldn't move without hurting himself. Nixs remained calm, using just the minimum force he needed.

"Say sorry to my friend," he commanded.

"I'm sorry, just let me go," stuttered the stranger.

Nixs released his hold, the stranger rubbing his wrist before quickly leaving. Rider had his mouth open in shock. Choosing to ignore everything that happened, Nixs slid into a booth not too far from them, placing the beers down on the table before being joined by Rider.

"I'm sorry. I shouldn't have left you alone."

"How did you do that?" Rider's shocked face had changed into a smile, which relaxed Nixs.

"My father in a Marine, so is my brother. I was taught a lot when I was younger."

Nixs took a sip of his beer. He hated speaking about his childhood with his family. He chose to come to Houston to be his own person. His family had wanted Nixs to also become a Marine but he had refused.

"They taught you how to disable a person?"

"I was trained on how to use minimal force to bring someone down, either with a simple hold like that or by using their own momentum against them. I also know how to strip and reassemble a gun, shoot a target over two hundred yards away, and also how to disarm someone. Although the most useful skill was how to tie knots." Nixs panicked when Rider blushed. "No...I mean...forget it."

Nixs pushed his dark hair up and out of his eyeline; it had finally grown too long for spikes. He drained the remaining beer in one swift go, still feeling slightly embarrassed. Signalling the empty bottle, he vanished to the bar without saying another word. A quick look back and Rider was still blushing. Nixs released a sigh as he reached the bar. *Why do I put a foot in my mouth around cute guys?* Returning to the both, he placed two glasses down. Rider lifted the brown liquid, taking a swig before he started coughing.

"Careful, that's a malt whisky. Its strong, but the taste grows on you." Nixs laughed. "Although if you don't like it. I can have it."

"It's okay." Rider said before coughing again. "Since you just nearly killed me, you have to answer my question. I love your hair but I'm guessing it's not your natural color…?"

Nixs bit his lip and smiled. He had dyed his hair and pierced his ear in order to distance himself from his old life. His family being Marines, they followed the rule of "don't ask, don't tell" and had refused to accept his sexuality, choosing to ignore it. Every time he had looked in the mirror, at the same hair his brother and father had, it brought up the negative memories.

"I even have a non-authorised tattoo."

"You have a tattoo? Can I see?" Rider's smile was wide.

Pulling his overshirt off and sliding up the right sleeve of his T-shirt. On the outer bicep just below the shoulder was the image of Wiccan, his cape flapping in the wind as he held a sword aloft in the air. Nixs had only had the tattoo for two months. He had been pondering the idea for a while, but Jordan always said tattoos were ugly. Once they had split up, Nixs had gone for it.

"Is that the master sword from Zelda?" Rider asked with a huge grin on his face. Shuffling forward, he reached across the table.

"Yeah. I know I'm a giant—"

"I love it!"

As Rider's fingers danced across his skin, Nixs had to grab his knee to stop the shiver that was trying to travel through his body. The soft fingertips tracing the lines of the character from Wiccan's waist all the way up to the tip of the sword. Nixs bit his lip again as he looked across the bar, trying to distract himself from Rider. There was no way he could look into those dark eyes right now.

"Does it hurt?" Rider asked, his eyes and fingers remaining on the tattoo.

"Nope, you're very gentle," Nixs said. Rider's eyes went wide, his hand pulling away quickly as he went bright red. "But to answer your question, it stings a little bit when it's getting done. Like someone dragging a sharp fingernail across your arm. Why thinking about getting one?"

"Oh, I don't know. I've always thought about it, but I hate pain."

Two more drinks later and Nixs couldn't remove the smile off his face if he wanted to. Rider was funny and whatever sadness that had been infecting him was now gone. The slight sway Rider had showed the alcohol was affecting him a lot more than Nixs.

"You're so cute," Rider mumbled.

"What?" Nix raised an eyebrow.

"I said this bar is so cute." Rider's eyes flicked away quickly. "I think I need the toilet. I'll be right back."

Nixs let out a small laugh as Rider wobbled as he got out the booth, slowly making his way across the room toward the restroom. Scanning the rest of the bar, the smile fell from his face when he noticed the guy standing at the bar looking in his direction. The blonde 90's middle-part hair that Nixs used to run his hand through now just made his skin crawl.

Jordan made his way over, biting his lip as he walked. "Hey, Nixs."

"It's Nickolas to you. Only my friends get to call me Nixs. What do you want, Jordan? Why are you even here?"

"I'm just here for a drink. Look, I'm sorry for what happened. I want to make it up to you. Try us again."

Nixs glared at his ex-boyfriend. Jordan stepped forward and started rubbing Nixs' arm, but he pulled it away instantly. When Jordan tried to slide into the booth where Rider had been, Nixs place his feet across the booth onto the soft fabric, stopping him.

"Sorry, that seat's taken by someone," Nixs said sternly.

"Come on, Nixs, we can get through this."

"No, we can't! We date for a little over year and then when I come home early because my TA class was cancelled, I find you in my bed with two other guys. God knows how long you were actually cheating on me and with how many guys! I should have listened to Wilson when he told me that you jump from relationship to relationship. It makes sense now why you were hitting on me while dating Leon. I don't want anything to do with you, just leave me alone!"

Jordan tried to reach for Nixs' hands, but he was quickly on his feet, arms crossed over his chest. It was then that a

Rider started heading back toward him, a huge smile on his face. Nixs was sure it was from the alcohol giving him courage, but as Rider reached the table, he pulled Nixs into a tight hug.

"Thanks for the best birthday—"

"Oh, I see how it is! You dumped me and went out and got yourself a little boy toy. Well, we'll see how long it lasts!"

"Get your head out your ass, Jordan. Me and Rider are friends, we're not dating."

"You could fool me. If you haven't already banged, then you will soon."

Nixs' gaze remained on Jordan but out the corner of his eye, he could see the smile drop slightly from Rider's face at the mention of just friends. As soon as Jordan insinuated they had slept together, Rider quickly looked away, the tips of his ears burning. *Does Rider actually like me?* Jordan turned and left the duo feeling awkward, Nixs slid back into the booth, followed by Rider.

"I'm sorry about Jordan. If someone's not interested in him, then he lashes out, and if someone is interested, he sleeps with someone else instead."

"You don't need to be sorry." Rider leaned on the table, arms stretched toward Nixs. "To be honest, I'm a little drunk so...I don't know for sure who Jordan is."

Nixs laughed loudly, the smile slowly reappearing on both their faces. The friendly chat came back thick. He didn't even realize his hand had ended up on top of Rider's until he reached for his drink. Nixs chose to leave it there since Rider didn't seem to have a problem with it.

Chapter 11

Cam

The gray clouds in the sky threatened to rain as Cam sat on a bench, his history book open on his lap but long forgotten about. He was still trying to find a solution for the problem he had caused. Rider had been extremely upset after Cam had forgotten to call on his birthday. It had been a week since and he could still hear the sadness in Rider's voice, the guilt coming quickly with each sigh. As his eyes raised from the photo on his phone, he noticed a girl with red hair across the quad. Cam slipped his phone into his pocket, grabbing hold of his backpack and book before sprinting towards her.

"Becca!" he shouted causing her to jump and drop loose sheets of paper across the ground. Apologising, he bent down and scooped up the papers, trying to sort them the best he could. "I'm so sorry. I didn't mean to."

"It's no problem, Cam. I don't think I've seen you since the BBQ over your mom's. I still laugh at that video of Rider falling into the pool."

During the summer his mom was adamant that she was hosting as big a BBQ possible. Cam would have been happy with just his small group of friends, but his mom had invited all of the Williams family, apart from Julian. Rider had used the moment to come out to his Aunt Sylvia and Uncle Mark, but, being nervous, he had tripped on his shoelace and ended up head-long in the swimming pool. Sylvia was more worried about Rider drowning than about him being gay. Jane had managed to capture the whole incident on camera.

"Do you have a minute to chat?" Cam asked.

"Actually, I'm heading back to my apartment. I just got my part for this year's production and need to start practising my lines for tomorrow's rehearsal. You can come with me if you want?"

The duo were soon in Cam's car driving across town. Originally, he hadn't understood why Becca chose to live an hour outside the campus, but her apartment was above a theater, and she often received free tickets to the shows.

Walking into the apartment, it felt like all Cam's senses were being attacked. Not one single piece of furniture matched any other. There was a worn-out red sofa flanked by a bright lime green wingchair on right, on the left a rustic brown chaise longue that looked like it had come directly out of the 50s. An antique clock hung on the wall next to a burlesque fan and a pink plastic flamingo. Cam took a deep breath and somehow smelled candyfloss, pizza, and blueberries all at the same time. Becca dropped down on the couch and pulled Cam with her.

"So how is my favorite bi guy?"

"Needing some advice. I messed up big style. I've upset Rider and I'm not sure how to make it up to him," Cam said, voice started to crack.

"Oh, Cam, I'm sure we can sort this." Becca pulled Cam into a tight hug. "Start from the beginning. Tell me what's happened."

Cam let out a sigh as he explained how the team had discovered about his sexuality and Rider, the negative reaction, and bullying. How he had wanted to prove them all wrong and after the game had been accepted as one of them, resulting in drinking till the early hours of the morning. It hadn't been till he got back to his dorm room and checked his phone that he had remembered Rider's birthday.

"You forgot your boyfriend's birthday?" Cam recoiled waiting for Becca to shout but it didn't come. "I've been there myself. The first year me and Dave were dating I forgot his birthday, it's actually what caused us to break up our first time." Becca patted Cam's hands when his eyes went wide. "I'm sure you and Rider will not break up. It's not like you're going to sleep with some random guy."

"Oh, don't even get me started about Fernando." Cam sighed.

"Who?"

"One of the other scholarship winners. Ever since he found out I'm bi, he keeps hitting on me even though he knows about Rider. He just won't take no for an answer."

"Fernando? Where do I know that name from? Wait... Dave's cousin?"

Confirming Becca's assumption caused her to roll her eyes hard. She pulled out her phone and Cam watched her compose a message. A response came quickly but this just caused her to release a sigh and slide through to her contacts list. Cam noticed Dave's name come up on the screen before Becca pushed the phone to her ear.

"Dave. Yes, yes…Dave stop talking for a second. Yes, I still love you but I need you to do something for me. You need to tell your cousin to back down, he keeps hitting on Cam. Yes, that Cam. Yes, that Fernando. Okay, thank you. I'll see you later this evening after I've run through my lines. Love you too, bye."

As she dropped her phone on the polka dot table in front of them, a smile spread across Cam's face. Becca jumped up from the couch and went to the kitchen grabbing a couple cold sodas out of the fridge, placing one in front of Cam without even giving him the option.

"So, what do you think I should do about Rider?"

"What did you do that time you had a huge fight?"

Cam took a deep breath in, he hated thinking about the misunderstanding that had almost cost them their happiness. "I got him a signed first edition of a book series he likes, but it was Jane that gave it to him. It was her that fixed things between us. I guess I could get him something he would love."

His mind wandered into the well of Rider factoids he had saved away. He needed something that said "I know you and I love you".

"Cam?" Becca nudged him to get his attention. "You've been quiet for about five minutes."

"Oh, sorry. Just thinking of ideas." Cam noticed Becca had her script in hands. "I didn't ask, what's the new show?"

Becca's eyes went wide as she burst into an explanation of the show and the characters. Cam smiled and nodded along hiding the fact that he already knew of *The Rocky Horror Show*, it being one of his mom's favorite films. Becca had managed to get cast as her favorite character, Magenta, and although she knew the lines inside and out, she still needed to practise.

"I thought it was called *Rocky Horror Picture Show*?"

"That's just the film." Becca laughed as if this was common knowledge to everyone. "The stage show doesn't have the word picture in its title."

Cam wasn't sure how Becca convinced him, but he soon found himself singing *Time Warp* with her. Despite his awful singing, he invested into the role, being pulled to his feet to do the actions of the dance with Becca. After the fifth performance, he collapsed back onto the couch, a bottle of water in his hand. Even with the script in his hand there were a number of times he had completely blanked what he was meant to be saying.

"I don't know how you're able to do this," he said as Becca was still dancing, not showing any sign of tiredness.

"You get used to it." Becca laughed. "Also repeating the lines over and over again in the rehearsal room helps. You can stay sitting but let's keep going."

Three hours later and Becca finally dropped down in the seat next to Cam, a bag of chips in her hands. Cam was surprised to find that while rehearsing, Becca refused to eat anything, claiming it to be a good motivator. He couldn't refuse a chip as she handed him the bag.

"I still don't know how you do it, I don't mean remembering all the lines. Getting up on stage with all those people watching you. All those eyes looking for any sign of failure."

"You're joking right? You play basketball. You literally go out every week with more eyes watching you than ever come to any of my shows." Becca jokingly punching Cam in the arm

"That's different. When I'm on the court, the crowd kind of fade away. It's just me, my mark and the ball. Even my teammates flow independently, I never look for them on the court. It's like a sixth sense, like we're all connected. I just know where they are, without even needing to look."

"Like the force?"

"You and your brother are so alike at times."

Cam's laughter brought a scowl to Becca's face. She tried to tickle him as vengeance, but he just sat there and laughed even more. That technique may work on Rider, but Cam was immune. After trying for a good five minutes Becca finally decided to quit.

"For me it's completely different. It's that electric feeling you get, the tingling sensation deep in your soul from people watching you perform. That connection with the audience on a spiritual level. You may do a show once, ten times, or even one hundred, but every time is different, feels different. Each crowd is different and that drive to connect with them makes it all worthwhile."

• • •

One hour later, Cam was back in his car, his mind fully back on his boyfriend. He had only gotten three blocks before he noticed a familiar face leaving an art shop. Pulling up to the curb, he honked the horn, summoning Jean over to him. As Jean climbed into the front seat, Cam noticed the bag.

"What you doing in an art shop this far uptown?" he asked, pulling away from the curb.

"It's the only place I can find Copic markers, or did you forget my major is art?"

Cam had completely forgotten that Jean studied art and how good he was at it. The equipment manager had started as an econ major but quickly switched without telling his parents. It had been Hugo that had accidentally let it slip one Christmas, making for a difficult family meal at the Livingston house. An idea sparked in Cam's head.

"I'm wondering if you could do me a huge favor. That night we went out drinking after our first victory, it was my partner's birthday," Cam said, pausing to see Jean's response. When a smile appeared on his teammate's face, he continued, "I completely forgot to call him. Now I'm in the dog house."

"I see dating a guy can be the same as dating a girl at times. So, what do you need help with?"

"I'm wondering if you can draw me something."

"Nothing naughty, I hope?" Jean joked.

Cam was soon telling Jean his idea for the drawing, a smile appearing on Jean's face the more he explained. It was different than the pieces Jean was used to drawing but he welcomed the challenge. When the car stopped at a red light, Cam pulled his phone out and quickly scrolled through till he found a picture of Rider that could be shared with someone else.

"Is this him?" Jean asked.

"Yeah, that is Rider." Cam smiled, but kept his eyes on the road.

"He looks normal...I mean..." Cam couldn't help but laugh at the panic in Jean's voice.

"I know what you mean. When Rider first came out as gay to me, I never even had a thought he might be. But he's very sweet and I want to make it up to him for forgetting his birthday.

"No problem. I already can see the drawing in my mind."

Cam could hear the pencil on the paper as he drove, by the time they arrived at the frat house Jean already had a mock up done. A smirk spread across Cam's face, *it's perfect*. Jean promised to draw the piece digitally and email him, but Cam was shocked when the email pinged over a couple of hours later. The detail of the art was fantastic, the image captured both Rider's love for Spider-Man and Cam's love for Rider. Pulling out his phone, he called the boy of his dreams.

"Hey," Rider said sadly.

"Hey, Ri. I know you're still upset—"

"I'm not." Rider's tone of voice betrayed him.

"Okay, well, anyway, I got you a special present." Cam hit forward on the email. "I hope you like it."

There was a loud gasp. The original idea was Rider meeting Spider-Man, but Jean had outdone himself. The piece had Spider-Man swinging through the city of New

York, the Empire State Building in the background. Rider was clung to Peter's back, his arms wrapped around his neck, a huge grin on his face. In Rider's backpack was a small pride flag sticking out the side, waving in the wind. In Rider's hand was a letter, a small amount of writing visible: *I'm sorry, Rider. Love, Cam.*

"Cam, I…" The words caught in Rider's throat.

"I am truly sorry, Ri, I never meant to forget to call. I love you so much."

"I love you, and I love this. I'm sorry for being angry. It's just so hard being so far away from you. I wish you were here." Cam laughed causing a change in Rider's voice. "No, I mean…I wish you were here."

"Oh!"

Cam blushed as he moved across the room to lock the door. He dropped down on his bed his hand already reaching for his crotch before Rider had even started talking again. Being so far away from each other, apart from sending each other pictures this could be the most intimate they could be.

Chapter 12

Rider

Study books were open on the desk, but Rider hadn't turned a page in over twenty minutes. His fingers drummed along the desk as his mind focused on his boyfriend. His thoughts had been all over the place in the last week. After Nixs had dropped him off and hugged him good night, Rider had found butterflies in his stomach. The same feeling he experienced when he first saw Cam in the principal's office. He had felt guilt all that evening, not only for the feeling but for flirting with Nixs at the bar. When Cam had called to apologise, he had felt a mixture of sadness and guilty. It had made their phone call slightly uncomfortable although Cam's present seemed to have rekindled their love.

Rider picked up his phone, there was still no call from Cam. He bit his lip, trying to focus on something else. After missing his birthday, there was no way Cam would forget about their one-year anniversary. Rider had believed throwing himself into his most recent assignment would be the best way to distract himself, but his notebook was still empty. Sighing to himself, Rider shoved his books into his backpack and his phone into his pocket.

Despite being in Houston for three months, he was still amazed how warm the evening air was for mid-November. Reaching the library, his phone still showed no missed calls. He held his breath and tried one last time to call Cam. *Sorry the number you are calling is currently not available, please leave a message after the beep.* Rider sighed and headed into the library.

The library at the University of Houston was larger than any he had previously been in, spanning eight floors. Taking the elevator to the third floor, Rider wandering up and down the stacks until he found the journalism section. His fingers ran along the books till he found the two he was after, *Investigative Reporters Handbook* and *The Elements of Journalism*. Tucking them under his arm, Rider walked toward the study desks on the other side of the library. As he approached, a person hunched over a laptop caught his attention, the artificial lights bringing out the blue in his hair. A smile appeared on Rider's face as he sneaked over to Nixs.

"Boo!"

A yelp came from the older student causing Rider to laugh. He slipped into the seat next to Nixs, apologising to the staff for shouting. The librarian glared at them both as she headed into the stacks.

"Sorry for getting you into trouble. So, this is your secret hiding spot. What you up to?" Rider asked.

"Oh, erm…nothing."

Nixs tried to hide his computer screen, but he was too slow. Learning from Jane, Rider grabbed the laptop and pulled it over to him, increasing the video to full screen. From Nixs' reaction, Rider believed it would be something erotic but the image on the screen showed a young Goku currently holding a Dragonball in his hands. He turned to look at Nixs who seemed to be extremely embarrassed. Rider's smile seemed to cause his blush to get worse.

"*Dragonball?*"

"Yeah, I know." Nixs pulled his laptop back and closed it. "I'm a nerd."

"Then call me a nerd also."

A confused look spread across Nixs' face, causing Rider to laugh. Although comics were his main thing, Rider was still an anime fan. He had never seen the original *Dragonball*, but he and Lloyd had watched *Dragonball Z* at least four times. It didn't take long before the journalism books were forgotten about, Rider shuffling closer to Nix while they both watched an episode. Rider's smile turned to a goofy grin when he saw Nixs mouthing the words along with the scene.

"How many times have you watched this?"

"Not that many," Nixs said, Rider refused to break his stare. "Fine, I think this is like my third time." Nixs turned to look away, making it difficult for Rider to hear the rest of the sentence. "This year."

The embarrassed smile on Nixs' face quickly twisted into an angry glare. Tracing Nixs' line of sight to a table three down from their own, Rider saw two students seated. A hulking brute of a student sat with his back toward them, the other student's fire-red hair got in the way of his eyes as he focused on Rider and Nixs. A weird look crossed his face, a mixture of jealousy and anger.

"Who's that watching us?"

"That would be Bane Sanchez. Remember when I told you about my freshman roommate?"

"The one you got into a fight with?"

"Well. After that happened, we…erm…kind of became a weird couple." Nixs smiled at the confused look on Rider's face. "How do I explain this? Bane definitely has a thing for guys, but he refuses to accept his feelings. Whenever we did anything, afterward he would pretend nothing had happened. In the end, I ended it between us."

"I'm…I'm sorry."

"You don't need to be sorry. I just don't have very good luck when it comes to dating."

Nixs started explaining about the bad dates he had been on and the bad relationships he had been in. A number of them had Rider laughing out loud, others awing in sympathy. He hadn't even noticed he was rubbing Nixs' hand until Nixs placed his own hand on top.

"What about you? Any evil exes?" Nixs asked.

"No evil exes. Actually, no exes at all," Rider said, swallowing the lump in his throat.

"Really? Someone as cute and sweet like you? I would have thought guys would have been lining around the corner to date you."

Rider wasn't sure why he didn't want to tell Nixs about Cam. A twinge of guilt spread through his body. Her pulled out his phone to try and avoid the question and to break the hypnotic gaze from Nixs' emerald eyes. There was still no message from Cam, but Rider noticed something else, the phone also didn't have any signal.

"Do you have any cell service?"

"Nope," Nixs said without pulling out his phone. "This building has a lot of metal in it. It stops any signal from reaching your phone."

Nixs closed his laptop and finally noticed the journalism text books that rider had placed down on the table. He looked around the library, confusing Rider, before he flicked through the textbooks and found a page third of the way through.

"I'm not supposed to help with your assignments, but you may find the third paragraph down helpful".

Acting as if he hadn't provided Rider the answers to his assignment, Nixs grabbed hold of the other journalism book and started to read a random page. Rider tried to read the paragraph but could feel Nixs' eyes on him. After attempting to read the same line for the fourth time, he looked over the top of the book, catching Nixs before he could look away.

"Hey you can't sit there and just watch me. That's not fair." Rider laughed.

"You're right." Nixs closed the book he had been pretending to read. "Let's get out of here. I'm hungry and you always look like you could do with food."

Rider smiled and closed his own book. Nixs pushed him back down in his seat and grabbed the books, walking the short distance over to a trolley before dropping the books down on top. "The library staff will put them back. This way we can get to pizza faster."

As the duo started to walk toward the elevators, Bane was still watching them, a scowl on his face. When they reached the table, Rider felt something gently slide around his waist, he looked down to see a hand pulling him close. He looked up seeing Nixs smiling, but it wasn't at Rider, he was looking toward Bane. The scowl on Bane's face dropped when the other student on the table noticed them moving past them.

"Fags," the other student said.

Nixs stopped, his arm pulling Rider closer, protecting him from the slur. "Really, Dwight? It has been almost three years and you're still going on with this crap? It's just pathetic. Maybe you and Bane should finally get over your homophobia."

Nixs stepped threateningly toward Dwight, which caused a yelp from the much bigger student. Dwight almost curled up in a defensive position in the chair. Nixs laughed as he wheeled Rider away from the duo, only releasing the hold on Rider once they were in the lift and the door had closed. Rider bit his lip as the elevator started moving downward, he was ashamed to admit it but he had really enjoyed having Nixs' arm wrapped around him. The butterflies had appeared the moment he had felt the touch on his hip, although now guilt spreading through him like a plague.

"I'm sorry about that, Rider. The other day Bane cornered me saying he wanted to get back together. I wanted to show him that I was over him. I didn't mean for you to get insulted."

"It's okay. I didn't…mind." Rider could feel his cheek heating up.

There was silence for the rest of the elevator ride although Rider was sure Nixs had shuffled closer to him when Rider had glanced away. The couple both tried to exit at the same time causing them to laugh before Nixs backed off, allowing Rider to go first. The politeness didn't end there as Nixs held open the door to the outside, As Rider stepped out into the warm evening, his phone burst to life. He quickly checked it, seeing he had three missed calls and four messages.

"Anyone interesting message you?"

"Nope." Rider looked down and could see Cam's name on his screen. "Just family."

He felt guilty for lying to Nixs, but also angry at Cam. His boyfriend had plenty of time to call for their anniversary, *why did it take him so long?* Thoughts of Cam were swept away when Nixs hand enclosed his own. The messages remained unread as he was pulled in the direction of the closest pizza joint. An hour and a half later, Rider was back in his dorm room. Holding his breath, he unlocked his phone to see one of the missed calls was from his mom, but the other two from his boyfriend. He opened the first message, and his stomach dropped.

Hey Ri. Sorry I couldn't call earlier, coach takes our phones on an away game so that we only concentrate on the match during the

journey. I saw your message and missed
calls, did you forget I told you about the
match? We won but I would have rather
been spending the day with you. I can't
believe I don't get to be with you on our one
year anniversary. I love you so much.

Rider felt like vomiting. Cam had indeed told him on
Sunday he had a match on their anniversary. While his
partner was trying to contact him, he had been watching
anime with another guy while being angry at Cam. Rider
could feel the tears starting to form in the edge of his eyes,
he felt like an awful boyfriend. It had to be missing Cam
that was causing his feelings for Nixs. He just needed to
clear his head.

He flicked through the photos on his phone—the
blonde hair, the dimples that appeared when he smiled, his
soft lips that he could feel when he closed his eyes... Each
image of Cam made his heart beat hard. He kept swiping
till he landed on the photo Trish had taken of the two at
The Met. A weak smile appeared on Rider's face as he
stared at the image, his eyes slowly closing as he fell asleep
fully clothed.

The sun lit up the room as Rider's eyes became heavy, he
had only been reading the textbook for thirty minutes, but
he was already bored. He was currently cursing himself out
for not going for food with Jason. Picking up his phone, he
let out a sigh when there was still no reply from Cam. The

moment he had woken, he had sent a message apologising for missing the calls. Before he could send another message, there was a knocking on the door.

"It's open, come in."

Another knock came.

"It's open!"

A third knock caused Rider to rise from his desk. He stomped across the room, the door was thin enough for whoever was on the other side to definitely hear him. Pulling the door open, the person burst through and grappled him into a tight hug. Rider was shocked, his voice struggling to work as a mouth connected with his, arms pulling him tight. As the kiss broke, Rider looked up, the blond hair falling in the way of the deep pools of blue, the dimples on full display.

"Cam? What? How?" A smile slowly appeared on his face as he looked into the face of his boyfriend.

"I couldn't not see you for our anniversary. I booked a plane ticket."

"How…how long are you here for?"

"Only a couple days, so we have to make the most of it."

Cam winked as he closed the door and locked it. Rider found himself being lifted up and carried to the bed. Rider wrapped his arms around Cam's neck, leaning forward and placing a passionate kiss on the lips he had missed. Once Rider was on the bed, Cam slowly removed his shirt, followed by his jeans. When he started taking his time with his boxers, Rider couldn't wait any longer, ripping them off in one quick motion.

Rider went to remove his own T-shirt but was stopped. Cam had a wicked smile on his face as he moved slowly down Rider's body, kissing as he went. When he reached the bottom of the T-shirt, he took it in his teeth, pulling it up and over Rider's head. The T-shirt was quickly discarded to the floor as Cam cupped Rider's package, giving it a gentle squeeze before his hands moved up and pulled both Rider's jeans and boxers off in one smooth motion.

Cam pulled Rider closer. Rider had missed the heat of the body next to him. Their lips quickly moved together, tongues massaged, rubbed up and down each other. Rider smiled when he could feel he wasn't the only getting excited. Pulling back slightly, he could see the smile on Cam's face that he loved. Before he could instigate another kiss, Rider felt a hand on his shoulder. He rotated in the bed to see another guy. The dark hair flashed blue in the light, his earring glimmering in the sun.

"Nixs?"

"Hey, handsome. Nice fluff," Nixs said, looking Rider up and down.

"What you doing here? Cam...I..."

As he turned, there was a smile on Cam's face. The jock's hand stroked up Riders side before coming to settle on Nixs' hand. Rider's head swivelled between the two guys, both their smiles slowly twisting into wicked grins.

"Don't worry, Ri. We can take turns," Cam said before gently pushing Rider towards Nixs.

Nixs didn't waste any time placing his lips onto Rider's. With Cam it felt like electricity was surging through his body, but with Nixs it was different; a cold chill pierced his lips, sending a shiver down his spine. Nixs' fingertips danced across Rider's skin, gently brushing past his nipples and down toward his crotch. Rider gasped as Nixs softly grabbed him, licking up Rider's neck, sending another shiver through his body. Before Rider could say anything, Cam leaned over and lightly bit Rider's neck, a gasp escaping the smaller teen's lips.

"You think he could take both of us?" Nixs grinned at Cam.

"Only one way to find out." Cam winked.

Cam and Nixs both leaned forward and kissed him at the same time. Rider lay still, allowing the pleasure to take over him. Both boys' hands slowly slid down Rider's body, wicked grins on both their faces. Their hands slid around Rider's back and over his butt cheeks, they soon landed at their destination. *Bang*. Rider's eyes jerked open, he gasped for air as if Cam was still lying on him. Rider searched the room for signs of either boy, but neither were present, only Jason.

"I'm sorry, Rider, I didn't mean to slam the door. I forgot my keys." Jason smiled as he walked across the room, picked up the keys, and slid back out, this time closing the door much quieter.

Rider's head fell back onto his pillow, his breath still staggered as his mind replayed the events of the dream. His hands slid up to his face as the tears started to fall; he tried to stem the flow as best as he could. Rider loved Cam so much, he didn't want to do anything to ever hurt him, but if that was true, then why was he also dreaming about Nixs?

Chapter 13

Rider

Sitting down on his bed, Rider watched the time on his phone tick down. Only five more minutes and he would have the whole night with just Cam. It had been three weeks since Rider had the dream involving Cam and Nixs and the guilt still ate at him. Nixs was sweet, attractive, and they had a lot in common, but Cam had allowed Rider to live the life he wanted. If Cam had been at Houston, Rider knew this wouldn't have been an issue.

Rider had actively decreased the time he spent with Nixs, hoping the distance would change his feelings into only friendship. This had been difficult due to his TA work increasing. Professor Hudson was meant to have three TAs, but Jenkins had recently quit, resulting in Rider picking up his work.

Taking a deep breath, he pushed his fellow journalist from his mind. The evening was only for him and Cam. Rider climbed off his bed and went to the mirror; he had slight bags under his eyes but apart from that looked the exact same he had met Cam. He had chosen to wear the same T-shirt he had been wearing that day, all black apart from the Batman logo etched in gray just above his heart. He pushed around his hair before abandoning it.

Pushing his glasses up his nose, he walked slowly back over to his bed, his gaze focusing on the artwork Cam had gotten him for his birthday. He loved the piece and had it printed and framed. It now hung on the wall over his bed so he could look at it every evening just before falling asleep. When the phone showed 6:01 PM, Rider smiled and hit the call button. In an instant, Cam's face appeared on the screen, the dimples on display from his smile.

"Hey, you," Rider said.

"Hey, Ri. How are you?"

"I'm okay, just missing you like crazy."

Rider loved the way Cam blushed, it started in the tips of his ears and slowly descended to his cheeks. He bit his lip softly before he blew a kiss toward the camera. Before Cam could return the kiss there was a noise from off screen, a soft muttering. Cam's eyes flicked above the phone before returning back to Rider.

"Who else is there?"

A face Rider was all too familiar with burst onto screen, pushing Cam out of the way. *What is Becca doing in Cam's room?* Becca was smiling and waving, but Rider couldn't hide the scowl on his face as Cam came back into the frame.

"What the hell, Cam?" he shouted.

Cam tried to explain, but he was drowned out by the anger in Rider's voice.

"We have hardly spoken in the last month. This was

meant to be just me and you, but you decided to invite Becca."

"Ri—"

"You both enjoy your evening!"

Without another word, Rider hit the end call button. The fire in his stomach vanished just as quickly as it had arrived. Guilt spread throughout him. He shouldn't have just ended the call; he should have allowed Cam to explain why Becca had been included in their special evening. Scooping up the phone, his finger hovered over the call button before he dropped it back to the bed. Rider took a couple deep breaths before he grabbed a towel and headed toward the shower room. A shower would allow him to relax, get his thoughts in order before he talked to Cam again.

Cam

Cam threw the damp towel into the wash basket before pulling on a fresh T-shirt. After the horrible defeat in his last match, Coach had doubled the drills. Cam and the rest of the team had blamed Oseman. After he complained he wasn't getting any game time, he had started instead of Cam. By the time they had been swapped, the score difference was too great for Cam to pull them back. After practise, Cam still had way too much energy thanks to his excitement for the upcoming call with Rider and had decided to go for a run, returning to his dorm drenched in sweat, and despite how much Rider would love to see him shirtless covered in sweat, he wanted to feel refreshed for their evening.

Quintin had invited Cam to go out drinking, but he had declined. There was plenty of time to drink with Matthews, but not often did he get a full evening with the man he loved. He ran his hand through his hair, he had yet to get it cut since starting college. The spring before his father had passed away, when Yorick had grown a mohawk, Cam's other best friend Bobby Davenport had challenged him to grow his hair long and it had reached his shoulders. While playing basketball against Edward Harris, Harris had "accidentally" caught hold of it. It had been at that point, Cam had decided to never let his hair grow too long.

The mess of his hair just reminded him of Rider, how he loved running his hand through the long dark locks. Checking the clock, he still had ten minutes until their call. Grabbing a bottle of water, he had just taken a sip when there was a knock on the door.

"Matthews, I told you, I'm not going drinking with you tonight."

Cam pulled open the door surprised to find Becca there. Her face was red, and her mascara was smudged from tears. He leapt out of the way as she entered the room and dropped down onto his bed, pulling a pillow into her lap. Closing the door, he walked over to his desk and waited until she was ready to talk.

"Me and Dave broke up."

"What happened?"

"He put the spoon in the sugar jar. That was too much. We are so over!" Becca said, throwing the pillow away.

"Come again? Cam said, a confused look on his face.

Dave had spent the afternoon over Becca's running lines with her. After four hours of singing, they were both feeling drained of energy and coffee was the best solution. Dave had volunteered to make them, but what Becca witnessed, horrified her. Dave had not only put the milk in before adding the water but after he had mixed the coffee, he had put the spoon in the sugar jar. The explanation confused Cam even more till Becca started going on about how it resulted in the sugar clumping.

"So instead of going out drinking with him tonight. It's me and you." Becca smiled, picking the pillow back up.

"I would love to, but I already have plans." Cam dodged out the way as a pillow came toward his head, causing him to laugh.

"Who with? Cancel them! This is me we're talking about."

"Sorry. No way am I cancelling on your brother." Becca's eye roll caused Cam to laugh even harder. "He should actually be calling any—"

The phone burst into life, demanding his attention. His excitement kicked in, making him forgot Becca was in the room. He hit the answer button, a smile spread across his face as Rider came into focus. The dimples came out when he noticed Rider was wearing his glasses. He could feel the blush spreading across his face as his boyfriend said how much he missed him before blowing a kiss. Cam almost blew one back when Becca caught his attention.

"Ugh. Why do guys have to be so cringey at romance?"

Cam took a second to look up at Becca, trying to signal

with his eyes to be quiet but Rider spotted the motion, demanding answers. Becca jumped of the bed and grabbed hold of Cam's phone, pushing him out the way. She started waving toward the small image of Rider.

"Hey, Ri. How's Houston?"

"What the hell, Cam!"

Cam grabbed hold of his phone again. Rider's face was full of shock and anger, his voice quivering with emotion. Guilt spread through Cam's gut, he should have told Becca at the beginning he was planning on talking to Rider and she needed to go, but he couldn't throw someone out who had just broken up with their boyfriend.

"I'm sorry, Rider. Becca just broke up with Dave, and she came over, but she didn't know it was our night. She's about to leave."

Rider started shouting again, killing any chance of an explanation. Before Cam could say anything else the call ended, the screen going blank. Cam was confused at what had happened, he dropped down on the bed, his eyes becoming wet before Becca pulled him into a tight hug.

"Cam, I'm sorry, I didn't think me being here would ruin your night. My brother is an ass at times. Call him back."

He shook his head. It wasn't the first time they had argued since starting college and the best technique Cam had found was to give Rider some space. He always came around after a while and was always super apologetic. It was the distance between them that was the problem, nothing more.

Becca smiled softly at him. "Okay, if you're not going

to call him then we are going out, getting drunk, and forgetting about both our boyfriends until they have calmed down."

"Boyfriends? I thought you and Dave were over?"

Becca rolled her eyes and threw Cam's jacket at him. By the time they were outside, there was already a taxi waiting to take them to Becca's favorite bar. Cam wasn't even sure when Becca had called for a cab. His eyes went wide, and his jaw dropped when they walked into the place. Not only was it a gay bar but it was a gay karaoke bar. He shook his head but before he could turn around to leave, Becca was pushing him further into the establishment. The beer Cam asked for was soon placed into his hand, Becca choosing to go for a cocktail instead.

"Please tell me you aren't going to be drinking plain beer all night?"

Cam didn't respond, a voice on stage had caught his attention. A smile slowly appeared on his face, as the Quintin admitted to the world that he couldn't lie about liking big butts. Quintin waved in their direction as he sprung into the second verse. A number of wolf whistles echoed throughout the room as Quintin spun around and started wiggling his butt toward the audience. Cam covered his eyes, embarrassed by the actions of his friend, questioning how much Quintin had already drunk. Once the song was over, Quintin swaggered toward Cam, only being stopped en route by a guy slipping a piece of paper into Matthews' hand.

"What are you doing in a gay karaoke bar and did that guy just give you his number?" Cam questioned.

"That would be a yes." Quintin smiled, looking at the number before he crumpled the paper up and put it in his pocket. "I'm here because you wouldn't come out drinking and the only person I could find was Morales. Did you know he was gay?"

Cam rolled his eye at the name of his teammate. "Yes, he told me after I came out during hell week."

An argument from behind them caused Cam and Quintin to turn around. Fernando stood next to Becca, in the middle of a heated debate about Dave, Becca, and clumped sugar. Cam wasn't sure how Fernando already knew about the incident, until Matthews explained how they had run into Fernando's cousin on the way out of college dorms. Sighing, the duo slowly inched away from the argument, the two already drawing stares.

"Anyway, why you here? What happened to your phone date with Williams?"

"We kind of had an argument and he hung up on me. I thought I'd give him some time to cool down."

"And the chick?" Matthews nodded toward the still-arguing pair.

"That would be who we were arguing over," Cam replied, causing Quintin to raise his eyebrows. "Not like that. That's Becca, Rider's sister. She dropped by just before Rider called and then he thought I wanted to spend time with her rather than him."

Quintin grabbed a beer for himself and a second one for Cam, who hadn't even realized he had finished his bottle already. They soon found an empty table, completely abandoning the duo whose fight had evolved from coffee-stained sugar to the correct way a kitchen should be laid out.

"I can tell you are upset about the call. Tell me, what's going on?" Quintin probed.

"I don't know. I love Rider so much, I think it's the distance getting to us. We're just on different wavelengths at the moment."

"Maybe you guys just need a break? Or how about getting laid? That always makes people a lot more easy-going. Do you not want to play the field a bit?"

"No," Cam said adamantly. "It's hard to explain but everything seems perfect when it's me and him together, it all just clicks into place. Even though we've argued a bit recently, afterward, no matter how upset or angry either of us are, it's still him I want to spend the rest of my life with."

A drink slammed down onto the table, interrupting the conversation. Becca looked angrier than when she had arrived at Cam's room. She started flicking through a book of songs she could perform.

"That guy is a jerk. Now that I've met him and know how arrogant he is, I understand why he keeps hitting on you."

"Morales is still hitting on you?" Matthew's jaw dropped.

"Don't get me started."

"That's got to make your assignment awkward."

Cam let out a long sigh. He and Fernando had been paired together for a history project, of which neither of them had started yet. It would require time spent alone with just Fernando, which Cam wanted to minimise as much as possible. He planned to do as much as possible by himself, then any of the group work crammed in a couple of days before the assignment was due in January.

"Can we just stop talking about Fernando for one evening and just have fun?" he demanded.

Becca was the first to take the stage singing along to *Touch-a Touch-a Me* from her show. As different members of the audience sang their own songs all Cam could think about was the night in Rider's bedroom, the first time he had heard Rider play and sing. Even in the loud bar, if he closed his eyes and focused, the words floated to him, the electric feeling burst through him.

"Come on, Walker, when you going to get up?" Matthews asked while lightly punching him in the arm.

"Have you ever heard me sing? I'll make your ears bleed."

"You're not that bad, Cam. You sounded good in my apartment," Becca said whilst looking for another song. Cam warned Matthews to drop the eyebrows. "I know, we'll do a duet, that way if they don't like you, I'll sing both parts."

"I'm going to need something strong to drink before I get up there."

Becca didn't even say a word, she instead climbed out of her seat and headed toward the bar. Matthews pulled the book toward him, smiling to himself when his finger tapped on *Never Going to Give You Up*. Cam sighed and rolled his eyes at Matthews drawing a laugh from his teammate. Becca returned with a smile on her face holding three tall glasses, not a single bottle of beer in sight. She dropped a glass in front of each of the boys, Matthews happily accepting it and taking a sip.

"Just because I'm dating your brother doesn't mean I like fruity drinks."

"Just try it," both Matthews and Becca said in unison.

"Fine," Cam grumbled.

Cam wanted to hate the drink, but he couldn't, the drink was sweet and fruity. Cam took a second sip and then a third, draining over half of the glass before he noticed the other two looking at him.

"I'm glad you like it, but calm down, they are strong." Becca laughed.

After two more pina coladas, Cam found a microphone in his hand, lights blinding him as he watched the lyrics start to appear on the screen. Somehow Becca had convinced him to get up on stage with her. She had promised the alcohol would make the stage fright easier, but all it was doing was making the words wobble on the screen. Becca had decided that the best song they could sing was the duet version of *Lay All Your Love on Me* from *Mamma Mia*. Her reasoning: they could sing it for their boyfriends.

Cam stood rigid as the music played into the crowded bar, the mic raised to his lips even before his part. Becca burst forth with the first verse, her theater genes kicking in as she started dancing around the stage as she sang, waving her finger at him as if they were in a relationship. The crowd hollered and cheered as she came and wrapped an arm around his neck. Cam sang quietly, trying to focus on the words on the screen despite knowing them from heart. *Damn Mom for being such a huge Abba fan.* As Becca danced around him, her energy slowly infected him. He was soon dancing around the stage, mirroring her actions. The crowd's cheers drove them both on further.

Becca pulled Cam down into a bow as they received a round of applause; even Quintin was on his feet clapping. Cam noticed a phone in his teammate's hand. It took them a couple of minutes to make it back to their table. A number of people stopped them en route to congratulate Becca on her singing voice. Only one person complimented Cam but once he refused to give the guy his number the compliments quickly stopped. Quintin was smiling and still messing with his phone when they finally reached him.

"You recorded it didn't you?" Cam quizzed him.

"I have no idea what you're on about," Quintin said, playing innocent. "Fine. Yes, I recorded it."

"And?"

Quintin refusing to look at Cam. "I may have sent it to Gomez."

The horror that spread across Cam's face caused Quintin to laugh. It was only a matter of time before Jane messaged him. As an apology, Matthews slid another drink into his hand. When Becca saw the video, she demanded her own copy, causing Cam to drain the drink. He closed his eyes, the world spinning as he dropped into an empty seat. When he opened them, he could see Fernando on stage ready to sing. Cam let out a sigh as the music kicked in, he knew the song and its meaning. He glared at his teammate as Fernando started to sing the song *Escape*, or more commonly called The Pina Colada Song.

When he was younger, Cam and his father had been in Central Park when someone had started playing the song close by. He had enjoyed the up tempo, but when he asked his dad about the strange lyrics, he was shocked. A guy bored of his wife had decided to have an affair only to end up meeting his wife. *Is this Fernando's way of trying to get me to cheat on Rider?* If it was, then Fernando was crazier than Cam had first thought. The second verse had hardly begun when Cam rose to his feet, staggering slightly. Explaining to Quintin and Becca, who were still rewatching the video, he was going outside for some air.

Cam walked out into the cold night air, the chill doubling the effect of the alcohol. He found a wall to lean against as the light rain drizzle cooled down his face. Pulling the phone out his pocket, an image of Rider slowly got wet as he tried to enter his passcode. After the third attempt, the phone unlocked. The front of the bar was too loud to talk, so Cam went to the side street. Hitting dial, he held his breath as Rider's voicemail kicked in. He smiled to himself; he wasn't going to miss this opportunity to say how he really felt.

"Hey, Ri, I'm sorry if this wakes you, although it is only..." He pulled the phone all the way to his face just to see the time clearly. "...ten thirty. I know you're probably mad at me because of Becca, but I promise she turned up after dumping Dave. I didn't know she was coming over and then I couldn't get rid of her before you called. You should know by now I'll do anything for you because I love you with every part of my body. I wish we weren't so far away. I just want to be with you and kiss those lips I miss so badly. I can't wait to see you in a couple weeks when we are both back in Belmont."

Cam bit his lip before he continued. "I can't wait to *be* with you. I've missed my fingers running through your hair, running down your spine, making you to shiver in anticipation. I know it's only a couple weeks, but I don't know how much longer I can last—my hand isn't working any more. I just feel like I'm going to explode, if you know what I mean. I wish you were here to *feel* how much I miss you. Anyway, I'll let you go, but we will sort out another date night, I'll even strip for you on camera. I love you, Rider."

Slipping his phone back into his pocket, the smile on his face vanished quickly as he turned to see Fernando watching him. Cam started to walk back toward the street, but Fernando stretched out his arms, blocking the route.

"I'm guessing you were calling Rider. What happened to your date? Quintin said that's the reason you couldn't go drinking with him, but here you are."

"It's none of your business."

"He says he loves you, but he's never there for you," Fernando said with a smirk. Cam just pushed past him. "As my girl Blu Cantrell says if it hurts, it just won't work."

"And what does she say about you being a jackass?"

Cam didn't wait for a response, instead entering the building and going straight to the bar. He needed another drink to get through the rest of the night with Fernando in the vicinity; ordering two whiskeys, knowing one wouldn't be enough. He slowly made his way back to the table where Quintin was currently sitting with a mysterious woman whispering in his ear. One of the glasses of whisky was empty by the time Cam sat down. The woman nodded at Cam before rising out of her seat and heading toward a large group in the corner.

"So, the old rumour is true, a gay bar is a great place to get women's numbers," Quintin said showing off five crumpled up pieces of paper. "I say no and they still give me it. Good thing Carrie-Ann isn't here."

Becca was back on stage, singing another musical song either Cam didn't know or couldn't understand due to the mixture of alcohol circulating his body. The most Cam was able to grasp was she wanted to fight gravity or something. Cam finished the second glass of whiskey by the time she returned to her seat.

"Can we leave yet?" he asked.

"Why?" both his friends asked.

The answer became clear as Fernando stepped back onto the stage, declaring his song was for a particular person within the audience. Cam knew that Fernando wouldn't be able to see his eye roll, but he didn't care, he did it anyway. He felt like vomiting as the song began, Fernando had chosen *Take a Chance on Me*. Even Quintin's face twisted up at the song choice before he looked over at Cam.

"Yeah, I think it's about to time to head," Becca said. "Matthews, it was lovely to meet you in person."

"You mean Manchews?" Cam laughed, a confused look

coming across Quintin's face. "Sorry, bit of an inside joke. I'll see you tomorrow."

Cam remembered leaving the bar, then the next minute his head was on a soft pillow. Everything in between was missing. It felt like he had only been asleep for an hour when he opened his eyes and was greeted by the sun. His eyes stung as he scanned the strange room he was in, it wasn't his dorm room. The duvet was purple, on the walls were posters for Broadway shows. A snore next to him caught his attention. Cam looked to the right to see a body lying next to him, the red hair a mess. Panic spread through Cam as he lifted up the duvet, a sigh of relief washing over him when he noticed he and Becca were both still fully clothed.

He tried to sit up, but there was a pounding in his head that made him give up. Instead, he grabbed his phone from the bedside table. He was glad that his drunk-self had plugged his phone in. The time confused him. *How can it be 11:30 already?* Cam tried to focus on the notifications on his screen, but it just caused his head to hurt more. He had two missed messages from Rider, one from Jane, and a final from Matthews. Before he could try and focus on the messages, the phone started to ring. The blur in his eyes stopped him from recognising the name on the screen, and the volume caused the pressure in his head to increase. Closing his eyes, he pressed the answer button. The voice sounded familiar but he his brain wasn't working.

"Cam?" said the voice.

"No, I'm sorry. This is Cameron Walker" Cam shook his head, it felt like it was full of syrup.

"Are you still drunk? You never replied to my messages, so I thought I'd call you." The voice laughed.

"Who is this?" croaked Cam, his throat dry.

"This is Rider Williams, your boyfriend."

Cam sat up sharply, immediately regretting the decision. His head started spinning fast, it felt like he was going to vomit. He took some deep breaths and tried to relax. He could feel the pounding in his temples as he regained his composure. There was giggling coming from the other end of the phone.

"Ri, I'm sorry—"

"Cam, you don't need to be. I'm the one who is sorry. It was my fault and my mistake. I hope you can forgive me?"

"Of course."

"Good. Now, let's talk about your night. It looks like you had a good time, but I do have one question: are you going to lay all you love on me or is that saved just for my sister?"

Cam's eyes went wide as the events of the evening flashed through his mind. He had completely forgotten he had gotten up and not only sang but danced in front of the whole bar. And Quintin had recorded and forwarded it.

"How did you see the video?" Cam asked as he rubbed his temples.

"Jane sent it to me, then immediately called me about it. She and Sam spent about two hours breaking down the video for their favorite part and where you could do with some more practise. I'm sure if you haven't heard from them yet, you will by the end of the day. I don't think I've laughed so hard for a while."

As he replayed the events of the night in his head, Cam suddenly remembered the phone call that had been busy and sent to voicemail. He felt the blush starting to spread over his face as he remembered exactly what he had said.

"You didn't—"

"Listen to your message? Yep," Rider confirmed. Cam sighed loudly, causing Becca to roll over. "What was with the sigh? I loved your message, I definitely *feel* the same way."

Cam's face felt like it was on fire as he listened to Rider's response to his own confession. He really wished he wasn't in Becca's bed at that moment, especially when Rider had explained in vast detail what they were going to do during Christmas break. Twenty minutes later when Rider finally said goodbye, Cam carefully slipped out of the bed and proceeded to the kitchen in order to get a glass of water and try and find some aspirin. It was another hour before Becca finally came out of the bedroom, looking even worse than Cam felt.

Chapter 14

Rider

Rider took a deep breath as he stood outside Professor Hudson's office. It was only two days till the university finished for Christmas vacation and three days till his flight back to Belmont. As he knocked on the wooden door, Rider was quickly summoned into the office. Rider had been called mainly due to Santos Jenkins quitting, one of Professor Hudson's other teaching assistants. Nixs was already sitting in one of the seats in front of the desk, a smile on his face in contrast with the worry on Professor Hudson's. He slipped into the remaining seat and looked toward Michele.

"Thank you both for coming. I have some bad news. So, not only did Jenkins quit as TA, but he's also pulled out of an important project that could result in a large amount of funding for the university. It's a bias analysis software that was yielding some very positive results. Due to the success so far, the board moved up the review process and I now need the project complete by the twenty-fourth."

"Bias software?" Nixs asked. Rider was happy he wasn't the only confused one.

"I am using artificial intelligence and an automated system to calculate the bias of an article and use the results to predict how the article may affect future events such as elections."

Both students nodded along with what Michele was saying, although Rider didn't really fully understand.

"I called you both in today to see what your plans for Christmas were and if you would be able to assist me. Don't look so worried, Nixs." Michele laughed at the face he was pulling. "You won't need to do any programming; your main role will be reading articles and assessing the bias in them for a control group to test the programming against. You will also need to monitor the results from the programming to ensure the predictions are correct. What do you think?"

"I'm doing the same thing that I do each year." Nixs smiled weakly. "So, I'll be able to help."

"Each year?" Rider asked.

Since starting at Houston, Nixs had avoided going home at Christmas, choosing instead to celebrate on his own. He was welcome at home for the holidays but with his parents and brother ignoring his sexuality, it made the situation awkward.

"What about yourself, Rider?" Michelle asked.

"Erm..."

Rider had his ticket printed and his luggage already packed, but the idea of leaving Nixs to do everything by himself made him feel guilty. He had also worked hard and didn't want to come across as ungrateful to Michelle for the opportunity. His feelings clashed strongly, his gut wanted him to remain and prove that he belonged in the advanced class, to prove that Michelle's optimism wasn't incorrect, but his heart yearn for Cam. It had been so long since he had seen his boyfriend and with them both being so busy it had impacted on the time they spent on the phone together. He wished he could just summon Cam here for the holidays, spend it helping the professor, and afterward head back to his dorm and just snuggle with Cam under the covers.

Then there was Nixs, who Rider could see smiling at him from the corner of his eye. Nixs would be alone for the holidays and have a mountain of work to do by himself. The friendship Rider had received from Nixs had helped with being so far away from Cam and his family. That if he ever felt lonely and Cam wasn't available, then Nixs was always free to talk. He didn't want one of his only friends in Houston to suffer while he was partying. Taking a deep breath in, he knew Cam would have his mom, uncle, and Gran and they had also made plans to meet up with Sam, Jane, and Lloyd. He wouldn't be alone. Rider swallowed the lump in his throat and made a quick decision.

"Sure, I can stay."

"Thank you, both of you. You're life savers." Michelle smiled with relief.

The duo soon sat behind a tall stack of articles that needed reading, grading, and compiling. With how high the pile was, Rider wondered if Jenkins had even read any of the articles. Five hours later, they had hardly made a dent in the pile. He was happy when Nixs re-entered the room holding a pizza box. They had both been so absorbed that they had forgotten to eat lunch. Rider scooped up a slice and devoured it in three single bites, making Nixs laugh.

"So, you going to tell me the truth?" Nixs asked, causing Rider to swallow the lump in his throat. He grabbed a second slice and chose to not look at Nixs. He had struggled looking him in the eye since the dream. "Why did you volunteer to stay? I thought you were going back home for Christmas?"

"Oh." He could feel a blush spreading across his face. "I didn't want to leave all this work for you."

"That's sweet, but what are you going to do for Christmas now?"

Rider hadn't even thought that far ahead. The university canteen would be closed, his dorm room didn't have a kitchen, and he was sure most restaurants in the area would be shut. Panic started to set in; it was too late to contact Professor Hudson and change his plans. While Nixs had been out grabbing pizza, he had already called the airline company and cancelled his ticket. He looked up to see Nixs smiling at him.

"I can tell by that face you have nowhere to go. Now you do. You are coming to my place for Christmas dinner. I'll cook for us."

"Nixs, you don't need to do that."

"It's okay. I've cooked for myself the last two years and eaten alone. It will be nice to have company this year."

"If you insist." Rider returned Nixs' smile. "Should we get back to business then?"

Two hours later and Rider sat on his bed, rubbing his ear. He had been on the phone for the last thirty minutes with his parents as he explained he wasn't coming home for Christmas. He told his mom it was due to his work as a TA that he wouldn't be able to make it. Somehow, she had taken this to mean he was ashamed of his small hometown compared to Houston and wanted to remain away. His father had taken the news a lot better, saying it was okay if he wasn't going to be there, but he had to call on Christmas morning.

Rider had also tried to call his best friend, but he could only reach Lloyd's voicemail. Jane had been disappointed but understood; she seemed to be swamped in not only college work, but also had been giving most of her free time to the homeless shelter. She was more interested in what Cam would say. Guilt flowed through him at the mentioned his boyfriend. He had been saving Cam till last, worried about the argument he knew would be coming.

Taking a deep breath in, he looked at the art piece on his wall before he hit the call button next to Cam's name.

"Hey, you, I didn't expect you to call. I just got back to my mom's house. It's at one you arrive on Saturday, right?"

"That's what I called about. Something's come up and I can't come back. I'm so sorry, Cam."

"What?" Cam cried. Rider flinched at the rise in his volume. "I don't understand. What's come up?"

Rider bit his lip as he started to explain the ongoing project. Although Cam wasn't talking, he could hear his breathing becoming deeper—he was angry. "I'm sorry I made you angry."

"I'm not angry," Cam said, his voice betraying him. "I just wish you hadn't waited until three days before you were coming back. I had arranged stuff."

"It only happened today. Also, what stuff?"

"Trish is coming to visit us. Well, now she's coming to visit me. I kept it quiet as a surprise, but I guess it's not needed anymore."

Rider was shocked, he had only talked to Trish the other day and she hadn't mentioned once that she was coming to visit them. The guilt from earlier hit him like a wall. *I shouldn't have cancelled on my friends, on Cam.*

"Can't you just come back? I miss you." Cam pleaded.

"I miss you too, but I can't. I've already cancelled my plane ticket. I have a lot of work with being a TA and I made a promise to the Professor."

"You also made a promise to me, Rider. You know what? Do whatever makes you happy."

Cam ended the call before Rider could apologise again. He tried to call back but after only one ring the call was sent to voicemail. The phone slipped from his hand, landing in his lap, along with a couple tears. It took twenty minutes before Rider managed to calm himself down. He picked up his phone, finding the correct number.

"Trish, I—"

"Sorry, Rider, I'm busy and not really in the mood to talk," Trish said, annoyance in her voice.

"Oh, okay. I'll try later?"

"I don't know, something *may come up* and I'll have to cancel last minute. Anyway, I've got to go."

With that, Trish ended the extremely short

conversation. Rider guessed during the time it took to stop his tears Cam had informed Trish. He felt awful—in a misguided attempt at trying to make one person happy, he had managed to make multiple other people upset, including his boyfriend.

The air was cool, and the sky was cloudy, but there was no sign of rain or snow as Rider walked toward Nixs' apartment. When he had called home, his mom had kept him on the phone for an hour telling him how it was snowing, about the Christmas dinner he would be missing, and the pile of presents that were under the tree that he couldn't open. By the time he had gotten off the phone, he was seriously regretting not traveling home. He hadn't spoken to Cam since the argument, but they were still texting each other, which Rider took as a positive. As he approached his destination, his pocket vibrated.

> Hey Ri. Thank you so much for the presents, I love them. I'm sorry I can't give you mine just yet. I don't know what you have planned today but I hope you have a nice time. Love you Cam X

Rider had ordered Cam's presents to be delivered home. He hadn't been sure what to buy Cam and before the argument he had called Trish for advice. After a three-hour discussion of how buying Trish a car wouldn't count as a present for his boyfriend, they had come up with a couple ideas, new sneakers for practise along with a New York Knicks jersey with Walker printed on the back. His original plan was to surprise his boyfriend on Christmas morning but still being in Houston, he had instead called Becca to convince her to drop off the presents, he had been chewed out by her.

It was around 3:00 PM when Rider headed towards Nixs' apartment. The present he had bought Nixs was twisting in his hand, this had been the first time he had been to a guy's house who was cooking for him. Swallowing the lump in his throat, he knocked on the door. It quickly opened, Nixs' smiling face greeting him as Rider was pulled into a tight hug.

"Merry Christmas, come on in."

The place was small but homey, the living room blending straight into the kitchen which had delicious smells wafting from it. A couch was positioned facing a TV and a table was set in front of the couch with cutlery already in place. A bookcase was positioned against one of the walls, full of journalism books and comics. Nixs dragged Rider to the couch, pushing him down and telling him to get comfortable.

"It smells amazing back there."

"It should, I've been in the kitchen since around ten. It should be ready in about thirty minutes."

Nixs sat down on the couch and positioned himself to both see Rider and watch the kitchen when he noticed something in Rider's hand. Rider swallowed hard as he handed the wrapped present over. With the short timeframe he had to buy a present, he wasn't sure how well it would go down. He had bought the older student a number of Wiccan and Hulkling comics.

"Wow, these are awesome. My favorite gay couple," Nixs said as he flicked through the first book. "I wish I had known we were doing presents, I would have got you one. Actually, wait here."

Jumping up, Nixs disappeared down the short corridor into a room hidden from view. When he returned, he was holding a book of his own, which he handed to Rider. It was a blank hardback notebook bound in leather.

"When I first started writing, I had to keep it from my family. It was in a book like that I used to keep it secret. I thought it would make a great starting notebook for someone who is going to become a great journalist."

The older student smiled and rested his hand on Rider's shoulder sending a shiver down Rider's spine. Rider bit his lip, his cheeks blushed as he thanked Nixs for the present. The emerald eyes seemed to twinkle against the Christmas lights hanging over the TV, creating something hypnotic that Rider didn't wish to break. It was the twitch in Nixs' smile which caused Rider to break his gaze.

"Is everything okay?"

"I…erm… It's Christmas so…" Nixs took a deep breath in and bit his own lip. "I want to tell you the truth. I, *like you,* like you Rider. I think you're sweet, handsome, and wonderful. I know you may not feel the same way and, if you don't, I'm completely fine with that. If you want to be friends, I accept that. You don't need to say anything and I'm sorry if I spoiled Christmas, I just wanted to be truthful with you."

Rider was shocked. He had been drawn to his friend since the moment they had met but he had never though Nixs might like him back. Rider took a deep breath and held it. It wasn't until Nixs nudged him that he realized he hadn't said anything. Releasing the air in his lungs, he looked into the emerald eyes.

"You haven't spoiled Christmas," Rider said causing a huge smile to appear on Nixs' face. A moment later, a chime called him toward the kitchen.

The room was small enough that Rider could feel the heat from the oven. As Nixs dished up the food, Rider took some deep breaths, calming himself and allowing the revelation to wash over him. He was feeling somewhat normal when a plate was positioned in front of him, Nixs sat down next to him as they both devoured the food.

Rider volunteered to do the dishes, but Nixs stopped him, opening what looked like a normal cabinet to reveal a dishwasher. Once the machine was loaded and turned on, they were both seated on the couch together. The TV was turned on and soon *Back To The Future Part 2* started playing. When rain started hitting the window, Nixs pull the blanket from the back of the couch and place it over both of them. As the movie progressed, Nixs' arm slid along the couch and down around Rider's shoulder. Rider smiled to himself and shuffled closer, resting his head on Nixs' shoulder.

The atmosphere was so relaxing that by the time the credits were rolling, Rider had rotated to be fully snuggled up to Nixs. Looking up, he could see Nixs was actively trying to avoid looking at Rider. Rider shuffled slightly, finally causing Nixs to look down at him. Again, he was absorbed in the emerald eyes as Nixs leaned forward. Their lips pressed together. The same feeling of ice from the dream burst through Rider's mouth and down his spine. He was shocked but didn't break the kiss, instead he pushed into it.

Rider soon became lost in the kiss, letting out a soft moan, and Nixs bit down on his lower lip. Their tongues massaging each other, a hand pulled Rider closer to him. Rider's hand was soon in the black and blue hair, clutching in pleasure. It wasn't until Nixs touched Rider's thigh that the spell broke. He leapt to his feet as the reality set in of what had just happened.

"Rider?"

Without responding, Rider's feet engaged. He was quickly out the door and into the storm that had moved in during the movie. The rain hit him hard in the face, but he didn't care, he just needed to get as far away as possible from what had just happened. The door slammed behind Rider as he entered his dorm room. Dropping onto his bed the tears mixed with the rain dripping from his hair. Before fully accepting himself, before he had come out, the thoughts of kissing another guy would have filled him with guilt and remorse. Cam had been there when he most needed him; not only did Cam save him from the bullies but also from his own self-hate. He still felt guilty for kissing Nixs, but those feelings of self-loathing were gone. If he was honest, he had really enjoyed kissing his friend. He felt confused.

Pulling out his phone, he loaded his photos. The first

was of him and Nixs together in a pizza joint. He had a huge smile on his face as Nixs wiped grease from his mouth. It was the night he should have been celebrating his anniversary. Rider swiped left on his phone and next came up the art Cam had gotten him for his birthday. The image changed to when Nixs had taken him drinking when Cam had forgotten his birthday. They were in a booth together, Rider laughing at something Nixs had said, and Nixs staring at Rider as if seeing something in him he hadn't seen before.

Rider kept flicking thought the photos before landing on the one Trish had taken almost a year ago. The white walls surrounded Cam and him, but they were lost in each other, the art on the walls completely ignored. Taking a deep breath, he flicked back to the photo from his birthday with Nixs.

Closing the photo app, he wiped away his tears, and swallowed all the doubt, guilt and uncertainty. He was making the right decision and deep down he knew it would all work out. He pressed the call button on the phone and after a couple of rings it connected, before the person on the other end could talk Rider started.

"Hey, I'm so sorry I left things the way I did."

Chapter 15

Cam

A pillow sailed across the room, startling Max who was napping on the bed. Cam had been excited to see Rider and spend time together but that had been destroyed due to Rider being too kind. *I know being a TA important, but could one project not wait till after the holidays?* Crossing the room, Cam apologised to Max, who was quietly growling in his direction. Pets on the head and a belly rub gained a tail wag as Max lowed his head back into snooze position. Letting out a sigh, Cam dialled Trish.

"Hey, CJ," Trish's voice echoed from a distance.

"Hey, Trish. Are…is that Yorick in the background?"

"What…no, just the radio."

"Oh, okay. You still coming for Christmas?"

"Yep, I'm literally packing my luggage now…*psst, put that down.* Why?"

Cam ignored the disturbance in the background, instead swallowing the lump his throat as he started to explain how Rider had cancelled his trip. Trish seemed to be angrier than him, as she promised they would have a great time, just the two of them. Cam couldn't help but smile when she reminded him how they had gone out on Christmas day to feed the ducks when they were younger. Despite ducks fly south for the winter, Trish had been adamant that the ducks would starve without fresh food in the form of frozen peas.

"He better not try to call me," Tish said adamantly.

"Trish, be nice to Ri. Just because he's not coming back for Christmas doesn't mean I don't love him."

"Fine!" She sighed. Cam could hear the eye roll. "For you, I won't bite his head off."

"You arrive at twelve thirty, don't you?"

The original schedule had Trish arrive thirty minutes before Rider's flight so they could surprise him. Instead, they were going to head straight back to Cam's home, by which time Uncle Roy should have arrived. A large bang came from the other end of the phone as Trish yelped before swearing loudly.

"You okay?" he asked.

"Grrr. Yeah, stupid suitcases fell off the bed and landed on my foot."

"You do know you're only coming for a week. You don't need to bring your whole wardrobe."

"Oh, CJ, how I wish that was true. A girl has to be prepared for all occasions. You think I'll need my sun hat?"

"Since it is literally snowing outside right now, I'm going to go with no." A shouting from downstairs caught Cam's attention. Max also heard the voice as he burst out of the room. "I think my mom needs me. I'll talk to you later, and, remember, go easy on Rider if he calls you."

As Cam approached his mom in the kitchen, he was denied the privilege of an easy first night back home. Thoughts of his missing boyfriend disappeared as he was put to work on a long list of chores that needed to be completed before his uncle arrived. By the time he fell into bed that evening, the refrigerator had been stocked with more food than twenty people could eat before it expired, kitchen scrubbed clean, living room hovered, and Max given a bath. Max was determined that he would not go in the water; Cam was sure he had gotten wetter than the German shepherd.

Despite being the tallest person at the airport, Cam still waved his arms in the air to draw Trish's attention. She was quickly wrapped in a tight embrace, a warm smile on Cam's face. The smile slipped slightly when he found himself battling three suitcases. Trish had decided that with her delicate frame she could only manage one case on her own.

"If you can only carry one, then how did you get four of them to the airport?" he challenged. When Trish refused to acknowledge the question, he decided to go in a different direction. "There is something different about you. Did you get shorter?"

"How dare you, Cameron James Walker!" she admonished, hitting him in the arm and causing him to drop one of the suitcases. "Did you not notice? It's the hair."

Cam had noticed the moment Trish had stepped off

the plane. Her hair used to be blonde, straight, and came down past her shoulder. Currently, her hair was curled up in tight spirals, the color gradually changing as it went from the golden blonde to a vibrant purple. Trish was in the process of explaining it was for her college course when they arrived at the car. After some squeezing Cam finally managed to get all four cases in the trunk. The journey back to his mom's went quickly, Trish managing to talk all the way about how her college experience was going.

Max greeted them as they entered the warm house only backing up when they brushed the snow off their heads that had gathered on the short trek between the car and the front door. The German shepherd wagged his tail hard, obviously having not forgotten Trish. She bent down and stroked Max, who couldn't stand still, constantly zigzagging between her legs.

"Mom?" Cam shouted.

"Kitchen, CJ!"

Walking into the kitchen, his mom and Uncle were sat at the table, cups of coffee in their hands. As Trish followed, there was confusion on both their faces. Only then did Cam realized he had completely forgotten to tell them he had gone to collect Trish and not Rider, in fact he hadn't told either of them that Rider was no longer coming.

"Trish!" Mary jumped to her feet and pulled her into a tight hug. "It's so wonderful to see you. I didn't realize you were getting in now, I was expecting to see Rider."

"Rider? Cam didn't—" Trish was interrupted by a wailing.

"Nooooo! My nephew has returned to the dark side," Roy joked, pretending to cry.

The whole room burst into laughter, causing Max to bark and circle around everyone's legs before he went back to the door. Even Max seemed to be waiting for the dark-haired boy. Cam's throat felt dry as he explained to his mom and uncle how Rider wasn't coming back for Christmas, although he left out the fight. He struggled to keep the tears in when his mom pulled him into a tight hug and apologised. Once she was sure Cam would be okay, his mom showed Trish to her room, leaving the men to grab the luggage.

"You sure you're okay, CJ?" Uncle Roy asked. Cam nodded as he grunted, pulling the cases out of the trunk. "I know long distance can be difficult, sometimes annoying. You may get into arguments, but if your love is true, you will both make it. I believe in you and Rider. Don't let me down."

Cam smiled weakly at his uncle as he was patted on the back. They both grabbed two cases each and headed back into the house. After delivering the luggage, Cam left Trish to freshen up. He dropped to his bed, being greeted by warm wet licks from Max. Picking up the remote from the bedside table, he turned on the TV and the DVD started to auto-play. A familiar voice echoed around his room, one that brought tears to his eyes every time he heard it. His father walked onto the screen to join Cam on the basketball court. Pulling Max closer as the scenes play out in front of him, it wasn't until he heard sniffles by the door that Cam turn away from the TV.

"CJ? I…"

Trish didn't say anything more as she walked over to the bed, climbing on and snuggling into the tearful Cam. They proceeded to watch the rest of the scenes before either of them talked again. Cam used Max to dry his tears as he stood up and ejected the DVD, storing it back in the special case Rider had designed for him for Valentine's Day.

"That was beautiful," Trish said as she tried to clear her cheeks from the mascara that had run.

"I know. It gets me every time. It's so good to see his face, hear his voice." Cam's voice cracked slightly from the emotion.

"Where did you get it?"

"It was my Christmas present from Rider last year. I had no clue what the disc was at the start. By the time it finished, me, Mom, and Uncle Roy were all in happy tears."

"Rider did this for you? Wow! I'm pissed at him for cancelling but this is unbelievably sweet of him. Damn, why did he cancel? This just makes me want to see him even more now."

Cam nodded in agreement before pulling his phone out his pocket and sending Rider a message saying how much he missed him. The phone hadn't been lowered before Rider had responded.

I miss you too and I'm still so very sorry I can't be there. Tell Trish I said hi if she still wants anything to do with me.

Cam smiled softly at the message. He had felt angry,

even slightly betrayed, when Rider had first called, but those feelings had slowly faded. He still wasn't ready to speak to Rider over the phone, he loved the smaller boy, but he knew that if they talked right now, they might end up arguing again, but messages like these made that call one step closer. Slipping the phone away, he and Trish headed back downstairs. The rest of the evening was spent with Trish telling his mom how much New York had changed since they had left.

Trish burst into Cam's room on Christmas Day. Despite having been awake for the last two hours waiting for others in the house to stir, Cam pretended he had only just woken up. Trish wasn't alone when she entered the room. Max sprinted across the room and jumped up onto the bed but misjudged where Cam was lying. Cam yelped and gasped for air and he pushed Max off his crotch as Trish exploded into laughter. He glared as she pushing a wrapped box into his hands.

"This was meant to be for both of you."

Cam started carefully removing the tape from the present. Normally, he would have ripped the gift wrap off in seconds but Trish hated people being slow with presents. He took pleasure seeing her squirm as he pulled out the box, before starting to neatly folding the paper. Trish pulled it out of his hands, scrunching it up before throwing it toward the corner, it landing in the trash bin without her looking. Cam opened the white box and pulled out a stained wooden frame. Rotating the present, he burst into a smile. In the frame was a photograph from when he and Trish had dragged Rider to their favorite burger joint in New York. Trish was positioned in the middle of them both, each resting their heads on her shoulders as they linked hands in front of her. All of them mid-laugh when the photograph had been taken.

"I love it," he said, giving her a hug.

"Good! Now, where is mine?"

Trish playfully punched him in the exact same spot she had at the airport when he pretended he thought they hadn't been doing presents. Rolling closer to the bedside table, he opened the drawer and pulled out a wrapped present, which matched Trish's hair color. The present was barely out of Cam's hands before Trish had decimated the gift wrapping.

"Are they the right ones?" he asked.

The smile on her face told Cam all he needed to know. Trish had been dropping numerous hints over the last few weeks about how her curlers were starting to die and she needed new ones, especially with her studying hairstyling at college. In their recent phone calls, she brought up the topic at least three times each call. She had never been very subtle, even when they had been dating. If Trish wanted something, it took around three hours before Cam knew what it was and the exact type he needed to buy.

"You know me so well," she said with a huge smile.

The next hour featured the family opening presents in the living room. Trish helped Max open his, of which by the time she had finished he had already destroyed two squeaky toys and devoured a whole bone. Cam didn't receive a new car again, but Uncle Roy had given him a gas card with $400 on it, which had prompted his mom to say Roy had spoiled his nephew. Cam had hardly used his car since arriving in Kentucky, so he was sure the card would last all the way till next Christmas.

Once all the wrapping had been collected and discard, much to the disappointment of Max who had been chasing around a scrunched-up ball while ignoring his actual presents, Cam slipping into the shower. By the time he climbed out, Christmas music was playing and there was a strong smell of turkey throughout the house. Entering the kitchen, Cam found his uncle in the kitchen chopping vegetables, but no sign of his mom.

"Where's Mom?"

"She had to dash out. Went just as you jumped in the shower but she shouldn't be long," Roy said. A knocking caught their attention. "Actually, that could be her now. Can you get the door?"

Nodding, Cam made his way to the front door only to be hit in the face by the cold upon opening it. A few flakes of snow landed on his nose, making him shiver. The woman on the stoop was not his mom. Her red hair clashed with the snow that was landing in it. Becca smiled at him as she pulled him into a tight hug. Cam wrapped his arms around the smaller girl.

"Merry Christmas, Cam!"

"Merry Christmas, Becca. What are you doing here?"

Stepping out of the way, he offered her to come into the warm house, but she declined. She didn't have long before she needed to be back at her parents. It turned out that the plan to stay at Dave's for Christmas had been cancelled after they had broken up again, this time over how Becca had bought the wrong type of popcorn for their movie night. She had bought sweet, but Dave had specifically asked for caramel.

"I'm here on a mission from Rider. Don't worry, I told him he was an ass for not coming home for Christmas. I'm completely on your side. Anyway, he begged me to bring this over for you." Becca handed him a gift bag with two presents wrapped in Spider-Man paper. "Don't mind the gift wrap. My mom used it to wrap Rider's gifts and I'm guessing she wrapped yours too. When do you head back to college?"

"The twenty-ninth. Despite it still being Christmas holidays, Coach has us training, so need to be back."

"Damn. I was hoping you would be going back on twenty-seventh. Dave messaged and we made up. Was hoping to get a free lift back to college to spend most the holidays with him. Anyway, I've got to head back, Mom is going crazy over how Dad got the car stuck in the snow going to pick up Uncle Steven and Julian. Have a good one, Cam, and I'll see you back at college."

Cam remained at the door, allowing the heat to escape as he watched Becca down the street, waving to her just as she disappeared out of his sight. Walking into the living room, a smile spread across his face. *I can't believe Rider still managed to get a Christmas present to me.* Opened the box-shaped one first, his jaw dropped when he realized they were top-of-the-line sneakers. Cam had mentioned only once during a phone call he was thinking of buying some new sneakers as his current ones were wearing down, but couldn't believe Rider had remembered that fact. The second present was soft in Cam's hands, he pulled away the gift wrapping and was quickly greeted by his family name in block writing and the number 22 under it, the writing emblazoned on the back of a Knicks jersey.

Cam grabbed his phone from his pocket and pulled up Rider's number. They had texted each other earlier, but he had so been missing hearing Rider's voice. After the wonderful presents, he wanted to hear it even more. His finger hovered over the call button when a noise came from the hallway. Trish and Max charged into the room.

"Why is there snow in the hall?" she asked, dropping down next to him.

Smiling at her, he explained about the unexpected visit from Becca, but his vision remained on the phone. He didn't know what Rider was currently up to, he planned to visit a friend who had also stayed at Houston to celebrate Christmas together. Instead of the call, Cam choose instead to send a quick message thanking the dark-haired teen for the wonderful presents. He hadn't even locked his phone before a response arrived.

> I'm so glad you like your presents, I was worried I had got the wrong team or even worse the wrong sport. I'm terrible at buying sports stuff. I'm sure whatever you got me will be amazing just like you. I hope you have a wonderful day.

"Rider by any chance?" Trish asked

"How did you know?"

"The big dumb smile you have on your face, and also the presents. I see he didn't accept my idea of a car, but I did suggest some options. Why not just call him? You obviously miss him and I'm sure he misses you just as much."

Cam bit his lip as he pulled Rider's number back on the screen, but before he could hit call there was another knock at the front door. Keeping his phone in his hand, he headed back toward the door. Pulling it wide open, he was greeted by a smiling face.

"Gran! I thought you were on a cruise?"

"Hi, CJ. It's lovely to see you, but its cold out here, so move out of the way."

He laughed as his gran pushed past him into the warmth of the house as she explained how because a number of crew on her cruise had come down with food poisoning, the cruise had ended a week early. His mom soon followed after, rubbing her hands to try and warm them up. Cam followed them into the kitchen and turned on the kettle while Gran pulled Roy into a tight hug.

"Roy, it's so nice to see you. It's been too long, busy with Joseph, huh?"

"Olivia, shhh!" Uncle Roy whispered, causing a confused look to spread over Cam's face. "Work has been crazy recently. You are looking wonderful as ever."

"Joseph?" quizzed Cam

"That doesn't matter, dear," his gran said, patting him

on his arm as he placed a coffee in front of her and his mom. "Where is your wonderful boyfriend?"

His mom started choking on her coffee causing Cam to pat her on the back. The commotion caused Trish to come and investigate. His gran was on her feet pulling Trish into a tight hug. "Are you back with Trish then?"

Cam's eyes went wide but this was nothing compared to Trish's response.

"No, no, no, no," she said as she waved her arms around.

He wasn't sure if he should be offended or not. It was the timer for the turkey that broke up the awkward conversation as his mom ordered everyone who was not Roy out of the kitchen. Cam spent the time before Christmas dinner filling his grandmother in on everything that was happening at college.

Several hours later and both Cam and Trish still felt stuffed when they were dropped off in front of Jane's house. Cam knocked on the door while brushing the snow out of his hair, Trish wiggling on the spot to keep warm. It didn't take long before the door opened, a confused young girl looking up at them.

"Hi, Sofia," Cam said.

"How do you know my name? Did Aaron send you?"

"Erm, no? I'm Cam, remember, I'm friends with Jane. This is my friend Trish."

Trish waved at Sofia who was now wearing a giant smile across her face as she noticed Trish's hair. She allowed them into the house only on the condition she could see it up close. Trish was all too happy that someone was showing interest in her new hair as she crouched down. Cam was glad when there were footsteps coming down the stairs, saving him from the discussion of colors that had just started.

"Cam, Trish! Come on up," Jane said, only coming half way down the stairs.

Cam almost had to pull Trish away from Sofia. As they entered Jane's room, he could see Sam sat on the bed, a social work book open on her lap. *Only Sam would be studying on Christmas day*. As he approached the bed, she jumped up and pulled him into a tight hug, almost strong enough to break his ribs. Sam has a soft smile on her face.

"Are you okay, Cam?" Sam asked with a worried look on her face.

He knew exactly what the question meant. "I'm okay. I miss him but there isn't anything I can really do." He turned to Jane. "I do have a question for you, who's Aaron?"

"Oh, Aaron is this sweet kid whose father owns the homeless shelter and runs the grief group that me and Sofia have been going to," Jane said, pulling him into a hug when Sam released him. "He and Sofia are always arguing about something. I think she actually likes him but won't admit it."

Cam dropped into a chair and allowed the three girls to take the bed. Jane's hand slipped into Sam's as she started telling them about all the hard work she had been doing for the homeless shelter. Both he and Trish were amazed at how much good Jane had done in such a short time. She had managed to reduce the shelters outgoings by thirty-eight percent but had increased their income by fifty-six percent. Not only had she arranged a charity drive, but she had found a government grant that the shelter could apply for.

"You are both so cute together," Trish said as Sam rested her head on Jane's shoulder.

"What about you, Trish? Anyone special in your life?" Sam asked as she squeezed Jane's hand.

The smile on Trish's face slipped slightly as she looked away. Cam was sure if she had been dating someone she would have told him. Jane seemed to also notice the look and wouldn't drop the subject until Trish revealed the truth. Cam's jaw dropped when she finally nodded in admittance. He even made an audible gasp at the boy's name.

"You're dating Yorick? Since when?" Cam demanded. Trish bit her lip. "Since when, Trish?"

"Since February," she said guiltily

"February? So, you were together when we came to see you in March, and you didn't say anything? I thought Yorick didn't even like you?"

Cam was extremely confused. While dating Trish, whenever he was hanging out with Yorick he avoided the topic of his girlfriend. Yorick always seemed as if he didn't like her, actively ducking discussing her. Cam had even tried to get the duo to hang out together alone, and when he had met up with them later, they had both been very awkward.

"Actual...erm...Yorick always liked me, but while we were dating, he didn't want to try anything since you were both best friends. That day we hung out, we both knew we liked each other, but our friendship with you was much more important. Once I knew you and Rider were together and you were happy, I thought why not ask him out. When you came to New York I wasn't sure how to tell you, I didn't want to spoil your trip with Rider."

"Is this the real reason no one else met up? Wait, is that the reason I heard him in the background when I called you?"

Trish reluctantly nodded. Cam wasn't angry that Trish was dating one of his best friends, but that she hadn't told him. The room grew somber until the three girls pulled Cam onto the bed and hugged him tight. Trish apologised to him, admitting she was just scared to tell him. He couldn't hold it against her, especially with how terrified he had been to tell her about his feelings for Rider. It would take a while for him to come to terms with it but he was happy for her and Yorick.

"Is Lloyd running late?" Cam asked. A sad look spread across Jane and Sam's faces. "What's wrong?"

"We've seen him, I think, four times since prom. He sometimes responds to messages but if you try and call him or visit there just is never a response," Sam responded.

"Lloyd?" Trish asked.

"Oh, sorry. I thought I told you about Rider's best friend," Cam said.

As he explained about the missing boy, Cam was shocked that Jane and Sam weren't aware that Lloyd and Yuki had broken up, although Rider had slipped it in during one of their longer conversations. Jane pulled out her phone, activating speaker mode and calling Lloyd. The phone rang three times before being sent to voicemail. Excusing herself,

Jane went out into the corridor to call Lloyd's house. She returned with a confused look on her face.

"Charles, Lloyd's dad, answered the phone. He said Lloyd wasn't home because he was supposedly over here with me and Rider."

"What? I hope he is okay," Sam said, pulling her own phone out and trying to call Lloyd.

"I told Charles the truth, that he's not here and that Rider isn't even back for Christmas."

A knock on the door quickly changed the subject as Sofia joined them, being bored by herself while her mom chatted with the adults. Sofia soon ended in Trish's lap, obsessed with the purple in her hair. Sam kept checking her phone, but it was Cam's that started chirping. A large smile appeared on his face when he saw the name on the phone.

"Hey, I'm so sorry I left things the way I did."

"No, Ri, I'm sorry. Being a TA in your freshman year is amazing, and I understand sometimes that means having to sacrifice some of your time. I just miss you so much and was just really looking forward to seeing you. That's why I got so mad."

"You had every right to be mad. I miss you like crazy. I really wanted to see you and do the stuff from your voicemail." Cam blushed slightly, trying to turn away as best as he could so the four girls couldn't hear him.

"I wanted to do stuff I can't say right now, also." He could feel the blush spreading from his ears to his cheeks

"Why can't you say?" Rider asked.

"This is why." Cam swiped his phone to speaker mode. "Everyone, say hi to Rider."

The room echoed with greetings. Cam tried to ignore the look on Trish's face. She was right, he should have called earlier. Trish's look wasn't the only thing that caught Cam's attention, there was a slight crack in Rider's voice. Rider had been crying, but when asked about it, he passed it off as just missing them all. It turned out that Sam had the perfect story to cheer Rider up, but before she started, she sent Sofia on a mission to get them all drinks despite the bottle of Coke already on Jane's desk.

"Sorry this story is a little too adult for Sofia. So, Jane was on the way back from shelter last week when she bumped into everyone's least favorite person. Darwin Brown." A hiss went around the room, Rider even joining in over the phone. "Don't worry it gets better. At first, he tried to act as if nothing had happened last year, and he even tried to hit on her." A wave of laughter ran through the group. "Anyway, after he could see our wonderful Jane wasn't interested in anything he had to say—"

"Or sell," Jane interrupted

"Well, Brown decided he was going to ask, and I quote, *where her f... friend* was. Jane didn't say a word but instead swung a fist at his face. Not only did she knock that jackass to the ground, it turns out she broke his nose."

"He deserves more than that after what he did to Rider." Cam said.

Jane blushed as Trish gave her a round of applause. Even Rider was laughing from the other end of the phone, sounding more like his normal self. He stayed on the call with them for another hour, only hanging up when Cam knew he and Trish needed to head home. Cam promised to call back when home, and that's exactly what he did. He abandoned Trish with his mom and uncle and went to his room to talk privately with his boyfriend who he truly did miss.

Chapter 16

Charles

Charles knocked on the bedroom door but there was no answer. Pushing the door open, he could see Lloyd was not at home. After the conversation with Jane on Christmas day, Charles had wanted to talk to his son, but Lloyd hadn't come home till late. Then on the twenty-sixth Lloyd was out of the house before Charles had even gotten out of bed, again coming home extremely late. Due to working early shifts for the last three days, by the time Lloyd had arrived home, Charles was already in bed.

Sighing at the empty room, Charles entered it. After the phone call with Jane, he was worried his son may be involved in something he shouldn't. *Why else would Lloyd lie about being with Jane and Rider? Why say he was going to see Yuki when the two had broken up?* Charles needed answers.

Walking around the room; everything seemed to be in its usual place. The photo collage on the wall hadn't been updated since Lloyd's birthday last year. The Lego Millennium Falcon at the foot of the bed was still sealed in the box. It had been a birthday present from Yuki, but Lloyd hadn't even opened it. In the closet, there was no evidence of anything, but his son hated folding his clothes. Charles wasn't sure what exactly he was looking for, but there was nothing out the ordinary. As he sat down on the bed, he could feel a lump under the mattress. He swallowed hard as he reached under, pulling out what looked like a journal. Relief flooded over him once he realized it wasn't drugs.

Charles was about to put the journal back when the curiosity got the best of him. Flicking through a couple pages, what he read shocked him. He bit his lip as he read one of the pages out loud to no one, hoping that if it was out in the open it would be proven false.

"Journal, you're the only one who I can tell. I feel so tired, it's all too much. I get home and I just feel like crawling into a ball and crying, but Dad might see. I can't let him see how pathetic his son really is. Yesterday, I had the pills in my hand, all I had to do was swallow and it would all be behind me, but I couldn't even do that. I'm worthless. Everyone would be better off without me in their lives."

His hands shook as he took in deep breaths, trying to calm down. Lloyd was a sweet, loving boy, he enjoyed spending time with friends, and was always laughing. There was no way he could be thinking like this, no way he could be thinking about harming himself. Flicking through the pages to identify when these were written, he hoped it had been Lloyd's thoughts before coming out, but there was no date anywhere. Charles moved towards one of the more recent pages and his stomach dropped.

"Rider isn't coming home for Christmas. He probably wants to stay as far away from me as possible. Everyone I love abandons me. Mom, Yuki, Rider, Sam, Jane. All of them are better off without me. If I hadn't been born, Mom would never have gotten ill. She and Dad could have had the perfect life, but I fucked it up like I fuck up everything."

If Lloyd was writing about Rider's Christmas, then these feelings are current. Charles wiped the tears from his eyes. He wanted to take Lloyd into his arms and make him feel better, but he didn't know where his son was. Picking up the book, he left the room, closing the door quietly behind him. He proceeded down to the kitchen where he poured himself a whiskey neat and proceeded to read the journal, waiting for Lloyd to come home. He wouldn't allow his son to suffer alone, they needed to talk.

It was close to eleven when the front door finally opened. Lloyd walked into the kitchen, a smile suddenly appearing on his face. Charles couldn't help but wonder how many times his son had faked his smile recently. Was he really happy to see his father or was he hiding the truth?

"Hey, Dad. How come you're up so late? I thought you had work tomorrow?" Lloyd asked as he went to the fridge to get a drink

"I rearranged my shift. I wanted to see how your day had been."

"Yeah. We went bowling and then out for some food. I'm sure Rider has been practising while he's been at college. Anyway, I'm off to bed."

Lloyd turned to head toward the hallway. Charles swallowed the lump in his throat. It was going to be a difficult topic, but he needed to be there for his son. "Lloyd? I need you to come sit down please."

Charles held his gaze until Lloyd realized he meant it. The teen slumped into the chair, the smile remaining on his face. Trying to find the right words, Charles took a deep breath to give himself a moment. After the third failed attempted, all he could do was lift the journal onto the table, his eyes focused on his son. Lloyd's eyes went wide, his lip started to quiver.

"Lloyd. I've read what you've been writing."

"It's…It's just a project for school is all," Lloyd said as his eyes dropped to the floor.

"I know you weren't out with Rider today. He's still in Houston and hasn't been home since he left back in August. I also know you and Yuki broke up. Please, Lloyd, just talk to me."

Lloyd tried to rise and leave, but Charles couldn't let him. He grabbed his son's arm, causing Lloyd to flinch. Charles wrapped his arms tight around the teen as the tears started to flow. Lloyd's breath became staggered—wild—as he struggled to get air into his lungs. It had been years since a proper panic attack. Placing Lloyd down onto the chair, Charles backed up toward the cabinet that contained the med kit, always keeping his eyes on his son. It took three deep intakes from an inhaler, followed by another three, to calm Lloyd's breathing. Once it returned to normal, Charles wrapped his arms around his son and stayed like that for several minutes.

"I really need you to be honest with me, Lloyd. Is what you wrote in that book how you feel?"

Tears were still falling as the teen opened his mouth, but no sound came out. Closing it, he looked away from his father and down at his feet as he nodded. Charles held his breath, rubbing his hand across his stubble as he tried to accept the truth.

"How long have you been feeling like this? Is it since you and Yuki broke up?"

Lloyd nodded again. The next question had been going through Charles's mind all evening, he struggled to even ask it. "Lloyd, I need to know, have you tried to hurt yourself?" Charles asked, his voice quaking.

"I can't do this," Lloyd responded. His feet trembled as he tried to stand, but he couldn't. He fell back into the chair defeated.

"Lloyd. Please answer me."

Tears flowed down Charles's cheeks as he waited for the truth. Lloyd's gazed remained on the floor as he pulled off his hoodie. A gasp echoed around the kitchen. It felt like all the air had been driven out of Charles as he looked at Lloyd's arm. From just below the wrist to up Lloyd's left forearm were a number of cuts. Some were close to healing, but the one that drew Charles's attention was around five inches long in the middle of Lloyds arm. There was still some blood trickling from it. It must have happened not long ago.

"I'm...I'm...sorry," Lloyd said, his head falling into his hands. An ocean of tears fell down his face.

Charles's hands were shaking. He wasn't sure what to do, what he could do. On instinct, he went back to the med kit and brought it to the table. He carefully cleaned Lloyd's wounds before gently wrapping them in clean bandages. He took short, quick breaths, worried that if he tried anything more, he might vomit.

"You...you hate me...don't you?" The words stumbled out of Lloyd's mouth.

"No, Lloyd. I love you so much." Charles pulled his son close. "I'm glad you're okay. I don't want to lose you. We will get through this."

The haunting thoughts Lloyd had been thinking, all of his stress and pain, was etched onto his face for the world to see. Charles wondered when the last time his son had actually slept properly. Putting Lloyd's good arm over his shoulder, he allowed Lloyd to rest on him as he carried his son up the stairs. Placing Lloyd gently down on the bed, the teen instantly curled up into a ball. Charles pulled the covers over his son, kissing him on the forehead and closed the door behind him. Whimpers and tears filled the uncomfortable silence.

Charles hardly slept, making sure to be awake before his son came out of the bedroom. Lloyd looked even worse than he had last night, his cheeks still stained from the tears. The bags under his eyes were dark as if he hadn't even attempted sleep. Before Lloyd could say anything, Charles pulled his son into another tight hug. Looking down at the bandages, there was a little blood that had managed to reach the outer layer. They were soon in the den, Charles changing the bandage. He breathed a sigh of relief when the wound didn't look infected.

"I'm sorry, Dad. I never wanted you to find out."

"Why, Lloyd? I'm your father. I'm here for you, not matter what it is."

"That's the thing, I don't know what this is. I don't know what's wrong with me. Yuki broke up with me almost a year ago and it hurts but it's more than that. There is just this feeling, like I've fallen into a pit and no matter how much I fight I just keep sinking." Lloyd's voice started to crack again.

Charles tried to be strong for his son. "Why didn't you ask for help?"

"How can I ask for help, when I can't even help myself?"

Lloyd's hand trembled. Charles was lost for words. He wished he could take all these negative thoughts his son was having—about himself, about the world, about his relationships—and scrunch them up, throw them in the furnace, and destroy them forever, but he couldn't provide that. Lloyd needed actual help, especially if he had already hurt himself. It was only a matter of time till Charles would come home and Lloyd would be seriously injured...or worse.

"Lloyd, we need to get you some professional help. Someone who understands what you're going through and what we can do to help you get better."

"No. I don't want to see a shrink. I don't want them to take me away from you and lock me up. I know I need help but I don't know how to do it. I don't know how to get rid of these thoughts."

"Okay, no doctor till you're ready. But you need to talk

to someone, and when I say talk to them, I mean properly talk to them. You need to say how you been feeling and what's going through your head. It doesn't need to be me. It can be someone like Rider."

"Rider doesn't need me. He doesn't want to hear my problems."

"Rider loves you, Lloyd, you're his best friend. Please, for me, just try." Charles voice quivered as he begged his son.

Lloyd slowly nodded at his father as he pulled out his phone. He tried to use the phone, but his hands were shaking too violently. Charles grabbed hold of his son's trembling hands and he punched out a message to Rider.

Rider

Pushing the door to his dorm room open with his foot, Rider struggled with the bag of groceries. Nixs had messaged yesterday, inviting him to celebrate New Year, but Rider had declined. He had yet to see Nixs in person since the kiss. They would have to meet at some point, but he had been enjoying talking to Cam every day since Christmas and wasn't ready to see the older guy.

Dropping the bag onto Jason's desk, the vodka bottle that had remained in their room since accidentally walking in on Jason making out with someone, fell to the floor. The roommates had only taken a couple sips since, but there was still over three quarters of the bottle. Picking it up, Rider placed it on the desk just as his pocket vibrated. Expecting a message from Cam, he was surprised to see a message from Lloyd. His best friend had been very difficult to get in touch with, only replying to messages, never being the instigator. Rider was worried before he opened the message.

I need to speak to you. If you're free.

Instead of replying, Rider hit the call button. It took five rings before a shaking voice answered the phone, he immediately knew something was wrong. He could hear Charles in the background talking to his son. *It's okay. You can do this, I'm here for you.* Lloyd hadn't even said anything more than hello but the emotion in his voice made it feel like being punched in the gut.

"Lloyd, what's wrong?"

"Ri…I'm sorry…I'm so sorry." Lloyd's voice quivered.

"What do you mean sorry?"

"I've…I've been having these really dark thoughts. I don't know what to do. I need help."

It felt like all the air in the room had been sucked out. This couldn't be his best friend. The sound of Lloyd hyperventilating came through the phone. Rider's head felt like it was spinning, he hadn't realized his best friend needed help. They used to be so in sync that they didn't even need to talk to know something was wrong. When younger, they would finish each other's sentences, try and call each other at the same time. Guilt spread through Rider. He had been too busy with Cam and his own feelings for Nixs, he had let Lloyd slip past him

"Lloyd, I…" Rider was lost for words

Lloyd started repeating the same words over and over—"I'm sorry". The voice became distant as the phone hit the floor. Rider held his breath, hoping nothing had happened, only breathing again when a deeper voice start talking.

"Charles. What's happening?" Rider own voice filled with emotion.

"How do I explain this, erm… So, I found a journal last night that Lloyd has been keeping. In there he wrote some…some fairly dark stuff. It was hard to read." Charles moved the phone away from his mouth as he spoke to his son. "Lloyd, none of this is your fault. You're not useless and I love you. Sorry about that, Rider. Lloyd's been feeling like this for a while now, and he's…he's also been hurting himself."

Rider gasped, tears starting to form in his eyes. The Lloyd he knew wouldn't hurt himself, he was so carefree and loving.

"I think he's suffering from depression, but he doesn't want to see a professional. I'm sorry to put this on you, but I thought maybe he can talk to you. If he talks to someone, then maybe he won't…" Charles didn't finish the sentence.

Rider could hear the older man getting choked up. "I want to see him."

"What?" Charles asked.

"Lloyd won't be back in school for a couple weeks and my lectures don't start again for another three. What about if Lloyd comes down and stays with me for a week? Maybe a change of scenery would help. He can tell me everything he's going through in person, and I'll do my best to help him."

"Oh, erm. Sure, but let me check with him." Charles's voice went quiet again. "Would you like to go see Rider? Lloyd, it was Rider's idea, of course he wants you there." Rider took a deep breath, moving the phone onto his other ear as he listened to Charles convince Lloyd that Rider was still his friend. "Okay, Rider. I'll check the flights and get Lloyd to call you back in a bit. Thank you for this."

"You don't need to thank me. Lloyd is my best friend, I'd do anything for him."

Rider stood by the arrivals gate waiting for Lloyd. Due to New Year, he had to wait an extra day to see his best friend, but he had even managed to get Lloyd to talk on the phone. It had only been about his schoolwork, but it was progress. As the passengers started appearing, Rider quickly located the blond spikes. Lloyd had a large goofy grin on his face as he waved. He pulled Lloyd into a quick hug before grabbing the suitcase the smaller teen was carrying.

"So, this is Houston? It's a lot warmer here. It was snowing in Belmont when my dad dropped me off at the airport."

As they headed toward the taxi stand, Lloyd happily rambled about how despite Belmont airport being so empty, he still somehow stood in the security line for forty-five minutes. If Charles hadn't revealed the truth, Rider would never have guessed his best friend was in such a dark place. As the taxi drove toward campus, Lloyd kept pointing out landmarks, but all Rider could do was nod and smile. If he opened his mouth, words would rush out and a taxi wasn't the right place for it.

"Wow, the campus is so much bigger than Belmont. I would get lost if I came here."

Lloyd kept talking all the way up to Rider's room. Opening the door, he allowed the younger teen in first. Rider closed the door behind him and placed the suitcase down. Before another word could be said, Rider crossed the room and pulled Lloyd into a tight hug. He could feel his best friend trembling underneath him, causing Rider to hug tighter. Lloyd's hands slowly slid around Rider's waist, still shaking but grabbing tight.

His T-shirt became wet from the tears. Rider couldn't hold back his own any longer. His best friend had been in so much pain for so long and he hadn't been there for him. Rider only released the hug when Lloyd's hands slipped away, rising to wipe his eyes. They soon sat on the bed in a side hug.

"Lloyd, you're my best friend. Always have been, always will be. I love you so much and never want to lose you. I don't know what I would do without you."

"I'm sorry. I just don't know what's going through my head." Lloyd looked away, but Rider pulled him back.

"Can I see?"

Lloyd nodded, slowly removing his hoodie and gently pulling up his long sleeve. The white bandage stretched from his wrist all the way up to his elbow. As the bandage was removed, Rider gasped as the scars. The sound caused Lloyd to start crying again. Pushing away the guilt he was feeling, Rider pulled him into a tight hug and allowed his best friend to cry.

"Lloyd, I'm so sorry this happened to you, and I wasn't there for you. If you start think you need to harm yourself again, please don't do it. Call me instead. I'll be there for you, any time of day."

He only received a simple nod, but it was something. Grabbing hold of Lloyd's shaking hands, Rider rested his head on the smaller boy's shoulder. Once the tears had slowed, Lloyd looked around the room. When the subject was changed to something not related to the self-harm, Rider knew Lloyd needed time to gather his thoughts.

"What about your roommate? I'm sure he won't like me being here."

"I've contacted Jason. He's fine with me sleeping in his bed until he gets back on Wednesday, then for that night we'll have to sleep together like the old days."

When younger, before Rider had gotten his double bed, the duo would sleep top to toe. Rider's head at the top of the bed, Lloyd's at the foot. Luckily, they had never once kicked each other, unlike Jane who managed to give Rider a nosebleed after which she had been made to sleep on the floor, even when he got his double bed. Lloyd rose up from the bed and went to his suitcase, pulling out a small med kit and a wrapped present. After Rider rebandaged Lloyd's arm, a present was placed into his lap.

"I don't know if you'll like the present, but I wanted to show you what you mean to me."

Rider smiled as he ripped off the gift wrap. He was confused as what sat in the plain white box: a Swiss army knife. Removing it from the box, he rotated the strange present. It was the red smear on the main blade which revealed what the present actually was. He looked at Lloyd for confirmation. The younger boy looking down at his feet but nodded.

"I thought, maybe if I didn't have access to it. That if it was with you then I couldn't...I couldn't cut myself anymore."

Clutching the present tightly in his hand, Rider pulled Lloyd close to him, kissing him softly on the forehead. There were no words he could speak that would show what the gesture meant. Lloyd took a deep breath before he started opening up about the dark feelings. Rider found himself biting his lip, struggling to hold back his tears. It had started early last year, Lloyd's mood would drastically swing, one moment he would feel like his normal cheery self and then next he would hate himself.

"When you guys invited me out, my head would say it was out of pity. That you didn't really want me there. You have Cam, Sam and Jane have each other. No one needs a third wheel"

"Of course, we wanted you there. We all missed you so much."

"I know, but my head won't accept that. It just felt like I was losing everyone. Slowly it built up and up until I couldn't take it. I sat there one night when Dad was at work. I had the pills in my hand, but I just couldn't do it. I left the house and when I reached the bench it was all a bit too much. Dad gave me the Swiss army knife for a present when I originally wanted to join the scouts. When I felt it in my pocket, I pulled it out. I wanted all the pain and feelings to go away, so I took the blade and cut. It's hard to explain but it made the pain go away for a while. Then it came back, and I cut again, and again.

"I ended up learning to mask the feelings. Hide how I truly felt with a smile here and a laugh there. I told my dad I was out with you or Jane or even Yuki. He didn't even know we had broken up till Jane told him on Christmas. Every day it felt like I was swimming in tar. No matter how much energy I exerted it didn't help. I ended up tired and sinking lower but if I stopped, I'd drown. I tried, I really did. I went to the prom with you, but then that student stopped me in the bathroom, he made me…he said exactly how I felt about myself."

"Student?"

"He was short like me but stocky with mousey hair. He pushed me down and told me how worthless I was. A different student came in before he could do anything, erm…Cam's friend, Quintin. I think he called the other guy Spencer."

"Fucking Octavius Spencer. Ignore that idiot, he's the one that spread my sexuality around school. I'm sorry anyone made you feel like that Lloyd. You are an amazing person. I don't know what my life would be without you."

Rider's stomach twisted in knots. If he had known the truth the evening of prom, Brown wouldn't have been the only one with a broken nose. Lloyd continued to explain how he had been feeling until Rider's stomach groaned. The clock showed it was well past lunchtime. They both laughed when Lloyd's stomach also groaned for food. The duo headed toward the door to find food, but as Rider pulled it open, they were greeted by a smiling face.

"Happy New Year, Rider."

Lloyd gasped loudly. "Yuki?"

Chapter 17

Lloyd

Sat on the bed, his trembling hand within Rider's hands, Lloyd had laid his dark thoughts out for Rider to see, and his best friend hadn't run. Taking in some much-needed deep breaths, his eyes stung from the tears. In the last three days, Lloyd had showed more of himself than he had shown in almost a year. When his father had first asked, it was the horrified look on his dad's face that made Lloyd hide everything for so long. He may have wanted to end it all, it would have eased his own pain, but that pain wouldn't have vanished, it would have been passed to his father and friends.

When asked if he wanted to visit Rider, his brain immediately jumped to the thought of arriving in Houston, but his best friend wouldn't have been there. Even on the drive to the airport, his dad had confirmed numerous times Rider would be waiting for him. It was lucky the Swiss army knife was in the cargo hold because the flight it had gotten a bit too much for Lloyd. The man next to him had thought he was suffering extreme fear of flying and given him a sleeping pill. Lloyd had woken as the plane was descending to land.

Although he could feel Rider's leg touching his, his best friend still felt a mile away until Rider squeezed his hand. Lloyd gave his best friend a weak smile, just as Rider's stomach growled. Less than a minute later, his own groaned. Both of them laughed out loud, for Lloyd this was for the first time in a long time it was genuine.

"If you're feeling up to it, do you want to grab some food?" Rider offered.

"Sure," Lloyd said with a weak smile.

Climbing off the bed, Lloyd took only a few steps before turning and rolling down his sleeve and scooping up his hoodie. He didn't want his bandages on display to the public. Rider waited at the door until Lloyd was ready, and after a couple of deep breaths, he gave his best friend a nod. The door wasn't fully open before Lloyd heard a familiar voice, a voice he heard in his dreams when he was able to fall asleep.

"Yuki?" exclaimed Lloyd.

The darkness flooded in, his hand shaking uncontrollably. *What's Yuki doing in Houston, in Rider's dorm?* Lloyd's fingers started to dig into his thigh, same as when he was pinned to the wall by Mr. Keats. Backing into the room, his head shook violently. He couldn't do this, he couldn't be around Yuki when he felt so drained from telling Rider everything. He bit his lip, and his breathing was ragged. Rider must have realized as he quickly stepped out of the room, pulling the door with him. Although the conversation in the hall was quiet, Lloyd could still hear everything.

"Rider? Was that Lloyd?"

"Yes, it's Lloyd. He's staying with me for a couple days as he needed some time away from home."

"Is he okay? I noticed bandages on his wrist."

"Erm…I think you need to speak to Lloyd, but, please, not today. A lot has been happening and I wasn't expecting us to bump into you today. It's going to be a big shock to him."

"What do you mean 'a lot has been happening'?"

Lloyd couldn't listen to any more, he stumbled backward to the bed. His whole body shook. He struggled to breathe as panic took over. Looking around the room for something, his eyes focused on only one item. The blade was soon in his hand, the bandages lying on the bed. Closing his eyes, the cold metal tip dug into his forearm. The sting came as he slowly moved his hand, but it only got an inch before it hit resistance. Lloyd opened his eye to see the horrified look on Rider's face, his hand stopping the blade. Rider grabbed the knife and threw it away. Nothing was said as Lloyd was pulled into a tight hug. Tears dropped like the blood down his arm.

There was silence in to room, Lloyd couldn't even look at his best friend. The guilt felt more painful than the knife, he had betrayed Rider's trust. Rider stood up but only long enough to grab the med kit from the table. The wound was cleaned, and Rider gently wrapped the arm. Lloyd's gaze had remained on the floor the complete time until Rider lifted his head. Worry etched his black eyes.

"Lloyd, why?"

"I don't know. It just hurt so bad seeing Yuki again and I just wanted it to go away. I should have waited for you to come back into the room, but instinct kicked in."

"Lloyd, I think you need professional help. I can only do so much, this…"

The tears started again. The fear of going to see a professional was too great. With the thoughts he was having, the actions he had done, Lloyd was sure they would take him away from everyone. Stop him from seeing his father, from seeing Rider. It all felt too much until Rider started rubbing his nose up and down Lloyds, the effect instantly sending a calming effect over the younger teen. Jane had always laughed at them for doing nose rubs, but it had been a technique they had been using since young and it always found a way to calm the stressed or crying person. Once the tears stopped, Rider pulled Lloyd into his arms, wrapping them protectively around him.

"I won't force you to go but you can't keep hurting yourself like this. I can't lose you, you mean so much to me."

The duo were quiet for some time, Rider refusing to leave his best friend's side. Even when Lloyd tried to go to the toilet, he was still by his side. Soon a weak smile appeared on Lloyd's face, the dark feelings slowly dissipating. He was afraid of bumping into Yuki, but the need for food was too great.

Settling down at The Burger Joint, Lloyd found himself laughing as Rider reminded him how when they were younger, their parents had taken them on vacation to the beach. They had managed to convince Jane to join them. One afternoon they had been exploring rock pools when the tide had slowly come in before anyone noticed. Rider and Lloyd had no problem getting wet, but Jane started panicking and crying. It turned out at the time she couldn't swim, which wasn't an actual issue with the water level only being five inches. As they both laughed, Lloyd reached over the table and took Rider's hands in his.

"Thank you, Ri. You mean so much to me. Even when I do something stupid, you're still there. If you ever need me, I'm there for you too." Lloyd took a couple deep breaths before he asked the question that had been eating at the back on his mind. "Why is Yuki here?"

"He's the resident advisor. He looks after the new students and is someone they can turn to if there is a problem. I was surprised when I first saw him here."

"And that's how you knew we broke up?" Lloyd asked, biting his lip

"Yep," Rider confirmed while nodded. "To be honest, I was shocked you hadn't told me. It's not like you to hide stuff from me. I mean, you called me while you were on the toilet because you had finished reading the reboot of *Deadpool* but now I understand why you hid it. I don't know if this will help, but Yuki asked about you constantly, every time I bumped into him on campus, he would ask how you're doing. I mean he…" Rider's phone vibrated on the table. The seventh time in the space of an hour Rider had received a message that he hadn't responded to.

"If it's Cam, you can take it."

"It's not Cam." Rider turned his phone and showed Lloyd the messages. "Yuki has been messaging me since he saw you in my room. I told him to give you space, but he really wants to see you. I told him not today and he's now asking about tomorrow. If you feel like it will be too much then that's okay, you don't need to see him."

Lloyd closed his eyes and took a couple deep breaths. Rider's hand squeezed his, helping to fight the anxiety. He was worried about seeing his ex, but the panic he felt earlier was missing. He wasn't sure if it was having Rider there but something felt different. It may not help but Lloyd hated the way they had ended it. He should have hugged Yuki one last time and not left him alone on the bench. *Maybe closure will help*.

"Okay. I don't know what I'll be like during it, but right now I think I can manage it."

"I'll be there with you throughout. As soon as it's too much, we will leave. Okay?"

Nodding at his best friend, Lloyd pushed the unfinished burger away. He was no longer hungry. Walking back to the dorm, the setting sun cast a darkness over the friends, the same darkness pushing its way into Lloyd's mind. By the time Lloyd was ready for bed, he was back to faking his smile. Climbing into the bed, a swinging Rider and Spider-Man looked down over him. Lloyd turned to face the wall, away from his best friend. He couldn't stop from releasing some tears. He shook slightly. He felt the bed shuffle and a warm arm wrapped around him, holding him tight. Lloyd could feel Rider's forehead pressed against the back of his head. The shaking slowed.

"Lloyd, it will be okay, I'm here for you."

Lloyd's eyes got heavy, the warmth on his back

managing to relax him as he slipped easily into sleep for the first time in months. The next thing he remembered was his face resting on Rider's chest, Rider's arm still wrapped around him. The sun was streaming into the room. The headache that normally surrounded him was gone. He hadn't woken once during the night, the first time since March. The relaxed feeling didn't last long as Lloyd remembered the promise to meet up with Yuki.

"Lloyd, you will be okay today. I will be there also," Rider mumbled from underneath him.

"How did you know what I was thinking?"

Rider shrugged before pulling his best friend into a tight hug. "You don't need to talk to Yuki until you are ready."

It was three in the afternoon when Lloyd was ready. His heart pounding as he stood in front of the door, hiding slightly behind his best friend. Yuki answered the door almost immediately, a large smile on his face as he ushered them both into his room. The Japanese flag above the bed had been in the same position in Yuki's old room. The carefully piled clothes on a chair reminded Lloyd of each time he had been over to Yuki's place. He recognised the picture on the desk. The photo showed them sitting across from each other, pizza stopping their hands from touching. It had been taken on their very first date. His heart pounded hard as he remembered all the positives of their relationship. Rider went to sit down on the chair when Lloyd caught his hand.

"Ri, do you mind if me and Yuki talk alone?"

"Are you sure?" Rider asked, squeezed the smaller

teen's hand. When Lloyd nodded Rider released his hand. "Okay, but I'm just upstairs. Promise me you'll come find me."

Lloyd didn't need to ask what the concerned look Rider was giving meant. He nodded at his best friend, which resulted in a smile and hug before Rider left Lloyd alone with Yuki. The older guy sat down on the bed, patting it for Lloyd to join him. Swallowing the lump in his throat, his legs were shaky as he crossed the room and sat down.

"It is very good to see you, Lloyd. I did not know you were coming down to see Rider, but it is nice to see you again," Yuki said with a smile.

"How have you…erm…you been?"

As Yuki described his third year of college, Lloyd struggled to focus, his mind kept returning to what he had done last night. The darkness started creeping in, his breath become ragged. It felt like there was lack of air in the room. He grabbed his leg to try and stop the shaking, hoping Yuki wouldn't notice, but it was too late. A worried look spread across the older guy's face.

"Lloyd? Are you okay?"

"I…I can't do this. I'm…I'm sorry."

Standing up, Lloyd's legs felt weak as he tried to take a step toward the door. Yuki reached out and grabbed his left arm, making the younger teen to yelp loudly in pain. Clutching his arm, his legs gave way under the pain, causing Lloyd to collapse to the floor. A burning sensation shot up his arm; the fire burst from his fingertips down to his elbow as a look of horror spread across Yuki's face. Yuki lifted Lloyd off the floor and placed him on the bed as the younger teen struggled to remove his hoodie. Dropping it to the floor, blood had reached the outer layer of the bandages.

"Lloyd, your arm? What happened?"

Tears started as the truth flowed out, how he had been feeling for almost a year, how the darkness had slowly infected and taken over his life, how he now struggled every day just to get through it. Sadness and guilt spread across Yuki's face as he learnt the truth, not saying anything till Lloyd had finished.

"Oh, Lloyd. I am so sorry you have been feeling like this and I am sorry that I made you feel like that." Yuki reached for him but retreated when Lloyd flinched.

"When we broke up, it felt like my heart had been ripped out. You were the love of my life and then you were gone. I was cast away. All my friends had someone and I was alone."

"Lloyd, I have thought about you every single day since your birthday. It took all my willpower not to message or call you, but I wish I had, because maybe you would not have felt like this. Maybe you would not have hurt yourself. You mean so much to me and to see you like this is so hard."

"I started to think that maybe it was me, that I was the problem. That you were going somewhere better and it's easier to get rid of the trash and start new," Lloyd admitted, trying to wipe away the stream of tears.

"Lloyd. You are not trash and never have been. I never stopped loving you. I never stopped caring. I have not been on a date with a single person since we broke up, as no one could replace you. It is the reason why I kept asking Rider how you were doing every chance I got. I only ended our relationship as I thought it would make it easier on you. You are young and I did not want you waiting around for me when you have so much life ahead of you. I do not know where you may end up going to college. I hated the idea of you following me here and things not working out, that you would despise me. Especially now that after I finish my degree my father wants me back in Japan. The tech world doesn't slow, and he wants me already working on the new systems to help people. I never wanted to cause you so much pain. I am sorry that I never called you." Tears were now streaming down Yuki's face, matching those on Lloyd.

Yuki opened his arms and unlike the last time they were together, Lloyd fell into them. The strong arms wrapped around him like they had during the winter solstice. As Yuki held him, the smell of green tea and incense surrounded Lloyd. The scents had always been so comforting. Even now they allowed him to relax, stopping the tears. Memories started flooding Lloyd's mind of all the times he and Yuki had spent together, finally settling on Yuki's birthday.

Lloyd had originally planned to spend the final day of summer with Rider but with Yuki's family being in Japan, he had surprised the older guy by turning up at his door with a card and flowers. He had spent the week before hunting down a florist in Belmont that stocked camellia. Lloyd had been adamant he wanted camellia after Yuki had explained how different flowers in Japan represented different things. Camellia represented humility, discretion, and perfect love, everything that represented Yuki.

The flowers weren't the only surprise Lloyd had up his

sleeve. Yuki had been missing a number of traditions from Japan and when Lloyd had discovered that there was a tea ceremony being held in Belmont on his boyfriend's birthday, it was something they had to do. With each part of the ceremony, Yuki would explain the meaning behind the actions. Lloyd had found it fascinating apart from the actual tea. He liked the smell of green tea on Yuki, but he did not enjoy the taste.

After the ceremony, the couple had found themselves in Raven Comics. After checking the racks for any *Deadpool* comics he didn't already own, Lloyd discovered his boyfriend at the back of the store. A huge smile etched onto Yuki's face as he held a book Lloyd had never seen before. It was the first in a series call *Black Jack*, which Yuki's mom had introduced him to when he had been younger. Without even giving Yuki a choice, Lloyd scooped the book out of his hands and proceeded to the register. The day had closed out with them in the pizza place they had visited during their first date, this time their hands had connected.

As Lloyd was released from the hug, he had a genuine smile on his face. The smile matched Yuki's, the tears long gone. The both held their position, their arms still around each other as they looked into each other's faces. Lloyd inched forward, followed by an inching from Yuki. Before either of them could make a full move there was a knocking from the door. Apologising for the disruption, Yuki proceeded to the door. A panicked student stood there, asking for Yuki's help.

"I am sorry Lloyd but one of the students need my assistance. I do not want things to end like this. Could I see you again tomorrow? Even if it is only a couple hours, I would very much like to spend it with you."

"I'd like that too, but I need to check with Rider first, just in case he has any plans for us."

Yuki nodded as Lloyd pulled his hoodie back on. Slipping quickly out of Yuki's room, a girl with pink hair replacing him, Lloyd walked through the dorm hallway quietly, the feelings in him rising. By the time he reached Rider's door, he was excited for tomorrow, the first time he had been excited in a long while. The hour he had spent with Yuki had managed to keep any darkness at bay and he wanted more. Knocking on the door gently, Rider pulled it open in a nanosecond. Lloyd couldn't help but laugh at the idea his best friend had been standing behind the door waiting for him to get back since the moment he had left Yuki's room.

"Did everything go okay? Are you okay?"

"I think so. I mean, I need a new bandage," Lloyd said, causing panic to spread across Rider's face. "No, not like that. At the beginning, I started to panic and went to leave. Yuki accidentally grabbed my arm and I think he opened the cut from yesterday."

The look on Rider's face eased as he picked up the first aid kit. "So, what happened?"

"I told him everything and he didn't leave like I thought he would. He asked if we could spend some time tomorrow together since someone came to speak to him now. I said I'd check with you?"

"Oh, erm…sure, as long as you are okay with it. I can

go to the library as I need to collect some new books for the next semester."

"Thanks, Ri. You're the best." Lloyd pulled Rider into a hug.

Holding his breath, Lloyd knocked on the door. Rider had made sure he would be okay alone before disappearing off to the library. The smile that greeted Lloyd was the same one that had greeted him many times before; there wasn't a single doubt on Yuki's face. Yuki stepped out the room, closing the door behind him before locking it.

"I thought we could go for a walk like we used to," Yuki said with a smile.

The duo walked quietly, their shoulders bumping together. The dark clouds in the sky had caused a cold wind to come in. Lloyd found himself shivering despite having his hoodie on. Stopping in front of a fountain, he felt something warm and soft wrap around his neck. He turned to see Yuki smiling as a scarf was wrapped around him. Lloyd tried to decline but the older guy refused to take no for an answer.

Not knowing how to respond, Lloyd turned his attention to the water feature. "What a beautiful fountain."

"It is. I normally walk down by Brays Bayou. It is very peaceful and relaxing but with the gray clouds in the sky I did not want to take you that far."

Although lectures hadn't restarted, the campus was always busy. The couple sat down on one of the benches, watching the students pass. A simple nod from Lloyd was all it took for an arm to be placed around him. Yuki pulled him close, Lloyd's head resting on his shoulder. In this moment, he questioned how he ever thought Yuki had never liked him and just been using him.

"I wanted to talk to you about what you told me yesterday. I am still very sorry you have been feeling like this, but have you seen anyone about it?" Yuki continued watching the students as he approached the subject as if it was a common thing.

"No. I'm worried with my self-harming they'll take me away."

Yuki turned to face Lloyd, a soft smile on his face. He explained how Lloyd was mistaken when it comes to seeking help with depression. No one was going to take him away from the ones he loved. They would help him battle the issue so that his loved ones wouldn't lose him. There were two helpful routes Lloyd could try, medicine and therapy.

"Antidepressants are not an instant fix to the problem. Taking them will not instantly make you feel better, but they will help. It may take time for the doctors to find the correct type and dosage, but it will slowly rebalance the chemicals in the brain. They will help increase your mood and help you sleep easier. When I saw you the other day, it looked you had not slept well for a while."

Lloyd remained silent as Yuki explain what would happen if he chose to speak to a counsellor: that they were trained to not only listen to how he felt but try and identify the root cause of what started his feelings; how to spot trends so he could stop the feelings before the even begin;

and that the counsellor was not there to judge Lloyd, only help him control his emotions.

"I never thought of it like that. How...how do you know so much about it?"

"Do you remember when I told you about my mother? How she became extremely sick and I had to go back to Japan?" Lloyd nodded. "During that period, my younger sister became extremely worried about losing our mother. She slowly fell into the same pit of darkness you describe. She spoke to me about it and I was able to find her help. It is only last week that she finally came off her medication, but she is in a much better place both emotionally and physically."

"Yuki, I'm sorry."

"You do not need to be sorry. She could not control how she was feeling, like you should not feel sorry for how you have been feeling. Sometimes it is not possible for anyone to control how they feel."

A large cold drop of rain hit Lloyd's nose, eliciting a shiver. Yuki jumped off the bench and offered Lloyd his hand. A smile spread across his face as he accepted the hand, being pulled to his feet. Lloyd had forgotten how caring and sweet Yuki was, the reasons he had fallen for the older guy in the first place. Despite the rain, the two walked slowly back toward the dorms, their hands entwined. By the time they reached Yuki's room, Lloyd clothes were drenched. Yuki's white T-shirt clung to him, semi-transparent as he pulled his jacket off, causing Lloyd to blush. He turned toward the door while Yuki changed, only turning back when a hand landed on his shoulder.

"Lloyd, you will catch a cold in those wet clothes. Here," Yuki said, holding a dry T-shirt for him.

Thanking Yuki with a smile, Lloyd tried to remove his left arm from the hoodie but flinched with pain. The wet fabric from the hoodie stuck to the bandage that wrapped around his wounds. Before he could even say anything, Yuki gently removed Lloyd's arm from the hoodie allowing it to fall to the floor. Lloyd couldn't do anything but look deeply into Yuki's dark eyes as the older guy pulled the wet T-shirt up and over Lloyd's head. The T-shirt landed on the floor also but neither of them moved, their eyes locked onto each other.

This time it was Yuki who moved first, wrapping his arms around the smaller teen, hands coming to rest at the base of his spine. Lloyd moved in, their chests touching as he wrapped his own arms around Yuki's neck. Lloyd wasn't sure who instigated the kiss, but he didn't care. As their lips connected, a surge of electricity shot through him, the hair on his arm standing on edge. It felt like no time had passed between them. Closing his eyes, he was sure he could hear wind, the sound of a lake. The bench back in Belmont where they first kissed. The passion that he felt back then was still present.

Yuki's hand slid up Lloyd's back, pulling the smaller teen closer. Their heart beats synched up. Lost in the moment, Lloyd tried to move his arm, but caught the bandage, causing him to yelp and break the kiss.

"Lloyd. I did not hurt you, did I?" Yuki asked worriedly.

"No, it was just my cut."

Now that the passionate kiss was over, Lloyd suddenly became very aware he was still shirtless. He pulled the T-shirt Yuki had handed him over his head. It was large on him, but he was happy it covered the obvious bulge in his pants. He had truly enjoyed the kiss, but there was one thing gnawing at the back of his mind that he had to know.

"The kiss, what does it mean?"

"I do not fully know. What I do know is I still have strong feelings for you, Lloyd, but I do not want to see you hurt when I eventually return to Japan. I also know that even if we are not together, I still want you in my life, even if just talking to you on the phone."

Lloyd had missed Yuki being in his life, not just because they had been dating, but because Yuki had been such a wonderful person just to sit and talk to. He was the sun hiding behind clouds on a rainy day. If Lloyd had a bad day, he just needed to wait, then Yuki would appear and cheer him up. Lloyd found himself smiling; he wanted Yuki in his life too. With a nod from the smaller teen Yuki approached, sliding his hand to Lloyd's and entwining their fingers. Lloyd leaned forward to kiss Yuki again when there was suddenly a pounding on Yuki's door.

"I am sorry, Lloyd." Yuki sighed. "This better not be another case of someone using their roommate's lipstick without asking."

Yuki kept hold of Lloyd's hand. As the door opened, Lloyd didn't get to look at the student; his brain focused on one thing and one thing only.

"Yuki? Come quick. It's Rider, somethings really wrong."

Chapter 18

Rider

Lloyd hadn't been able to stand still all morning. Since the moment he'd left Yuki's room last night, Rider had been worried something bad might happen and Lloyd would self-harm, but when his best friend had returned with a smile on his face Rider had finally relaxed. As the elevator rode down to the first floor, Lloyd's pacing brought a smile to Rider's face. As the door opened Lloyd jumped.

"Relax, Lloyd, everything will be okay. You were so happy last night. I'm only going to the library and shouldn't be more than an hour. If anything goes wrong or you start feeling that darkness creeping in, come find me. Promise me."

"I promise," Lloyd said. He didn't smile but a squeeze of the hand showed Rider he was telling the truth.

Lloyd stepped out of the elevator, turning left, then right, before turning to look at Rider who pointed to the left. Thank you came just as the doors closed, causing Rider to laugh as the elevator descend to the entrance. Exiting the building, the clouds in the sky threatened to soak him. The darkness of the clouds made Rider's thoughts focus on his best friend. They had spoken a lot over the last three days, but he was still amazed at how deep the darkness had penetrated his best friend. Hiding such a huge secret had been slowly tearing Lloyd apart to the point that he had started harming himself.

Guilt flooded Rider at what he was hiding from the world. When he had come out, he had promised not to hide anything anymore, but he had yet to tell Cam about the kiss with Nixs. Even though he hadn't seen the older guy since Christmas, the kiss still managed to infiltrate his dreams. Not only was he hiding the truth from his boyfriend, Rider was also hiding Cam from Nixs. There had been numerous times to come clean, but something in him had always stopped him. *Will my secrets devour me like Lloyd?*

With the guilt came anxiety, what if he was not the only one who was hiding a secret? When he had first attended Houston, Rider had never expected to discover someone like Nixs. Someone fun and attractive, someone who had an instant effect on him, the way Cam did. It had only been three months but if he could have found someone like that, what was stopping Cam from finding his own Nixs?

Rider was lost in his thoughts when he walked into someone, the force causing him to land on top of the other person. The duo weren't the only thing to hit the ground, only a couple of inches away were three small bags of green leaves and one of white powder. Rider rotated his head to see his face was inches from Jay.

"If you wanted to top me, you only needed to ask." Jay's hands travelled down to Rider's butt and squeezed; Rider jumped off him. "Oh, don't go, that was fun."

"Jay, what the fuck! I have a boyfriend and you know that," Rider growled as Jay scooped up the bags before rising to his feet. "And that the hell was that?"

"You never seen weed before? Come on, just because you have a boyfriend doesn't mean we can't bang. Why else would you keep bumping into me?"

Rider opened his mouth but decided to close it. He simply shook his head and proceeded toward the library, making sure to bump his shoulder into Jay's as he passed him. Before he entered the building, he quickly pulled out his phone, smiling when he saw there were no messages from Lloyd. Despite how busy the quad was, the library was almost empty. It didn't take him long to find the three books he needed for his next modules. He exited the stacks just as the door to the elevator opened. Rider recognised the blue-tinged dark hair instantly. He wasn't quick enough to retreat back behind the wall of books before Nixs spotted him, a smile spreading on the older guy's face as he headed over.

"Hey, Rider, I haven't seen you since Christmas."

"I…I've got to go, sorry." Rider's hands were shaking; he dropped the books on the nearest shelf and tried to walk past Nixs.

"Rider?" Nixs placed his arm out to stop him from

moving. "What is going on? Why are you avoiding me? Is it about what happened on Christmas?"

His stomach twisted in knots as Rider's breath became heavy. He closed his eyes as he tried to center himself. It felt like he had been punched in the gut; the world was falling apart around him. Cam's face appeared in his mind, the dimpled smiles that brought him so much happiness. His legs felt like they were going to give way until a hand landed on his shoulder. Nixs had a concerned look on his face, Rider dropped his shoulder causing the hand to fall of it.

"I'm sorry, I didn't mean to—" Nixs started to apologise.

"No, Nixs, I'm sorry. I've been lying to you, well, more like I haven't told you the full truth. I, erm...I have a boyfriend, he's called Cam. He doesn't go to this college, but we've been dating for over a year now. That time we met in the library last year was actually our one-year anniversary. I should have told you sooner, but I thought you wouldn't like me if you knew. I'm sorry I didn't tell you sooner."

"Oh...I'm sorry, I should have actually asked. I didn't even think you might have a boyfriend. I thought that with how much time we spend together, then snuggling up at Christmas and the kiss, that you liked me."

"I snuggle with my friends."

"Okay, but you didn't say you didn't like me," Nixs said with a hopeful smile.

Rider bit his lip as he looked down at the ground. He took a few deep breaths, focusing on the image of Cam in his head. He needed to tell Nixs the full truth, but he didn't want to destroy their friendship. As he raised his head, he looked directly into the emerald eyes of Nixs which made what he was about to say much harder.

"I do. I do like you—a lot—and that's the problem. I love Cam and don't want to hurt him. The kiss was an accident, a nice accident, but it can't happen again. Being so far away from Cam has just been difficult; we were arguing, but it's no excuse. I feel like I cheated on the guy who was always there for me." Rider's hands were shaking again.

"Rider." Nixs reached out and held his hands to calm the smaller boy. "I'm sorry. If I had known you had a boyfriend, I would never have kissed you. I should have clarified with you, made sure you were single rather than just wanting to be happy. I think you're cute, funny, and definitely sweet, and that's why I wanted more for us, but I would never want to compromise your relationship."

Knowing Nixs had the same feelings for him made it hard to hold back the tears. Rider loved Cam with all his heart, but it was also pounding hard for the boy in front of him. No matter what he chose, one would be hurt. Closing his eyes again, it was Cam he saw a future with, it was Cam he wanted to be with. Rider needed to get out of the library, he needed to call Cam and hear his voice. Rider apologised to Nixs again and started heading for the exit, this time Nixs allowed him passage. A sad but understanding look was on the older boys face.

As the cold air hit him in the face, all the air rushed back into Rider's lungs. Rider could still feel the guilt, but at least his hands weren't shaking anymore. Before he could move, there were footsteps behind him. Rider held his breath, hoping it wasn't Nixs, and only allowed himself to breathe when a guy with desert-blonde hair came running out of the library. He looked familiar but Rider couldn't think why. The student soon stopped in front of him.

"You're Rider, right? I need to talk to you."

"Yes, that's me. And you are?"

"Jordan."

Rider suddenly remembered where he knew the person from. The gay bar that Nixs had taken him to for his birthday, Jordan was the person arguing with Nixs. His ex-boyfriend Jordan. Rider took a sharp breath in.

"What I wanted to know is if you want to sleep with me? Nixs blatantly wants you and I think if we sleep together it would be revenge for him dumping me."

"What? No! I have a boyfriend—and it's not Nixs. I'm not going to just sleep with some random person I don't know."

"Oh, come on, every guy cheats. It's in our DNA. We don't follow our heart or head, we follow what's between our legs. Once we get a taste, then it's only a matter of time. A guy can only last so long until the pressure builds up and then they explode. They need to relieve themselves somehow, so why not explode with another guy?"

Panic flooded Rider's senses. He had felt *that* pressure when he had kissed Nixs, he had even dreamed of doing more than kissing with Nixs. The message Cam had left him before Christmas started playing in his head, how Cam had started to feel that pressure. They had planned over Christmas to relieve both their stress, but then Rider had cancelled.

"No! I love Cam and I know he loves me. He wouldn't do anything like that to me." Rider's voice quivered with doubt.

"All guys do it. I mean you and Nixs looked very cozy in that booth at the bar, and I heard you in the library. You kissed at Christmas. You say you love your boyfriend, but you cheated on him. A kiss is cheating, right? You're telling me you have never once thought about riding the Nixs train? It's only a matter of time, you'll see."

The panic warped into despair, Rider didn't need someone to remind him that he already cheated on Cam. His heart started pounding, adrenaline spiking as he ran toward his dorm. He needed to contact Cam. He needed to admit the truth and say how very sorry he was. A few raindrops hit his face as he reached the building. He took the stairs two at a time, not wanting to wait for the elevator. Pushing open the unlocked door, he found the room empty. Lloyd was still not back from spending time with Yuki.

Dropping to his bed, Rider's hands trembled in fear as he pulled out his phone. A voice call wasn't going to cut it. He needed to see Cam's face, show how truly sorry he was and how he would do anything to make it up to him. Hitting the FaceTime button, it took a couple rings before the call was answered...but not by the jock Rider wanted. The face in front of him was red, with sweat on his brow, and his silver hair all a mess. Rider could only see from the chest up, but the guy had no shirt on.

"Who are you? Where's Cam?" Rider spluttered.

"I'm Fernando and you are?" the guy said without much care for an answer.

"I'm Rider."

A wicked smirk appeared across the face of the guy on the other end of the video call. Fernando adjusted himself so he was lying down on an unmade bed, his head resting on a pillow. Rider knew the bedding, it belonged to Cam, but his boyfriend always made sure his bed was neatly made.

"You mean Walker hasn't told you about me? I'm his lover. We just finished fucking. He's in the bathroom cleaning up for round two."

"What?" shouted Rider. Panic shot through him like bullet.

"He said it had been way too long. That he couldn't wait any longer or else he would explode. I gave him relief and by God I can tell you he needed it. Something about his plans for Christmas being messed up. I mean, I was here just to do our group assignment, it was him that pushed me onto the bed. Ripped my T-shirt and pants off before I could even ask him what he was doing. I mean, I tried, but his mouth was a bit full to answer, if you know what I mean."

His mind was racing so quickly. Had it been his fault for not going home that had caused all this? "You're lying. Cam wouldn't do that!"

"He did. How many times have you seen a naked guy in someone's bed, and they *haven't* had sex? Anyway, got to go now. Bye!"

Fernando did a slight wave before the screen went blank, returning Rider to the home screen. Fear washed over him, his breathing becoming sporadic as panic started to set in. He hit the call back button.

"Sorry the number you are calling is currently not available, please leave a message after the beep," said the automated system.

Rider shook his head, not believing what he heard. He ended the call and then immediately called back.

"Sorry the number you are calling is currently not available, please leave a message after the beep"

"No, no, no. This…this can't be happening."

Rider pulled Cam's hoodie up and over his head, letting it fall to the floor. It felt like the room was a hundred degrees. His hand was shaking so badly he could barely get to the number he needed to call. Holding his breath, he waited for his best friend to answer his call, but he knew in an instant Lloyd wouldn't. A phone on the table started vibrating, playing the Spider-Man theme music. Lloyd had left his phone in the room by mistake. Tears fell, Rider felt lost at what to do. Picking up the hoodie that once meant a lot to him, he threw it on the ground. His eyes circled the room for an answer before finally settling on an item on the desk. Rider stood up, walked over to the desk, and grabbed hold of the bottle of vodka.

Chapter 19

Sam

Sam sat at the kitchen table trying to write an assignment on dealing with homesick children, but she was struggling to keep her attention on the laptop. Not only did it remind her of the home she couldn't return to due to her father's problem with her sexuality, but Sofia sat across from her asking any question that jumped into her head. She could also hear Jane practising on her electronic drums upstairs, a muted bang echoing around the house rather than the actual sound. Saving the assignment, she to give Sofia her full attention.

"You'll never guess what Aaron said at group today…?"

"I don't know, what?" Sam said, smiling at the younger girl.

"He was watching *Harry Potter*, so I asked him who he liked more, me or Hermione. He said he would choose Ron!"

Laughing, Sam confirmed she would have picked Sofia. Last week, Sofia had accidentally let slip that she liked Aaron and wanted to hug him. Aaron on the other hand seemed not interested or was hiding it very well. The banging from above came to an end, footsteps moving towards the stairs as Sofia continued to talk about the things Aaron had done recently to annoy her. Sam smiled as Jane walked into the kitchen, but a knock from the front door caught their attention.

"Sam!" Val shouted from the entranceway.

A confused look spread across Sam and Jane's faces, neither had been expecting anyone. She walked cautiously toward the door, Jane behind her with a hand on her back. A smile spread across her face as she was greeted by her brother. Although he was named after his father, Sam's brother had always chosen to be called by his middle name, Anthony or Ant. Ant pulled her into a tight hug, she hadn't seen him since her father kicked her out, although they had been in touch by text. Once he finally let her go, he waved at Jane who seemed to be suspicious of the older guy's presence.

"It's lovely to see you, Ant, but why are you here? Won't father be mad if he catches you?" Sam asked.

"I'm here because I'm taking you home. I know Jane and her family have been wonderful looking after you, but you should be at home. The girls miss you, I miss you, and Mom misses you."

"What about your dad?" Jane said, crossing her arms over her chest. "He doesn't want Sam there because she's—"

"Bisexual?" Ant asked with a smile. Sam looked down at her feet unable to keep eye contact. "I don't care what my father wants. I want Samantha back at home, and I don't care that she's bisexual or that she's dating you. I'm happy she has someone kind in her life."

Jane and Sam's mouths dropped. When Sam had come out to her parents, she hadn't mentioned she was dating anyone. Her friends knew, as did Val, but as far as she knew, that was it. Ant laughed at the look on their faces and reconfirmed he was absolutely fine with it.

"To be honest, I've known for a while. Why did you think that when you brought that awful car to the garage it kept passing inspection? I'm the mechanic who worked on it, fixed any issued free of charge because you were Samantha's escape from our father. I knew that as long as you had access to that car, my sister had an out."

Ant had discovered their secret long before anyone else. It had been their second date, when Jane had dropped Sam off at home. After a quick check of who could see them, Jane had gently kissed Sam. Sam had been so invested in the kiss that she had missed her brother's car drive straight past the house.

"I didn't want to spoil the moment. I sat around the corner for another twenty minutes just in case."

Sam stepped forward, wrapping her arms around her brother and kissing him on the cheek. They had always been close, but not only had he accepted her, he was defying their father to take her back. Not even her mother had been brave enough to rescue her. After confirming to Jane and Val he wouldn't allow any harm to come to Sam, Ant helped Sam load her bags into the car.

"Text me when you get there. And text me to make sure

you're okay. And text me to say what is going on." Jane's face twisted into a scowl when Sam started to laugh. "I mean it. If you don't, I'll come over there myself and drag you back here. Ant, look after her."

"You have my word, Jane," Ant promised, making a cross over his heart.

The drive to her parents was quiet. Nerves were setting in. Their father had never gone back on a decision, no matter how badly it had turned out. One summer he had invested in a company he thought would be the next big thing, but as soon has the price had started to fall, their mother had begged her husband to cut his losses and sell but he refused. When he finally sold the stock, it had been worth 1% of what he paid, resulting in the Keats family missing their holiday that summer.

As the car pulled into the driveway, Sam's hand was shaking until Ant took hold of it. He promised everything would be okay. Sam took a deep breath as she followed her brother into the house.

"Eric, is that you, darling?" Their mother's voice came from the kitchen.

Sam was barely in the house before she heard her name echoing from upstairs, followed by stomping feet coming down them. Smiles were on the younger sisters' faces as they both grappled her from the sides. The commotion drew the attention of the woman in the kitchen, their mother's face in shock at the sight of Sam at the front door. The distance between them vanished in an instant, Sam being pulled into tight hug as her mother let out a few tears.

"Samantha, I've been so worried about you. I love and

miss you so much, but you shouldn't be here. Your father will be home any minute now."

Despite the disagreement from her younger sisters, Sam nodded at her mother and turned to leave, but soon found her path blocked by Ant who refused to let her go. He was tired with the way their father dictated their lives and believed Sam should be living back under the same roof as her family. Ant had hardly finished trying to convince her to stay when the door opened, the face of Eric Keats twisting into anger at the sight of his own daughter.

"What the hell are you doing back here? Did I give permission for you to come home?" He spat in Sam's direction.

"What is wrong with you?" Ant demanded, stepping in front to shielding her from his vicious words. "She's your daughter. It doesn't matter who she's dating or what makes her happy. It's none of our business."

"She is my daughter, so therefore it is my business. It's my parental right to know. Now get out my way or I will make you," their father snarled.

"Girls, you head upstairs while your father and brother talk." Their mom spoke quickly as the twins vanished up to their room, the door shutting quickly after them.

Ant raised his palms to show he didn't want trouble, but he stayed between his father and Sam the whole time. Sam's heart was beating hard, she was sure it could stop any moment. Ant wanted to talk calmly about Sam returning home and how their father needed to accept his daughter being bisexual. As Ant took a step forward, something caught him in the side of the head causing him to stagger to the side. Sam's eyes went wide, and her jaw fell as her father's punch connected to Ant's jaw. Panic washed over her; this was all her fault. She wanted to move, get between the two men to protect her brother, but her legs refused to work. Standing upright again, Ant rubbed his jaw.

"Ant!" their mother shouted.

"His name is Eric! He is named after me and he will be called that. No more calling him by his middle name."

"I hope you enjoyed that," Ant said, spitting some blood out of his mouth. His father's face twisted into more rage as the red liquid hit the white carpet. "Because you won't get to do it again. You won't lift a finger against anyone in this house ever again."

Their father swung again but Ant was ready this time. He blocked the punch with ease and pushed his father backward, away from the women he was protecting. The older man's head banged off the front door. Moving toward the children again, fists raised, it was their mother that stepped in between the two males. Sam was frozen in place, she had never seen such a ferocious look on her mother's face. Pointing a finger at her husband, their mother stopped him in his tracks.

"Eric, stop this now! You will not hurt any of my children."

"A dyke and an idiot who can't follow orders? Are you kidding me, Julia? They need to be put in their place, so they grow up properly."

"No, you need to be put in your place. You can't go around terrorising your children. You can't go around terrorising other people's children either. I know what you did to that young man, how you cornered him. Charles Fellows came around the other day to speak to us about what you did to his son last year."

Sam's hands where trembling as her mother explained how their father had cornered Lloyd, blaming him for Sam's sexuality. She wasn't sure which was worse, the fact that her father had demanded one of her best friends stay away or that her father would scare someone so sweet and kind as Lloyd. Shaking her head from side to side, it made sense why she hadn't seen Lloyd in the last couple months.

A snarl appeared on her father's lips, his eyes flaring with anger. He wasn't used to be talked back to by anyone. Their father stepped forward and grabbed hold of his wife's arm, but their mother slapped him, causing him to stumble back in shock. "You will not put your hand on me or my children again. Get the hell out of my house!"

"This is my house!"

"No, Eric, this is my house. Only my name is on the deed. My parents bought me it before you had an actual job, remember? The job you only got in the first place thanks to my father. Now get out of here before I call the police!"

Their father stood there with a snarl on his face, until their mother reached for the phone in her pocket. Turning around, he stormed out of the house without saying a word. Ant dashed forward and locked the door behind his father. Sam burst forward, wrapping her arms around her mother. Ant was soon dragged into the tight hug.

"I'm sorry I didn't do that sooner, Samantha. Trust me, I have no problem with who you are or who you are dating.

Ant told me it's your friend Jane? She's a wonderful person," her mom said, tears in her eyes.

The three were soon sat on the couch in the family room. The door was closed to protect the twins from hearing anything as their mother revealed the truth, the bruises she had been hiding from the children for years. Ant wanted to go straight to the police, but their mother declined. Their father had the money and contacts to fight any charges against him. It was Sam that convinced Ant to not go after their father.

It took two hours before she had been able to break away from her family. Her phone informed her she had missed calls from Rider, but she chose to call her girlfriend first. Jane had been shocked, offering to come around and check on her, but Sam declined, wanting time to settle back in. She was also slightly worried her father would turn back up despite the locksmith who was currently changing all the locks. Ant had agreed not to call the police as long as the locks where changed.

"So, you sure you're okay, Sam?" Jane asked.

"Yeah, but I'm worried about Lloyd. Rider told me the other day he had been going through some stuff and was going to visit him in Houston, but I need to check he's okay. I can't believe my father cornered him like that."

"I understand. Tell him I'm asking about him too."

"I will. I love you, Jane. Call you later?"

"Sure. Love you too. Bye"

Sam took a deep breath as she dialled Lloyd, hoping he would answer. Every time she had tried to call him, even on Christmas, the call had gone straight through to voicemail.

A smile spread across her face as she heard the line connected. The smile didn't last very long, Sam knew something was wrong the instant Lloyd spoke. Lloyd was in tears.

"Lloyd, what's the matter? What's going on?"

"It's Rider!"

"What about Rider? I had missed calls from him."

All color drained from Sam's face as Lloyd explained what was currently happening in Houston. Her hands were shaking as Lloyd said he needed to go and call Jeremy and Susan. Before he disappeared from the call, Lloyd promised he would call her back. Sam already had tears running down her face as she called Jane back. How could Rider be in the hospital?

Fernando

Fernando gasped for air as he placed the basketball down on the ground, wiping the sweat from his brow. It might still be the Christmas break, but when fellow students invited Fernando to join them for a quick match, he couldn't say no. Basketball flowed through his veins, there wasn't much more that could keep his attention. He would have happily played longer but he had a project due the first week back and both him and Walker hadn't even started it. In fact, Walker had been avoiding spending any time alone together.

It was a surprise to discover Walker was into dudes, even more when Walker had turned him down. He may have hooked up with fifteen guys and two girls last year, but they always came back wanting more. In fact, the two women were just because Fernando had gotten bored with how easy he could pick up guys and wanted to see if he could get a girl to sleep with an obvious gay guy. Once he had his fun, Fernando moved on. Walker was the first guy to turn him down and it bothered him greatly. Even the flirting at karaoke hadn't warranted a smile. Fernando was sure if he and Walker spent more time together or he got Walker's boyfriend out of the picture then the star of the basketball team would fall into his bed.

To try and make that happen, Fernando had approached the History Professor, Mr. Finn, and asked to be partnered with Walker due to both being busy with the basketball and how they could work together during down time at practise. The lie had worked and now it would be just him and Walker all afternoon. After thanking his fellow students, Fernando walked toward the dorms, the sun beating down on him, causing him to sweat even more. He was only ten minutes late for the afternoon of studying. Walker opened the door quickly with a look of annoyance.

"You're late," Walker said, looking Fernando up and down. "And you're drenched. Did you swim here?"

"No, but I went by a brothel. I still have plenty of stamina if you want to go a couple of rounds?"

Walker sighed and rolled his eyes. He didn't welcome Fernando into his room but left his door open as he took place in the chair by the desk. Walking into the room, Fernando could see history books already scattered out on the desk, notes already in place. When he couldn't find a second seat, Fernando dropped down on Walker's bed, shuffling backward to rest his back against the wall and shoving the duvet out of the way. He was still way too hot from the hour of basketball he had just played.

"So, what do we have to do for this assignment?" he asked.

"Don't worry, I've done the majority of the hard stuff. It should only take us a couple hours to knock it out, and then it's ready to hand in," Walker answered while flicking through the books, his eyes remaining on the assignment.

"I'm sure you are very good with the hard stuff. I'm all for knocking it out with you."

Walker shook his head and glared at Fernando. The duo fell silent, Fernando concentrating on notes that Walker passed. The fellow jock wasn't lying when he said most of the work had been done. Walker had already completed the research, indexed everything, and started to compile the list of references. All that they needed was a little more research and then to organise the structure and flow of the assignment. The sun outside shone into the room, making it unpleasantly warm as Fernando squirmed on the bed, messing it up even more.

"You got any water?"

"Sure," Walker said, reached into the small fridge that was just below his desk and passed Fernando a bottle of chilled strawberry water.

"Thanks. I'm gagging for it." Fernando winked at Walker as he took the bottle, allowing one finger to stroke along the outstretched hand of his teammate.

"What the hell!" Walker shouted, rising to his feet.

"You know what? I'm taking a break. I'm going to the toilet."

The door slammed shut as Walker exited the room, a scowl on his face. A minute later, there was a chiming originating from the desk. Fernando got up from the bed and grabbed hold of Walker's phone; the image on screen showed a FaceTime coming from a boy with dark floppy hair. Rider's name was etched across the top of the screen. From previous discussions, Fernando knew that was the name of Walker's boyfriend. A wicked smile came across his face as he leaped back to the bed, pulling his shirt off before he hit the answer button. A confused face came onto the screen. Fernando wasn't sure if the guy had been crying or if it was raining where he was.

"Who are you? Where's Cam?" the boy stumbled.

"I'm Fernando and you are?" Fernando said, purposely acting as if he didn't care who he was. Planting the seeds of doubt, he hoped it would result in Walker being in his bed.

"I'm Rider."

Fernando laid down on the bed, making sure the camera caught his smooth chest but falling no lower than his navel in order to make it look like he was completely naked. Panic spread across the dark-haired teen as Fernando lied about having just finished having sex with Walker. He glanced at the door, hoping Walker wouldn't appear until after the call. Rider's eyes flicked about, trying to compute what he had just heard. Fernando smirked as he decided to push even harder.

"He said it had been way to long. That he couldn't wait any longer or else he would explode. I gave him relief and by God I can tell you he needed it. Something about his plans for Christmas being messed up. I mean, I was here just to do our group assignment, it was him that pushed me onto the bed. Ripped my T-shirt and pants off before I could even ask him what he was doing. I mean, I tried, but his mouth was a bit full to answer, if you know what I mean."

"What? You're lying! Cam wouldn't do that!"

"He did. How many times have you seen a naked guy in someone's bed and they *haven't* had sex? Anyway, got to go now. Bye!"

Fernando waved at the screen as he hit the end call button. With a quick flash of inspiration, he set the phone on airplane mode. Walker would find out the truth eventually, but it would be fun while it lasts. Placing the phone back down in the exact place it had been before the call, he had only just made it back to the bed when Walker burst through the door, a confused look on his face.

"Why the fuck do you have your shirt off?"

"I was just trying to cool down. I was hot from basketball, and your room is like a furnace."

Walker crossed the room and opened the window. "There! Now put your shirt back on and also get the hell off my bed. You've messed it all up. It was nicely made till you sat your ugly ass down on it."

"We can mess it up even more if you would like?"

The deep growl from Walker gave all the signal that Fernando needed. He knew not to push Walker too far without a retreat plan. Standing up and sliding his shirt back on over his head, Fernando dropped into the chair, allowing

Walker to make the bed again. Once he was satisfied with the bed, Walker grabbed his phone and notes. Luckily for Fernando, he didn't notice the phone was on airplane mode. The duo continued working for another hour in near-total silence before Fernando decided they had completed enough work and that he needed food.

"Do you want to get a bite?" he asked, causing Walker to glare at him. "I promise I won't try and hit on you at all. Look, I'll even invite Q-Tip, who can play the good chaperone."

Fernando pulled out his phone and quickly called Matthews while Walker had yet to decline. It didn't take much convincing to get Matthews to go, Fernando had hardly gotten his sentence out before he had agreed.

"Q-Tip is in. What about you, Python?"

Walker looked at his phone briefly before slipping it into his pocket. "I was thinking I would have received a call or text, but they must have been busy. I guess I can go for some food with you both," he agreed reluctantly before rising to his feet and grabbing a hoodie from the closet.

The duo headed out, meeting Matthews on his way up the stairs. The smile on Fernando's face only grew larger the longer Walker didn't notice his phone. The three spent most of the evening discussing their current season performance and where they believed their performance could get better. It was only once the discussion of basketball ended that Matthews brought up the idea of going out for a drink. Both Fernando and Walker agreed but were confused when their fellow teammate chose the karaoke bar.

"What can I say? I enjoy singing," Matthews said.

A few drinks and a couple songs later and the trio lost track of the time. It was late when they had arrived back to the dorms. When they all split for the night Walker still hadn't noticed his phone was on airplane mode. Fernando may have been going to bed alone, but he was going with a giant grin on his face.

Chapter 20

Rider

Rider's eyes were red and sore. He had been crying for the last thirty minutes, but the tears kept coming. Three more calls to Cam had been diverted to voicemail and the four texts hadn't even been delivered let alone read. Even the calls to Jane and Sam had gone to voicemail. Rider had lost count of how many vodkas he had drunk. He didn't like the taste and the first glass had burned the inside of his throat but it made it easier to drink. He couldn't taste the alcohol anymore.

The guilt flowing through him was even stronger than the tears. Rider blamed himself for everything that was happening—he should have been honest with Cam, explaining the kiss and his feelings in order to find a solution. He should have gone home at Christmas. It wasn't just Cam he felt he had ignored, if he had reached out to Lloyd more, maybe his best friend wouldn't be in such a dark place.

Rider refilled the glass when a banging in the hallway

disturbed him. Trying to rise to his feet, he collapsed back into the chair. The alcohol had a much stronger impact on him than he had been expecting. Using the desk for stability, he stood up and slowly made his way across the room. Hoping it was his best friend, he was disappointed to see a man standing further down the hall that was not his Lloyd. Rider had to focus hard to realize it was Jay that was approaching.

The older student had been dropping weed off to one of the wrestling team. While leaving the room, he had accidentally slammed the door. Rider turned away from Jay mid-explanation and headed back into the room. Without any invitation or rejection, Jay followed Rider into the room, dropping into the chair at the desk when the younger boy dropped onto the bed, glass in hand.

"For someone still two years shy of being legal, you've had a lot of vodka," Jay said, picking up the bottle. "Something wrong?"

"It's Cam. I think he's sleeping with someone else," Rider said, draining the glass.

"Wow! Okay, I may have something that can help. How about I roll you a nice joint? Or if you want something a little harder, I've got something new, much stronger than weed."

Rider shook his head, he hadn't taken drugs before and he wasn't going to start now. Before he knew it, he was explaining everything that had happened. The phone call, the voicemail, the kiss, the guilt. Saying it out loud caused his stomach to twist and writhe, it made everything more real. Jay sat and listened without saying a word until Rider had finished talking.

"A kiss that the other guy started, and you bailed on is not cheating. Your boyfriend fucking someone else is definitely cheating," Jay said, looking at Rider with a soft smile which slowly turned into a smirk. "So, why not get some payback? Me and you, we'll record it and send it to him. Show him what he's missing out on."

"No, I won't do that to Cam. A kiss was too much. I'll never do something like that again, even if he is sleeping with Fernando."

"Come on, you know you want to."

"I said no!" Rider growled.

"Fine, at least let me pour you another drink."

Nodding, Rider passed his glass to Jay. His head felt like it was swaying, he couldn't stay sitting down. Rising to his feet, he started pacing, anxiousness biting at him. He let out a sigh at Jay's stretched-out arm, the glass half full. Grabbing the drink, he took a deep swig before pacing again. After the fourth pivot, half the liquid was gone but something felt different. A strange sensation flooded him, it wasn't the alcohol or guilt, it was something else. He looked at Jay before staring at the glass, but his eyes seemed to struggle to focus. Rider's leg's buckle under their own weight but Jay grabbed him before he hit the floor, helping him to the bed.

"Take it easy Rider. You've drunk a lot"

Once sat down, Rider closed his eyes trying to regain his equilibrium. A few seconds later, Jay sat next to him. The deep breaths didn't help shift the fogginess clouding his head. His heart felt like it was pounding while also missing a beat. As he opened his eyes, he couldn't seem to sense anything around him. His vision was blurred, and everything felt far away. His head was aching as Jay leaned forward and placed his lips on Rider's. Pushing as hard as he could, Rider jerked backward. The kiss with Nixs was an accident, but he wanted nothing like that from Jay.

"Don't worry, Rider. I'll make it feel better. We both know we want this, there is no point in trying to fight it."

Something pinned Rider down to the bed, but he couldn't understand what was going on. Hands were touching him, but it took all his effort to even realize it was Jay. Rider's mind focused on the one thing that mattered to him—Cam. He needed his boyfriend, he wanted to make things right and tell Cam the truth. The tears flowed down his cheeks again.

"No, Jay. Get the fuck off me," Rider stammered as he tried to fight back.

Flailing, his foot hit Jay in between his legs. It had been an accident, but Rider used it to escape. He pushed Jay off him and leaped to his feet, but his legs refused to work as he fell to the floor. Under the bed, Rider noticed Lloyd's pen knife. He grabbed it as he shakenly rose to his feet, pointing it at Jay.

"Stay the fuck away from me. I said no, Jay. Get the—"

Rider didn't get to finish the sentence as a stream of vomit hit the carpeted floor. The room was spinning, his heart was racing, his insides were burning. He reached for his phone but dropped it, the screen smashing and landing in the vomit. His legs were too weak to hold him as he crashed to the floor. Starting to shiver, he couldn't control his body. Jay stood up from the bed, panic on his face. For a second, Rider thought he was going to help, but instead, Jay turned and sprinted out of the room. Rider's insides were freezing and boiling at the same time. He struggled to get air into his lungs. He reached for the chair to try and pull himself up, but he lacked the strength in his arms. The chair came tumbling down to the floor as Rider's vision slowly faded to darkness. Blinking didn't help to bring back his sight. His heart started slowing along with his breathing. There was movement from the door, a voice that sounded familiar, but he couldn't identify its owner.

"Hi, Rider. I'm sorry I came back a day earlier than I said, but—" The voice suddenly stopped. "Rider!" the voice shouted. "Elliot, quick, go down to the first floor, room one-oh-four. You want to get someone called Yuki. Quickly, go now! Rider, stay with me, can you hear me? Rider?"

The sounds in the room became muffled. The person who had dropped to the floor next to him felt miles away. Rider knew a hand was touching his arm, but he couldn't feel it. He couldn't respond to the voice, his throat refused to work. The world slipped away, the darkness in his eyes spreading to all areas of his being.

Chapter 21

Cam

Yawning loudly, Cam stretched in bed before rubbing the sleep out of his eyes. It had started as something quick to eat, but somehow Matthews had convinced them all to get up and sing *I Want to Break Free.* That one song had spanned into four hours, resulting in Cam getting back to his room just after one in the morning. He was amazed that his body still woke him up at seven. Grabbing his phone, a sad look spreading across his face when he noticed there still wasn't a single call or text from Rider. It was unlike his boyfriend to go this long without sending a message, even during an argument he would still send him a good night message.

Good Morning Ri. I hope you're okay and I haven't upset you or anything. I miss you.

An error appeared on his phone as he hit send. Cam was confused as he hit send a couple more times but nothing happened. Ignoring the error, he hit the call button but the cell didn't even connect. Cam restarted his phone but the call to Rider still was still rejected. When he noticed the small airplane in the corner, he felt like slapping himself. He wasn't sure how the phone ended up in airplane mode. He was sure he had set it to silent while studying with Fernando but he must have hit the wrong icon. Setting the phone back to the default mode, he jumped when his phone vibrated out of his hand. He picked up it up to see he had eighteen missed calls, seven from Rider, three from Lloyd, two from Jeremy, one from Jane, and four from Becca, which had all been in the space of the last thirty minutes.

Cam didn't get to look at the mountains of messages or call anyone back before there was a pounding on his door. Climbing out of bed, he quickly made his way to the noise. He pulled the door open enough to poke his head out, hiding his bare chest in case it was Fernando. His jaw dropped at the state of Becca. Her eyes red, tears still rolling down her stained cheeks. Cam opened the door fully and Becca burst into the room, wrapping her arms around Cam as she cried more. He couldn't understand what she was saying through the sobs. Placing her on the unmade bed, he grabbed tissues from his desk.

"Becca, what's wrong?"

"I've been trying to contact you. It's Rider. He's in the hospital. Somethings happened, he's unconscious, Cam. We need to go to him."

He couldn't believe what he was hearing. He grabbed his phone and went through the messages; each one confirmed Becca was telling the truth. Still not believing it,

Cam tried calling Rider, but the call didn't connect. There was a soft knock on the door, a silver-haired boy stood there, a sad look on his face. Cam waved Dave into the room with shaky hands. Dave placed the bag he was carrying down and pulled Cam into a tight hug. He had agreed to help them drive the fifteen hours it would take to get to Houston, he didn't want to leave Becca alone at a time like this. Grabbing his bag, Cam shoved clothes into it before collecting his phone charger. Both he and Dave had to help Becca up from the bed, her legs not working at the moment. Cam bit his lip, until he saw it with his own eyes, there was no way he believed his boyfriend was in hospital.

Cam showed the duo to his car, wiping a tear out of his eyes. He needed to focus, there had to be a reason to what had happened. Lloyd's message said they found Rider with an almost empty bottle of vodka, but Rider hardly drank, let alone enough to pass out. He threw his bag along with Dave and Becca's into the trunk, slamming it closed as the couple climbed into the back of the car. A voice called from the other side of the parking lot. He turned to see Matthews making his way over. The smile on his friend's face dropped off when he noticed the sadness on Cam's face.

"Walker? What's going on? Where you off to so early? I thought we were getting pancakes this morning."

"Matthews, sorry I need to go. Rider, he's…he's…" Cam's voice cracked as a couple tears escaped. "He's in the hospital"

"What!? Why?" Quintin's eyes went wide.

"I don't know. We are driving down there to see him. Can you—"

"Tell Coach? Sure. Message me later. Let me know what's happening, okay? I'm here if you need me."

Cam couldn't even answer, all he could do was nod as Matthews pulled him into a tight hug. Thanking Matthews, he climbed into the car and got the three of them on their way. Dave was trying to calm Becca, but Cam's mind wouldn't allow him to focus on the conversation. Cam bit his lip, as thoughts of the last time he walked into a hospital room flooded his mind. The heart-wrenching feeling of seeing his father in the hospital bed, eyes closed. Cam wasn't sure he could go through it again. Rider had managed to ease the pain of losing his father, but it was still raw. There was no way he would survive losing Rider.

After three hours, Cam pulled over to gas up the car, Dave volunteering to take the next shift. Cam was glad, having just been holding the tears at bay, he wasn't sure how long he could last. He slid quietly into the back seat, Becca pulling him close and resting her head on his shoulder. Her tears had stopped, but her eyes were still red as she sipped the water Dave had bought from the gas station.

"He probably just drank too much. He's always been a lightweight." Becca laughed softly.

Cam laughed but he wasn't convinced. Rider couldn't handle his alcohol, but he always knew when to stop drinking. The joke was simply Becca's defence mechanism, the same one she shared with her brother. When in serious or stressful situations, they both start telling jokes. Even Dave was trying to join in with the jokes to cheer them both up.

"I'm sure he'll be up and writing an article about this by the time we even get there."

The trio made good time, reaching the hospital just before 10:00 PM. Dave volunteered to park the car as Cam and Becca dashed into reception. Cam struggled to breathe properly as he walked the halls of the hospital, the memories of his father rushing back. They were directed toward the ICU on the sixth floor. The elevator stopped at every floor en route, causing his anxiety to increase with each stop. Once the doors opened on the sixth floor, they both started sprinting in the direction of Rider. Entering the waiting room, they were greeted by Lloyd, wrapped in Yuki's arms.

"Cam, Becca!" Lloyd broke out of the older man's arms and dashed at them both. His cheeks stained with tears as he wrapped his arms around Cam.

"Lloyd, how's Rider? What happened?" Cam stammered as he hugged the smaller boy.

"He's stable but we don't know what happened. Rider's roommate came back and found him on the floor. Jeremy is currently talking to the doctor. We been waiting for the test results all day."

"Is he awake?" Becca asked

As soon as Lloyd shook his head both Cam and Becca burst into tears. The restroom door opened as Susan came out; Becca rushed into her mother's arms. Yuki moved over and hugged Cam before he wrapped Lloyd in a defensive hug. It was all too familiar to Cam, the grieving family, the waiting for the doctors. He felt like he would break if he didn't find something to distract him. He turned to the two men in front of him. It had been so long since he had seen either of them. As Cam's eyes looked over Lloyd, he noticed the bandages wrapped around Lloyd's arm.

"Lloyd?" Cam said pointing at the bandage.

Being pulled to the plastic seats, his mouth hung low as Lloyd explained about his depression and self-harming, how it was the reason he had come down to spend some time with Rider. Cam didn't even say anything, he pulled the smaller boy into his arms only releasing him when Jeremy came out of a door to the left of them, shaking the doctor's hand. The group quickly gathered around him.

"He is still unconscious but stable. He has a large amount of alcohol in his system and the doctors believe this could be a suicide attempt."

Cam wasn't the only one shaking their head in disbelief. Over Christmas, Rider had been saying how much he had been enjoying his course and how he wanted to spend time with Cam. No way was it a suicide attempt.

"There isn't much we can do at the moment and visiting hours have come to an end for the day. We will head to the hotel and try and get some rest. Come back first thing in the morning and check for any changes," Jeremy said.

Becca nodded at her father before taking her mother's arm and heading toward the elevator. Jeremy patted Cam on the back before heading toward the two women. Cam felt lost, helpless. He didn't know how Jeremy was being so strong at the moment.

"Lloyd, are you coming with us?" Cam asked.

"No. I'm…I'm going to stay with Yuki tonight but if you need me, you can call. Any time."

Cam understood, they all needed that one special person at the moment, but his was lying in a hospital bed. He nodded, receiving hugs before heading toward the elevator that was being held. The group was quiet on the way to the hotel, Cam even turning down the option for food. He couldn't eat at a time like this. When he reached the hotel room, he slipped into the bed fully clothed, his mind trying to process everything that had happened in the last twenty-four hours. There were tears from the other side of the room, Dave whispering to Becca that everything was going to be okay. Cam closed his eyes but couldn't fall asleep, constantly rotating all night until a knock on the door came at 8:00 AM.

Jeremy bought everyone breakfast wraps, but Cam couldn't even eat half of his. His hunger had been left back in Kentucky. It took ten minutes for the group to sign in before they reached the ICU, any hope that something had changed over the night was short lived. Rider was still in the same state as yesterday. Cam bit his lip and nodded when Becca asked if she could go in before him. He soon found himself sat in an uncomfortable chair in the bland waiting room. Dave was playing around with the vending machines, he seemed to be the only one with an appetite at the moment. Susan had joined her daughter in Rider's room, leaving Cam with Jeremy.

"How you doing, Cameron?" Jeremy asked softly, his strong calm demeanour still on show.

"I…I…" Being the only ones in the waiting room gave

Cam the ability to start crying. Jeremy didn't say anything, instead wrapping an arm around him and pulling him close. "I lost my father and now I could lose Rider. I don't know what I would do without him. He pulled me back from such a dark place, he made me feel like a person again."

"I know you are worried, Cameron, but Rider will pull through this. He is one of the toughest kids I've ever seen. You won't lose him, Rider cares too much for you to leave you just yet. After what happened last year, the pain in his eyes…I never thought he would be happy again, but you gave him that. You helped him not only come out but accept who he really is. Out of anyone Rider could have ended up with, I'm glad it was you, Cameron. I'm glad your Rider's partner."

Cam's words got caught in his throat. Jeremy had shown he was okay with Rider's sexuality, but this was the first time he had ever referred to Cam as Rider's partner. Smiling weakly at Jeremy, he was pulled into another hug as Dave wandered back over, arms full of chips and sodas. The silver-haired boy had struggled to know what anyone would want so had bought one of almost everything in the vending machine. Cam took a can of Coke out of instinct more than need. Behind Dave was a timid student. He was tall, blond, and had a guilty look on his face.

"Mr. Williams? My name is Jason, I'm Rider's roommate."

Jason extended a hand to Jeremy who ignored it, pulling the tall student into a hug, thanking him for finding Rider when he did. Cam was shocked to discover Jason had found Rider in their room convulsing on the floor. Dave simply patted the student on his back. When Cam introduced himself, his cheeks heated up with a blush spreading across his face as Jason explained how he knew everything about Cam. Rider hadn't been able to stop talking about him.

The smile vanished from Jason's face, being replaced by a haunted look. "I know you probably don't want to hear this, but I want to say sorry. It's my fault that Rider is in this state."

"What?" Cam and Jeremy echoed at the same time.

"The vodka, it was mine. I shouldn't have left it in the room. I never thought Rider would drink it. I'm so very sorry."

A weak smile appeared on Jeremy's face as he placed a hand on Jason's shoulder. "This isn't your fault, Jason. Its college, people drink. You couldn't have known this was going to happen."

A polite cough came from behind the group. The doctor Jeremy had been speaking to yesterday was stood there, clipboard in hand and a sad look on his face.

"We have an update on Rider. We can rule out any alcohol-related reason for his condition. The level of alcohol in Rider's body was high but nowhere near the limit to cause someone to fall unconscious." The relief on Jason's face was almost immediate. "We are still waiting for the results from the last few tests, but we believe we have discovered the main cause. Can I ask, have any of you ever noticed Rider take any kind of drugs?"

"No!" Cam shouted louder than he'd meant to. "I mean, Rider is very anti-drug. He doesn't even like taking aspirin when he has a headache. He always said he would never do drugs."

"I agree with Cam," Jason added. "There is this student at the university that supposedly sells drugs and Rider always looked disgusted when anyone talked about it."

"Then this may come as a shock to you all. We have discovered an extremely potent drug called fentanyl in Rider's system. We believe the low level is thanks to the vomiting, but he suffered an allergic reaction to the drug. We believe there is potential damage to his kidneys and heart. It was lucky Mr. Alighieri discovered Rider when he did."

Cam's hand rose to his mouth in horror, Jeremy was shaking his head and Jason's eyes were wide. Dave, on the other hand, wore a confused look on his face as he double-checked with the doctor to be sure he said fentanyl. Dave was studying medicine at college and had recently studied the drug in his chemical compound module. It was a very strong opioid used for extreme pain relief and normally only issued by hospitals. Cam fell back into a chair, the conversation with the doctor lost on him. His mind lost in the many unknown ways how something so horrible could have gotten into Rider's system. It wasn't until Becca's hand landed on his shoulder that he was pulled out the trance.

"Cam? We're going to go get some food. Would you like to join us?"

"No, thanks, I'm not hungry. Can I...can I go in and see him?" Cam asked. The clock on wall showed two hours had gone by.

"Sure." Becca smiled softly, her cheeks still stained from recent tears. "We shouldn't be too long."

Cam waited until he was alone before he rose to his feet. He took three deep breaths before pushing the door open and taking a step into the room. His heart was pounding at the body lying in the bed, a number of machines beeping at its side. The only sign Rider was still with them was the up and down movement of his chest and the constant chirp of the heart monitor. It took all his energy to take the first step forward, moving around the bed toward the seat near Rider's head.

"Rider, I'm here," Cam said, slipping his hand into the smaller boy's and squeezing softly. "I hope you can hear me. I want you to know I love you so much. Please come back to me. I'm so sorry we fought recently. I can't do this without you. You are and will always be my life. I love you, Rider Williams, there will never be another you."

The tears came thick and fast as Cam's hand trembled. He took some ragged breaths, trying to calm himself when he felt something in his hand. Looking down he could feel it again, a weak squeeze. Cam held his breath as he looked at Rider, the chest was still rising and falling, the machine chirping. It took a minute, but Rider's eyes started to shift and twitch. A smiled spread across his face as his boyfriend's eyes opened.

"Rider?" Cam whispered softly, jumping to his feet.

"Cam?" Rider's voice was hoarse. "Where am I?"

"You're in the hospital"

Rider tried to sit up but gave up after the third attempt. Cam wanted to run out of the room and grab everyone, but he was frozen to the spot. He was terrified that this was all a hallucination and once he moved it would all fall apart around him. He quickly started telling Rider how much he loved him, how sorry he was for not being there when he was most needed.

"Cam, please," Rider said weakly. Cam stopped when noticed Rider crying. "I'm…I'm…I'm the one who's sorry."

"You don't need to be sorry."

"I do. This year, at college. There was this guy, Nixs."

"Your TA friend?" Cam asked. Rider had only ever spoke positively about the other student, Cam hoped he wasn't involved.

"I…I liked him. The way I like you." Rider cried, squeezing Cam's hand.

Cam let out a soft sigh leaning forward and kissing Rider softly before resting his forehead on his boyfriends. People in love could still like others and Cam was fine with that. It was only natural to find others attractive. Cam gave him one more kiss, confirming his feelings were completely fine and understandable before sitting back down and holding Rider's hand in both hands.

"It's not just that. At Christmas when I cancelled on you, he invited me over to his to celebrate Christmas. While I was there, he kissed me and I didn't immediately push him away. I cheated on you and I'm so sorry." The tears were coming even stronger now.

"Ri, it's okay," Cam said squeezing his hand. "It was one kiss. We can get through this together. I love you so much."

"Then there was Jay. I told him no but he wouldn't stop. He pinned me down—"

"What?" Cam yelled.

"I was drinking and he came in the room, I was telling him about the kiss and he made me a drink. I started feeling weird, then he pushed me down and started kissing me. I didn't want him to, but he tried to do stuff that I don't fully remember. I only just got him off in time."

Panic and anger coursed through Cam. Whoever this Jay person was tried to rape Rider and the drink the he made must have been how the fentanyl got into Rider's system. It took all of his energy to not pull out his phone and call the police immediately. There would be time for that but for now Rider needed his attention. Cam reached over and wiped his boyfriend's tears away.

"Ri, whatever that guy did to you, it is not your fault, understand me. None of this is. I'm sorry I wasn't there when you needed me. I love you, okay? I mean that with all my heart. We will be okay, you'll be okay."

"I…I love you, Ca…."

Cam's eyes went wide as Rider's closed. His chest stopped moving, the chirping over Cam's shoulder became a flat sound. Several alarms sounded around the room. Cam squeezed his boyfriend's hand tight and shook his arm, the chair behind him crashing to the floor as he jumped to his feet. His heart pounded hard as his boyfriend refused to react to any stimulation.

"Rider! Rider! Please come back to me! You have to wake up, Rider. I love you! Please, I need you."

The door burst open, the room flooded with white

coats and blue scrubs. The doctors and nurses surrounded the bed, pushing Cam back and away from Rider. Their hands separated, causing Cam's heart to shatter. He couldn't focus on what the medical staff were saying, his eyes refused to leave the still body. Despite his protests, he made to leave the room as a crash cart was brought in. The seats were only meters away but Cam couldn't move from his spot by the door, his legs gave way as he slumped down to the floor, his head in his hand as the tears burst from him.

"Cam?" Jeremy said.

Cam barely had the energy to raise his head, his eyes struggling to meet that of Rider's family. He didn't need to say anything, he couldn't say anything. His words had been trapped in the room when he had been forced out. The sound from the room beyond told everyone everything they needed to know. Becca was soon on the floor with Cam, both wrapped in each other's arms as Jeremy struggled to hide his own tears, his strong façade finally breaking.

Cam stood in front of the plain looking door, his hand shaking on the handle. It had only been a week, but it had felt like a life time. The days had been dark, full of tears and sadness. He now stood at Rider's dorm with Susan and Jeremy. They had come to collect Rider's belonging. Cam took a deep breath as he pushed the door open. The three were greeted by an empty room, Jason had promised them the time and space they needed to strip the room of Rider's essence. As he stepped over the threshold Cam could smell fresh paper, Rider's normal scent.

The room was so familiar. Cam had seen it numerous times on video calls but now it felt so much smaller. Rider's aura was all around him. Cam's heart caught in his throat at the image of Rider swinging through the New York City skyline with his favorite superhero. His boyfriend had the artwork printed and hung on the wall. The smile on his face did not last long as his eyes fell to the neatly folded gray hoodie that sat on the bed.

Instinctively, he moved away from the hoodie, falling onto Jason's bed, tears falling from his eyes like they had all week. His father had given the hoodie to him and in turn he had given it to Rider. It had always been his good luck charm, even when it was wrapped around the small frame of his boyfriend. Maybe if Rider had been wearing it that night, things may have ended differently. It only took seconds before Susan joined Cam on the bed, pulling him into a tight embrace. Her hand stroked through his hair.

"Cameron, you got to stay strong. I know it's hard now, but things will get better," Susan said weakly as if she didn't even believe her own words.

The three of them took their time collecting and packing Rider's belongings. Cam picked up the Spider-Man clock that sat on the desk. Rider had been so happy on the phone when he had described how Yuki had surprised him with it. Cam wrapped it carefully in bubble wrap and placed it in the box. He picked up Rider's phone from the table, Jason had cleaned the vomit from it, but it was no longer in working condition. All the messages he had sent to Rider were now lost to the aether. By the time the room was clean of any sign of Rider, each of them had broken down into tears. All they could do was try and carry on.

Chapter 22

Yuki

Yuki held Lloyd tight in his arm, both had done a lot of crying since the moment they had seen Rider on the floor. It had been a week, but the pain was still so raw. Yuki kissed Lloyd on the forehead as he tried to slow the teen's tears. Lloyd had stayed in Houston an extra week after what had happened, but in a couple hours he would be on a plane back to Belmont. Although he hadn't said it out loud, Yuki didn't want Lloyd to leave. With the depression and what had happened to Rider, Yuki was worried Lloyd may do something stupid. Only two days ago, Yuki had come back from speaking to admin office about Rider to discover Lloyd on the bed with blood running down his arm. He had run over and quickly wrapped a bandage to stop the bleeding. Yuki couldn't even be mad; all Lloyd had wanted was to feel anything else than the sadness that had been suffocating them all week long.

"Lloyd, you cannot blame yourself for what happened."

"But what if it was me. What about if me telling Rider

everything that was happening in my head, how the darkness felt overwhelming, put too much pressure on him. What happens if all my problems were the reason why he had been drinking? I shouldn't have told him, I shouldn't have told anyone."

"I am glad that you told people. We can now start helping you. I know that what you told Rider is not what caused this. When I wanted to see you, I could tell from his messages how much he cared for you, that all he wanted was the best for you."

The tears slowed as Lloyd reluctantly nodded at Yuki, wrapping his arms tightly around his waist. Yuki's heart fluttered as he welcomed the hug. The love he had for Lloyd was staggering, he didn't want anything bad to happen to him. In all honesty he wanted to be with Lloyd, but he couldn't; Yuki had made a promise to his family that once he had finished college in America he would return. He would help his father run the company and support his family like a good son should.

"I want to get help. After seeing the pain that Susan, Jeremy, and Becca are going through. I can't do that to my father. I need help to stop me from hurting myself. Yuki, will you help me?"

"As best as I can." He smiled softly

Before everything that happened, Yuki had briefly explained the options Lloyd had, but this time he broke down everything he knew about the medication and the type of counselling his sister had received. It didn't take long for Lloyd to agree that the best starting point was to speak to a doctor about the dark feelings. Using his phone, Yuki did a quick search for the number of Lloyd's doctor. By the time the phone call had ended, Lloyd had arranged an appointment for two days' time. Yuki squeezed the younger boy's hand, who smiled back at him.

"Yuki, I know this is asking a lot but…will you come with me?"

"Of course," Yuki said. He didn't even need to contemplate it. He had promised to be there for Lloyd and if it meant the price of a plane ticket then he would happily take that blow.

Booking a seat on the same plane as Lloyd, Yuki began placing clothes into a bag when there was a knock on the door. Cam had promised to leave the dorm key after they had cleaned out Rider's belonging. Smiling at Lloyd, he walked to the door and opened it to see an older student there. He had met the student before, the florescent light catching a glint of blue in the hair. The student reintroduced himself as Nixs although Yuki was sure last time he had introduced himself as Nickolas.

"I'm sorry to bother you. I was just up at Rider Williams's room and there was no answer. He hasn't been answering my messages since last week and his phone keeps going to voicemail. I'm worried I have pissed him off."

"Oh…" A sad look spread across Yuki's face. "I guess you have not heard. A week ago there was…an incident and Rider was…well, he was rushed to the hospital."

Nixs' jaw dropped and his eyes went wide. He had been under the impression that Rider had been ghosting him, he had even written him a letter to apologise for everything that had happened between them. Nixs handed the letter to

Yuki, asking for him to deliver it before he wandered away confused. Yuki didn't even get to say another word before Nixs had disappeared. He turned back into the room, the letter still in his hand. Lloyd was on the bed, tears in his eyes again. Yuki swallowed hard, he must have heard the whole conversation.

He smiled weakly while walking over and wrapping his arms around the smaller boy before placing a soft kiss on his cheek. "Things will be okay, Lloyd. It will take time but things will get better and it will stop hurting. I promise you."

Yuki had just finished packing when another knock arrived on his door, softer than Nixs'. Cam's eyes were red, the dark circles under his eyes looked worse than they had yesterday, the teen didn't look like he had slept at all in the last week. Cam slipped the keys into Yuki's hand and thanked him for allowing them to collect Rider's things.

"Before you go, a student called Nixs came by with a letter for Rider. I thought it was best to give it you," Yuki said softly, handing Nixs' letter to Cam.

Cam's face twisted up as he shoved the letter into his pocket before giving Yuki a tight hug, causing Lloyd to run across the room and join in. Cam didn't remain long, Jeremy and Susan were waiting for him at the car.

The flight to Belmont wasn't busy and they had been offered double seats each, but Yuki had chosen to remain seated next to the smaller boy. Lloyd may have spent the last week sleeping in his bed and, although nothing had happened, Yuki just wanted to be close to Lloyd. Ever since the kiss, Yuki had wanted to reveal truth, that he still loved him and wanted to be with him, but with everything that had happened with Rider and the looming threat of Yuki having to go back to Japan, he didn't want to put Lloyd through more hurt than he had been.

"Thank you for coming with me." Lloyd smiled weakly as they climbed out of the taxi.

"Anything for you."

Yuki stood nervously outside Lloyd's house, a place he hadn't been in almost a year. Before he had left for Houston, he had walked past a number of times, each time having to stop himself from knocking on the door, hoping for just one last glance of his ex, but he had never been lucky. Lloyd opened the door and Yuki carried both their luggage into the hallway. They were hardly into the house before Charles burst from the kitchen, wrapping his son tightly in a hug.

"Lloyd, I'm so sorry. Jeremy called me. Rider—"

"Dad." Lloyd bit his lip, barely held back his tears. "Can we...can we not talk about that right now?"

Charles nodded and pulled his son back in for a second tight hug which broke Lloyd's flood barrier. Yuki could see Charles was holding back his own tears. Once the hug broke, Lloyd disappeared toward the bathroom for tissue. Yuki held his breath as Charles turned to look at him. He hoped Lloyd's father didn't blame him as much as he did himself about the state Lloyd was in. Relief coming across him when he was greeted by a weak smile from Charles.

"Yuki, it's good to see you. Thank you for being there

for Lloyd this week and coming back with him. It's good to see you both together."

"It is good to see yourself also, Mr. Fellows."

"Call me Charles."

"Sure. I am glad Lloyd was able to get an appointment. I just hope the next two days will not be too difficult."

Yuki and Charles tried their best to distract Lloyd over the next two days. That evening, Yuki found himself wrapped around the younger man whispering into his ear that everything would be okay as they both drifted off to sleep. The hardest moment had been when Jane and Sam came over the following day. Yuki had to take over the story of what had happened to both Lloyd and Rider as Lloyd broke down in tears. Lloyd was still blaming himself for not taking his cell phone with him. Sam blamed herself for not calling Rider back first and Jane blamed herself for ignored Rider's call, worried that she would miss a call from Sam needing her after returning home.

He had done his best to reassure them all, they couldn't take the blame for this. Even after they had composed themselves, not much else was said that day, each lost in their own thoughts. What brought a smile to his face was when the two girls had pulled Lloyd into a hug and told him they were always there for him and how they would be checking on him a lot more. A small laugh echoed around the room when Jane threatened to kill the smaller boy is she found out he had self-harmed again.

The night before Lloyd's appointment, Yuki found himself thinking about his sister and mother, who he had almost lost. When he had first seen Rider in the hospital bed, his mind had warped back to the hospital in Tokyo, his mother all frail, tubes hooked up to her. She had been diagnosed with stage three lung cancer. When he had left for the states, she was such a strong woman, but when he had returned, she hardly resembled herself. After a hard-fought battle, she had finally been given the all-clear but that image of her in the bed had haunted Yuki ever since.

The image must have haunted his sister also. It had been Yuki that walked in and find his sister Hikaru unconscious after overdosing. Rushing her to the hospital, she final revealed the darkness clouding her mind. The same darkness Lloyd was feeling. It had been a challenging battle and Hikaru was doing better but that didn't stop Yuki from worrying about her. Both his mother and sister's afflictions had made him even more determined to return and support his family.

Ducking out of the meal with Lloyd and Charles early, Yuki sat outside the house as he called his family. He needed to know they were all okay, that his mom was still cancer-free, and that Hikaru was still keeping the darkness at bay. When he finally returned, his eyes were slightly watery, which he hid from Lloyd, not wanting to worry him.

Yuki sat in the doctor's waiting room by himself, Lloyd had been called around ten minutes ago. Charles had tried to get the time off work but had been unsuccessful. He had taken Yuki aside that morning to thank him for everything he was doing for his son, how he was glad that Lloyd wasn't going to the appointment alone. Throwing the magazine he had flicking through four times down onto the table in front of him, Yuki looked back up at the clock on the wall. His leg bouncing from nerves, he just hoped this would help the boy he loved.

"Nervous for the Fellows kid? What's his name again, Laid?"

Yuki turned to see an old woman sat two seats away from him, a friendly smile on her face.

"Lloyd," Yuki corrected her only to find out she had been joking to try in order to relax him. "Yes, I am slightly nervous."

"Don't worry, it will all be fine. Life normally is."

The old woman stretched over and patted him on the shoulder. It turned out that Mrs. Bell actually lived next door to Lloyd and his father and had been friends with Lloyd's grandmother before she had passed away. When Mrs. Bell asked how Yuki knew the Fellows, it caused him to squirm in his seat. It had always been a difficult subject for him to talk about. In Japan the younger generation where a more accepting of LGBT people but the older generation still looked on it with shame.

"I'm a…family friend."

"Oh, I thought you might have been Lloyd's partner," Mrs Bell said with a smile. Yuki's eyes went wide, and he scrambled for words. "You just had that loving look in your eyes when he headed into the doctor's office. I've also seen his homosexual flag through the window."

"Oh, well…I do not know what I am to Lloyd, but I do know what he means to me." A soft smile spread across Yuki's face as he looked down at the ground.

"And what would that be, sweetie?"

"I think he's my…" The smile grew on Yuki's face as he got the courage to say it out loud. "My soulmate."

Yuki never heard Mrs. Bell's response as the loudspeaker summoned her to her appointment. His heart was pounding hard. He had only said it out loud once, but now that the words were out in the universe, Yuki was sure Lloyd was the one for him, even if it wouldn't work. It was another ten minutes before Lloyd left the doctor's office, paper in hand. Walking out of the building, Yuki wasn't surprised to discover the doctor believed Lloyd was suffering from major depression and anxiety. Not only had the doctor given the teen a prescription for anti-depressants but the doctor had also managed to arrange a counselling session for him.

"The session isn't with my normal doctor so I'm going to have to check with my dad to see if we can afford it, but, if so, I have an appointment next week with a Dr. Greenwood."

Yuki pulled the teen into a tight hug, happy in the knowledge that Lloyd was on the road to recovery. It would be a long, difficult road, but he believed in his soulmate. Leaning forward, he gently pressed his lips to Lloyd's. It only took seconds for Lloyd to press back hard, grabbing hold of Yuki tightly.

"Thank you," whispered Lloyd as his cheeks started to glow red, his lips in brushing distance of Yuki's. "For everything."

Chapter 23

Cam

June 22nd

The summer sun beat down on Cam, causing a bead of sweat to roll down his neck and continue down his back. The lack of wind made the heat feel double the strength. He took a number of deep breaths as he looked down on the grave in front of him. The graveyard was quiet, the only other people present were five rows over, a small group dressed in black, crying over a coffin being lowered into the ground. Cam knew the grief they were going through, his hand trembling as he placed the white roses down on the grave in front of him.

"I'm sure he would have loved them," his mom said, patting him on the shoulder. Once she was sure he was okay she headed to a bench not far away, giving him some privacy.

Cam bit his lip hard, almost drawing blood when a hand slipped into his and squeezed softly. He turned and smiled weakly at the boy next to him. Rider returned the smile and rested his head on his boyfriend's shoulder. Cam's gaze returned to his father's grave. It had been two years since he lost him, but the pain hadn't truly vanished. When Rider had been in hospital fighting for his life, Cam had felt guilty he had never come to see his father since they laid him to rest. The first year was too painful, but on the second anniversary of his father's passing he had made a promise.

Rider had also agreed to accompany him, despite the trial in Houston. His boyfriend had been adamant a couple days in New York would not change the outcome. He had already been called to the stand and given his evidence and was no longer needed for questioning. Cam had tried to convince him to stay in Houston where he was needed, but Rider had only confirmed that he was needed at Cam's side. A weak smile spread across Cam's face as his head made contact with the shorter teen.

"I know I never got to meet your father, but if he is just half the guy you are, then he was an amazing person," Rider said.

Panic shot through Cam as he noticed Rider swaying slightly. Despite Rider's claims that he didn't need any help, Cam wrapped Rider's arm over his shoulder and walked him to the bench where his mom sat. They had misjudged the distance from the bus stop to the graveyard, resulting in Rider becoming tired. Although needing to sit, Rider was actually proud of himself, it was the furthest and longest he had been outside without needing a break since being released from the hospital.

That day in the hospital, Rider's heart had stopped for

forty-two seconds making him officially dead. The doctors had managed to restart his heart and stabilize him, but with the potential damage caused by the drug, they had refused to release Rider. In the two months he was a patient, Rider got tired of the doctors poking him for tests and everyone else treating him like he was a fragile plate. He had argued to be treated exactly the same as before the incident, but he quickly learned his body had been through a lot. At the start, he had found it extremely exhausting just walking up and down the stairs. Over the last three weeks he had slowly been building up his strength.

"Are you okay? Is it your heart?" Cam asked.

"No. I'm just a little tired." Rider's smile relaxing Cam slightly. "I'll stay with your mom while you talk to your dad."

Cam stayed by Rider's side until his boyfriend glared at him. Slowly making his way back over to his father's grave, he turned one last time to make sure Rider was okay. His boyfriend was already lost in conversation with his mom. Cam took a deep breath and closed his eyes as he tried to focus on everything he wanted to talk to his father about.

"Hi, Dad. I'm sorry I didn't come to see you sooner. I know I'm a bad son, but it was just too painful. I've got some...erm...big news for you. I'm bi. Mom says you would have been okay with it and, well...she always did know you best, that's why I brought Rider to meet you. See, Rider is... he's my boyfriend and I'm sorry I didn't bring him to meet you sooner. I know how you hated when I kept secrets, but I didn't know how to tell you." A small laugh escaped Cam. "I didn't know how you would react. I mean I know you're gone and you can't react, but still. Knowing you, you would have just shrugged and asked when were we next going to see the Knicks.

"I'm sure you would have liked Rider. He's not that much of a fan of basketball, but he plays the guitar beautifully and loves Iron Maiden. He makes me so happy. If it wasn't for him, I would still be that husk I was on the day I lost you. I miss you so much. I wish I could have seen you just one more time. I promise I'll come and visit you more often. I mean, Trish keeps telling me she's going to kick my ass if I don't come see her more often, and then there are Bobby and Yorick who I miss hanging out with. I promise I'll come visit you every time I'm here.

Cam took a deep breath in, wiping away a couple tears before resting his hand on top of the gravestone. "You're always with me, watching everything I do. I know you can't respond, but I need to know, I hope I've made you proud?" He waited a moment. Cam didn't actually expect a response, but when a small breeze caught a tear rolling down his left cheek, he couldn't help but smile. "I'll catch you around, Dad."

He waited until he was sure the tears had gone before turning to face his boyfriend and mother. Rider needed someone strong, with the trial and everything that happened Cam didn't want to show him more tears. The couple sat quietly, peacefully, as his mom went to speak with her husband. Wrapping an arm around Rider, Cam gave him a kiss on his temple, drawing a smile from the dark-haired teen.

When they finally left the graveyard, Cam flagged

down a cab and the trio were quickly en route back to their hotel. The heat and distance had taken a lot out of Rider who had decided to have an afternoon nap. His mom had planned to meet up with some of her old friends, which left Cam alone to meet up with Trish, of which he was already running forty-five minutes late. He hadn't wanted to leave until Rider had fallen asleep. As he walked toward the door of Starbucks, Cam kept his eyes forward, ignoring Trish, who was glaring at him through the window.

Cam made sure to grab a coffee before he turned and headed toward Trish, who sat at the same table she had taken Rider to during their first meeting. Trish wasn't alone, Cam hadn't seen Yorick since he had left for Belmont. His friend looked nervous, his gaze remaining on the floor. Cam took a sip of coffee, surprised by Yorick's current look. The blond Mohawk was gone, shaved to stubble. Yorick had loved the Mohawk so much he had happily gotten suspended from school for refusing to cut it.

"Hey, Trish, Yorick. It's good to see you."

"Hi, CJ," Yorick said, shifting uncomfortably in his seat. It was then that Cam remembered what he had learned at Christmas. With everything that had happened, it felt years since Trish had told him she and Yorick were dating.

"I'm so sorry for being late," Cam said, giving Yorick a fist bump before pulling Trish into a tight hug and whispered into her ear the reason. "I was making sure Rider was okay."

"I forgive you, now sit," she instructed him

Cam did as he was told, dropping into the seat on the other side of the table. He sipped on his coffee as Trish tried to take Yorick's hand in hers. A smile spread across Cam's face as Yorick pulled his hands back. He remembered how scared he was to tell his best friends he was dating Trish originally, worried they would think she would split up their friendships.   Trish rolled her eyes in her boyfriend's direction causing Cam to laugh loudly. Maybe talking about something different would allow his friend to feel more comfortable.

"So, Yorick, what's up with the hair?"

"Oh!" Yorick looked up and smiled as he ran his hand through the stubble on his head. "Well, I, erm…I donated it to locks for love. It's a cancer charity that uses real hair to create wigs for cancer patients. Trish talked me and Bobby into it." Yorick turned and smiled at Trish until he realized what he had done and looked back down at the ground.

"What was with the look?" Cam said innocently, causing Trish to roll her eyes again.

"Well…I…erm…you see, CJ…I…erm…me and Trish, I mean…"

"We're dating," Trish said proudly, having enough of beating around the bush. She grabbed hold of Yorick's hand.

Cam faked shock, which caused panic to spread across Yorick's face. He tried to shake his girlfriend's hand off him, but she refused to let go. Despite the fun he was having, the glare Cam received from Trish made him admit he had already known since Christmas. Yorick still looked guilty, his gaze remaining on the floor until Cam reached over and patted his old friend on the knee, confirming everything was okay between them.

"Don't worry, Yorick. I'm completely fine with you dating Trish. I mean you're no Edward Harris—"

"How dare you!" Yorick responded before the three burst into laughter.

"I joke, but I'm glad she has someone to make her happy. I can't think of anyone better for her. In fact, I'm seeing someone myself—"

"And they're fantastic," Trish cut in causing Cam to roll his eyes. He completely agreed but he wasn't going to admit it to her.

"What's her name?" Yorick asked, more relaxed than ever.

"Rider Williams," Cam said proudly.

Yorick turned to Trish for confirmation who just nodded. The lump in Cam's throat that normally came with telling people the truth was no longer there. In fact, it hadn't been there since he had almost lost Rider. He was now proud to tell the world of the man he loved. As he came out as bi, Yorick rose to his feet and pulled him into a hug and congratulated him. They had always been close, but that hadn't been the reaction Cam had been expecting.

"I thought you would have been slightly surprised," Cam said.

"That would be because of Harris," Trish said. "After he saw you and Rider last year, he started telling everyone at school you were gay."

"No one really believed him, but it was out there for everyone to know," Yorick said. "It was just kind of a thing, then when Bobby came out as gay most people just accepted it."

"Wait, Bobby came out as gay?" Cam said.

When Cam had lived in New York, he, Yorick, and Bobby has been almost inseparable, being known as "The Trinity". They spent most their time together, were on the basketball team together, and had shared all their secrets with each other. It had been Trish, Yorick, and Bobby that Cam hadn't wanted to leave when he moved to Belmont. With how open they had all been, he was surprised that Bobby hadn't actually told them, but he completely understood. Although Cam was now proud to tell people about him and Rider, he still remembered that fear of people discovering the truth.

"Yeah, and I couldn't be prouder of him," Yorick said, before Trish gave him a glare. "What?"

"You shouldn't just out people. I knew about CJ, but I would never just tell people."

"I'm not just outing him. When Bobby said he couldn't come today, I asked what I should do if anything about him or his sexuality came up. He said it was fine because its CJ and he trusts him. Anyway, what was I saying? Oh yeah. With people having accepted Bobby and your supposed sexuality being known, most had already come to terms with it. So, tell me about Rider?"

Cam couldn't help but blush, apart from Trish and Quintin, he wasn't used to people asking about Rider. It was difficult to put into words, but the dark-haired teen touched a part of him that he didn't realize existed till they had met. He soon had his phone out showing off pictures, bringing smiles to both Trish and Yorick.

"He's cute," Yorick said before laughing at the worried

look on Trish's face. "Don't worry. You're the only one for me."

"Enough about Rider. What's been happening with you?" Cam asked.

Cam soon found himself laughing as Yorick informed him of everything that had happened during their senior year in high school. He and Trish had tried to keep their relationship quiet but when Harris had found out he had gotten angry, he'd tried to kick Yorick off the basketball team. The coach had thought Harris had let the captaincy go to his head and then stripped of it, with Yorick receiving it instead.

"Speaking of basketball, I have to head. Got practice in about an hour. You can come along if you want, CJ? Bobby and the other guys will there, just like old times."

He hadn't played basketball with Yorick or Bobby since his father had passed, but Cam declined the invite, he would need to be getting back to Rider shortly. Needing another cup of coffee beforehand, he walked Yorick out of Starbucks and hugged his friend goodbye, promising to stay in better contact. Grabbing a latte, he pulled out his phone and sent a quick congratulations message to Bobby, making a mental note to call him later. Cam made his way back over to Trish, who pulled him close and gave him a peck on the cheek, which caused Yorick to glare as he walked past them outside.

"Now that Rick has gone—"

"Rick?" Cam questioned with a laugh. He knew Yorick hated people shortening his name.

"How's Rider doing?" Trish choosing to ignore Cam.

"I worry about him constantly despite him telling me not to. He was too tired to come out with me and I was tempted to message you and call it off, but he said if I didn't come then he would come by himself."

"Just like him, always thinking of others. What is he going to do about college?"

Rider had to drop out of Houston University, not just his freshmen year but permanently. It was three days after his heart stopped when he had finally woke and was able to talk to people again. The first thing Cam had arranged was for the police to be informed about the attempted rape and the possibility of Jay using fentanyl on Rider. After speaking to the police, Rider had decided that he couldn't go back to Houston, the pain of what had happened was just too great and he didn't feel comfortable or safe there. Cam and his family had all agreed, volunteering to collect his belonging while he was still in the hospital.

"Rider hasn't made any plans yet. Once the trial is over, he's going back to Belmont to live with his parents."

"What about you?" Trish said, worried about her friend.

"I don't know. I don't feel like I can leave Rider alone. I know he will be safe at his parents', but I just don't want to be away from him. Especially with what happened."

When Cam had called Trish to tell her Rider was in hospital, he hadn't been able to tell her everything. She had called him every day, but the full explanation was a conversation they needed to have in person. He bit his lip as he began to explain how Rider had been feeling alone and isolated from him, mixed with feelings for another guy that had resulted in Rider kissing someone else. His boyfriend had felt so guilty he even gave Cam the option to end their relationship. If Rider hadn't been in hospital at the time, Cam would have hit him over the head for suggesting something so stupid. He loved the dark-haired boy; one accidental kiss would not end their relationship.

"I'm not mad at Rider, I love him. This other guy, Nixs? He better not come back around or try and contact Rider again. He even wrote him a letter; can you believe that?" Cam said, his face twisting into annoyance.

"Really? What did it say?" Trish asked, sitting forward.

"I don't know, I threw it away. I just want to get back to normal, just me and him."

"What about your college? Your scholarship?"

The annoyance slipped from his face, replaced with a simple smile as he shrugged. An alarm from his phone chimed, a reminder to check up on Rider. Cam grabbed an extra coffee for the trip and Trish ordered two drinks before they both headed back to the hotel. Trish was adamant she was going to see Rider even if she had to wake him up. Pushing the door to their room open slowly and quietly, Cam poked his head in to see Rider sitting up on the bed, a book in his hands. Rider's smile grew when he noticed Trish behind Cam. Trish walked over to the bed and handed one of the cups to him. Rider reached out, his hand slightly shaking as he grabbed hold of the hand, thanking Trish before he placed it down on the table without taking a sip.

"Is everything okay Rider? It's your favorite, hot chocolate with a caramel shot, whipped cream, and mini marshmallows."

"Erm…I…" Rider stuttered as he looked down at his book.

"After what happened, at the moment Rider can't drink anything that he didn't make or is sealed," Cam said. "I'm sorry, Ri, I completely blanked when Trish ordered two drinks,"

"No, I'm the one who's sorry," Rider said directing it more at Cam than Trish.

Trish didn't even question what she had just been told, instead climbing on the bed and pulling him into a tight hug. Rider thanked her for understanding before they both summoned the jock onto the bed to hug with them. Cam happily accepted.

Rider

Rider stretched out, finding the bed empty. It took him a couple minutes to remember Cam had gone to meet up with Trish. Rolling over, he reached for his phone, seeing three texts from his parents and one from Lloyd. The first message from his parents had been to check how he was, the following two were panic texts when he hadn't responded. It had only been two weeks since Rider had gotten angry and shouted at his parents. They had been smothering him, not allowing him to go more than ten paces without one of them there. He knew they were afraid of what had happened, but all Rider wanted was to get back to normal. Since the outburst, they had reduced their constant worry to a couple texts a day. He sent a message back to his mother confirm everything was okay and he had been asleep.

The message from Lloyd was just confirmation he would be at the courthouse tomorrow with Yuki. Rider took a deep breath; the trial had been draining. Three days after confessing to Cam, after his heart had stopped, Rider had finally woke and was able to explain to everyone, including the police, what had happened. That same afternoon, Jay was arrested, although he denied any involvement. Jeremy and Cam had been outraged when the police charged Jay with only assault for the drugging and possession with the intent to sell. They had also wanted him tried for sexual assault of Rider.

Four days ago, Rider had been called to the stand to present his statement which had been nerve wracking. The prosecutor had asked him questions he was ready for, but the defence had tried to skew his answers, trying to insinuate that he couldn't be trusted because he had freely been drinking. Yesterday, the police had given evidence about drugs found during the arrest and today had been Jay's turn on the stand. The trial was scheduled to end tomorrow, the only issue standing between Rider and justice was Jay being defended by his father. Although he practising law in a different state, even Cam's Uncle Roy had heard of Jacob Augusts II. He was a vicious but extremely successful defence lawyer, doing anything he could to get his client found not guilty. Roy couldn't remember a single case Jacob had lost in the last three years.

Trying to distract himself from tomorrow, Rider pulled the *Spider-Man* book Lloyd had bought him out of his bag and opened to the page he was on. He had managed to make it five pages before there was a click from the door, Cam poking his head into the room very cautiously. His boyfriend walked carefully into the room as if he could break just by him being there. Cam was quickly followed by Trish, a sympathetic look on her face. Rider was happy she had come back to the hotel, scared he wouldn't see her before flying to Houston tomorrow morning.

Rider felt guilty as he placed the drink down that Trish had bought him. It was difficult to explain, he sensed a haunting feeling whenever someone gave him a drink. It could have been from his mom, Becca, even Cam, but when someone handed him a drink that wasn't sealed, his hand started shaking and he struggled to breathe properly whenever he tried to raise it to his lips. The doctors believed it was an induced panic attack and it would slowly disappear over time. Cam apologised to them both as he broke the hug on the bed, the three coffees he had drank were pressing on his bladder.

"So, how are you doing, Rider?" Trish asked.

"I'm doing well. I still get tired when I exert too much energy, but the doctors say it will get better."

"That's good, but how are you really doing?" Trish glared at him

"How do you do that?" Rider laughed softly. He was positive she could read people's minds. "I feel so guilty with Cam missing his freshmen year. He was dropped from the basketball team which meant he lost his scholarship. He gave up his dream for me, and I know I shouldn't, but I just feel so guilty."

"Gave up his dream? You mean he didn't tell you either?"

Rider was surprised as Trish told him the truth. While he was in the hospital, Cam had received a call from Coach Lieberman. Due to the strict rules around missing practise even in extreme circumstances a player had to lose their spot on the team. The coach had been extremely sad to cut Cam but that wasn't the full reason she had been calling him. She had spoken to the dean of the college and explained how Cam's grades were outstanding, how he had quickly become one of the most valuable players on the team and the difficult situation Cam found himself in with a family member. Cam had blushed when Coach had confirmed his boyfriend was considered his family. Although he would lose his scholarship for that year, the dean had agreed with Coach and had allowed her to offer Cam the Issel Scholarship again, although it meant he would have to repeat his freshman year.

Rider's jaw hung low, Cam hadn't told him about being reoffered the scholarship. Trish confirmed she had only just found out in the coffee shop. Rider struggled to keep a smile off his face, the feeling of guilt easing up. Cam could still study history and fulfil his dream of becoming a history teacher. There was a cough, which caused the duo jump. They turned to find Cam had been listening to them talk.

"Cam, why didn't you tell me?" Rider asked.

"Because I haven't even decided if I want to go back yet. I don't want you thinking I'm choosing a college over you. I'm sorry for not telling you"

"You have to go back! You made your dad a promise

and I'd hate you missing out due to me." Rider pulled out his best puppy dog look.

"I wouldn't miss anything because of you, it's my decision. I would never blame you."

"Can we at least talk about it?"

Cam smiled, agreeing to his boyfriend's demand. Rider climbed to his feet and crossed the room to give him a tight hug. He felt a lot better than he had in the graveyard; the sun was lower in the sky and the heat outside was much cooler. He managed to convince the other two to go out for a walk, tired of being holed up in the hotel room. As they walked, Cam kept complaining they were walking too fast and it may tire Rider, causing Rider to shake his head. They were only three blocks from the hotel when Rider came to a stop, not from being tired, but due to the shop in front of him. He smiled as he entered the tattoo studio, despite the pleas from Cam.

"Are you sure you are should get a tattoo. What happens if you pass out during it."

"I will be fine. Trust me."

Cam pulled an unsure face but followed Rider and Trish into the store. Taking a seat, Rider already knew the design he wanted, a phoenix on his upper left arm. The mythical creature rises from the ashes and only becomes stronger. It was the perfect metaphor of himself, with everything that had happened this year, but also with his relationship with Cam. There had been bumps in the road, but they were even stronger than they ever had been.

Chapter 24

Rider

Rider winced slightly when Cam accidentally bumped into him as they climbed out of the cramped airplane seat. He rolled his eyes at the panic on his boyfriend's face and confirmed that his heart was absolutely fine. His new tattoo that Cam had nudged was still a little painful. The protective wrapping had been removed this morning, as advised, bringing a smile to Rider's face as he admired the phoenix that now soared up his arm. The artist had informed him it would take a couple days for any pain to subside.

As they duo waited in line for people to disembark from the plane, Rider pulled his suit jacket on and straightened his tie. Mary had only been a couple rows in front of them but somehow had beaten almost everyone off the plane. By the time the couple finally arrived in baggage claim, she had already collected their cases and was ready to go. Rider took a deep breath as he stepped out of arrivals into the heat of

Houston. It only took a couple minutes before his parents arrived, pulling the trio into tight hugs.

"You okay, Ri? You said the other week you were getting over needing an afternoon nap," his mom said as she messed with his hair.

"That was my fault," Cam said with a guilty look. "We went to see my father and it took a lot out of Rider."

"It was one nap. You all need to calm down," Rider told them, crossing his arms over his chest. "Anyway, where is Roy?"

Roy and Becca had driven to Houston University in order to collect Yuki and Lloyd. Becca had been adamant they would have become distracted if she didn't go along and they would meet the group at the courthouse. Rider pulled out his phone, they had two hours until the trial resumed. As he climbed into car, squashed between his boyfriend and father, Rider closed his eyes and took a deep breath. He just wanted the trial to finish.

It had been a week since he had given his testimony, but he still didn't feel clean from it. The prosecutor had instructed him to simply explain in his words what had happened that evening. What he hadn't been ready for was the cross examination where the defence had challenged him on every little detail. Why had he been drinking that evening when he was underage? Could the alcohol have affected his memory of the events? Could the drug have already been present in the vodka? They had made him feel like the villain. That night, after giving his testimony, he had told his family he was going for a shower but spent thirty minutes crying under the flowing water. When he finally came out of the bathroom, his eyes had been red and sore. Cam must have noticed but did not mention anything.

As the car progressed toward the courthouse, Rider leaned and rested his head on Cam's shoulder, keeping his eyes closed. He did not open them till the car came to a stop. He smiled as he accepted Cam's hand out of the car. Mary chose to keep his mom company as she went to park the car, leaving the three men by themselves.

"So, what happens today, Dad?"

"Roy was telling us all evidence was finished being presented yesterday. The prosecution and defence have their final statements, then the jury will deliberate. In a small case like this, it should only take around an hour or so. We should know the result by then end of today."

The three were halfway up the stairs to the courthouse when his father put an arm out, stopping the teens from moving. Standing near the entrance was Jay, in his expensive suit and with his hair no longer tied up in a ponytail but loosely cascading over his shoulder. It was obviously a ploy by his father to make Jay look both younger and more innocent than he was. Rider turned and walked back down the steps, taking a deep breath in and out, when he opened his eyes, he noticed his sister standing in front of him.

"You scrub up well. Why can't you look like this every day?" Becca laughed as Rider rolled his eyes.

Rider greeted his sister, best friend, and Yuki with a hug before being summoned to take their place in courtroom three. Sliding in-between Cam and his father in the front row, Rider's eyes locked onto the back of Jay's head. He felt a hand patting him on the back and he turned to see Roy softly smiling, having just sat down with Mary and his mom. Roy squeezed his shoulder as the bailiff called for everyone to stand as Judge Shan took his seat. The prosecution was called first to give her closing statement.

"Ladies and gentlemen of the jury. Over the past three weeks, you have heard first-hand what happened on that night in January. You heard from witnesses that stated the defendant has offered to sell them marijuana. He was also arrested in possession of marijuana, as it is only one step to offering harder substances. When the victim collapsed, did the defendant try and gain help? No, he ran. Running is not a sign of an innocent man. It has been brought up that the victim was underage when he was drinking but that does not change the fact that the victim was assaulted. He did not volunteer to take that highly addictive, dangerous—and often fatal—substance. In my honest opinion, there is only one way you should all vote, guilty."

Rider could see his father nodding along with every single one of the comments the prosecutor had made. He was amazed that his father hadn't climbed to his feet and applauded. A hand slipped into Rider's, as he turned Cam was not looking at him but instead focused on Jay, anger flickering across Cam's eyes. A man in an expensive suit and a more expensive haircut—Jay's father—stood up, he patted his son on the back before he proceeded to the jury.

"Ladies and gentlemen of the jury. Mr. Williams may have ingested fentanyl, I am not debating that. It is not my job as the defence to tell you where the substance could have come from, that is the job of the prosecution—and they have not done that. They would have you believe that it was my client that gave the substance to Mr. Williams, but they have not proven this without a doubt. They have produced no solid evidence that my client gave Mr. Williams the substance. They have not even been able to produce evidence that my client has access to the substance. The only evidence presented was hearsay events, a small personal amount of marijuana, and the word of the victim, who in his own testimony confirmed he had drunk copious amounts of vodka before my client arrived, therefore impeding his memory of events. During that evening my client panicked and ran from the scene due to the underage drinking. He has already shown in this court how remorseful he is for that action. I close my statement with this, the law states the prosecution must prove without doubt that my client is guilty, and they have not done that, therefore you must vote not guilty. Thank you, ladies and gentlemen."

The judge released the jury to start their deliberations and soon Rider found himself outside in the Texas sun, his loved ones all surrounding him. Despite his father and Becca's optimism it was Roy that was the voice of logic and reason. Rider actually felt more relaxed that at least one other person in the group thought that the defence had been extremely well structured and was incredibly strong.

"If somehow that asshole is found not guilty, then we will go to civil court and win there," his father announced.

"No," Rider said, shaking his head, causing everyone to look at him. "If we lose here, Jay's defence will be just as strong, if not stronger, in civil court. I just want this all over with."

"You sure, Ri?"

Rider smiled weakly and nodded at his father. The twenty-eight minutes it took for the jury to debate seemed to be the longest twenty-eight minutes of Rider's life. Relief flowed over him when they were summoned back into the room knowing that it would all be over soon. His father took the short time as a positive sign, Rider not so much as he bit his lip while the jury re-entered the room. Rider found himself holding his breath when the jury foreman confirmed they had reached a verdict.

"Your Honor, the members of this jury find the defendant not guilty in the case of possession with the intent to sell. The members of this jury find the defendant not guilty in the case of assault."

A gasp came from his mom and his father swore under his breath. He suddenly felt Cam's hand pull out of his as it clutched hard around the arm of the chair, the knuckles going white from the pressure, as Cam ground his teeth. Rider let out a long sigh, it wasn't the result he wanted, but now he could start putting it all behind him. Whimpers came from behind him as Becca tried to hide the tears. Jay had a huge smile on his face as his father patted him on the back. The judge quickly thanked and dismissed the jury before calling an end to the trial. The prosecutor was lost for words, she was sure this had been an open and shut case. All she could do was apologise to Rider for letting him down.

"Ri, I'm so sorry. If I hadn't been with Yuki that day, I

could have helped. If I had come straight back to your room after the rain, I might have been able to catch him, been the evidence you needed."

"Lloyd don't think like that," Rider said, pulling the smaller boy into a tight hug. "None of this is your fault. You did absolutely nothing wrong. Life can be difficult, and it often doesn't go the way we want, but we always need to fight back. I'm not giving up, so you shouldn't either."

As Rider and his family started the slow walk out of the courtroom, he suddenly heard a snarl come from both Cam and his father. Looking over to the other side of the steps, Rider saw Jay and his father who were shaking hands with the counsel that had made up Jay's defence team. Rider had to get Mary, his mom, and Becca to stop the two men from charging over there and assaulting Jay themselves. Even Lloyd was grinding his teeth; he was sure his best friend would have charged also if Yuki's arms hadn't been wrapped around him. Apologising to his family before asking for a minute alone, Rider walked slowly over to Jay.

"Don't be long, and don't say anything stupid," Jay's father said to Jay as he noticed Rider approaching, then he turned and carried on down the stairs toward the car that was waiting for them.

"Rider, I…erm…I'm sorry." A sympathetic look was on Jay's face

"No, you're not," Rider called him out. The look on Jay's face changed to a smirk.

"You're probably right. I'm guessing you're angry at me like that lot." He flicked his chin in the direction Rider had just come from.

"At first, I was scared for my life, that I might never see the ones I love again. I was terrified to touch anyone in case they did to me what you did. I still can't drink anything created by someone else. For a while, I was angry—at what you did to me, what you tried to do to me, and at myself for not stopping you sooner. Now? No, I'm no longer angry at you. I pity you. You may have been found not guilty, but you will have to live the rest of your life knowing exactly what you did to me. How you hurt not only me, but so many people with your stupid actions. You have to live with the fact you almost took someone's life. I don't feel angry at you, I feel sorry for you. That you need to take substances just to be able to feel something. Me? I have my family, my friends, and the love of my life. I don't need a substitute. Have a good life, Jay."

Rider turned around, not allowing Jay to say anything to him ever again. He walked back over to his family, friends, and, most importantly, Cam. Weak smiles were on their faces as they all agreed with him; it was time to head home and try and move on with their lives.

Chapter 25

Lloyd

Lloyd scowled as his ball slid too far to the left and into the gutter. It had been way too long since he had been bowling and it had definitely affected his game. He grabbed the ball and took his second throw, hitting nine out of ten pins. He nodded to himself and then turned and smiled at his best friend. Rider stepped up to the lane, sending the ball screaming down the lane and smashing into the pins, getting a strike. Lloyd's smile quickly turned into a glare. It had been three weeks since the trial but today was a day just for the best friends, like old times. Rider turned around smugly, cheering as the final score finished at 178 for Rider to Lloyd's 154. As he raised his arms in triumph Lloyd noticed something dark sticking out of the edge of Rider's T-shirt.

"Ri, what's wrong with your arm?"

Rider's eyes went wide, and he tried to drop the subject, but Lloyd wasn't having any of it. Breaking out his puppy dog eyes, he whimpered till his best friend finally gave in. Pulling the sleeve of his T-shirt up, Lloyd was greeted by a tattoo. The black bird raised from Rider's bicep up to his shoulder, wings stretched out in flight as the tail feathers wrapped around the back of his arm.

"When did you get a tattoo?"

"When Cam and I went to New York. You like it?"

"Absolutely, it's awesome. I would love one, but I think Dad would kick my ass if I got one."

Rider laughed loudly. It turned out he hadn't told his parents he had gotten a tattoo, until two days ago when coming out the shower his dad had spotted it. Rider had actually enjoyed his father shouting at him for once, it made him feel like everything was back to before the incident. Jeremy had even threatened to stop him from coming out to meet up with Lloyd.

The duo left the bowling alley and slowly walked toward the lake as Lloyd found his pocket vibrating. He smiled as he read Yuki's name on the phone screen, but he rejected the call, quickly composing a message.

Hey you. Don't worry, I'm just out with Rider at the moment but I'll give you a call later.

They both sat down on the bench that overlooked the lake as the friendly conversation slowly changed to more delicate subjects. Since the fateful day of the incident, neither had really discussed the moment—it was a taboo subject. Doctor Greenwood, who Lloyd had been seeing for his depression, had instructed him to share more with the ones he loved. He needed to express his feelings so people knew exactly what was going on in him and so they could help.

"I still can't believe that guy was found not guilty," Lloyd said. Rider simply shrugged. "Ri, that night. I really thought I had lost you."

"I keep telling people it will take a lot more than that to stop me." Rider laughed as he turned and looked at his best friend. The joking smile slipped from his lips. "I'm sorry I made you feel like that Lloyd. I'm glad Jason came back early."

"Me too." A weak smile appeared on Lloyd's face. "I also want to thank you. It sounds bad but seeing you…you know. Seeing what your parents were going through, how much pain they were in. It was the kick start I needed to get help."

Lloyd swallowed the lump in his throat; he hadn't told Rider he'd been seeing Doctor Greenwood and had been on antidepressants since January. Being in hospital for two months and then the trial, Lloyd had through the time wasn't right. Taking a deep breath, he told Rider about his weekly counselling session and how they had been a great help in identifying the dark thoughts before they found a way into his head. There had been times in the last month that he had felt drained, but there were larger gaps between the negativity. Lloyd bit his lip as he waited for his best friend to respond; the large smile spreading across Rider's face eased the younger teen.

"Lloyd, that's fantastic to hear!" Rider exclaimed, pulling him into a tight hug. "So, you haven't self-harmed?"

"I've only done it once since I told you. It was after your

crash in the hospital, when we all thought the worst. I found everything overbearing and wanted to just feel something else. Yuki had left the room for a meeting and I ended up cutting myself. There are still dark days, but they seemed to be further apart and now I know who I can turn to when I feel overwhelmed."

The truth was, Lloyd wasn't sure he would ever be free of the feelings that haunted him, but he was now fighting with all his might and that's what had made the difference. He hadn't allowed the feelings to control him, he was the one in charge. Sam and Jane had also kept their promise and randomly dropped by when he wasn't expecting, just to make sure he was okay and not self-harming.

"It's made it very difficult to jack off, not knowing when those two were going to show up," Lloyd admitted, causing Rider to laugh. "But I have learned one thing from all this. When the days are the darkest, that's when you find the thing that gives your life light."

"That's fairly poetic for someone like you," Rider teased.

"I do listen in English sometimes. Anyway, I decided what I'm going to do for college. I don't want others to go through the same thing as me, or if they are, I want to be able to help. I'm going to train as a counsellor."

"That's fantastic Lloyd, I'm sure you will be a great counsellor and I'm always here if you need someone to practise on." Rider smiled at his friend. "I hope you know that I love you."

"I know...as a brother" Lloyd laughed, but Rider didn't.

"No. You're more than that to me. I just love you."

Lloyd looked into Rider's black eyes and could see he was telling the truth. Without even saying another word, Rider wrapped his arms around his best friend and Lloyd couldn't help but blush as he rested his head on the tall guy's shoulder, a soft smile on his face as words slipped out of his mouth.

"I love you too."

A gentle breeze passed over the two, the sun low in the sky causing the horizon to glimmer a warm orange. As Lloyd watched two birds ducking and diving over the lake in an endless dance, he felt happier than he had in a long time. They both sat in each other's embrace, neither talking as nothing else was needed. He had no idea why he ever questioned his friendship with Rider because in that moment they had never been closer.

"Gay!" someone shouted. Moving out of the hug, Lloyd turned to see a younger teenager on his bike with a couple of friends who were sniggering.

"Yes, I am, why? You interested?" Rider said with a straight face.

The smile on the kid's face dropped as he stumbled for a response. Lloyd and Rider started laughing when nothing came and the group of kids cycled away, but not before flipping the duo off, which just caused them both to laugh even more. Rider took hold of Lloyd's hand, who squeezed back as he smiled.

"Speaking of gay. How are you and Yuki doing? I notice you went back to his place rather than fly back to Belmont with us after the trial."

Lloyd swallowed. Since the incident, he and Rider hadn't approached the topic of Yuki—even he and Yuki hadn't approached the topic. "He calls me at least twice a week to make sure I'm doing okay."

"And?" Rider smirked at him.

"Yes, we've kissed." Lloyd could feel the blush spreading across his face, Rider's gaze was too much. Lloyd swallowed as he told his best friend the truth. "I also slept in the same bed, and we've had sex a couple of times since we reconnected but I'm not really sure what any of it means. Yuki hasn't brought up the topic of what we are doing and I'm too afraid to. I'm worried if I say anything he'll realize it's wrong and we will go back to not being in each other's lives. After next year I know Yuki has to go back to Japan, but I just want to spend time with him before he goes."

"I'm sorry it's not clear, but I'm glad he's back in your life."

Lloyd simply nodded before falling back into the arms of his best friend. The duo spent a while longer on the bench before heading in the direction of Cam's house. Cam had returned to Belmont with Rider; he had missed too much of the year for it to be worth going back for his final exams, and with his scholarship being removed, Cam hadn't thought it was even worth trying. Lloyd declined the invite to join Rider, leaving his best friend to be with his boyfriend. Turning, Lloyd started to head home, pulling his phone out and calling Yuki, a smile spreading across his face as the older guy answered.

"Hey, you," Lloyd said as he walked slowly toward his home.

"How was your day with Rider? Is he doing okay?"

"He's good, we went bowling."

Lloyd entered his house and smiled at his father who came to greet him. He dropped down on the couch in the den and continued to chat with his ex, a huge smile on his face as Yuki talked about how his exams were going. Lloyd could happily sit and listen to Yuki talk for hours, he just wished he had the courage to tell him how he truly felt. That he loved Yuki with all of his heart.

Chapter 26

Rider

Rider waved goodbye to Lloyd as Cam's arms wrapped around his waist. It had only been five hours since he had left his boyfriend, but having spent almost every minute together for the last three weeks, Rider has missed Cam considerably within those five hours. Following Cam to the bedroom thinking they were going to make out, he was disappointed to find Cam had the laptop on. Rider pounced onto the bed but only Max joined him as Cam sat back down at his desk. The German shepherd lay across Rider's legs and started licking his face, making him laugh. He had read online that animals had a sixth sense for when people had been injured and Max definitely had this sense, as since Rider had returned to Belmont, Max refused to leave his side when they were together.

"Ri, I've made a decision," Cam said, drawing Rider away from the dog. The University of Kentucky website was currently on the laptop screen.

A smile spread across Rider's face. "And?"

"I think I'm going to take the scholarship again. I want to do my father's memory justice."

Rider wanted to get up and hug his boyfriend, but he was tired from exerting himself during bowling and was currently trapped under Max. Instead, he waved his index finger at Cam, summoning him over. The jock seemed to understand and crawled on the bed over to Rider, wrapping his big arms around him and bringing an even bigger smile to Rider than the one he already wore. In the last three weeks, Rider had tried to convince Cam to take the scholarship and each time Cam had been unsure, not wanting to leave him. As Rider tried to double down and confirm it was the best choice, Cam placed his finger over Rider's lips. Instead of talking, he kissed the tip of Cam's finger, causing the jock to blush.

"I had an idea. I don't know if you will want to, but it's the only plan I have that allows me to study history and be with you. I want you to come to Kentucky with me." Rider's eyes went wide, but before he could say anything, Cam continued, "You don't need to worry, it will be different. I thought we could get an apartment together, that way you don't need to worry about who you're sharing with. Becca graduates this year, so you won't have to worry about her, and I've been checking the journalism courses for you. They aren't as good as Houston, but their course is still good and they're still open for late admissions."

Cam rose from the bed, grabbing the laptop before he settled down again with Rider resting on his chest. Rider was shocked how much research Cam had done while he had been out with his best friend. He had lists of all the different types of journalism modules the university offered, gay friendly housing areas in Kentucky and information on how to apply. Rider couldn't lie, he had loved being at college and studying the subject that interested him the most. If he went to Kentucky there would always be Cam around for him, he wouldn't have to worry about being lonely again. Even if there were people like Jay at Kentucky, he would still be living with Cam.

"You've done a lot of research I see."

Rider couldn't help but laugh when Cam showed him the "congratulations but bye" poster he had designed for Becca. "If you don't want to go then I won't force you. But I can't be away from you, Ri. With how close I was to losing you, it would be too much."

"I…erm…I can't promise anything, but let's talk to my parents about it."

"Should we go over or just call them?" Cam asked excitedly

"I meant tomorrow. Tonight is just me and you time." Rider winked.

This was the first evening that they had a house to themselves, and Rider did not want to waste that opportunity. Grabbing hold of the laptop and closing the lid, he placed it on the floor before he rotated and laid on top of Cam, pinning him to the bed. Since being discharged from the hospital, the two had kissed but it had always been more of a peck than full-on passionate makeout. With the potential damage to his heart and kidneys, Cam was panicked Rider might end up hurting himself. After almost five months of teasing, Rider couldn't take any more.

Leaning forward, he pressed his lips to Cam's. After what Jay had tried to do to him, Rider had worried about kissing Cam, that the feelings would have dissipated, but the electric charge shot through him, spurring him on. As Cam placed his hands on Rider's lower back, Rider kissed him harder before biting Cam's lower lip, causing the jock to release a soft moan.

"Rider, are you sure you'll be okay?"

"I'll be fine, but if I'm going to college for you then you're doing this for me."

"Fine." Cam smirked before he got a weird look on his face. "Erm…let me put Max out in the hall. I'm not going to be able to do anything with him watching me."

Rider laughed as Cam picked up Max over his shoulder and carried him out the room despite the whines from the German shepherd. The promise of treats later managed to convince max. Just as he reached the bed, Cam turned and wiggled his butt at Rider before slowly bending over and picking up the laptop. Rider had to bite his own lip to stop from growling at the sight. Cam placed the laptop back on the desk and his shirt and jeans onto the floor. Rider's eyes went wide as his boyfriend turned on the spot, showing off his new jockstrap. He had never been so turned on by a piece of sports equipment before. As Cam reached the bed Rider pulled him back down with a kiss, his hands slowly drawing circles on Cam's naked chest. He tried to remove his own shirt, but it got halfway over his head before Cam leaned forward, kissing and biting the smaller teen's neck. Rider gasped loudly.

"Cam!"

"That's my name."

Rider had missed this closeness with Cam. Now that he had it, he was going to make the night last.

Rider's eyes went wide, and his jaw went slack as he took in what he was hearing. From the way they had acted in the last four months, he was sure his parents would been against him going to another college out of state, but they were even more supportive of the idea than Cam. Rider sat at the kitchen table as discussion of accommodation and timings went on around him. All he had asked was what they thought of Cam's idea but now everyone was making plans without any input from him. As he turned to look at Cam, his boyfriend had a guilty look on his face.

"You already spoke to them about your idea, didn't you?"

"Maybe," Cam said, his gaze on the table. "I'm sorry, Ri. I just wanted to know what they would think about it before I asked you. I was worried that asking you so soon would cause you to immediately reject the idea, but it was your mom who said someone as strong as you could take it."

"We just want the best for you, Ri. Ever since you could read, you wanted to be a journalist and I don't want that dream to come to an end. In the last couple years, you have been through hell, but me and your father just want the best for you, want to see you succeed. If you don't want to go to Kentucky that is okay, you could enroll with Lloyd and join Sam and Jane at Belmont, or you don't need to go to college at all. We love you no matter what you choose."

"Here, here," his father said over the top of the module selection book for Kentucky.

Rider glared at the three other people in the room, but he couldn't hold it. He was glad his mom was starting to relax and allow him more freedom. Cam's hand slipped into his own, a soft smile on his boyfriend's face. Rider released a contented sigh; he knew what he wanted, and he knew what must be done. Pulling the laptop that sat in front of Cam over to his side of the table, he loaded the late admissions page. With each data box he filled Rider found the decision easier.

Cam's infectious enthusiasm seemed to fill Rider over the course of the following weeks. He had yet to hear back from Kentucky, but Cam had already started looking at apartments they could rent together. He was in the middle of showing Rider one above a theater when Rider's new phone started ringing. He had tried to recover his old phone, but even replacing the screen and battery had not solved the issue of it refusing to turn on. He had instead got a new phone and the number calling was not known. He recognised it as a Houston number but the only number from his time in Houston that he still had was Jason's, having got it from Cam after they had gathered his belongings.

"Good afternoon, Rider, this is Professor Hudson."

Rider hadn't spoken to the professor since she had offered him to stay on over the Christmas period and work on her project. He had been too afraid to drop out himself or talk to anyone from the college. It had been his father that had broken the news to Professor Hudson that Rider would not be returning to Houston.

"Hi…erm…Professor. How did you get my new number?"

"We had your parents' details on file. Do you have a minute to talk?"

"Sure."

"I'm sorry to call you out of the blue. I received a call yesterday from the University of Kentucky requesting your transcripts and my recommendations on you as a student. I just wanted to let you know that I told them that you were a brilliant student and an amazing TA despite only being in your freshmen year." The laugh from the other end of the phone relaxed Rider. "I just wanted to say how truly sorry for what happened to you, Rider. You are a bright teenager and didn't deserve something so despicable to happen to you. I am also sorry that you are not coming back to Houston, but I understand. I can see you going far in the journalism world, and I can't wait to read your first published article. You should hear from Kentucky in a couple weeks, but I'm sure you will be accepted. They would be crazy not to accept you. I wish you all the luck in the future, Rider."

"Professor, I…I don't know what to say. Thank you for everything."

They both quickly said their goodbyes, Rider ending the call with a smile on his face. He explained to Cam what Professor Hudson had said, which resulted in his boyfriend being even more excited, knowing that Rider was almost guaranteed to get into Kentucky. Rider's eyes fell back to the apartment they had been looking at before the call. As Cam clicked on the next photograph, an image on the wall stood out, one of a red-haired girl and a silver-haired boy.

"Cam! We are *not* moving in to my sister's old apartment!"

"Fine." Cam rolled his eyes. "I'll keep looking."

The summer went by in a blink of an eye. After being accepted into Kentucky, the couple went into a whirlwind of things to do, including finding a place to live. Before Rider knew, it was the night before he moved away. Cam had left three days earlier in order to make the final arrangements for their new apartment, and would meet Rider at their new house on Saturday. Rider currently found himself in his old bedroom with old friends. His mom had wanted to arrange a big family get together but it wasn't what Rider wanted, he wanted a quiet time with his best friends.

Sam was at the top of the bed with a plush elephant in her arms, Jane sat on the floor with her back against the bed, and Lloyd had just sat down on the chair at the desk. Rider had managed to get Cam's father's guitar out of Lloyd's hands before he had done too much damage to it, joining Sam on the bed. The guitar was still in the same perfect condition it had been when Cam had given it to him for valentine's day, although Rider was sure it had been Mary's idea.

"You looking forward to Kentucky?" Sam asked.

"Of course, he is, to get away from us lot," Lloyd said, only just managed to avoid the elephant aimed at his head.

"I'll miss all of you all a lot, but that doesn't mean I

don't care about you." He pointed directly at Lloyd who smiled back. "I'm just on the other end of the phone. I'm excited for Kentucky, but also nervous. I know nothing bad will happen but…"

"We understand," Jane said resting her head on his legs. "It's just another fork in the road. I'm sure this one will turn out much better."

Jane's words sparked inspiration as Rider lifted his guitar and played a couple of bars before he burst into the song. One by on the group slowly joined in with *Good Riddance (Time of Your Life)*. Rider was glad everyone had joined in on the song, or else he was sure he would have ended up crying. As the song came quietly to a close, Jane and Lloyd climbed onto the bed as the group hugged. Before any of them could move, Jane pulled out her phone and took a picture of them all together, the boys sandwiched between the girls. The photo showed them all as the happiest they had been for a long while. Lloyd demanded a copy, he wanted to start rebuilding his collage.

The next morning, Rider hugged Lloyd close as he stood by his father's car. His best friend had stayed over last night, not wanting to miss him leaving for Kentucky. He had missed saying goodbye the first time around and he wasn't going to miss out this time despite it being 5:30 AM. Charles yawned, having agreed to collect his son, in case Lloyd had been upset. He patted Rider on the back before going to speak to Rider's father who was currently trying to stop his wife from crying for the third time since they had woke up.

"I'm going to miss you, Ri. It's been so good having you back home," Lloyd said, his eyes tearing up.

"I'll miss you too, Lloyd. Just remember, I might not physically be here, but I'm always there for you. No matter what time it is, just give me a call if you need me. Okay?"

"I promise."

He pulled Lloyd close and give him a kiss on his cheek. His love for his best friend was so great that Rider was almost in tears when they finally set off. It was a lot harder than the first time. The journey to Kentucky was quicker than it had been than the one to Houston. Rider held his breath as they pulled up in front of what looked like a normal building. Cam had managed to find them a street-level apartment that was the lower half of a house. They had their own access to the building that led straight out onto the street, whereas the upstairs apartment required access from the rear of the property. Rider jumped out of the car as his father went to look for a parking spot. He smiled as he knocked on the door; he could hear sounds behind it. As the door opened, Rider became extremely confused. The jock standing in front of him was not his boyfriend.

"Williams! You finally made it. Come in, come in." Quintin smiled

Rider followed Quintin to the family room, where a guilty-looking Cam sat on the couch. He wasn't sure what was going on, but it had been almost a week since he had seen Cam. His boyfriend started to open his mouth, but Rider stopped as he pulled him into a passionate kiss, drawing a whistle from Quintin, causing Rider to laugh mid-kiss.

"Rider, I should have told you sooner. When I showed you this apartment, you loved it, but we wouldn't have been able to afford it by ourselves. So, I spoke to Matthews about it and he said he was sick of living in the dorms. He already agreed to taking the smaller bedroom. The apartment is easily big enough for all three of us and I know I should have told you before we moved it but are you—"

"Yes," Rider said still inches away from Cam's face. Quintin had only ever been friendly to him, supported their relationship before others in school knew about it, and had defended Cam from the frat. He was one of Cam's best friends and Rider had no problem living with the other jock.

"I told you he wouldn't have a problem with it, Walker. Can you believe he stayed up all night preparing this big ass list of reasons, hoping he could convince you to change your mind?" Quintin laughed. "Anyway, where is your luggage?"

There was a knocking signifying his father was there with the first load of boxes. Knowing that he had a proper apartment this time rather than sharing a dorm room, Rider had brought more of his belongings. The unpacking was slow mainly due to the fact that when his father had found out that Quintin was also on the basketball team with Cam the conversation had quickly devolved into a discussion about sports. Rider rolled his eyes and moved into the bedroom with a box of what looked like clothes. Removing the clothes and hanging them up in the closet, his eyes went wide as he reached the very bottom of the box, a smile on his face as he pulled out wrinkled stack of paper.

"'The Weight of a Secret'," Rider said out loud to himself.

Sitting down on the bed, he began reading over his old article. He may have only taken one semester at Houston, but Rider was two paragraphs into the piece and had already found areas he would change and adapt to fix the flow. By the time Cam came to check if he was okay and confirmed they had finished talking sports, he had already made a number of changes. As they entered the living room, there was a rolled-up poster in Quintin's hands. Rider bit his lip; he knew exactly which poster it was. Trish had bought it for him it, the first time he had met her. As Quintin unrolled it, a smile spread across his face.

"Be yourself, everyone else is taken. I love this! It has to go up in here so everyone who comes in see's it."

Quintin's enthusiasm could even dwarf Cam's. The group had gotten through most of the boxes before Rider's father had to leave, but the group had come to a stop a number of times as Quintin had demanded to know the story behind items Rider had brought with him or wanted Rider to play something on his guitar. As he walked his father back to his car, the other two had promised they would keep working despite the TV being turned on as soon as the duo had left the room. Reaching the car, Rider hugged his father tight.

"We are just on the other end of the phone if you ever need us. Enjoy your time here and please stay away from vodka. No scaring us again."

"Don't worry, I'm staying away from all alcohol," Rider confirmed.

"After how he took care of you the last seven months, I know Cameron will look after you. You're in good hands with him, Ri." His father paused, pulling him into a hug. The hug didn't last long, but it meant the world to Rider. "I better head back to your mom. Love you, Ri."

"I love you too, Dad."

His father climbed into his car and waved before putting the car in drive and pulling away. Rider stood watching until the car turned a corner and vanished from sight. He headed back into his new apartment, and as he entered the living room, his eyes again went wide at what Quintin had in his hands. Rider loved the artwork Cam had gotten him for his birthday, but he had kept it hidden behind the couch for a reason. He didn't want just anyone seeing it as it made him look like such a huge fanboy.

"Williams, this is awesome! That's you with Spidey, right?" Quintin asked. Rider just nodded. "Where did you get it?"

"It was a present for my birthday from Cam." Quintin turned to the blushing jock and nodded his appreciation of the gift. "I think its great piece. I'm more of a Deadpool fan myself."

Rider suddenly found himself becoming overly animated while he discussed the reasons why Spider-Man was superior to Deadpool. He'd had this argument with Lloyd many times, but it was entertaining to see how much knowledge Quintin had about comics. Back in Belmont, Rider would never have guessed that the captain of the basketball team was such a fan of comics. He was in the middle of telling Quintin about Lloyd's collection when he noticed Cam smirking at him.

"What?"

"Still my lovable nerd, I see." Cam laughed

"Hey! I'm a geek not a nerd and don't you forget that."

Cam

The harsh florescent light stung Cam's eyes, the smell of disincentive burned his nostrils. He slowly walked down the hallway, legs weak since he had been pulled out of class. The whiteness of the walls made him feel claustrophobic. He needed to be back in class, working on his assignment instead of being in the hospital for something that couldn't be happening, he was too strong to be here. It felt like the hospital was closing in on him with each step forward toward the doctor. Cam could hardly breathe as he stopped in front of a white lab coat, not understanding any details what was being said.

"Mr. Walker, I am so sorry we need to meet like this. An unknown aneurism burst in your father's head. It was quick and he wouldn't have felt much pain. I am so sorry for your loss."

The doctor placed his hand on Cam's arm, but it felt like it was burning. He pulled away and demanded to see his father. Cam knew that once he got to look at the body, it would be obvious to everyone that it was someone else and there had been a mix-up. The doctor nodded his permission, holding the door open. Wiping the tears out of his eyes and walked into the room, he held his breath as he approached the body on the bed. Hands trembling, he slowly pulled back the sheet that was covering the face.

Cam gasped as the sheet fell to the floor. He was right, it wasn't his father on the bed, but this was just as bad. His whole body shook as his gaze fell on the pale body of his boyfriend. It felt like someone had punched him in the gut, all the air escaping him. He couldn't remain in this room. He needed to get out of the hospital. Cam turned and started to run as fast as his legs would carry him. He ignored the voice of the doctor shouting as he picked up speed, slamming open the doors as he went. With one last burst of energy, he smashed through the final door and into the warm sun that cascaded down onto his face. Looking up too late, he went crashing into an older man.

"I'm so sorry," Cam apologised as the man got to his feet.

"It's okay, CJ."

Cam's eyes went wide, his jaw hung low as he struggled to find any words. His father hadn't aged a day since he had passed. His smartly-trimmed blond beard looked like it had just been cut, his hair was perfectly in place despite the wind that was blowing at him. Cam stood frozen in place as his father stepped closer, a soft smile on his face. As he wrapped his arms around his son, Cam couldn't stop himself crying. He had dreamt of this moment for so long, but he was still confused. His father had died. When the hug finally ended, his father wiped away the tear that was still clinging to Cam's left cheek.

"Dad, how are you here?"

"I'm not, this is a dream." His father confirmed. "I saw you in that hospital, how you saw Rider on the table. This isn't the first time you've had this dream, is it?"

Cam shook his head.

"You can't keep blaming yourself for what happened to Rider, just like you can't blame yourself for my death. What happened to Rider was extremely sad, but you had nothing to do with him ending up in hospital. If anything, what you said to him in the hospital…your love is what kept him going."

"How do you know what I said to him in the hospital?"

A smile spread across Terrance's face as he explained to his son that just because he was gone from the world, it didn't stop him from watching over him. He had felt so bad that he couldn't be there for his son when he was in so much pain.

"So…you don't hate me for being bi? Or that I'm dating a guy?"

"Does Rider make you happy?"

Cam held his breath but nodded, he could never lie to his father.

"Then why would I hate that you are dating him? You care so much for him and it's obvious he cares for you. Your mom was right when she told you I wouldn't have a problem. All I've ever wanted was for you to be happy, my son. Do you remember what you asked at my grave? Of course, I'm proud of you, CJ. You're the best thing I have ever given to the world."

Cam smiled at his father, his eyes wet. He went for another hug and slipped straight through him. His father was starting to fade as Cam tried to grab hold of any part he could. His father shrugged at him, confirming his son he was simply waking up.

"I love you, CJ. Take care of that boyfriend of yours and I'm always here when you need me. I'll catch you around, CJ."

The sun in the sky seemed to increase in intensity, Cam found it hard to keep his eyes open. As he blinked, the hospital parking lot faded, being replaced with pastel-blue walls. The warmth that was wrapped around him transformed into a duvet. The sun had managed to get through just a sliver of the curtains and right into Cam's eyes. He rolled over to see his boyfriend next to him, perched up with his phone in his hand. As he watched Rider, the dream that seemed so important just minutes ago had already started fading from his memory.

"Good morning you," Rider said he noticed Cam was awake. "I hope Quintin didn't hear us last night."

Cam laughed as he remembered how he and Rider had spent their first night in their new apartment together. They had gotten slightly passionate, which had resulted in them being slightly loud. He was sure Matthews would make a joke when they finally got out of bed, but right now all he wanted to do was hug Rider. Cam pulled the smaller teen to him as he placed his soft lips onto the boy he loved. Despite Rider's claims of needing the bathroom, Cam kept him in his arms for another five minutes. He only allowed Rider when he threatened to pee on him.

"So, what do you want for breakfast?" Cam asked with a yawn.

"Pancakes?" asked Rider as he climbed out of the bed.

"You always say pancakes." Cam rolled his eyes but

couldn't help but laugh when Rider started doing puppy dog eyes at him. "Fine, pancakes it is."

As Rider headed to the bathroom, Cam entered the kitchen. Looking out the window over the sink, whatever sun had woken him up was now hidden behind dark clouds. Cam pulled out the ingredients that they had collected from the store after finish unpacking yesterday and started work on the pancakes his boyfriend loved. He had just poured the first in the pan when Matthews entered the kitchen with a smirk on his face.

"I guess you heard us last night then," Cam said as he flipped the pancake.

"Just a little but it's okay. It just means that next time I see Carrie-Ann, we'll have to be louder." They both laughed. "Speaking of Carrie-Ann, would it be cool if she came over in a couple weeks? I know Williams and her never truly saw eye-to-eye."

"This is also your house too Q-Tip." Matthews rolled his eyes. "If you want to have Carrie-Ann over, then invite her. If anything happens between them, me and Rider will just go to a hotel and be as loud as we want."

"You mean last night wasn't the loudest you could be?"

Although Cam offered him pancakes, Matthews declined; he already had plans with Jean, and was already running twenty minutes late. He gave Cam a fist bump before heading toward the door. Rider settled down in the living room as Cam finished frying the pancakes. Pouring syrup over them, he carried the two plates into the other room, noticing Rider looking silently out the window.

There was a steady wave of rain drops hitting against the pane of glass sending a shiver through Cam.

"Are you okay, Ri?"

"Oh!" Rider seemed startled by Cam's voice. A smile spread across Rider's face as he nodded. "Yeah, I'm okay, just thinking."

"Good things, I hope?" Cam said as he placed a plate of pancakes in front of Rider.

"Yeah. I was just thinking about how I hate the rain and how it always curses me, but I still love the sound of it hitting against the glass." Cam smiled as he agreed. "Do you know, it was a day like today when I was asked to guide you around the school. It was the final day of the school year and Principal Simmons called me into his office. At first, I thought it was about the article I wrote about the cheerleaders cheating, but instead he told me about a new student starting next year and they needed a guide. Imagine how different our lives might have been if I had said no."

"You wouldn't have. You were too much of a nerd."

Rider hit Cam in the arm, causing the jock to drop some syrup onto his jeans. Cam only laughed as he placed a syrupy kiss on Rider's cheek. Sitting and eating the pancakes and listening to the rain, Cam knew he loved Rider with all of his heart. What had happened in Houston had not fazed them as a couple, but had brought them closer together. There was no way he would lose him ever again.

Chapter 27

Rider
Eight Years Later

R ider stood looking around a room he hadn't stepped foot in for years. The last time he had been in the room was when Principal Simmons had been telling him that Brown was expelled from the school for trying to assault him for a second time. He couldn't believe it had been nine years since they had finished high school. *What an odd number of years to host a reunion.* Mr. Simmons's name plate was no longer on the desk. Rider had been surprised when his mom had informed him Principal Simmons had somehow made superintendent. At the current moment they were meant to be in the gymnasium with Jane, but Cam had wanted to have a look around the school again, this time giving Rider the tour, and they had ended up at the place they had first met. After five minutes of being in the office, Rider was now bored. He turned around to look at Cam, who seemed extremely nervous.

"Are you okay Cam?"

His boyfriend took in a deep breath before he nodded. Rider tried to walk toward the door, but Cam stopped him. He took hold of Rider's hands and looked longingly at him. Rider couldn't help but get lost in the deep pool of blue that Cam called eyes. Even after all this time he was amazed at how much he loved his boyfriend's eyes. Leaning forward to kiss Cam, he was only greeted with a small peck. Cam's hand was shaking slightly as he smiled at Rider.

"That day I thought I lost you. I don't ever want that feeling in my life again," Cam said.

Rider smiled softly. After seeing the pain on Cam's face when he had been recovering, he never wanted his boyfriend to feel that also. Cam pulled him closer, this time kissing him with passion. Rider tried to keep the kiss going but he couldn't stop himself from laughing as Cam's beard tickled him. In the last year, Cam had grown a stylish beard, but now he looked even more like his father. Rider had found it hot but there were times when they kissed the hairs caught his nose causing him to laugh. The laugh soon stopped and turned into a gasp as Cam dropped to one knee, a black box in hand.

"Rider Williams, will you marry me?"

"Are you serious?"

Cam nodded, showing Rider the platinum band in the box.

"Yes! Of course, yes!"

Cam jumped to his feet, kissing Rider again before slipping the ring onto his finger. Rider traced the platinum ring that now sat on his finger, a tear forming in his eye as he smiled at his fiancé. He could still remember the point where he was struggling to accept himself and now, he was engaged to the man of his dream. Thinking about dreams, this all seemed a bit too similar. Rider pinched his leg and when it hurt, the smile doubled.

"I had a dream once that was exactly like this, except we were on top of the Empire State Building and at the beginning all I was wearing was a towel."

"I can take the ring back and wait till we are next in New York. Ask you there instead? I can even bring a towel." Cam stretched out for the ring, but Rider snatched his hand away from his fiancé and snarled.

"There is no way in hell you're getting this ring off me."

"Good," Cam said.

The couple kissed once more before heading to the gymnasium. Rider took a deep breath as he walked into the building. It took a couple seconds for him to realize that the room he stood in wasn't the same one his prom had taken place in. The gym was large enough for two basketball courts and there was plenty of space even before the bleachers were pulled back. Cam tapped Rider on the shoulder, he had been standing still, blocking the entrance.

"You okay?" Cam asked.

Rider nodded. "There is just something about this place that feels off."

"They built a new gym over the old one about two years ago. We should hurry up, we're blocking the entrance and I can see Jane over there all by herself."

They started heading in the direction of the lonely woman before a face Rider hadn't seen in years caught him. Informing he would catch Cam up, he quickly slid off to the side. His smile beamed as he walked over to Darius Hogarth. Rider hadn't seen Darius in person since he left Belmont High, but he had contacted him a number of times over the course of his college life. Darius had originally contacted Rider after finding out about the incident, but soon Rider found himself turning to his old mentor to bounce ideas of him for articles. Rider pulled his old teacher into a hug.

"Rider it is so good to see you. I heard about the news, congratulations."

Rider's eyes went wide. He had only had the ring on his finger for a maximum of ten minutes. The panic subsided when Darius started talking about how he knew the editor of the *Belmont Tribune* and it had been him that let slip that Rider had just received a job offer. After graduating, he taken a number of smaller journalism posts, but when a position had opened up in his hometown at a paper read across the state, Rider had applied. He had never believed he would get the job, but he had received an offer last week. His hand rubbed across his face, but he immediately regretted it when Darius eyes went wide; the ring was on full display.

"Rider, when did you get married?"

"Oh...erm...well. Cam literally just proposed, but no one else knows yet. Can you promise not to tell anyone?"

"Absolutely, my lips are sealed. I wish you more luck that me and Hamish. We still haven't set a date yet. We can't do it during the school year and if we do it during the school holidays then there is a much higher chance one of the parents or the board may find out."

During one of their long phone conversations, Darius had been asking how living with his partner was going and Rider had ended up asking if the teacher was dating someone. Rider had been shocked to discover Darius was engaged to Coach McClay, he could still remember his gasp when he was told it was his old gym teacher. This year would mark ninth years of being engaged but Darius was worried that if any of the parents found out, they could create problems and he or Hamish could lose their job.

"I'm sorry you haven't been able to marry like any other couple. I can't imagine how hard it must be having to hide your relationship from the school board."

"It's okay. We have some good friends who are happy to hide it for us," Darius said. He looked away from Rider as he blushed. "Your man is waving at you, better get back to him. We'll catch up soon? And congratulations again."

"Absolutely and thank you," Rider said, giving Darius another hug before heading across the room.

Cam and Jane were sitting at an empty table, Jane was currently in the middle of telling Cam about the new changes she had implemented at the homeless shelter she donated her time to. She had recently started showing the owner's son the ordering systems and the overall running of the shelter. Thanks to her degree and the hard work she had done helping the shelter, Jane had been hired by a local firm that helped failing businesses get back on their feet. The firm received payments months after the business was back to being successful, but to Jane it was about helping people, not making money. Due to this, she was currently in the process of creating her own company, which would only charge enough to keep her business running instead of trying to make a profit, the increase in workload caused her to reduce her volunteering, hence Aaron starting to take over what Jane did for the shelter.

Rider sat down between Jane and his fiancé. While listening to the conversation, he found himself rubbing his thumb over his scar. He held his hand under the table, hiding the ring from view. He hadn't been this nervous to bring up a subject with Jane since that time in Quintin's bedroom when he came out. Cam's hand landed on his knee, giving him the courage he needed. Rider took a deep breath before turning to Jane.

"Jane, I have some..." Rider's mouth froze up as he saw two people advancing in their direction. There was no way he could tell Jane the news with Quintin and Carrie-Ann there. "I...erm...I'm glad you could make it tonight. Sam said you've been busy and may have to miss it."

Cam was soon on his feet greeting his old friend in a tight hug. Quintin had graduated a year earlier than either Rider or Cam. He had reluctantly moved out when he had gotten offered a contract for a smaller basketball team. He wasn't making millions and his games wouldn't be aired on national TV, but the opportunity had been too good to pass up. Rider just smiled at the duo as they sat down at the table, any chance of telling Jane the news was long gone. Despite the unexpected arrival, Rider was still happy to see Quintin and Carrie-Ann and that the two of them were still together.

Rider also had come to calling Carrie-Ann a friend. When he had been living with Quintin, she had come and stayed over a number of times. Having been away from her parents, her personality had changed over the years. She was humbler and more respectful to people. Despite the change, the thing that had brought him and her closer had happened by complete accident. One evening, the basketball team bus broke down, resulting in Carrie-Ann and Rider having to spend the evening together, just the two of them. Rider had been flicking through the TV channels when *The Justice League* film just started to air. He had expected Carrie-Ann to roll her eyes or say some sarcastic remark, but it never came. Instead, her eyes were more focused on the TV than his were.

It turned out Carrie-Ann loved the DC comics including the films and shows. That evening they had ended up forgetting about the film and talking about their favorite characters. Rider had laughed when Carrie-Ann had said her favorite was Harley Quinn, although her favorite male character matched Rider's—Jon Kent, A.K.A. Superman's son. He had been extremely surprised by that revelation due to Jon being bisexual in the comics. She had definitely come a long way since Belmont High. When they had found a quiz online to do, Rider was shocked to find out Carrie-Ann knew the films even better than he did.

After everyone had hugged each other "hello", the conversation quickly changed to what the group was currently up to. Quintin was still with the team but looking at retiring soon, wanting to spend more time with Carrie-Ann. The restaurant Carrie-Ann had managed to get a job in had become so popular the owner was opening a second location and had chosen her to be the manager.

"I had the best interviewee yesterday. Shelly Winter's turned up looking for a job and when she realized it was me interviewing, her face dropped."

The conversation was soon interrupted by another duo arriving. The ginger hair was easy to identify, the goatee Myers sported made him look older than he was. He looked sheepish standing there as if he still felt guilty for accidentally revealing Rider's secret to Spencer. Rider offered Myers and his date a seat. The girl with Myers looked very familiar but Rider didn't know where from, the only person he remembered having shoulder length platinum blonde hair in school was Aisha, but the girl sitting in front of him wasn't her. Aisha had blue eyes similar to Cam, but the girl in front of him now had soft emerald eyes.

"I'm sorry if this comes off as rude but do I know you?" he asked.

"Yes." The girl smiled. Her voice sounded so familiar.

"Noah?" Rider asked, his eyes wide.

"I go by Charlotte now."

The last time Rider had seen her, she had still been in hospital recovering from a violent attack. When she had returned to school for her final year, she received a lot of abuse from some of the students and originally her parents wanted to pull her out of Belmont High and finish her final year with home study or in a private school. She had started thinking maybe her parents had been right until Michael had randomly appeared one afternoon and threatened to kick the bullies' asses. With the support of her parents and Michael, she had slowly transitioned and now felt comfortable with who she was. It had been a long road, but she was happy.

"Did they ever find the people who attacked you?" Rider asked

"It was Brown," Quintin spoke up, surprising the group.

"What! You knew?" Myers said angrily and rose to his feet but Quintin soon calmed him.

"I found out after the attack. He had come to school to sell some drugs and let it slip that the people who did the attack owed him money. It was also Brown that told Spencer that you were trans. I managed to record Brown admitting everything and after school that day I went to the police with the recording. Brown gave up the two attackers fairly quickly, but because he didn't actually tell them to attack you, but rather only hinted at it, and because this was only his first offence, he only got six months in jail."

Charlotte smiled and thanked Quintin, she had always wondered how the detectives had identified them so quickly. The officer assigned to her case had only said they had come across some strong evidence that identified the potential offenders. Cam offered to get Rider and Jane a drink, he was soon joined my Quintin and Myers. The group gasped when Myers bent down and gave Charlotte a kiss before heading toward the bar.

"You and Myers?" Jane asked beating Rider to the question, even Carrie-Ann looked interested in the answer.

"Yeah. It's difficult to explain. He was there through some of the most difficult moments in my life. He was so caring and supportive during my transition. We got really close and then one evening while we were watching a film, I kind of questioned if we were in a relationship due to how much time we spent together. He…erm…kissed me, and that confirmed it. Then about nine months ago, we, well, we kind of got married," Charlotte said blushing as she raised her hand up to show the ring.

"That's wonderful" Carrie-Ann smiled, Rider agreeing as he slid his hand into his pocket.

Carrie-Ann soon sat talking to Charlotte about everything that had happened at their wedding. Rider smiled as he looked around the room, happy how different everyone was since they had left Belmont High, how much their lives had all changed for the better. As he looked toward the bar to see what was taking the guys so long, he suddenly noticed Jane was glaring at him.

"So, when were you going to tell me?"

"Huh?" Rider bit his lip as he slid his hand even further into his pocket.

"About you moving back. Is it true?"

Rider was going to kill his sister, apart from his parents, Becca had been the only other person he had told he was moving back to Belmont. "Yes, it's true. I was hoping I could tell you, Sam, and Lloyd all at the same. I got a job at the *Belmont Tribute*. It will be a bigger challenge than what I've previously been doing and with the *Tribute* covering world news, it will also allow me to travel more, like I always wanted.

Jane pulled him into a bone-crunching hug. "Congratulations, it's amazing but what about Cam?"

"What about me?" Cam said as he arrived back. Rider happily accepting the Coke.

"Cam's coming back with me too. He's been in contact with Belmont University, they are willing to accept his credits from Kentucky and he can complete his final year here."

"Wait? What?" Quintin said, a confused look on his face. "I thought you finished a year after me? You were definitely in your final year when I moved out the apartment."

Once they had finished their degrees, Cam and Rider had taken a couple years working hard and saving up so Cam could go back to college and get his teaching degree. He had always wanted to teach history and it had been Rider that had pushed for him to go back and get the degree. Once Cam completed one more year, he would be a qualified history teacher, just like he had promised his father. Quintin pulled his friend into a tight hug to congratulate him.

"It should be Rider that is getting the congratulations. Not only does he start a new job soon, but the paper is going to publish one of his articles immediately."

Rider couldn't help but blush. He had reworked the piece since he rediscovered it in the old apartment and it had been attached with his application for the *Belmont Tribune*. "The Weight of a Secret" no longer just covered the part of Rider's life where he was trying to understand who he was while also hiding himself from the people he loved. It now included the part of his life after he accepted his sexuality, about finding the man of his dreams, and how his life had changed for the better.

"Not drinking tonight, Williams? I noticed Walker brought you a Coke?" asked Myers

"I don't drink alcohol. There was an...incident at college and I'm now teetotal."

A voice from behind Rider said, "What, you get too drunk and wake up with a chick? Yeah, that would be terrifying to a fag."

Spencer was walking over to the group with a smug look on his face. Cam and Jane started to rise out of their seats, but they were stopped by Rider's hand on their shoulders. It was comforting to know Jane and his fiancé would protect him from someone like Octavius Spencer, but Rider no longer needed it. Having grown so much since college, he had only gotten stronger. He could deal with someone like Spencer all by himself.

"It wasn't the fact that she was a chick that scared me but that it was your sister." Spencer growled at Rider who just smiled back. "Have you not got over this thing about making people feel smaller just to try and make yourself better? Everyone else has moved on, become a better human being, and you're still stuck in the past. I do have something to thank you for though, Spencer. If you hadn't told everyone at school I was gay, I might have never fully accepted who I am or become the man I am today. You can go home tonight knowing that it was because of you I'm with Cam and that I'm happy."

"Well...erm...faggots like you—"

Rider's eyes went wide as a fist connected with

Spencer's face, knocking backward and to the floor. Blood started to leak out of his nose, which was bent at a weird shape. The short jock had tears starting to form in his eyes as everyone's gaze fell onto him.

"Oh, I'm sorry Spencer. The floor was wet and these are new shoes. I slipped. I didn't mean to punch you," Quintin said with a smile on his face. "Although, you were being a dick."

"My fucking nose," Spencer mumbled through the blood. "You broke my nose. I'm going to my son's soccer match tomorrow."

"You? You have a son? Someone had sex with you?" Jane asked through laughter.

Spencer climbed off the floor and glared at everyone before he stormed away to a wave of laughter. Rider didn't like physical violence, but even he couldn't help but laugh at Spencer, karma finally catching up to him. The rest of the evening went along pleasantly without any real issues. Close to the end of the evening Cam was called up on stage, it was tradition for the student who had been named prom king during their senior year to do the speech at the reunion. Rider got to his feet, but he was stopped by Jane.

"Where you going? It's Cam's speech."

"I have heard Cam practising this speech for the last three weeks at home. By now I think I could give the speech. It involves thanking everyone who came, how many of us couldn't recognise each other, and how he was happy so many people were better off now than when we were in high school. Now if you don't mind, I am going to the toilet."

Rider walked to the back of the gymnasium and quickly located the men's toilet. As he entered the restroom, he wished he had stayed to listen to Cam's speech. His eyes went wide as he turned and sprinted out the room as quick as he could. This was the second time it happened, why was he jinxed? Rider had walked in on Quintin and Carrie-Ann making out again.

Chapter 28

Rider

The three friends walked through the cool air towards Joe's Diner. Rider was famished, he had expected there to be food available at the reunion. He dashed the last twenty yards making the other two hurry. Pushing open the doors, he noticed a table in the corner had already been acquired. Sat at the table were Sam, Lloyd, and Yuki, all with large smiles on their faces. Rider slipped into the table next to his best friend who quickly wrapped his arms around Rider, congratulating him on moving home. Rider rolled his eyes, he couldn't wait to scold Becca in person. Cam slid in next to Rider and Jane took the seat next to her girlfriend.

Rider was already ordering his food while Sam was informing Cam of the recent changes. She and Jane moved in together three weeks ago, their apartment close to Jane's job. Her mom had not only fully accepted that she was bi, but she also treated Jane like her own daughter. Her father had not seen her since the day her mother had kicked him out the house, but Sam was in no hurry to see him again. Cam was amazed when Sam started explaining her job as a social worker.

"How do you do it? It must be difficult."

"It can be. There are some cases where you know the kids are being mistreated, but the parents are doing everything they are told to do, so my hands are tied. Then there is the opposite where the kids don't want to leave the parents and the parents are really nice people, but they just can't cope. It can be very taxing at times, but when you help a child and you see the happiness on their face when you find the perfect loving family for them, it's all worth it."

"You're fantastic." Cam smiled.

Rider agreed, he thought Sam was fantastic too. He knew there was no way he would be able to be a social worker. He knew nothing about kids, for a start. It wasn't just Sam who had a challenging job based around children. Lloyd had succeeded in his goal and graduated from college with a degree in counselling and was now an assistant counsellor at Belmont High.

"My job is nowhere near as hard as Sam's. I mean, I had a student come to me the other day because he was worried he had a porn addiction. He watched it twice a week. At his age I think I watched it twice a day," Lloyd said causing the whole group to laugh.

"Shit!" Rider shouted, startling everyone, including the waitress who was just bringing over their food.

"You don't have an assignment you forgot to do?" asked Jane drawing another laugh out of his friends.

"No, I just remembered I need to call my parents.

Remind them to not lock me out." As he slipped past Cam, he leaned close and whispered. "I want to tell my parents first."

Cam just nodded as Rider headed outside of the diner to make the call. Making sure the door was closed and his friends were talking before he pushed the call button on his phone. It only took four rings before his mom appeared on the screen. Rider thought it was better to do this over video call rather than a voice call. Taking a deep breath, he released it slowly before informing his mom he had something important to tell her. Panic spread across her face.

"Is it your heart?"

"No, it's not my heart. It's good news," he said with a smile.

"Okay, let me just get your father."

Rider flinched as she shouted loudly off-screen. It took three more loud, shrill calls before his father finally appear on the screen. Even then it took another couple minute for his parents to find a position that would allow them to both appear on the screen at the same time, finally settling on sitting down on the couch. When they were finally comfortable, Rider took another deep breath. He didn't think telling them would be this difficult.

"I've got something to tell you both."

"Is it your heart?" his father asked, eyes going wide.

"No! It's not my heart," Rider yelped a little too loud. He turned to face the other way when he noticed his outburst had caused his friends to look out the window. "Erm…well…Cam proposed."

There was a gasp from his parents, a huge smile appearing across his mother's face. His father told Rider to wait a minute as he brought the phone closer to them and started messing around with it. Rider wasn't sure if his father was trying to activate screen recording until there was a ringing on his parents end and by magic suddenly Becca appeared on the call squashing his parent's image.

"Hey, Rider. Mom, Dad? What's going on?"

Rider could hear some crying in the background of Becca's line. "Everything okay, Becca?"

"Don't mind that. Dave is just trying to get Emma to sleep. You know what he's like with her, takes him five times longer to get her down than me. Anyway, what's up?"

"Tell her, Rider," their mom said excitedly.

"Tell me what? Is everything okay? Is it you heart?"

"Oh my God!" Rider threw the arm that wasn't holding his phone into the air in disgust. "There is nothing wrong with my heart. In fact, everything is great. Cam just proposed."

Rider pulled the phone away from his face as Becca started squealing in excitement before their mom joined in. His father was simply shaking his head at the two women but had a huge smirk on his face. Rider simply rolled his eyes wondering if it was a bad idea to tell them now when any of his friends could walk out the diner at any moment.

"Please tell me you said yes!" Becca asked but didn't give him a chance to respond. "Actually, please tell me you said no. You can't get married before me that would just be unfair."

"Of course, I said yes," Rider confirmed with a laugh. A blush spread across his face when Becca cheered again.

"So, when do we get to congratulate our son in person?" his father asked

"Well, I'm out with Lloyd, Jane, and Sam right now but I shouldn't be back to—"

"No not you. Our other son. When do we get to congratulate Cameron?"

Rider's jaw dropped as his father burst out in laughter, shortly joined by Becca. Before he had come out, Rider had been terrified to tell his father he was gay, not knowing what would happen, how after he was forcibly outed, he hadn't slept that night, thinking his father was going to come into his room and attack him, but now he questioned how he was ever afraid. He had a fiancé that his father happily called son. Rider swallowed the lump in his throat as he tried to hold back the happy tears.

"I'll bring him back with me."

"Good. Bring the others and also pick up Mary. We should all be celebrating together."

"Oh yes, we can't forget about Mary," his mom agreed.

"What about me?" Becca demanded putting on a fake hurt face that she hadn't been summoned.

"We are not driving to pick you up," Rider joked causing Becca to stick her tongue out at him.

"It's too late to drive there now. I'll get Dave to drive us over in the morning."

Becca didn't stay on the call much longer, she had to try and organise a babysitter for tomorrow. His parents congratulated him once more before they also disappeared off the call to start organising a party at last minute. Slipping his phone back into his pocket, he took a deep breath and looked at the platinum ring on his finger. *How was I so lucky to end up with Cam?* He turned and headed back toward the group of friends hoping Cam hadn't eaten all of his fries. He had just reached the group when Jane dropped her phone onto the table.

"You guys are engaged? Since when?" Jane questioned.

"Damn Becca. I am going to kill her." Rider was more shocked at how quick she had messaged Jane. "Yes, we're engaged. Cam asked just before the reunion."

Finally, he took his fiancé's hand and showed off the ring. The couple were quickly pulled into hugs by everyone, congratulations flying around as Lloyd demanded more milkshakes for everyone to use as a toast. When everyone had finally returned to their seats, Cam wrapped his arm around Rider causing his heart to flutter with love.

"Who's taking who's surname?" Sam asked, a huge grin on her face.

"Oh, he's taking my surname," Rider said immediately before Cam muttered a syllable.

"What? Why? I asked you to marry me, shouldn't you have to take my surname?"

"I am not having a name made up of two different exercises!" Rider defiantly said, making everyone laugh.

Cam glared, confirming that this discussion wasn't over before he leaned forward and placed a kiss onto Rider's lips, causing Rider to go red. As the milkshakes arrived, each of the friends gave a small speech about the couple, which just caused the blush on Rider's face to get even worse. On the positive side, Cam was blushing, and his dimples were on display. It was Lloyd who questioned how Rider's parents took the surprise while he stretched across the table to dip his fries into Yuki's milkshake, bringing a smile to the older guy's face.

"They are super happy. They asked when they get to celebrate with their son in person."

"I thought you were stay with them this evening?" Yuki asked with a confused look on his face.

"I am, but they were talking about Cam."

"What?" Cam yelped

The milkshake his fiancé had been in the middle of drinking shot out of his nose and across the table. Sam yelping as it almost hit her. The group laughed as Cam started to go neon red, dabbing up the liquid with napkins. Even with milkshake coming out of his nose, Rider knew there was no one else for him. He had no idea how he ever questioned their relationship back in Houston.

"My parents want everyone to head back to theirs to celebrate."

"Yes!" echoed a chorus of Lloyd, Sam, and Jane.

"Erm…I guess that's decided then." Cam laughed.

Becca

Becca kissed Dave on the cheek and left him to try and battle with Emma. Their daughter always fought against being put to bed but then always complained she was tired the next day. Sinking down on the couch, she grabbed hold of her glass of wine and took a sip just as her phone started ringing. Becca found it weird that her mom was trying to FaceTime her. Normally, her mom would just send a text. She placed the wine glass out of sight knowing her mom would complain if she was seen drinking wine at 9:30 PM on a Wednesday.

Answering the phone, Becca was surprised to not only see both her parents on the call but also her brother. She felt panic flood her guts as her mother said Rider needed to tell her something. It had been a long time since he had been in the hospital, but the doctors had said back then that the damage to his heart may never fully heal, and Rider would have to take it easier than most people.

"Tell me what? Is everything okay? Is it your heart?"

Becca's eyes went wide as she heard the news. Cam had proposed. They had only been dating nine years. Her and Dave had been together for eleven years and he had still yet shown any signs of asking her despite the huge number of hints she had dropped. There had been one time they were out shopping for a present for Dave's mom and Becca had stopped to look at engagement rings, literally pointing to a ring and saying to Dave, "Wouldn't that look good on my finger?" Dave's response had only been that it wouldn't look good on his bank statement.

"Please tell me you said no. You can't get married before me, that would just be unfair."

The family started laughing. Becca was so happy for her younger brother, she still remembered the phone call from her mother to inform her of how Rider had been assaulted at school because he was gay. She had been adamant she wanted to talk to him, confirm how proud she was of him. During the call she could hear how nervous he had sounded and how shy he was to approach that certain subject. Rider had come a long way from that shy nerd. The conversation quickly turned to organising a party to celebrate. Becca's eyes fell onto the clock on the wall. Even if they set off now, they would reach her parents' house until around two in the morning.

"I'm so happy for you, Rider. I can't wait to see you and Cam tomorrow. Don't get too drunk tonight, we don't need another trip to the hospital." Becca laughed when Rider rolled his eyes. She was sure Rider hadn't touched a drop of alcohol since the incident, but it had been long enough now that she could get away with joking about it. "I'm going to go and arrange someone to look after Emma, but we will see you tomorrow. I love you all."

"Love you too, Becca," Rider said, a smile on his face.

Becca hit the end call button and grabbed the glass of wine, downing it in one motion as she sent Jane a quick message. Her little brother was getting married. She poured herself another glass but sat it down on the table before rising and heading towards her and Dave's bedroom. She had already started placing some clothes on the bed when Dave walked into the room.

"She is finally down. You're not leaving me, are you?" He laughed while looking at the pile of clothes.

"You would be so lucky."

Back when they were in college, they have broken up a number of times for stupid reasons. Three years ago, Becca had accidentally gotten pregnant and nine months later her and Dave had greeted Emma at the hospital. Since that day, they had never split once. They still argued at times but the break-ups over small pointless things were long gone. All that was left was the love she had always felt for the silver-haired man.

"Do you think you could get your mom to babysit Emma for a couple days?"

"Sure, she loves having her, but why? I thought we were going shopping tomorrow." Dave sat down on the bed and started to refold the clothes Becca had unsuccessfully folded.

Becca couldn't help but smile as she told Dave about the conversation she had just had, how Cam and Rider were engaged and how they needed to go to her parents to see them tomorrow.

"It's about time!" Dave said with a smile on his face.

"You can't really talk." Becca held up her empty ring finger

"Well, technically with all our breaks they have been dating longer than we have."

Becca rolled her eyes and threw a T-shirt at him, which he grabbed mid-flight and folded it. As she struggled to pull the suitcase down from the top of the closet, Dave got to his feet and grabbed it, setting it down on the bed, and started adding their clothes to it. As she watched the case being filled, a soft smile spread across Becca's face. Walking over, she placed a kiss on his cheek. They may not be married, but she loved him so much.

Cam

The group had split at the diner with the majority heading toward Jeremy and Susan's while Cam and Rider proceeded to pick up his mom. As they pulled into the driveway, Cam could see the light of the TV in the family room. Rider jumped out of the car but Cam remained in his seat, his eyes closed as he took a couple deep breaths. Cam had spent the last year building up the courage to ask Rider to marry him but he hadn't actually told his mom that he was going to propose. In his heart he knew Rider would say yes, but there had still been a small part of him that thought it was too good to be true and he didn't want to build up his mother's hopes. He didn't move again till there was a soft tapping on the window next to him. He turned to see the worried look on his fiancé's face. He turned the engine off and climbed out of the car.

"You okay, Cam?" Rider asked as he took Cam's hand and squeezed it.

"Yeah. I—"

"Never told your mom?" Rider smiled.

Cam nodded and explained how he never found the right time to tell her. Only two other people had known he was preparing to propose. Trish somehow already knew, when Cam had called her about how they were both moving back to Belmont. Mid conversation she had interrupted and asked if he was going to ask Rider to marry him.

"I tell you, she is a witch. There is no other explanation to it."

"Who was the other person?" Rider asked through the laughed.

"Oh." A smile spread across Cam's face. He had broken his promise to tell her when someone special came into his life. He hadn't made the same mistake twice. "My gran."

They walked slowly toward the house, hand in hand as Cam told Rider how excited his gran had been when he had told her. Every time he had called her since, the first thing she would ask was if he had done it and Rider's response. Cam took out his keys and slid it into the door, it felt so strange coming home after living away for the last eight years. The duo soon heard Mary shouting from the family room.

"CJ, I didn't expect you home so early." Mary jumped to her feet when she saw Rider and pulled him into a tight hug. "And you brought Rider with you. If he's staying over, no naughty stuff under my roof."

Cam struggled to keep the smirk off his face as he looked over to Rider. That ship had long sailed, multiple times. He asked his mom to sit, and she soon started to panicking, thinking something was wrong. Rider seemed to glare when she asked him if it was his heart, which caused Cam to laugh and pull the smaller man close to him. He wrapped his arm around Rider's waist as he searched for the correct words. It wasn't until he looked Rider in the face that he could get them out.

"Mom, I've loved Rider for years. I loved him before I even knew I was bi…and there was only one thing left to do."

"You haven't adopted, have you? I'm too young to be a grandmother."

"No. Me and Rider are engaged."

Rider didn't even get time to raise his hand to show the ring before they were wrapped into a super tight hug. Cam could barely breathe from the pressure from his mother. Mary kissed Rider and congratulated him, but when it came to Cam he found his mom using her stern voice.

"Cameron James Walker. How dare you not tell your poor mother your plans? Next, you'll be moving without telling me."

"You didn't tell her?" Rider said, a touch of worry in his voice.

"She's joking, Ri. I told my mom we were moving back before anyone else."

She ran out of the room, which drew a confused look from both men. Cam scratched at his beard as he sat down on the couch, Rider flopping down next to him, wrapping both arms around Cam's right one. His mother's voice flowed from the hall; she was talking to someone. Coming back into the room, her cell phone was pressed to her ear.

"One minute while I put you on speaker." Pulling the phone away from her ear, she messed with it till Cam grabbed hold and hit the speaker button, placing it down on the coffee table.

"Hey, CJ. Your mom says you have some big news to tell me?" Uncle Roy asked, a slight crackle on the other end of the phone.

"Yeah we do. Me and…." The phone crackled again. "Is everything okay?"

"Everything is fine, I'm just in England at the moment."

"Okay?" Cam pulled a confused face but carried on. "Anyway, Me and Rider are engaged."

"That's absolutely wonderful boys. I can't believe it, my god son marrying another man. It's like a fairy tale, and here I was afraid to tell you I was gay. I know what paperwork you both need to complete, so once I get back next week, I'll start work on it and waive my usual fee."

Cam couldn't help but laugh. He hadn't even given any thought to about the process of them both getting married, all he knew was he wanted to marry Rider. He was glad his uncle knew the process and even more grateful they were getting his help for free. Roy was very successful and sought-after lawyer, being a named partner at his firm and his rates normally started at $1,000 just for an hour of his time.

"Roy, you don't need to do that for us," Rider said softly

"Roy? It's Uncle Roy to you now." He laughed. "And that's what family is for. Congratulations to both of you. What are you doing to celebrate?"

Cam's eyes went wide, he had almost forgotten the Williams were waiting for them. Once they had managed to get Roy off the phone, the three were quickly in the car traveling the short distance during which his mom kept asking questions that Cam did not have answers to such as *when will the wedding be?*, *where were you going to have it?* and *who gives who away?*. Rider could at least answer one question, his best man was going to be Lloyd. Cam was hardly out of the car when Susan pulled him to a tight hug, kissing him on the cheek. He struggled not to blush when she thanked him for finally getting one of her children to get wed. Susan was soon replaced by Jeremy as he patted Cam on the back and congratulated him.

In the living room, their group of friends were seated under the photograph that hung on the wall. It was no longer a photograph of just the four Williams, over the last eight years extra people had slowly been added. First Becca had put up an argument over how long she and Dave had been together and that he should be added, even though they split up two weeks afterward. Rider had then got upset that Becca's boyfriend had been added but his hadn't, so a new photograph was taken that included Cam. The image that hung there now always brought a smile to Cam's face. Rider still had his mop of hair and smile as he leaned against Cam. Becca still didn't look amused, but this time it was due to trying to keep Emma entertained long enough for the photographer to do his job.

A glass of champagne was soon pushed into his hand. Everyone but Rider currently had one as everyone started giving a little speech about Cam and Rider. His heart pounded hard as Jeremy confessed that he couldn't wait to add Cam to the Williams family. Susan had started crying in the middle of her speech when she brought up how if it hadn't been for him moving schools, Rider may never had accepted himself. Even Cam found himself choked up as his mom talked about how proud his father would be right now, he was glad he didn't need to say anything.

As Rider was in the middle of telling everyone how the proposed went down, Cam slipped out of the room and headed to the kitchen, pulling his phone out as he went. It took only seconds for Olivia to answer the phone.

"Did you ask him yet?"

"Hi to you too, Gran. I thought I'd call and see how you were doing." Cam smiled as he sat down at the table.

"Screw how I'm doing. Did you ask Rider yet?"

"He said yes."

Out of everyone, it was his gran that Cam had so much to thank for. He had originally been scared of asking Rider to marry him to the point he trembled even just thinking about it. It was her who sat him down and made him realize that if he loved Rider, he didn't need to be worried about asking him. All he needed to do was find the perfect location and everything else would fall in to place. She had also helped with that location. Cam's original idea was to propose at a basketball match on the big screen until his gran had pointed out that Rider wasn't a sports fan. It had been her idea to find somewhere that meant a lot to them. After going through the list, Cam had narrowed it down to two locations. One was by the lake where Rider had fallen in, it was the place where he had given the smaller boy his hoodie and the first place he had realized he may have feeling for him. The other was the principal's office, the exact spot where Cam had first laid eyes on Rider. When they had been contacted about the reunion, she had been right, everything had fallen in place.

"So, when is the wedding?"

"I don't know yet. We need to sit down and talk about it, but we are currently at Rider's parents' celebrating."

"If you're celebrating then you shouldn't be on the

phone with me, CJ. Go and have a good evening and come see me in a day or two with that wonderful fiancé of yours."

Hearing someone else say fiancé sent a shiver down Cam's spine, the smile on his face getting even larger. He said goodbye to his gran and hung up, but he didn't climb out the chair. Instead, he called a different number and waited. It took seven rings before the voice came through the other end of the phone.

"Good evening, Mr. Williams," Trish said, he could hear the happiness in her voice.

"How? How do you do that? Are you psychic?"

"No, you doofus. When you called yesterday, you were super nervous, even more than when you first wanted to talk to me about having feelings for a guy. It was obvious that you were going to ask him soon."

"But how did you know he said yes?"

"It's Rider. Of course, he was going to say yes." Trish's voice dulled as she moved away from the phone. "Yorick! He did it today, you owe me twenty bucks."

"Damn it, I really thought he would have done it on their anniversary. Let me guess, Rider said yes?" Yorick's voice said in the background.

"Yep."

Cam couldn't help but smile at how happy his best friends where for him and Rider. He soon found himself tell Trish the exact same story Rider had been telling when he had walked out of the family room before she had put Yorick on the phone and made to tell him all over again. They both demanded all the details, but Cam was already looking like he was running out of time; he could hear someone heading toward the kitchen. Promising to call them tomorrow with every detail, he said his goodbyes. Cam had just slipped his phone back into his pocket when Lloyd walked into the room. He had been sent by Rider to find out where he was.

"Sorry, I had to make a couple of calls, but I can come back now." As soon as Cam stood up, Lloyd pulled him into a tight hug.

"I'm so happy for you both."

"Talking about both, I didn't expect to see Yuki. I thought he had gone back to Japan? Are you both back together?"

A soft smile crossed Lloyds face as he shook his head. Yuki spent the majority of his time in Japan working for his father's company but every three or four months he would come back to Belmont for a couple weeks to connect with US companies. While he was here, Lloyd spent most his time with the older guy, including spending almost every night with him in his hotel room as if they were dating. Then Yuki would leave and they would keep in contact, but it wasn't the same as a long-distance relationship.

"It's like we both love each other, but we never say it out loud to each other. It feels like if we do, we will break… whatever it is we have together."

"But are you happy?" Cam asked, a slight worry in his voice.

Since the moment in the hospital when Lloyd had explained to Cam everything that he had been thinking, Lloyd had changed. He was no longer just Rider's best friend, he now meant a lot to Cam. Although he could always turn to Trish for advice, when Rider had been in hospital it had been Lloyd that he had turned to for comfort. They had both been going through something similar with the potential loss of Rider and it had made them both so much closer. It was no longer just Rider that Cam would defend to the death, he would protect the younger man also.

"Yeah." Lloyd smiled. "When he is here it's amazing. It's like nothing has every changed and I enjoy every second of it. When he's not here, I have my work and I still go on dates. He keeps telling me that he hopes I find someone to care for me like you do for Rider."

"I'm sure you will, but I'm still keeping my fingers crossed for you and Yuki."

"Thanks. Rider was saying you're moving back here and finishing you teaching degree in Belmont. What you got planned after you graduate?"

"Well get a teaching job hopefully. Why you ask?"

"Rumour has it the current history teacher at Belmont High is going to retire at the end of this year. Want to come work with me?"

Cam laughed as he patted Lloyd on the back. He had promised his father he would become a history teacher and that was now closer than ever. The idea of working with Lloyd back at his old high school brought a huge smirk to Cam's face, he knew it would be an amazing experience.

Chapter 29

Rider

Rider squinted out of the cab window as it drove down a street he was unfamiliar with. He was nervous to be back in Texas, but at least this time it was in Austin and not Huston. Cam had offered to come with him, but Rider had declined. Not only had Cam promised to go help his gran, but this was something he needed to do on his own. Rider needed to see him alone, he had stuff on his mind he needed to say. The cab soon stopped in front of an apartment complex, Rider swallowed the lump in his throat and handed the driver the money.

Rider had been extremely nervous on the flight, even questioning if it had been the correct idea to come all the way instead of just doing this over the phone. He wasn't sure if it was the nerves or the hot Texas sun that was causing him to sweat so badly. He ducked into the entranceway of the complex and took some deodorant out of his backpack. He wanted to smell okay for his reunion. Rider took the stairs and soon found himself in front of a strange door. Rider took a deep breath and held it as he knocked on the door. He could hear noises from inside the apartment. The door soon swung open, a smiling face greeting Rider.

"Hey, Rider. It's great to see you," Jason said before pulling Rider into a hug.

After the incident and the loss of his phone, Rider had hardly any interaction with anyone from Houston. Cam had Jason's number due to organising collecting Rider's belonging and Rider had taken the number and stored it in his new phone, making sure to message Jason. It wasn't a constant communication, but a text message here and there, but one topic they had never discussed what had happened the night Jason had found him on the floor.

"Come on in," Jason said when the hug finally ended.

Rider followed him into the house, glad to be out of the hot Texas sun. As they walked into a large room, on the left-hand side was a living room area and on the right an open-plan kitchen only separated by a row of cabinets. There were half packed boxes scattered around the room. On the coffee table was a framed photo of Jason with his arms wrapped around a Black guy that looked familiar, but Rider couldn't think where from. Sat on the single seater was a gray short-haired cat, looking in the direction of the men. As Rider sat on the couch, the cat jumped down and headed in his direction.

"That's Oliver, don't worry if he doesn't…" Jason's face became shocked as the Cat jumped up into Rider's lap and settled down. "He normally doesn't take to people apart from myself." Rider guessed it was possibly the same sixth sense Max had.

"Have you just moved in?" Rider asked as he stroked Oliver, looking around at the boxes.

"Actually, I'm moving out. I was offered an amazing job in New York that I couldn't turn down. Half my stuff is coming with me to a much smaller apartment up there and the other half is going to—"

The door to the apartment exploded open causing Rider to flinch, Oliver simply looked up before settling down. A child around the age of ten sprinted into the room, leaving the door open before stopping and looking at Rider with a confused look. The blond hair and tanned skinned matched that of Jason. The Black guy from the picture on the coffee table arrived shortly after, slightly out of breath whilst shaking his head.

"Sorry, I tried to keep him out, but you know what he's like."

"It's okay," Jason said with a smile. "Rider, this is my younger brother Dante, and of course you may remember Elliot."

Now that Jason had said the name the memory came flooding back to Rider. Elliot had been the person who had helped Jason move into the dorm room and, as Rider had discovered on the night he had come out to Jason, Elliot had also been Jason ex-boyfriend. As it turned out they were back to being an item again. After he had finished college, Jason had struggled to get a job in the theater so had gone back to living with his parents which had worked perfectly for his mother, who had decided she wanted to go back to work full time. He had instead spent his time looking after Dante. During this time, Elliot's father had gotten sick and instead of being a driver for the company, Elliot had returned to run the company for his father, allowing the two to reconnect. The spark between Jason and Elliot hadn't extinguished between them despite the time and now it felt like they had never been apart.

"That's why the belongings that are not coming to New York are going with Elliot." Jason confirmed.

"Is it true you play guitar?" Dante asked randomly.

"Oh…erm…yeah," Rider said, looking at Jason for an explanation.

"I was telling Dante about you yesterday when he found out you were coming. He only just started learning to play guitar himself and he's excited. He wants to learn to play Dolly Parton, thanks to my mom's taste in music."

"Virgil wasn't happy when he heard about that," Elliot said rolling his eyes.

"Why not?" Rider asked.

"Well, he still hasn't really come around to the whole gay thing. He thinks me looking after Dante and our parents having a gay couple next door may influence Dante," Jason said.

"But Uncle Dom and Justin are fun. They play fun music and bake me cookies," Dante said not really understanding what his brother was saying.

Jason had explained to Rider about Dominic and Justin, an older gay couple who lived next door. When Jason had first started questioning his sexuality, the older men had been there to support Jason on his journey to self-discovery.

They had never pushed him in one direction or another but allowed him to find his own way, always offering an ear when he needed someone to talk to. The hope Jason had found from Dominic and Justin support; Rider wished that he could someday give someone that same type of hope in the future.

"You think Virgil's reaction to Dom and Justin is bad?" Elliot said as he headed toward the kitchen area. "Virgil used to work for my dad's trucking company, but when he found out that not only am I gay, but how me and his brother were dating again, he quit on the spot. Something to do with not liking being away from his girlfriend for long periods of time but the timing of him quitting was way to coincidental,"

He opened the fridge and grabbed a can of beer. Leaving the fridge door open he turned back to the group only to be greeted by a loud meow from Oliver who was glaring in his direction.

"I will not take that tone when you come live with me, Mr. Twist," Elliot said returning his own glare.

"Mr. Twist?" Rider asked.

"Oliver Twist. I had to name my cat after my favorite play, but as I said, he doesn't take to many people, and he definitely doesn't like people leaving the fridge open. Sadly, my new place doesn't allow pets so he will be living with Elliot for the time being."

"Just means you have to come back often. Anyway, would you like a beer, Rider."

"Thank you for the offer, but no thank you. In fact, I haven't had alcohol since the incident."

The room went quiet apart from Dante who wanted to know what the incident had been. The topic was not something Rider wished to tell someone so young and by the worried look on Jason's face neither did he, but luckily Elliot came to the save as he quickly got Dante's attention saying they needed to pack his case before he went back to his parents tomorrow. Both of the men let out a sigh once the bedroom door was closed. Before Rider could say a word, Jason started apologising for not doing more for him.

"I'm so sorry about what happened to you, Rider. I should have said this sooner, but I was terrified to say it to your face and over text wasn't the right place. I feel so guilty, I mean, it was my vodka in the first place."

"Jason, you shouldn't ever feel guilty. None of this is your fault and never has been. We should have had this conversation sooner so I could tell you thank you."

"Thank you?"

"Yes. Who knows what would have happened if you hadn't come back when you did?"

"But if me and Elliot hadn't spent ten minutes making out in the car, we could have potentially caught the guy. Stopped it from ever happening in the first place. If I hadn't bought the vodka or if I took it home with me over Christmas, then things would have been different."

"I've been through every what-if scenario since it happened and although it was one of the most terrifying things to ever happen in my life, I wouldn't change anything," Rider said proudly.

"Really?"

"Yes, because otherwise I wouldn't be the man I am

today. I wouldn't be where I am today." Rider grabbed his backpack and rummaged around until he found the item he was looking for, an ivory envelope. "If things changed then I might not be with Cam now and I might not be marrying the man of my dreams.

He smiled as he passed over the wedding invite to Jason whose eyes went wide. "You want me to come to your wedding?" Jason said, his eyes a little wet.

"Of course, I want you at the wedding. There may not have been one if you hadn't come back to college early. Not only did you save my life that day, Jason, you allowed me to reconnect with Cam." Rider smiled softly.

Jason climbed out of his chair and crossed the room, dropping down next to Rider and pulled him into a tight hug while confirming he wouldn't miss it like he had the trial. The guilt at the time of the incident had been so intense for Jason that he could only submit a written statement and not attend court. By the time the door to the bedroom opened, Rider had reiterated that Jason had nothing to feel guilty about three more times and Jason had finally accepted it.

"Hope you're not making a move on my man," Elliot said with a laugh.

"I don't think you need to worry about Rider since he invited us to his and Cam's wedding."

"Thank God. I said it back then and I will say it again. He's cute, I'm worried he'll steal you from me."

"No chance," Jason said pulling Elliot close for a kiss.

Rider couldn't help but laugh at the dynamic between Jason and Elliot. He could see some similarities between them and him and Cam. It made him miss Cam even more, even if he was only away from his fiancé for a night, it was still strange after spending the last eight years seeing each other every day. Rider was happy that he had made the trip and that Jason could put the past behind him like Rider had himself. The rest of the afternoon went by in a blur of stories, which seemed to keep Dante entertained, mixed in with food, drinks, and Rider teaching Dante how to play the start of *Jolene*. By the end Rider questioned why he had been so panicked to come.

Chapter 30

Cam
November 21st

Cam looked at himself in the mirror, taking in the gray suit he found himself in. *Why did we choose gray again?* It looked good on him in the shop, but now that he was in it on the day, he was sure his hair clashed with the color. Maybe they should have gone with navy to highlight the blue in his eyes. Scratching his beard, he wondered if he should have a shave, but that would mean he would have to get undressed again. It had somehow taken him two hours to put the suit on in the first place, he was sure he would run out of time.

He was messing around with the Batman cufflinks Lloyd had bought him as a present when there was a knock on the door. He turned to see his mom and Uncle Roy entering the room. His mom had a streak of mascara running down her cheek as another tear escaped her eyes. She tried to pull Cam into a hug but he backed away, not wanting to get his suit stained. Instead, she took his hand and smiled at her son.

"CJ, you look so handsome. Your father would be so proud of you right now."

A smile spread across Cam's face; he knew his father would be proud of him, although he wished his father could be here to see him on his big day. He went to respond but closed his mouth. He had been so nervous this morning that he had already vomited once and hadn't eaten anything. Instead, he leaned forward, placing a kiss on his mom's cheek while squeezing her hand. Cam hoped he didn't have to speak too much during the ceremony.

"Your mom's right, kid, I've never seen you so well dressed. When you were born, I would have never guessed you would have been marrying a guy," Roy said. A confused look came across Cam's face as he looked at his uncle. "No...that sounded bad. I didn't mean I thought you were straight. I meant because of the stupid people who were fighting against equal rights. I...erm...just ignore everything I've just said. You look fantastic, CJ, and I can't wait to see you at that altar."

Cam allowed a simple thanks to slip past his lips, not wanting to take the chance of vomiting again. Grabbing a tissue from the desk, he cleaned his mom's mascara smudge before he pulled both of them into a tight hug. Roy had to pull Mary away before she started crying again. A vibrating on the desk got Cam's attention. Walking over, he noticed he had a message from Matthews.

I just arrived at the venue but you're not

here, neither is Williams and it's currently
locked up. The wedding is today right?

A smile spread across Cam's face as he shook his head. Quintin had been involved in the planning of the wedding after Cam had selected him as his best man. During that period, he had kept getting the date of the wedding correct but the time wrong believing the ceremony was at 10:00 AM and not 2:00 PM. It had been so long now that Cam was sure he was joking, but sent a full explanation response just in case. A moment later, Matthews replied.

My bad. See you soon

Putting his phone on the desk, he sat down carefully on the bed, not wanting to crease his suit. The door to his room burst open, surprising him as Jane and Sam entered, with Sam scolding her girlfriend for not knocking. The confused look on Cam's face asked the question of why they were here.

"We are here to make sure you're doing okay, Cam," Sam said with a smile.

"And so you don't get cold feet or get drunk singing Abba and leave a very raunchy voicemail," Jane laughed, causing Cam to roll his eyes.

"No Lloyd?"

"He's with Ri. Making sure he doesn't get cold feet or think you're having sex with someone else and getting drunk," Jane said causing Sam to shake her head.

Cam had been furious when he had discovered the

reason why Rider had been drinking that evening. He couldn't believe Fernando had not only answered his phone but made Rider believe they had just had sex. What had made it worse was he and Matthews had Fernando over to their apartment a couple more times before Rider had told him the truth. It had been one evening when Rider had been very uncomfortable that he retreated to the bedroom that the truth was finally revealed. Cam had thrown his teammate out of the house instantly and Matthews had only backed him up once he was told why. The rest of the time Fernando had been at Kentucky, Cam had only interacted with him when he had to, otherwise he blanked him.

"What's the matter with Trish? She's in the family room looking very pissed off—even Yorick can't get a smile out of her," Jane said.

The knot in Cam's stomach tightened. When they had been planning the wedding, Rider and Cam had agreed they would both have a best man. Cam had chosen Matthews due to how long they had lived together and the closeness between the two. Trish took this as an insult and had been angry at him since finding out when she had arrived three days ago, only talking to him when she had to.

"Don't worry I already know how I'm making it up to her, I thought it would be wonderful if she read something during the ceremony. It also means that Yorick is sitting with his girlfriend."

Cam had kept his promise at his father grave to visit more often. Every couple months he would go to New York, not only to spend time with Trish, but also a full afternoon with just him, Yorick, and Bobby. He had been so happy when both of them had confirmed they could attend the wedding, especially when Bobby asked if he could bring his boyfriend.

Jane and Sam pulled him into a tight hug which he was happy to receive. When he was finally released, he took a deep breath and looked out the window. The dark clouds threatened to rain, but that wasn't going to stop him from marrying Rider.

Rider

The light from outside cast a shadow over the bed that Rider was lying on. His laptop was sitting precariously on his chest as his eyes flicked over the screen. He closed the lid and threw the laptop onto the bed.

"Never again! That was the last time!" he said to himself.

It wouldn't be the last time, Rider had read and reread his wedding vows over one hundred times in the last week alone, yet he still didn't think they felt right. It was too late to make huge changes; it was only an hour till the ceremony. His thumb started tracing up and down the scar on his wrist, the nerves building without anything to focus on. He sat up, grabbing hold of the laptop and reopening it, his eyes started to look at the vows again as he read aloud.

"I once was asked to write what should have been a simple essay about the word love. I found it difficult. That was, until you came into my life, Cam. You allowed me to realize that I was worthy of love and that love is found everywhere. When I was younger, before anyone knew I was gay, I feared never finding someone…but you gave me more love than I could have ever asked for, you made me realize the love is for everyone too. But now that we are standing here in front of our families, our friends, and the people we love, with everything that has happened to us, both good and bad, I realize one important thing. *Our Love Is For Ever.* I love you, Cameron James Walker, with all my heart, and although I've done stupid things in my life I know it was always you I was destined to be with."

Rider sighed heavily. "Is it enough? Is it enough to say how I feel about him?"

"It sounded good to me," Lloyd smiled from behind Rider's guitar.

Rider still wasn't sure how could one paragraph explain how he truly felt about Cam. Rider's eyes moved from the screen to the window, small raindrops were now falling on the pane. He had woke up blinded by the sun, but by the time he had gotten out of the shower the dark clouds had appeared. After he had finished putting on his suit, the first rumblings of thunder came and now there was rain. Rider couldn't help but smile to himself, of course it would rain on his wedding day. He had to keep up the water curse, after all. As his eyes fell back down to the laptop, there was an almighty screech.

"You are never allowed to touch my guitar ever again!" Rider said.

He stood and crossed the room, picking up the guitar. He and Cam had still been looking for their own apartment, so the majority of his belongings were currently stored in his old room. As he glared at his best friend, Lloyd was trying hard to look anywhere but at the guitar.

"Why did you decide to have your wedding so close to Thanksgiving?" Lloyd asked, trying to change subject

Rider blushed. It was him that had chosen the date. When he had first suggested the day, he had ended up getting angry at Cam. His fiancé had known it was their anniversary but hadn't been aware that it would have been their ten-year anniversary. Rider's blush doubled when his best friend said how romantic it was.

"It's a shame that Yuki couldn't come," Rider said softly as he finally set down him laptop.

"He was saying he has this huge project on at work and he couldn't get away." A sad look was on Lloyd's face.

Rider turned to hide a smile from his best friend. He had actually been on the phone to Yuki yesterday where the older man had informed him, he had manged to get someone to cover for him at work and planned on surprising Lloyd at the wedding. A gentle knock came from the bedroom door, distracting both boys. Rider's father poked his head around the door before he came fully into the room. Rider couldn't help but laugh, it was strange seeing his father in a suit compared to his normal jeans or work overalls. His dad asked Lloyd if he could have a moment, and the young man happily gave up the groom-to-be. Rider stood as his father walked over, he pulled Rider's bowtie loose and retied it.

"Ri, I know you have been through some crap in your life, but looking at you today, I have never been prouder of my son. You're amazing and you will only continue to do amazing things." His voice cracked slightly.

"Thanks, Dad." Rider himself starting to get chocked up.

"Are you ready?"

"As much as I will ever be."

"Okay, then let's go get you married."

His father turned and left his son. Rider did one last look around the room. He picked up the gray hoodie that was on the bed, he had been using it to try and relax his nerves. He took one last smell, still amazed how after all this time Cam's hoodie till smelled like him. Folding it carefully, he set it down on the table by his laptop. He gently closed the bedroom door and walked down the stairs. His parents, Becca, Dave, and Emma, along with his best man were all waiting for him. He smiled at everyone and brushed his hair out of his eyes. He pulled open the door to see the car waiting to take him to the venue. Rider took a deep breath and smiled.

He was ready to start this new chapter of his life.

Acknowledgements

The ups and downs keep coming in Rider and Cam's complex L.I.F.E., but could have been a lot worse if it wasn't for a number of people. So, I, Rider, and Cam want to thank the following...

As always, I want to thank Craig G from Deep Hearts. Even when you're getting me to edit some of the hardest sections I've ever written, you do it with care, love, and kindness. I couldn't ask for a better editor unless you want to give me a larger word count. The constant anecdotes in your notes keeps me going during some of the long editing periods. You are even happy to let me spam you with my never-ending stream of ideas, so thank you. I'd also like to thank John R also from Deep Hearts for always being excited when my work lands in his inbox. To Francisco for proofreading my work, it must be annoying to proofread a British author writing an American story, so thank you.

Thank you to my partner Ben. I doubt LGBT YA books will ever be your thing, but I still love when you check on me and see how my writing is going. Thank you for still supplying me with drinks and snacks during my long writing sessions. Thank you to my family for not only supporting me but for also being big fans of the series itself, and telling others about it. As always, a huge thanks to Aaron and ML, my close friends and beta readers, who like to insult me when I do bad stuff to *their* cinnamon rolls. Thanks to Jake Martinez for allowing me to reference his characters from *The Mixtape to My Life* and for allowing them to appear in the future.

To Craig H, you are my best friend and best man in life and gaming. You keep encouraging me no matter the topic and it pushes me to be the best person I can. Like with Lloyd, we both have been through dark times but I couldn't have come out the other side without you. To all my fans who cheer me on, ask questions about my books or just promote my work in general. It is with your help that my book has been able to reach such a wide audience and I hope that the same happens with *Our L.I.F.E.* My interactions with you all are some of my favourite parts of writing.

Finally, too you, the reader. As always, it doesn't matter if you are gay, bi, straight, or one of the other wonderful sexualities in this world. Whether you are still in the closet, just come out, or have been out for years; know you are valid, you deserve happiness, and you are loved. From the bottom of my heart, thank you for continuing to be part of Rider and Cam's story.

Rider, Cam and the Gang will return in…
L.I.F.E. is Too Short

About Felyx Lawson

Felyx Lawson is a writer from the mysterious land of North East England who writes LGBTQ+ slice of life stories. He lives with his partner and they are saving for their own house. He knew he was gay from a young age but only fully accepted and embraced it in his mid-twenties.

He's an avid gamer and will fight anyone to prove the SNES is the best console. If he isn't writing, he can normally be found playing on his PS5. His favourite place to visit was Japan, not only for all the awesome manga, anime, and collectables, but also for the peaceful atmosphere even in one of the busiest cities in the world.

Books by Felyx Lawson

Main L.I.F.E. Series
L.I.F.E.
L.I.F.E. Too
Our L.I.F.E.

Spin-Off L.I.F.E. Books
Twins for Life

Also from Deep Hearts YA

Hunting Rabbits in the Dark
S.W. Ballenger

Hawk has the perfect life with the perfect girlfriend that he's loved since seventh grade. He's built his whole world around her, and he knows that once they graduate and enter the adult world, he's going to marry her and they're going to start a family.

This rock-solid life is shaken after a chance encounter with his former childhood best friend, Gabe. He's now the quarterback of the rival school's football team, tall, rugged, handsome...all of which awakens feelings Hawk thought he'd buried long ago.

When tragedy destroys Hawk's perfect world, he turns to the only one that can help him through—Gabe. With his best friend's help, will Hawk be able to rebuild his world and regain his footing? Or will he sink so deep into depression that he'll never escape?

Available now in ebook and paperback